Stories by M.T. Bass

Crossroads
In the Black
Lodging
Somethin' for Nothin'
Untethered
Article 15
Dephying the Laws of Physics

Murder by Munchausen Series
Murder by Munchausen
The Darknet
The Invisible Mind
Motherless Children

White Hawk Aviation Stories
My Brother's Keeper
Jungleland
Racing the Dream

MURDER BY MUNCHAUSEN

THE TRILOGY: BOOKS 1 THROUGH 3

MURDER BY MUNCHAUSEN
THE DARKNET
THE INVISIBLE MIND

BY

M.T. BASS

AN ELECTRON ALLEY PUBLICATION

MUDCAT FALLS, U.S.A.

Electron Alley Corporation
The Herald Building
732 Broadway Avenue
Lorain, OH 44052

This book is a work of fiction. Any references to historical events, real people, or real places are used fictitiously. Other names, characters, places and events are products of the author's imagination and any resemblance to actual events or places or persons living or dead is entirely coincidental.

Copyright © 2024 by Electron Alley Corporation

All rights reserved, including the right to reproduce this book or portions thereof in any form whatsoever.

Manufactured in the United States of America

Edited by Elizabeth N. Love (www.bee-edited.com)

ISBN 978-1-946266-26-2 (Hardcover)
ISBN 978-1-946266-25-5 (Trade Paperback)
ISBN 978-1-946266-10-1 (eBook)

www.mtbass.net

The characters and incidents contained herein are fictional. Any resemblance of persons, living or dead, may, in fact, be a violation of copyright statutes.

Murder by Munchausen

A NOVEL BY M.T. BASS

For Lightnin' S. Norton

The Three Laws

1. A civilian-owned and operated synthetic humanoid entity may not act in any manner so as to engage in or cause any harmful or offensive contact against a human being or, through inaction, allow a human being to come to harm.

2. A civilian-owned and operated synthetic humanoid entity must obey the directives and orders given it by human beings except in those instances where such directives and orders would conflict with the First Law.

3. A civilian-owned and operated synthetic humanoid entity may protect its own existence as long as such protection does not conflict with the First or Second Laws.

Federal Technology Administration Regulations

Obviously, crime pays, or there'd be no crime.

~G. Gordon Liddy

The Warehouse

The abandoned building in the Warehouse District was dark and cold. I didn't have glass on the AnSub, but we were picking up an RFI signature that was an eighty percent match to the A-VIN profile. My Smith & Wesson eM&P was out and humming in my hand, ready for me to take a shot. Behind us the SWAT team was spreading out into position to monitor our visual feed from outside so they wouldn't jam the ambient signals with their tac gear. We went passive on our glass as soon as we entered the building.

I looked over at EC, my partner, pressed against the far wall covering the left side of the industrial cavern, which was piled high with discarded junk—desks, chairs, pallets of boxed materials and strange hulking machines that no doubt once fabricated some kind of pieces-parts necessary for the stuff consumers once found they absolutely-positively could not live without in their daily drone lives—all collected from businesses that absolutely-positively no longer existed. The quiet was oppressive and haunting. We both strained for an aural clue to the location of our quarry, since the electronic intel was still too weak to pinpoint within the building.

We slowly wove around the junk, deeper and deeper into the room. I led. EC followed, constantly adjusting the ePD scanning app to search and map the room. I muted the tactical channels and stripped most of the data from my view to let him work the tech and comm. It's too distracting. I needed to maintain focus. I needed to be able to react.

This particular Android Subject apparently went off the rails and killed a luckless pedestrian on his way to a bodega for some iced tea or bottled water to quench his thirst. A one-in-a-million occurrence, but every so often it still happens. Anyone who believes technology is infallible is a fool. The incident didn't appear all that nefarious when first reported, but shortly thereafter the Atlas data stream went dark and patrol called our unit in. It quickly became obvious we were dealing with a malware hit, not a malfunction. The luckless pedestrian was actually not so luckless, being on what appeared to be the winning side of a particularly nasty termination suit with his ex, who we suspected had outsourced the final settlement to extra-judicial parties.

It might not make sense, but the beloved Media tags it "Murder by Munchausen." For a price, there are hackers out there who will reprogram a synthoid to do your dirty work. The bad news: no fingerprints or DNA left at the crime scene. The good news—at least for us—is that they're like missiles: once they hit their target, they're usually as harmless as empty brass. The trick is to get them before they melt down their core OS data, so you can get the unit into forensics for analysis and, hopefully, an arrest.

EC's scanner returned a hard ping. His quick double blink put his cross-hairs up on my lens and I followed his eye line to the northwest corner of the building. I swept my eyes up and down to acknowledge and we slowly headed in that direction. As we moved, the RF signal narrowed and confirmed bogey lock with a low growl in my ear buds. EC swung out from the left and unshouldered his shotgun. Good old-fashioned blast power often came in handy to buy some time. Like I said, *usually* they're harmless, but usually just ain't good enough odds for me.

My Smith & Wesson started flashing yellow in my glass. It took the data hand-off and started frequency ranging, seeking the optimal setting for its electro-magnetic pulse to take down the AnSub. We slowly and methodically cleared the warehouse, aisle by aisle, until we got to the very corner of the building where the android had parked itself, facing out the window towards the city lights. In sleep mode, I could see its right eye's red optic laser reflect off the window pane as it lazily pulsed. We spread out as quietly as we could with our weapons trained on the synthoid perp. EC pulled the restraining bolt from his webbing and held it up. If we could get it in without discharging our weapons, there was less chance of frying any lines of code that the forensics guys would whine on endlessly about.

I nodded. I had frequency lock on the droid's GMC—Gyro & Mobility Chip—and kept my weapon pointed at center mass. Precise aim isn't critical but improves effectiveness and tends to minimize collateral damage to nearby appliances. EC moved in swiftly and smoothly. Since they all, literally, have eyes in the back of their heads, there's just no sneaking up on a droid like you can a human, so the best thing is to get it over with as quickly as possible and hope their reaction protocol has not been tampered with to ignore the RFID chip in our cop badges.

EC was within arm's reach when I saw both eyeball scanning lasers reflect off the window pane as the droid came alive. It spun quickly and reached for EC's neck. I reacted instinctively and double-tapped the synthoid with my Smith & Wesson. It's like tasering a human and, since it's just a machine, there's some entertainment value in watching the spastic jerking of arms and legs as the control signals are scrambled then flatlined.

The AnSub collapsed in a heap. EC kneeled down to place the restraining bolt in the small of its back, then radioed SWAT to stand down. He pulled his Department-issued *Google Glass* off and wiped the sweat from his forehead with the back of his arm. He looked up and, catching his breath, sighed, "Thanks, Jake. He was going for my throat."

"All in a day's work," I answered, holstering my pistol. The droid's mechanical strength would have made short work of EC's windpipe. "Besides, I couldn't let him ruin that lovely singing voice of yours."

EC smiled.

I winked back.

He knew he couldn't carry a tune.

~~~

The Meat Market

Misbehaving synthetic humanoids don't go through the normal booking process, of course, but we still bring them in through the sally port at the precinct house to be logged into evidence and lockered up until the forensics guys can do their digital autopsies. The sheriff's deputies who run the jail are always glad to see us because it gives them a chance to make fun of the one group of regular cops who are even lower on the social pecking order of the station than they are.

"Well, well, well…If it ain't the Geek Squad, again," snickered Deputy Ernst, raising his voice to announce our arrival to his squad. Ernst was a hairy ape of a man perfectly well-suited physically to supervise the swing shift band of gorillas in the "Meat Market."

"Great to see you, again, Deputy," I said with extra maple syrup dripping from my words.

"Look, guys, it's the Dynamic Droid Duo." Ernst's troop started to gather around him. "Bringing in Suzie Sexbot for solicitation, again?"

I could hear EC grinding his teeth beside me in the squad car. It was the one case we would never live down and the grief we took over it bugged the living crap out of him. But, pervs come in all shapes and flavors. We don't pick 'em. "Come on, partner. Take it easy. At least we're still loved more than Internal Affairs—*I think.*"

EC hopped out of the car and rushed off to get a gurney.

I got out and opened the rear door on the squad car. I had taken to handcuffing the synthoids when we brought them in as a subtle way of mocking the Meat Market crew. Maybe it was too subtle, so I decided to put on a little show.

"You…have the right to remain silent…"

As I recited Miranda to the droid sprawled in the back seat, I pulled it halfway out of the car and deliberately slammed its head hard on the car door a few times.

"Watch your head, sir."

I pulled it the rest of the way out and tossed it on the concrete floor in a heap, then pulled out my baton and whipped it to full length.

"…If you cannot afford an attorney…"

I smacked the sprawled out replicant human in the small of its back and the back of its thighs as hard as I could, the slaps of baton metal against synthetic skin reverberating off the concrete block and tile of the sally port. The groans and sighs of the Meat Market apes accompanied my performance as they watched and heard me do what they only wished they could.

"…Do you understand these rights as I have explained them?"

EC returned pushing the gurney and smiling at my antics.

For good measure, I kicked the torso where ribs would be, then took a deep breath and turned to Ernst. "Sorry you had to see that, Deputy. But sometimes it feels good to get it all out."

I collapsed my baton. We lifted the synthoid up and dropped it hard on the gurney. As we pushed it slowly past the swing shift of the Meat Market, their eyes followed us out with a combination of shock, envy, and animal hunger twitching in their fat faces.

"Feels good. Yeah. Feels good," I muttered to myself, but purposely loud enough for them to hear.

EC worked hard to suppress a laugh. When we got to the elevator, he asked, "Was that really necessary?"

I thought for a moment. "Yeah. Yeah, it was. Sometimes you've got to feed the beast."

"But everyone knows I.A. cleared you of the worst."

"Doubt is a powerful force, my friend. Like gardens, rumors need fertilizing and reputations need weeding."

Down in the basement, we transferred custody of our evidence to Gus. I scribbled my name at the bottom of the form and slid the clipboard to EC.

"You got this?" I asked him.

"Maddie?"

I nodded.

"Yeah. Go on. Get out of here."

"Thanks, partner." I headed back to the elevator to go up to my old haunt in Robbery/Homicide, where the coffee would be hot and company might be, if not more inviting, at least more visually pleasing — if Maddie was, indeed, there.

~~~

Robbery/Homicide

"What? No donuts?" I asked no one and everyone as I loaded up a cup with coffee. Maddie's desk chair was empty, so I scanned the squad room for her.

"Well, well, well…look what the cat dragged in," Lt. Sands said as he sauntered over to the coffee pots from his office.

"Hey, boss. What's new?"

Sands shook his head as he set his official police department cup down to fill it. Our careers crossed paths in Robbery/Homicide—his on the way up, mine on the way down. After the *"Incident"* and the Internal Affairs investigation, he crafted my out into the Geek Squad, saving my pension and giving my idle hands something to do during what would otherwise be interminably long and empty hours of a forced retirement.

Sands held up his cup and we clinked in mock toast. He took a sip without ever taking his eyes off of me. "Maddie?"

I shrugged, then nodded. Sands knew the back story of how I took all the weight and kept my former partner's jacket clean.

"She's around," Sands said. "What's new down the alley?"

EC and I had our offices in an annex building literally down the alley from the precinct, reaffirming our status as outsiders. It bugged EC because it made him feel like an exile, but I was just as glad to be as far away as possible from the bureaucratic and political bull crap in the House. I'd had my fill of it in my career. "Murder by Munchausen. Hopefully, the forensics geeks will find the signature of the re-code man for us."

Sands nodded, then said, "We never did work a case together."

"No, Lieu. Never did."

"Shame. Maddie says you were good."

Still am." I winked, spying Maddie stepping off the elevator. You couldn't miss her red hair, even when it was pulled back in a pony-tail, though I preferred it when she let her natural curls free to flow down her shoulders. More of an off-duty thing for her. "Speak of the she-devil."

Sands smirked and shook his head. He knew. Saw it in my face, no doubt. He turned to go back to his office. "Good to see you, Jake."

"Yes, sir."

Sands stopped and scowled back over his shoulder. "Don't call me sir."

"Yes, sir." I cracked a smile.

Sands shook his head and walked back towards his office. He warned Maddie as they passed in the aisle between the desks, "You've got a visitor, detective."

Maddie stopped and looked over at me. She arrested the smile that started curling on her face for the benefit of the squad room and shook her head. She slowed her usual manic pace and took deliberately measured steps towards me. "Detective."

"Detective," I answered as politely and officiously as she had greeted me. I shuffled over to her desk. "How is your day going today?"

Maddie exhaled a long, heavy sigh.

"There, there. Tell Jake all about it."

"Nothing to tell. Just the usual."

"Ah, humanity at its best being bad."

"Something like that. So what brings you out of the Alley?"

"Drop off for forensics."

"Another disorderly droid in public?"

"Actually, murder this time."

"Oh, *do tell.* It sounds positively marvelous."

"Well, no…nothing like what you *real* cops see every day." I scanned the crime scene thumbnails spread out on her *iSlate* screen. "That looks like a nasty one."

"Hooker in an alley—a *real* alley. Messy business. Completely unnecessary, but…"

"Yeah, I can see." I tapped the screen to open the gallery and swiped nonchalantly through the pics, then zoomed in on a body shot. There was something familiar about the mutilation of the body. "Hmmm."

"What?"

"Ah, nothing. What have you got to go on?"

"Zip. Zero. Nada. The scene was as clean as a whistle with regards to the perp. Too clean. Three days now and the case is starting to stink like fish and unwanted house guests. I really don't want it to go cold."

"Hmmm."

"You don't think a droid…"

"Nah, too vicious. Too animal," I mumbled, shuffling the pictures back and forth. It was gruesome, but there seemed to be a signature there. "Unless…"

I'd have to check my library of paper books, but there was something in the messy crime scene I had seen before.

"Dinner?" I asked.

"Yeah…I don't think so," Maddie did the *Price is Right* product arm swing toward her desk. "Gotta lotta work to do."

"Sure."

"But…"

"The door will be open. I'll be up late. I've got some research to do."

"About what?"

"I don't know, yet. Something caught my eye."

"You're the best. We could use any help we can get."

"Sure thing." I smiled looking forward to later, but wondering what it was I saw that was so familiar in that crime scene.

~~~

Old School

"There's Pinot open on the counter," I called out when I heard the front door to my flat open and close.

Good, I thought to myself, assuming Maddie got out of the House early. But then the clink of bottles as the refrigerator opened and closed told me it wasn't her.

"You don't mind, right?" EC asked as he sauntered into the living room holding up a Shiner Bock beer. "Holy calamari, what's going on in here?"

I had open books spread out and blanketing the sofa, love seat, leather lounge chair, and coffee table, spilling off onto the surrounding floor. "Research."

"Whatsamatta, the net down or did you forget to pay your bill again?"

I shrugged. "You can't think outside the box when you're locked in the box."

"That's what I love about you, Jake. You're so *old school*." EC shook his head. "I half expected to catch you watching *Ren and Stimpy* or *Pee-Wee's Playhouse*."

"Ah, the classics…but, no, Maddie hates 'em."

"I'm not interrupting anything, am I?" EC looked around for Maddie.

"Nah, late night. She's still on the job trying to crack a hard nut of a case."

"And is that what this is all about?"

I nodded, looking around at all the mess of open books. I had a pretty extensive library of dead trees. People scoff, but predictive AI searches always lead you to predictable places. Noticing my wine glass was empty, I stood up and stretched out my back muscles. "Yeah. I thought I saw something in the crime pics in the murder book. Something odd about it. Something you can't put into words, so how do you Google it?"

EC followed me into the kitchen. *Do tell. I love a mystery.*"

"Classic hooker in the alley scenario. The mutilation got my attention." I poured myself a healthy portion of Pinot Noir. "Something about the way the intestines were thrown over the shoulder and wrapped around the neck like a scarf."

"You've got an eye for details. Always have."

"It's a blessing and a curse." I took a sip of wine, then leaned on the island in the kitchen across from EC. "So, what brings you out slumming?"

"Got any snacks? I'm famished."

"What am I, your butler? Check the pantry. You know where everything is. Might be some nuts or chips or something."

"Guess I'm still wired from taking down that AnSub. It felt good. And, you know, a real case."

"Yeah. It did." I watched EC dig around my cupboards. He pulled out a bag of pretzels and tried one. He gave me a look that told me they were long beyond stale, then tossed the bag into the trash and dug deeper into the pantry. "Still too soon?"

"Huh? What?" EC asked coming up with an unopened bag of Famous Amos chocolate chip cookies. "These go good with beer, right?"

"I like 'em. Evidently, it's an acquired taste, though. Or so I've been told repeatedly by a certain female detective."

"What the hell." He popped a cookie in his mouth and washed it down with a gulp of Shiner. "So, the hooker? The intestines?"

"Puzzle pieces. You know. And there was a nice neat 'Y' incision, so it wasn't just an unschooled gutting out of rage."

EC popped in another cookie and crunched it up.

"I thought I might find something in the library."

"You do have an awesome collection."

I sighed and sipped my wine. "There's just something about ink on a page that can't be replaced or replicated with pixels."

"But nothing, huh?"

I shrugged my shoulders, mentally leafing through the volumes I had pulled down from the shelves in my study.

"I just didn't want to go home, yet, you know," EC finally confessed. "You and I, we had a good day and I didn't want that to go away yet."

I nodded. EC lost Pattie, his wife, in a car wreck back in January. "Yeah, it was something, wasn't it. I thought for sure the droid was going to rip your Adam's apple out."

EC chuckled. "It was a stroke of luck nailing him in that warehouse, huh?"

I popped a cookie in my mouth, grabbed the bottle of Pinot, and sat down at the kitchen table.

EC brought the bag of cookies over and we replayed the case and the capture from the top, so he wouldn't have to go home just yet.

~~~

Maddie

After I found the sediment in a second bottle of wine and EC had put a dent into the second half of a twelve pack, he headed back to his empty split-level in the 'burbs and I ended up in the leather lounge chair staring aimlessly at crime photos from the last century, flipping pages one way and back the other without focus, lost in inebriated thoughts of murder and Munchausen, EC's friendship and loneliness, a promising law enforcement career gone south, and rebounding into very different kind of partnership with my ex-partner.

The next thing I knew, I woke naked in bed beside her, trying to solve the mystery of just when she had finally gotten to my apartment. All I could remember was sleepily padding after her as she led me to the bedroom. A dream, perchance, but no. No dream. There I was spooning against her, feeling her warmth and her steady breathing against my chest.

I came up from nuzzling into her neck and noticed Maddie's shield and department-issued service weapon on the nightstand. I always found the Glock to be a rather soulless firearm. It never spoke to me like a 1911 or Colt *Python*. All they do is work, coldly and efficiently, but I suppose in the rather corporeal world where we spend our days cold, soulless and efficient is what you really want when your life is on the line.

Then it struck me.

"Jake?" Her voice was morning hoarse. "Don't."

"Huh? I—"

She grabbed my arm draped across her chest and held me to her. "Stay."

"Okay." But in my mind, I was trying to remember where in the puzzle pieces scattered on the furniture and floor the book was with the crime scene photo that had floated to my consciousness.

"I'm sorry I was so late. Sometimes I get a bit obsessed."

I tightened my embrace.

Maddie sighed heavily. "You know…"

"Shhhh." Never spoken of and only ever acknowledged in intimate moments like then, there is a toll your soul pays with every homicide you work.

No one wanted to work with Maddie when she was assigned to the precinct. It wasn't chauvinism. There were plenty of women in the squad already. But it was more than the discomfort of a change in the familiar routine or the extra burden of showing a newbie the ropes added to the weight of the daily grind of crime solving. Or even the jealousy of watching a thoroughbred fast-tracking her way to a command slot. Nope. Maddie was young and beautiful and, of course, a redhead, with all the usual attendant baggage and a smart mouth to boot. No one—not even some of the female detectives that walk that way—wanted to ride with that temptation every day.

Stupid me tempted fate, though that wasn't why I found myself at the other end of the alley on the Geek Squad.

Maddie's phone rang and she instinctively groaned. The ringtone identified it as the station house. She answered it and "uh-huh-ed" her way through the call. I knew the days off we had planned together were toast.

"Another one," she sighed wearily after she hung up.

I held her for the briefest of moments, then she rose to leave me.

~~~

John's Diner

The best buttermilk pancakes ever in a tsunami of maple syrup. Hard, crisp bacon and a huge glass of milk. That and about a gallon of coffee helped shake the sediment of Pinot grapes out of my brain. I wondered, briefly, how EC was doing. He was pounding down the Shiners pretty hard.

I passively let the sugar and caffeine work their magic on my biologics, gazing blankly out the window at the mid-morning traffic on Detroit Avenue. No crime books. The *iSlate* dark. Just me and breakfast. At some point, I'd have to decide what to do with my two days off, since my previous plans with Maddie had been overcome by events. But I didn't have to decide just then.

"So, where's Red?" Amy asked coyly, sliding onto the booth bench across from me and slapping her paper waitress order pad down on the table. *John's* is old school, too. Amy, though, is twenty-something. She slowly pulled an undone strand of blonde hair back off her face. "Flying solo?"

Her tone was a little too perky and a little too pregnant with expectations. Those days were over, though. At least for now. "Murder and mayhem in the big city. You know how it goes."

"Yeah, Jake. I do know how it goes." Amy cracked an alluringly half-crooked smile.

I smiled back. Temptation abounds. Just then, my phone started vibrating on the table. I looked at the screen. It was Maddie.

Amy scowled and grabbed her pad. She leaned over the table as she stood up. "I get off at the usual time…"

I watched her pirouette and sashay towards the kitchen.

"Hey," I answered Maddie's call.

"Hey. Got a quick minute and wanted to call. You know, sorry and all about having to rush off this morning." Her jaw was locked unsmiling in crime scene mode. I saw frustration in her eyes.

"Duty calls. I get it." Not every mate did. It's one of the advantages of keeping it in the family. "All day pass?"

"Well, if forensics ever moved faster than a snail's pace," Maddie said loudly, turning to direct her comments over her shoulder at the crew in bunny suits working the scene behind her. Then back to me, "I could get myself sprung maybe in time before the Fire Escape Grill closes?"

The fire escape in question was the one on the back of my building and the grill, my charcoal Weber. Old school. "I'll talk to the proprietor and have him keep the kitchen open."

"Thanks, Jake. I need it."

"The usual?"

"Yes, please." She paused, looked off screen to her left, and listened. I ignored the muffled voice and followed Amy with my eyes as she carried an order from the kitchen to a table. "Sorry. Gotta go."

I nodded. "Okay."

The screen went dark.

Hadn't planned on grocery shopping on my day off, but what the hell. I decided to go by the West Side Market. And I'd probably have to pick up all the crime books strewn about the place. No doubt a mood killer for Maddie after a hard day at the office. Great. More domestic chores. But not yet.

I tossed a generous tip on the table and grabbed my stuff. As I passed by on my way to the register, I put my hand on the small of Amy's back, feeling her young muscles clench in a familiar way.

"Try to stay out of trouble, you," I said lowly into her ear.

"Is that personal advice…*or professional?*"

"I'm just a cop on the beat, ma'am."

"Stop by anytime, officer."

I paid my bill and left.

~~~

The Fourth Estate

"So…where's your partner?" the inquiring reporter ambushed as I stepped out of John's Diner.

With the wisps of warm memories of Amy's body still dissipating in my mind, I reflexively responded by guardedly asking myself, *Which partner?*

"Ah…*yeah*…I meant EC." He had no doubt caught the warmly confused look on my face. "I know from the Atlas scan app that Maddie's on the job."

"Are you stalking me now?"

"Slow news day."

"No, it's not. It never is. How long?"

"Oh, 'bout half a short stack."

"Asshole. Why didn't you come in?"

"Professional courtesy? Maybe? Didn't know if you were on duty or not since you were solo and—*so, who's the blonde?*"

I followed his eye line into the diner to Amy who was waving at us. I waved back. "Put a sock on it, ya mook. She could be half your age."

"Yeah, but a man can still dream, can't he?"

I kept those thoughts to myself.

Jamal was an indie but a good one. He mainly did tech stuff, but he had found a niche for himself in my little corner of the world where electrons collide with corpuscles on the wrong side of the law that kept his byline—E.J. Quick, probably his maiden name—on millions of screens on an all too regular basis. He swears he created the whole Murder by Munchhausen tag. He's probably right, but I'd never let on that I thought so—or that I even read his stuff, which I did. It was more fratricidal ego hazing than professional discourtesy. Jamal was a good guy. I liked him.

"That was a nice catch on the droid."

"It's why the city pays me the big bucks."

"So, spill. Got the data dump yet?"

I rolled my eyes. "As if…"

"Come on. The vic was Judge Mullaney's third-second cousin or something. Right?"

"Damn Irish. Kill one and they all take offense. Anyway, you know the lab squidlies in forensics. Their clock speeds ain't exactly set to the Naval Observatory."

"But you'll let your favorite journalist know as soon as the results come in."

"Journalist? You flatter yourself."

"Hey, let me get a pic—so my editor knows I'm not just sitting around in my pajamas making stuff up." Jamal spun and pressed himself to my side, holding out his phone to take a selfie with me. "Is that a pistol? Or are you just glad to see me?"

"Did you at least get my good side?"

"Jake, you don't have a good side."

~~~

Edgewater

When I've got nowhere to be, there's no place better than being at the lake. Also, public parks are nearly exclusively occupied by humans. Synthoids don't need R&R, so the few there to pick up trash are uniformed in Metroparks logoed jumpsuits and are easy to avoid.

So, I hoofed it back from *John's* to the building that I "inherited" from Mom and Pop, where my apartment was above what used to be their shop. My sister took it over, but couldn't clean up the mess left behind after probate and I bailed the building out of IRS purgatory with a chunk of my settlement stash. It was okay between us. I had no interest in a flower shop and Karen made an honest go of it, but her heart really wasn't into floral arrangements either. So, no hard feelings.

But now, the shop was a big empty man cave for my play things. I rolled the Indian *Chief Dark Horse* out the garage door that led to the alley out back. It's my preferred mode of travel since motorcycles don't have a "Rochester" chauffeur mode—and I *hate* putting my life in the hands of self-driving cars.

I cranked the engine and headed down to Edgewater to hang and watch the waves crash. The sound aurally scrubbed my mind, clearing my thoughts. Funny, how not thinking can help you think.

I sat for a long while on the rocks, then wandered the beach, which was mostly abandoned in the middle of the week—at least 'til the day was pushing noon, when the people watching got a little more interesting as folks started gathering like lint and hair in a drain trap. You can never turn it off completely, even when you're off duty. Always making judgments and sizing up intents, whether it be ill or otherwise. An involved couple meeting to share a sandwich. A scattering of businessmen brown-bagging it to seek out a little serenity in the middle of the work day. Teens who should be in school but weren't, with no ill intent except to escape the educational warehousing for a day. The ones that always draw closer scrutiny are those who sit in their cars, especially on a warm, sunny day. Their visages are always the least social, rarely smiling, staring like hungry panthers at prey. My eye is immediately drawn to the license plate number. Like I said, you can't turn it off.

But I was off duty, so I walked back, then east out around the marina and the power plant to Whiskey Island. Pumping my legs helped the thought process a lot, too. Somehow, I solved many a tough case wandering aimlessly about the city. There was nothing really to noodle over on my case with EC—at least until the forensics guys finished up analyzing the synthoid's hardware, firmware, and software. We had the AnSub; we just needed the accomplice who programmed the murder and the perp who paid for it. But Maddie's case was still festering in my mind, chewing on my gray matter like the waves gnawing and eroding the shoreline.

I got back to the water's edge on the north side of the island and mindlessly watched an ore boat breech the break wall to head upriver to deliver its mined goods.

"Another one," Maddie said when she got the call from the House that morning.

The Trilogy: Murder by Munchausen

I didn't need to see those photos to know what that meant and the look on her face when she called from the crime scene confirmed it: the same person had committed both murders. It was early, but no doubt the thought had already put down roots in the back of her mind that she may have just caught a serial murder case…and that brings a whole new set of calculations into the equation. Some of it is bureaucratic and procedural and exceedingly annoying—like when do you actually invite the brass to start looking over your shoulder with a microscope at every little thing that you do and when do the federal frat boys at the F.B.I. crash the party and then the whole public relations nightmare with the media. I don't mind sparring one-on-one with Jamal and his ilk, but standing in front of a pack of hungry news cameras and microphones to feed their pathological need for attention? In a way, it is its own Media by Munchausen. No thanks. Been there. Done that. Been second, third and fourth guessed by every expert out there with their own blog and by-line. But, come to think about it, Maddie would probably look great and sound smart streaming onto all the big screens at the end of the media pipeline. She might like it. Me? Not so much.

On the other hand, the hunter in us all can't help but feel the adrenalin rush of being on the trail of "big game." Hell, it's not even my case, but I got a mainline dose of it just looking at the crime photos. Homicides are usually just messy and emotional, no mystery or matching wits with a mastermind. You're essentially cleaning up the temper tantrum of a toddler armed with a deadly weapon. But it's a completely different ball game when the act of taking a life becomes some sick mode of self-expression. And unlike the unsolved cases that can take their toll over time with their lack of answers, a serial case eats you alive because you're not looking back asking 'why.' You know there is a new victim coming, so you're looking ahead and asking 'who' and 'when,' feeling powerless to stop what you know will happen.

I knew Maddie's mind had already started going there, wondering about the third vic.

So, while the hunter in me yearned to join the pack, the lover in me wanted her out. But I knew that would never happen. This was the kind of case careers are made out of…and she knew it, too.

I walked back to my bike with selfish thoughts swirling unverbalized in the back of my head and disrupting any professional attempt to connect dots into a usable and meaningful pattern.

~~~

The West Side Market

Mel, the Butcher, saw me coming and waved his cleaver at me. I waved back and slowly meandered down the crowded aisle of the open market, mentally taking note of the produce and bakery offerings along the way to his stall.

"The usual?" asked Mel as I stepped up to his counter.

"Yeah. A couple of Freddies, please." Mel didn't know who Fred Flintstone was, but he knew that—whoever he was—he liked his steaks extra thick. I watched him saw off a couple of cowboy rib steaks that would barely fit on the Weber. I mentally drifted back to the butchery in the alley.

"You got a big case?" Mel asked in his thick Slavic accent, noticing my faraway look. "You look like you got a big case."

"Me? No. No big cases for me anymore." I shook my head. "Maddie, though…"

"How is Miss Madeline?"

I sighed out loud.

"Jake, Jake, Jake…" Mel shook his head and wagged his butcher knife at me. "Don't screw this one up, too. She's a good lady."

Maddie and I used to stop at the West Side Market for gyros when we were just work partners and wander up and down the aisles scoping out the food items, since we both share a passion for good eating. You wouldn't think that a career woman cop would be such a good cook, but she knew her way around the kitchen. I found that out later, during my suspension, when she came by to cheer me up with plateful after plateful of gourmet goodies. Truth be told, I'm just an animal flesh searer. She's the one with the culinary artistry. Mel knew the same thing from her interrogation of him on different cuts of meat, like she was wringing a felony confession out of the butcher.

"Yeah, I know. I know. That's what everybody tells me."

"Well, then, you should listen to everybody then. *Huh.*"

"Just throw those Freddies over this way."

The steaks landed with a satisfying thud on the counter top, like a heavyweight boxer hitting the canvas. I smiled and slipped Mel bank scrip for the meat—more than they weighed out to—that I'm sure went right into his pocket. The government tried hard to take the cash out of society, but that just ain't how people are in the real world.

"You listen to everybody, my friend. *Listen.*"

"Sure, Mel. Sure."

I saluted and wandered on down the aisle, listening instead to the voice inside my head and doing my people-perp watch of the crowd.

I missed it more than I admitted—at least to the outside world—being a people cop, I mean. I guess the Poindexters EC and I go after are people. Barely. Not exactly the usual stuff of crime statistics, anyway. Just not much sport in it really, just digital ones and zeros for evidence, mainly, and a geeky computer nerd at the end of the trail. Maybe that's why I latched onto Maddie's case so quickly, but I didn't really believe that. Just playing *iPsych* on myself—something that I got too much of a taste of from the Department shrinks.

The Trilogy: Murder by Munchausen

I mean, just being so close to a real flesh and bloody crime investigation, I could feel the heat of passion, anger, ambition and a tinge of fear, like standing close to a radiator. Truth be told, it's a pretty intoxicating cocktail. But the bottom line is that there is somebody doing bad things to people…very bad things that have to be stopped. And there was something there in the crime pictures that I saw but didn't yet see.

The faces in the Market dissolved into a blank, fleshy canvas as I sliced through the crowd like a shark through a school of tuna.

And I'm sure my eyes looked just as cold and empty to the schooling shoppers.

~~~

The Fire Escape Grill

Unconsciously, I sorted the books scattered around the loft into two piles as I tidied up the place for Maddie. I had thoughts of running the vacuum, but, well, I got sidetracked by black-and-white eight-by-tens from a hundred years ago or more. I re-shelved the bigger stack of books and towered the other off in an out-of-the-way corner, hopefully where it would stay out of Maddie's eye line. I surveyed the joint. The place was clean enough. I just had to ensure footprints weren't left in the dust and that all other possible work-related distractions were properly tucked away out of sight.

I went out to preload the Weber and Frank the Feral Cat was there waiting for me with an impatient look on his face, so first I took care of his needs. He followed me into the kitchen to keep an eye on me like the wary feline that he is. I took his tuna back out to the fire escape and he eyeballed me as I dumped charcoal into the stovepipe starter and stuffed it with scrap paper from the precinct. As he settled into wolfing down his meal, I sat down on the fire escape and dangled my legs over the edge with a beer, soaking in the long summer sun. In the winter, with the trees stripped of their leaves, I can just barely make out the lake through the cuts between the houses and apartment buildings. Once spring comes, it's gone, so I watched the traffic and the birds and the occasional pedestrian as I waited, slowly and methodically stripping my mind of thoughts like old paint off of woodwork.

"Hey, Jakie," Maddie called out what could have been minutes or hours later or maybe even days.

"Out back!" I answered.

A few minutes later, she climbed out on the fire escape with her lawn chair and a glass of red wine. She plopped down and took a long sip. "Hey, Frank."

Frank acknowledged her arrival with a long, impatient look up from his tuna.

"Oh, my God. That sun feels great," Maddie exclaimed. "Bring it on. Bring it on."

"Hungry?"

"Mmmm…I will be."

"Mel says 'hi' and that I should pay attention more—to you, that is."

"Yeah? Maybe you should take his advice"

I looked back at her over my shoulder.

She smiled wearily.

I wasn't going to be the one to bring it up.

"Exact same M.O." Maddie sighed heavily. "Definitely dealing with a sick puppy."

I nodded. I understood completely.

"You got anything?"

"A gut feeling."

Maddie nodded. She understood that if you force it, like a bird in the bush, you flush it and maybe never see it again.

"I—"

"Later. We've got all night." I got up and took her hand to lead her inside to the bedroom.

The Trilogy: Murder by Munchausen

She didn't resist.

After, we lay naked for a long while, not speaking, then I got up and lit the grill. I watched the sunset.

Maddie appeared behind me, dressed only in a tank top and a pair of short shorts. Her hard, well-exercised and well-tended body teased beneath the thin fabric. Her hair waterfalled down across her shoulders like I like it. She sipped at the glass of wine she had poured when she first arrived and admired the setting sun. She sighed contentedly.

"Yeah."

"Yeah."

We don't call it the Fire *Escape* Grill for nothing.

Eventually, the coals glowed orange hot and I started searing the cattle flesh. Maddie went in to rattle around the kitchen to prep our side dish. We sat in our lawn chairs in the dusk at the end of the daylight, eating our steaks and talking about sports, work politics, city politics and what we should do on our vacation together in the fall—everything except the five-hundred-pound gorilla of a subject in the room—until we ran out of ways to avoid it, so we went to bed to wrestle more tenderly this time and fell asleep.

"Sands says he'll hold off going to the brass," Maddie said when we met at the coffee pot the next morning as she made her way to the shower. "But if it starts getting too much play in the media…"

"He'll have no choice," I finished her sentence. "Obviously."

"Yeah. Managementspeak."

"Got anything?"

"Precious little, except the profession of the victims and the eviscerations. The Bunny Boys picked up some DNA material, but with the revolving door on their panties, who knows where that will lead."

"Well, start practicing your media doublespeak."

Maddie rolled her eyes and took a sip of coffee. "What about your Munchhausen Murder? Anything back from the Wonder Kids?"

"Oh, I imagine Q will have something for us this morning. I'm just glad EC has the patience to endure his techno-babble. I sure don't."

"Always at the mercy of technicians," Maddie whined sympathetically.

"Press '3' for all the ways that technology has not made your life better…"

We dressed and armed ourselves for the work day, then went our separate ways.

~~~

The Grease Monkeys

The first stop EC and I made was the back room in our building known as Mechanical where the grease monkeys tear down apprehended synthoids in a half-assed autopsy. Bob and Puff were hunched over our droid bickering like the old married couple they practically were. EC cleared his throat.

"Hey there, guys," Bob said in his sing-song way, standing upright and wiping fluid off his hands with an oily rag. He was the rounder and jollier of the two. Puff, tall, lean and curmudgeonly, just grunted and kept poking around the wires and tubes in the torso through the abdominal access panel.

"Spring a leak?" I asked, pointing at Bob's hands.

"Yeah, you know, boy, it's a funny thing…" Bob smiled and chuckled, adjusting the glasses on his face. "Some of the bio-hydraulic lines in the legs and rib cage were ruptured. Nasty take down, I guess. Huh?"

Puff stood up straight, bringing some kind of electronic module from inside the droid to the tip of his nose to examine, squinting at it to bring its label into focus. "The *Dermal-Lite* on the back of the thighs had lateral impact impressions…like from a baton." He squinted my way. "You wouldn't know anything about that, would you?"

I shrugged innocently.

Puff looked at EC, catching his smirking half-smile, then

grunted and dove back into the guts of the synthoid. "Right. *Idiots.*"

"So what's the story on this unit?" EC asked.

"Well, I'll tell ya, guys," Bob wound himself up with a deep breath, "it's a standard Omega Gen-3 chassis, but there's definitely been some special modifications."

"Chop-shopped?"

"Yeah, yeah, yeah—but these guys aren't hacks. They seem to know their way around bio-robotics pretty well. And they didn't use cheap gray market replacement parts. All OEM stuff, but they mixed and matched from the Big Three. Look here, a Fanuc Dexterity Control Unit," Bob pointed into the abdomen of the synthoid, "mated to a Mitsu BLC. And over here's a GD mobility module." Bob shook his head. "I don't know how they got their hands on a military grade mobility pack."

"But the Gen-3s aren't as vertically integrated as the earlier designs, right?" EC asked.

"True. True," Bob's bald head bobbed up and down. "And swapping out subassemblies is a pretty effective way to get around the embedded RSHA protocols to defeat the Three Laws."

"Yeah, so, they're all Frankensteins to one degree or another, right?" I asked.

"True. True. You can't do it all with just software. But this one—"

"The mobility module," Puff said curtly. He stood up again, twirling what looked like a hip ball and socket assembly in his hands. He squinted one eye shut towards EC and I. The stare down seemed to last forever.

"He's right, you know," Bob finally interrupted. "That's the wild card."

"How so?"

"Generals need to know where the grunts are, but not the enemy," Puff explained without elucidating the matter.

"Yup. Army synthoids aren't permanently latched to the Atlas grid like civilian units," Bob said. "Otherwise, troop movements could be seen by the bad guys. I couldn't begin to tell you how they hacked into a mil spec GMC, but this is definitely post graduate work—maybe even Ph.D. level."

"Post hole diggers?" I asked to lighten the mood.

Puff glared at me.

"Did you get the black boxes pulled?" EC asked quickly before another staring contest got under way.

"First thing we did, fellas," Bob answered. "Got them over to Q yesterday morning."

"Great. Thanks, guys." EC headed towards the door.

I took a last long look at the tangled innards of the murder weapon. I looked over at Puff. "Serious, huh?"

He ran his fingers through the thick shock of his graying hair. "As a heart attack."

I nodded and followed EC out.

Puff's squinting eyes tracked me the whole way out the door.

~ ~ ~

Q

EC planted himself at his desk and began mining his inbox for word back from the code analysts. I sat down and pulled a pad of paper out of my desk to start my daily "To Do" list. Old school. But scrawling out my hopes and dreams in long hand was always more effective for me than doing it online and stuffing them into a cloud somewhere—who knows where. Out of sight, out of mind—and people wonder why nothing ever gets done.

Our Elba was called "Exit Alley," back behind the precinct building in an abandoned warehouse that the city foreclosed on and put forth a minimal effort to renovate in order to get us out of the hair of the "real" cops. It drove EC crazy. I was just as glad to be off the chain of command's immediate radar—especially now with the cold shadow of a possible serial killer hanging over their heads. Maddie's case would ratchet the tension in the squad room up for everybody.

Our "offices" were nothing more than a big open bullpen with desks and a few file cabinets. We did have a couple of conference rooms/interrogation rooms along the side wall that got more use out of HR and their endless training sessions, than they did wringing confessions out of reluctant perps. Usually by the time we apprehended a hacker, their will to resist—usually as weak to begin with as their upper body strength—had evaporated. There were four other officers exiled to the Geek Squad. Two of them had actually requested the duty, having come up through IT, white collar crimes, and forensic accounting. None of them had seen the street in their entire crime fighting careers like me and EC. They hung out with Q and his gang on their breaks—*as if…*

"Bingo! Q's got something for us," EC exclaimed and I watched his lips flap as he read the email from our resident forensic programming genius and reverse hacker. Q had some kind of shady past that was never mentioned by anyone in the squad and that tickled my interest not one bit, *or byte,* depending upon your technical orientation. EC hopped to his feet. "Come on, Jake. He says it's something we need to see for ourselves."

I made a show of lumbering reluctantly to my feet and shuffled after EC. The Brainiacs were in another part of the warehouse, in offices much nicer and more climate-controlled than ours, which boiled in the summer and froze in the winter. Thank you, Mr. Mayor.

Q's world was one of cubicles and the quiet tap-tap-tapping of keyboards, like a constant depressing rain against a windowpane. He greeted us at the door and motioned us into a severe white conference room with modern white furniture. You almost had to shield your eyes from the glare. The pale green paint somebody viciously picked for our decor was already peeling, even though our side had been renovated at the same time as the lab's. EC and I sat on one side of the table. Q sat across from us and pulled out a printed out report on…*more white paper!* How could the Brainiacs sit in such brightness all day long and not get even a hint of a tan?

I sat back in my chair. EC leaned in to listen intently to Q. That wasn't really his name. I tagged him with it because I refused to engage lab rats on a personal level. Evidently, he actually knew who James Bond was and even Ian Fleming—one point in his favor—and took a shine to his new nickname, so it stuck. He was also able to affect a scruffy unshaven look, being one of the few males in the colony who could actually sprout whiskers, so he didn't look fourteen. Another point. And if I was being completely truthful, he had a gritty attitude about rules that I found appealing—but I never let on.

"We've found some recurring subroutines and library links in the coding that are *very* interesting." Q laid out sheets of paper filled with typed gibberish cascading across the page. His index finger darted into different lines of code like peccadilloes until it finally stuck on one line of code highlighted in yellow. "And this call out here is particularly intriguing."

That's odd, I caught myself wondering. *Q? Paper?*

"And why is that?" EC asked with interest.

"Well…" Q shuffled more papers in a file folder and pulled out another couple of sheets. "It is an external call out into a cloud bank that has, well, evaporated."

Techno mumbo jumbo, I thought. "Okay…"

"It is obviously a ploy to keep forensic evidence out of the synthoid's firmware by putting it where it wouldn't be found or would be destroyed after the mission was concluded."

"How would they do that?"

"It might be triggered by an event, like the crime, or time deadline or even sensor input, like a spike off the RFIDs in a cop badge." Q scratched his whiskered cheek loudly. "It's a new twist. Actually, quite creative."

"Well, where is this cloud bank?" EC asked.

"And that, gentlemen, that is the funny thing…" He folded his hands on top of the papers and stared first at EC, then me.

"What?" I asked impatiently, but not from Q's transparent attempt to build suspense. My spider senses started tingling at 'quite creative.'

"Commercial services are required by the Public Utilities Commission to keep LUDs—*Local Usage Details*—on cloud account activities, which can be subpoenaed."

"So, we need to get you a subpoena?" EC's voice betrayed reluctance at the prospect of official paperwork.

"Well, I would say yes, if I thought it would lead us somewhere useful. But I already know that it would be a dead end."

"And how do you know that?" I asked.

Q rolled his eyes and feigned a Spanish accent, "'Cause we don't need no stinking subpoenas here."

"At least not unless we want it to be admissible," EC noted impatiently. Q was even starting to irritate my partner.

"But there's no sense in wasting all that time and judicial goodwill when we know there won't be anything useful to be *admissible.*"

"And we know this how?" I asked again, a bit more sternly.

Q stared back at me. "I've read the I.A. transcripts on your…*incident*—"

"Those are sealed," I said. "Or are supposed to be."

"Yes. *Quite.*"

"So?"

"Then you do understand." Q swept up the pages of printed out code. He tapped the edges square on the table and slid them into the file folder. He reached to his belt and pulled off his Android *Alpha-Bit* and placed it on the table between us like an ante in a poker game.

"That's not department-issue," EC noted.

"So, report me." Q stood up and motioned silently towards the door. "You in or out."

EC and I pulled the *iNodes* from our belts and anted up. As far as the Atlas grid was concerned, we'd still be sitting in the conference room with Q.

Q rounded the table and headed out.

EC and I looked at each other, stood up, and followed him out of the conference room and down the hall, offices on the left and a cubicle farm on the right.

When Q got to the end of the hall, he pulled out a burner and tapped swiftly on the screen, then silenced the alarm on the emergency exit and held the door open for us. We all went out into the alley that separated us from the precinct house. Q produced a flat piece of hard plastic from nowhere like a magician, slid it between the latch and the jam, then pushed the door shut behind us. He squinted up at the security camera to make sure its blinking red light was out. He gave us a smirk.

"Lovely aroma," EC said, sniffing the air and eyeballing the dumpster.

"What can I say? My gang loves Indian food," said Q.

"So, the cloak and dagger routine…for why?" I asked.

"*For why*, because the LUD breadcrumbs lead back to the NSA. And Samantha noticed in her pattern analysis that the logic loops therein are, shall we say, bureaucratically bloated and inefficient."

"Samantha?" EC asked.

"You'd like her. She's cute." Q winked.

"NSA?" I asked.

"A lazy copy and paste job. It appears to be a routine to access metadata."

"But why? How did a domestic dispute gone awry end up in a hack into the NSA?" I wondered out loud.

"Hey. Me, I'm forensics. Remember?" Q asked pointing his finger into his own sternum. Then he wagged his long, skinny index finger between EC and me. "You are the detectives. So, detect."

"Okay, so email me your findings," EC said.

"Uh-uh." Q shook his head and handed EC the thick manila file folder. "Breadcrumbs. I don't want any knocks on my door—personally or professionally."

EC and I looked at one another.

Q pulled the emergency exit door open and stepped back inside. "You guys coming back in?"

"Nah. I think I need some air—fresh air," I said, looking up at the security camera. "I think we're gonna take a walk."

"Suit yourselves." Q pulled out his burner. "I'll give you a minute or two to clear the alley before I turn big brother back on. This gonna take long?"

I looked at EC. He shrugged. "Give us an hour."

"Excellent. Since I'm off the grid, I've got some errands to run." Q smiled cryptically. "Ping me once and I'll clear you back in to adjourn our meeting and get your *iNodes.*"

Q slipped back into the building.

EC and I headed down the alley to *Cutty's Deli,* where we knew we'd be away from prying eyes and ears…*and lenses.*

I looked back over my shoulder at the security camera and saw the red light come back on.

~~~

Cutty

Cutty was a retired cop who developed an expertise in deli meats during his twenty-five years on patrol as well as some pretty strong opinions on the proper assembly of a great sandwich and the improper pollution of coffee with anything other than real dairy cream and real sugar from real sugar cane. His place was always busy, even though it was around the corner and tucked away from the Justice Center. It was a place where plea deals got made, because prosecutors and public defenders checked their indignation as well as the Bill of Rights at the door and where cops spoke freely and frankly about the facts—admissible and otherwise—of their cases clear of the mist and fog of Department policy and political correctness. Although there was no sign on the door, the place was always completely devoid of politicians, both civilian and those wearing blue. Oh yeah, and no one from Internal Affairs—past or present—ever showed their face there. Evidently, Cutty had some history with them, too. Most of the good ones do—or so I'd been told by Cutty. He was my training officer went I first got out of the academy.

EC and I got a booth in the back and it wasn't long before the ex-cop appeared at our table dressed in a stained white apron.

"Howdy, boys." Cutty swirled amber liquid in a department mug that had never been stained by coffee—at the precinct or in its afterlife at the deli—and took a sip. His affinity for Scots Whiskey was well known. "The chili is a particularly good batch today."

"Are you kidding me?" EC snickered. "I've got to ride with this guy for the next five days."

"I'll do it. Make it a five-way," I said to Cutty, pushing away my unopened menu, then scowled across the table at my partner. "EPA and EC be damned."

"That's the spirit."

"Then give me a pastrami Reuben," EC countered. "With slaw."

"Nice. Fighting fire with fire. It's going to be an aromatic tour."

I shrugged my shoulders.

EC smirked.

"I heard you scooped up the droid that iced the judge's son. Nice work." Cutty winked. "But…what about the Geppetto pulling the strings?"

"Funny you should ask." EC tapped the envelope from Q with the forensics report. "Appears to be complications."

"Always are…Always are."

"Yeah, but these might be of the *federale* variety," I sighed.

"Ouch. Sorry to hear it. No one needs that." Cutty paused to peer at me over his mug. After another sip, he grinned and added, "Just ask Maddie in a week or two. How's that case working out for her? Word is that she'll be surrounded by pressed suits and starched white shirts before too long."

"Don't get jealous now, Jake," EC teased.

"Actually, I feel sorry for the suits. She has a knack for getting her way. Trust me. I know."

"You've always played with fire," Cutty said.

"I'm not the only one with third-degree burns on his soul."

"Yeah, but most people wait for the afterlife." Cutty winked. "I'll put in your order."

We watched him head back behind the counter.

"So, what do you think about Q's report?" EC asked when Cutty was out of earshot.

"A breadcrumb."

"You want to follow it? Knowing where it could lead?" EC sighed heavily. "I ain't got the energy to be sparring with DC's boys—especially if they're spooks."

I pondered for a moment. "I wonder what it really means. You heard Q. Anybody can hack into anyone's short hairs if they want. Why would this guy want? It's a local judge. A local crime. No need to go all *Mission Improbable* about it. Maybe, like Q said, he's just a lazy cut-and-paste kind of guy."

"Cutting and pasting from the NSA? That's a special kind of lazy."

"Inside or outside. That's the question."

"I hope it's outside. You know there's no way we'll get any help from the Company minions." EC arranged and rearranged his silverware.

"Depends upon what he was tapping into and why. Maybe, just maybe, the worker bees don't want the ruling class to know there's air leaking out of their tires."

"And just who would you talk to about that?"

I tapped my chin with my index finger. "Hmmm. I might know a guy who knows a guy."

"Yeah, well, I don't want to know."

Cutty returned with our lunches. *Bon appétit.*

EC and I traded evil smiles as we prepared to load up our intestines with ammo.

~ 52 ~

~~~

The Federales

EC went back to the precinct to retrieve our iNodes and start data mining known associates of the victim and his spouse to prep for our interview. I headed down to Lakeside, then took a right over to East 9th and sat on a park bench across the street from the Federal Building. I took out my latest burner phone and dialed a number inside.

"Yeah, can I get a pizza to go with no anchovies?" I got the response I expected from the familiar voice inside and pocketed my phone. *Secret Service, my ass.* That place had more holes in it than the Pacific Fleet after December 7th.

The engineers and programmers do a good job and most people can't tell the mechanical droids from the human drones on the street even at a reasonably close distance. More likely, though, is that they just stopped paying attention, like ignoring regular people in the crowd every day. If you know what you're looking for, though, you can spot them easy enough. Of course, after the last year or so, I'm a bit more tuned into them, like a fisherman reading the surface of the lake for a school of walleye. They're still digital creatures, not analogue like us humans, so their movements are just a bit too crisp and hard-edged, even from a distance, mostly at the knees and elbows. Of course, it's even more obvious when you come face-to-face with one. Too many muscles in the human head, including the big, fat one between the ears. But it's getting harder, though, because the industry is always getting better, especially with the new active plasma biologic materials they are developing. And research showed that people react subconsciously to rhythms of bodies around them, so the Gen-3s even mimic the diaphragm movements of breathing and have nano-motors to generate pulses in the neck and wrists.

What struck me most, though, as I observed the activities on the plaza across the street, was just how many synthoids there were wandering around the Federal Building. I started making mental notes, as was my habit, and eventually noticed the same droids circulating randomly around the plaza. *Ah…security droids.* No doubt the first line of defense in any attack against the government. I wondered what my Secret Service pal thought about his job description being automated.

Eventually, my "pizza" got delivered.

"J-man," muttered the tall, dark-suited civil servant as he wandered by my bench. His eyes were shielded by government issued Ray-Bans. He stopped at the East 9th Street crosswalk and looked up at the traffic camera perched above the signal lights.

I stood up and meandered to the corner, then crossed Lakeside against the light. Cloak and dagger crap. A bit overly dramatic, but a small price to pay.

Eventually, we crossed paths again at Short Vincent Street and headed down Superior Avenue to the library. If you knew where to go, there were still dark holes deep, deep in the stacks, safe from prying eyes. Nineteenth Century literature was an appropriately dim corner of our modern day Orwellian reality.

The Trilogy: Murder by Munchausen

"You off grid?" He hissed between his glowing gritted teeth. He still had his sunglasses on, like the cheesy Federal LEO that he was.

I nodded.

"Good. So, how's tricks?"

"Can't complain." I shrugged off the question.

"Yeah, well, I could, but where would it get me?"

"Maybe promoted to a GL-9?"

"Funny, Jake. Real funny."

"Yeah, I'm a riot. That's what I.A. put in their report. So, now I've got *that* on my permanent record."

"So, how can I help you today, Citizen?"

"I don't know. Maybe I can help you."

"How so?"

"How about spook code infecting my murder investigation?"

"Huh. Homeland Security? Insecure? Imagine that. Is this that judge's kid?"

I nodded.

"Interesting…"

"Ya think?"

"No. Not really." He sighed heavily. "Do you know how many lines of code it takes for the federal government to rule the plebes?"

I shook my head. "Or wait. Is this a joke?"

"Sadly, no. Nobody does. And that's the problem."

"I'll bet it's gotta be at least as voluminous as the tax code."

"Yeah, well, at least the private sector is anal about their magic pixie dust."

"Capitalism. You gotta love it."

"You'd think, but…You know the only real competition in

civil service is in the area of mudslinging and backstabbing."

"I thought the NSA was a cut above anyway—especially on mudslinging. You know, the new J. Edgars, the ones with brontobyte-sized files on everybody, born and yet unborn, and the total lack of fear or ethics to use them to protect themselves and their own dark wants and desires."

"NSA? Well, that's different. Those guys are bad ass."

"So again I ask, why is their code polluting my crime scene?"

"And how do you know this?"

"Really? You want my source?" I feigned outrage since I knew he knew.

"Q, right?"

"He's good. At least that's what EC tells me. And he is actually pretty effective when he's not in one of his moods."

"I'm surprised he doesn't work for them."

"Him? The NSA? Never." I shook my head and fingered the bindings of books on the shelf. "Q wouldn't be caught dead working for *The Man.*"

He answered with a Federal-sized grunt of indignation. "You got something for me?"

I took out the page with the code that Q highlighted. "Don't get any Inspector General types involved, okay? I just want to know if this guy is inside or outside of government."

The *Federale* snatched the page out of my hands and skimmed over it. "Jesus. How can anyone stare at this crap every day, all day, and not go mad."

"And not go mad? I think you answered your own question. Q is anything but even-keeled."

He nodded, folded the page back up and stuck it in his suit jacket. It was actually nice that not everyone in government dressed like a golf pro. "I don't know where this will lead, but you understand that I'm not sticking my neck out too far on this."

"Of course."

"But I'll chum the waters and see what kind of carp comes to the surface."

"Carp or crap?"

"Neither one is good eating, so what's the diff?" He pulled down a volume from the shelf. "Read much, Jake?"

I nodded.

"You would." He smirked and showed me the cover: *Frankenstein* by Mary Shelly.

"I'm more of a fan of her husband."

"Who's that?"

"Never mind. Let me know if you hear something." I started to turn to head out of the stacks.

"Hey, hey, hey—what about me? You know how this works: *Quid pro quo.*"

"What do you want?"

"I don't know…*something.*"

I had to stop and think, really think about selling out Maddie and whether it was worth it, but nah. Sure, he'd score points giving the local F.B.I. guys two floors down a heads-up on a serial killer case coming their way, but it's Maddie and I hate to admit it: I am sweet on her. *And,* I hate bureaucratic backscratching—it's unsightly like the simian grooming on Monkey Island at the zoo; but, ugly as it is, it's the way of the world. Of course, there had yet to be any *quo to quid.* Besides, he owed me from last time, so by my scorekeeping, I was still ahead.

"I might have something juicy for you, but not yet."

"What?"

"Don't worry. It'll be good." I turned and headed out of the stacks, calling back over my shoulder, "Though actual mileage may vary."

~~~

Mrs. Victim

Now that we had the murder weapon and we were starting to get some leads on the reprogrammer, it was time to chat with the judge's daughter-in-law and, from what EC found in his search, he hinted she might be a doozie.

We made a good Mutt and Jeff team. EC liked doing his homework and researching the hell out of an interview. I preferred to be more of a blank canvas so that my impressions weren't colored by information already smeared on my psyche. It's important to get a clean read on a person of interest, and if you're painting-by-numbers, sometimes staying inside the lines takes your eye off the big picture. EC got it. So did Maddie—at least when we were professional partners. It's not so easy now. But, you know, things always change.

The Widow Mullaney agreed to see us in their penthouse apartment a couple of blocks down the hill from the bodega where her husband was programmed out of existence. After our formal introductions, EC sat down across the coffee table from her and took out his *iSlate*. Laying it on the table, he hit 'Record' and pulled up his research notes.

I drifted over to the huge picture window that looked out over the mouth of the river from the east bank. Out on the lake, an ore boat hovered near the break wall, waiting for a railroad drawbridge to rise.

I closed my eyes and listened to her voice answer EC's basic opening who-what-where-when questions—like a polygrapher trying to get a baseline reading. Her voice was smooth and calm, yet her thoughts were carried forward with a strong undercurrent of authority, like a doctor who actually deals with patients on a regular basis—and effectively, too, though she would probably be a nightmare to the nursing staff.

"So, did you and your husband have any registered Personal Services Assistants?" EC asked, going down his list of questions like a head coach calling in the next play in the game plan to the quarterback.

I turned from the window to put a face with the voice in time to see her shake her head in a measured way that didn't ripple or disturb her straight, shoulder-length blonde hair.

"Of course, the building has several in service for maintenance, housekeeping and, obviously, to patrol the parking garage, but we had no call for a PSA for ourselves," she answered coolly and evenly.

Her face was cut in a sharp kind of way that matched her voice, giving her beauty a hard, perhaps dangerous, edge. It held an expressionless cast as she spoke, like an eight-by-ten glossy promo shot or an ID badge portrait. She looked up at me with hard blue eyes. I smiled but got no ping back.

"What about work?"

"The usual orderly duty droids at the Clinic. I believe my husband's law office had them for library retrievals and returns. Typical stuff. Nothing very high-level. I am a geneticist. We don't do surgical or office procedures, just basic patient management and movement functions. I prefer human staff in my office."

Right, because getting up in a droid's grill isn't nearly as satisfying as berating a fellow human being, I thought to myself. Synthoids are all programmed to take so-called "Droid Rage" completely passively, which doesn't really work too well in being an emotional pressure relief valve for the human. Though every once in a while it makes for fairly entertaining watching when a registration holder decides to post a vid-log of someone who totally loses it with technology. It's good there's no such thing as assault and battery on inanimate objects—they're basically indestructible to a barehanded human anyway—but it does give one in my line of work pause when you imagine that kind of rage precipitating a domestic abuse call or murder scene. And some people wonder why we still carry guns.

As EC continued on with his questions and Mrs. Victim responded with her emotionally flat-lined answers, I surveyed the room and noted a discernible lack of testosterone in the ambiance.

"So, your husband wasn't living here anymore, right?" I interrupted.

She broke engagement from EC and looked up at me.

EC knew what I was doing and watched her like a hawk.

I smiled.

She smiled back with the slightest crack of her lips. "Why would you say that?"

I shrugged and did a panoramic sweep of the room. "I just get that kind of vibe."

"Vibe?"

"Yeah, you know, we're guys. We still mark our territory like the animals we are. Sometimes it's an 'I Love Me' wall or display case. Other times more subtle: trophies from our life's adventures…and conquests scattered about."

Her brow furrowed for the first time during our interview.

"I don't sense it. Not in this room, anyway." In reality, the building's doorman had tipped us off.

Behind the glossy mask, her gears were turning so hard you could practically hear them grinding like a first generation robot.

I smiled.

She finally broke and smiled back with the smallest of shoulder shrugs. "It wasn't something that we wanted out there for public consumption, even with family."

"A rough patch? Or something more serious?" EC probed gently.

Mrs. Victim sighed and finally the needles moved. "I think Alec might have overreacted a bit, but…"

"You?" I tried but couldn't keep all of the accusatory tone out of my voice.

She nodded.

Her hard professional demeanor slipped noticeably, but I wasn't sure if it was just part of her disarming bedside manner act. "Attorneys?"

She nodded.

Of course, EC had already found that out from the scuttlebutt at Cutty's, though no paperwork had been filed yet with the court.

"We don't have to tell you how these dots lay out on the page, do we?" EC pressed a bit. "It just happens all too often."

She looked back to EC, more guarded now.

"Prenup, I presume?" I asked.

"Of course."

"Another dot, then."

"I see." Her voice turned icy, so much so I swear I could see her breath. "Well, then, I suppose I should talk to that lawyer of mine about these dots you seem intent upon connecting."

"Now, Missus Mullaney—" EC tried to calm the waves.

"That is *Doctor* Mullaney," she scolded, then stood up.

EC sighed, then stood up.

I shoved my hands deep into my pockets and took a last look about the penthouse.

"I think we are finished here." She addressed us curtly as if we were hospital staff.

"Yeah…for now." My eyes tracked back to hers. No more smiles.

EC swept up his *iSlate* and we left the Mullaney apartment.

"I'll bet she's a hell of a good doctor," EC said on the elevator ride down.

"Scare the sick right out of you," I agreed.

~~~

Prime Time

"Uh-oh," EC muttered through gritted teeth as he spied the news vans from channels three, five, eight and nineteen parked haphazardly out front like they were fire trucks and the precinct house was ablaze. Instead of hoses, axes and water cannons, cameramen wrestled with cameras, microphones and anchorettes-in-waiting. We cut down to St. Clair and came around back. For once, I bet, he was glad to be exiled down the alley. I wondered if Maddie might be wishing the same thing by the end of the day, but I doubted it.

We don't have a lobby or a desk sergeant, just a cubed off entryway with a couple of intentionally uncomfortable chairs. In one, Jamal sat smiling like a loon.

"Look EC, a reporter," I said in a hushed, reverent voice as if I had spotted an extinct spotted owl. "You hardly ever see one around here."

"Yeah. It's kind of like finding honesty at City Hall," Jamal snickered.

EC grunted. He waved his badge over the keypad to unlock the door and went inside, leaving me alone with "the Press."

"So, whatsamatta? Didn't you get invited to the really big show?" I teased.

"Since when did any truly useful information ever get

released or exposed at a *really big show?* It's just a kabuki dance for the cameras."

"And that brings you here? For why?"

"So, how's Maddie handling it?"

"Don't know—and probably won't 'til later. Haven't seen her since we went on duty."

"Well, you tell her that if she ever needs a friendly ear to talk to…"

I rolled my eyes.

"Yeah, well…"

"Seriously. You are here, *for why?*"

"You know that Sands and PR weren't going to take any questions from me, so what's the point? I can replay the stream and get what I need from the talking heads at my leisure—with a strong drink in my hand—and then I'll have the exact same info everybody else has without standing around pathetically begging for scraps."

"And being the crusading pursuer of truth, justice and the American way that you are…"

"Actually, I came across an interesting tidbit about Mister and Missus Mullaney that I, oh, I don't know, thought might have some currency on the information meat market."

"Oh, well, then, step into my office." Instead of sweeping my badge over the keypad, I held open the door out to the alley.

Jamal threw out his lower lip in an exaggerated pout.

"Trust me, you don't want to go in there." I shook my head. "Come on, I'll buy you a cup of coffee."

"And a danish?"

"And a danish," I sighed wearily.

With the press vans out front, the food trucks parked around back. Even so, they probably did a better trade, what with the rush of blue soon to be scurrying out to stay off camera. I bought Jamal his low-fat latte and a bear claw. I got black coffee. We wandered to the back corner of the fenced-off parking lot and sat on the hood of a patrol car.

"Good luck," the reporter said, surprisingly sincere.

"With what?"

"Prime time."

"How's that?"

"Oh, I don't know. This kind of thing can swell a gal's head, what with all the attention and notoriety. I'll bet she'll look great on camera—not like you."

"So you're saying I should be worried?"

"You tell me."

I thought about it for a minute. "Maddie's definitely on her way up the food chain, but in her heart and soul, she's a cop, not a suit. It's in the family DNA."

Jamal nodded and gnawed at his pastry. "But…"

"But what?"

"That incident down in The Flats."

"What about it? I was cleared. *Officially.*"

"Sort of."

"Yeah. So?"

"How discreet are you guys—you and Maddie? You know that my intrepid colleagues will spare no drop of rare and precious journalistic sweat to dig up dirt to juice their ratings and page views. And you, my friend, are dirt. Internal Affairs may have cleared you, but they didn't clean you up any."

"Hmmm."

"I know you can take it. What about Maddie? Especially, if there's not a quick arrest and the investigation starts to drag on. It's good to be the hero. Not so much being the goat day in and day out—especially when bodies are piling up."

"I guess we'll see, huh? She's a good detective."

"Those ain't the skills she'll need for this."

I took a loud sip of coffee.

"Anyway, good luck."

I shrugged. Truth be told, Jamal's reporting on the incident precipitating my suspension was fair. Not necessarily pretty, but fair.

"You know that the judge's son was not such a nice guy. With his family connections on the bench, he had things pretty well stacked up against his soon-to-be ex. She doesn't have much juice outside the Clinic."

"Yeah, we picked up on that right from the start."

"Did you also pick up on his extra-curricular marital activities?"

"Ah, no. Do tell."

"I believe it kind of fouled up his lawyer's play with the pre-nup," Jamal smiled. "They did a good job of keeping it under wraps for a while, but it's not something the judge can sweep under the rug. Unless…"

"Unless the missus was wading in the same waters."

Jamal shrugged. "I hear that some of the women were, shall we say, hourly workers."

I nodded. "So he had needs, needs that maybe his hygienic and antiseptic obsessed wife did not care to indulge in. It happens."

"Sure, but here's where it gets interesting: Maddie's second victim."

"Oh no…" I froze in mid-java sip.

"Oh…*yeah.*" Jamal polished off his bear claw, licked his fingers and took a huge gulp of his latte. "I don't think it will come up today in the presser. Not likely anyone even knows yet. You didn't. *Does Maddie?*"

I lied with a shrug of my shoulders.

"But, rest assured, eventually someone's going to step off the sidewalk and into the gutter with me on this one."

"And how did you come to have this tasty morsel?"

Jamal put his shocked face on. "Do I ask you for the recipe to your Cajun rub?"

"Fair enough. But what are you going to do with that info?"

"Well…I just don't know yet. I'm working on a story, but the timing has to be right. If I release it right now, it will get lost in the thundering hooves of the media stampede heading Maddie's way right…about…now." Jamal looked over at the precinct building. A tide of uniformed officers ebbed out the back door towards the food trucks. He chuckled to himself. "Oh what a tangled web we weave…"

"…when first we practice to believe." I hid my concern over Jamal's information behind my coffee cup.

"Well, right now, it's actually just a thread that needs to be pulled a bit more. We've got to stay ahead of those pancaked-faced Bozos and Bozettes to find out what it means."

"What do you mean 'we,' Kemo Sabe?"

"You don't think this information is of value to you personally, as well as professionally."

I nodded slowly. It was—or would be.

"Just remember who's your pal." Jamal pulled out his phone and surfed to the stream of the press conference going on inside the precinct house. He held the phone up so I could see the screen. "You want to watch?"

I shook my head. I'd hear about it later. First hand.

Jamal smiled. "And you thought the geek squad was going to be low profile. *Sucker.*"

I looked at Maddie answering a question. She looked good, even on the small screen.

"When was the last time a camera crew came down the alley to your offices?"

"Well, let me think—like never."

"Yeah, well, good luck with that." Jamal looked at his phone. "She looks good. You're a lucky guy. You'll need it."

"Good luck with what? The press? Or Maddie?"

"Both, my friend." Jamal hopped down off the hood of the squad car and sauntered off. "Thanks for the bear claw."

~~~

The Flats

I sat in the dim twilight of the dying day on my sofa, staring at the stack of books in the corner that deserved a serious second look—especially now with Jamal's G2—to compare to the crime scene shots of Maddie's now infamous "film at eleven" worthy murders. Before, my interest in her case was a personal, say, curiosity. Now EC and I were going to get sucked into the media wave like into a rip tide. I hesitated before diving in.

The case that brought so much grief into my life was, of course, political. Maddie and I had "inherited" it because the Captain wanted to put fresh eyes on a high profile murder, after consuming so much time and department resources with so little results. We had been on a streak and just put away a butcher, a baker, and a candlestick shaker in short order, after they had killed a wife, a lover, and the last one a rival by smashing in his head with—wait for it—a candlestick, respectively and in that order. Instead of the gratitude of the city, we got a case that stank like the garbage truck servicing all the downtown restaurants.

Dr. Mullaney's apartment overlooked the Flats—the industrial lowlands around the river stitching its way up from the lake like a nasty knife wound that has always been the cultural equivalent of the Chilean Triple Junction, where commerce, crime and the creatures of *haute couture* have long collided for fun and profit. Amazingly, one of the dinosaurs from the Industrial Revolution times still spits out steel, fed by the ore boats off the lake. The rest lay abandoned. One has been turned into a hydroponic vegetable hothouse and tilapia farm, but the stink of industrial agriculture isn't much better, just different. On the West Bank, establishments cater openly to the baser needs of the city's citizens: liquor, drugs and women. Safely separated by the river, the East Bank is home to condo boards and gourmet cuisine that is really just a facade to the well-heeled's pursuit of the same baser needs. Crime, like magma, oozes between the cultural tectonic plates into the streets and alleys on both banks of the river. Most times it gets left alone, until blood is spilled.

Maddie's pedigree hearkened to the East Bank. I'm more a West Bank Joe—more *Harbor Inn* than *Ritz-Carlton*. Maybe that's why the Captain gave us the case. He knew I'd bulldog my way through the bull crap, but that Maddie would keep me on a short enough leash not to pee on the wrong hydrants. The best laid plans…

I just remember sitting in the interrogation room after I shot the Councilman's son as the weight of the city's political machine just began to bear down on me. I could feel Maddie's presence on the other side of the glass. It was almost telepathic, but we were always connected that way somehow. I could hear in my head the counterpoint of her thoughts, cursing me and thanking me for going into the parking garage alone and coming back out with four fewer bullets in my Glock. The Councilman's son deserved it. It was a good shoot, but, still, he was a Councilman's son. Hell, the Councilman deserved it, himself, being as dirty as he was, but that wasn't our case. We just needed to find out what happened to Sara Ann. And we did. Unfortunately, I scorched my career in Robbery/Homicide in the process.

It was ironic, then, that my current case centered on the East Bank luxury condo of a judge's wife and Maddie's victims were West Bank working girls. And now, again, we'd be going down into that circle of hell known as The Flats. Only this time we did not ride as partners.

I needed to do my homework. So first I watched a replay of Maddie's press conference in the growing dark, then flipped on a light and cracked the books.

~~~

Partners

"Did you see?" Maddie blurted out the first thing when she got to my place that night. She was uncharacteristically bubbly. "How'd I look?"

I looked up from my book. "Mmmm…a little too, um, formal for me. I prefer your Casual Friday Night look."

"Yeah. I had to go out at lunch to buy this stupid thing." She looked herself up and down in the dark pinstripe pantsuit, then shook her head. "I gotta get out of this monkey suit."

"You did good," I called out after her as she went into the bedroom to change. I meant it. She handled the press like a trainer holding the leash at the Westminster Dog Show. But that wouldn't last long. And like an overbred AKC pedigree, media types have a mean streak lurking in their DNA: MDS—*Media Derangement Syndrome*. "What did the brass think?"

"The weasel from downtown said I need to work on tightening up my answers to questions."

"Corporate is never happy with what anyone does outside their building."

"But Sands and the Captain were pleased. At least Sands said so."

Lt. Sands was a standup guy, but the Captain weather vaned freely with the political winds. That's how he got there. "Good."

Maddie came back barefoot and dressed in only a classic Joe Montana *Forty-Niners* jersey three sizes too big for her. He was making a big comeback in the NFL. Robots don't get concussions, but after the initial battle bot novelty wore off, the League realized that they needed on-field personalities to keep the fans engaged, so they started mining the Hall of Fame to give their rosters some soul. She carried a couple of wine glasses filled with a red of some sort and offered one to me. We clinked and drank, then she nested in against me on the sofa. She softly hummed a tune I didn't recognize as she sipped again.

I knew I had to tell her what Jamal told me. I also knew it would dampen her mood—to say the least. Hell, I wasn't happy about it. Working a case is hard enough without complications and entangling a serial spree with another high profile murder vic was definitely a complication—for me as well as Maddie. I didn't have to imagine how she would take it. Partners know. But I had to tell her…eventually. Right time. Right place. And now didn't seem to be the right time, until she forced my hand.

Maddie's gaze eventually settled on the stack of books in the corner like dust in a moonbeam. She stopped humming and sipped. She was thinking about her case. I knew I had better get it over with because waiting would only make it worse.

"The press came to see me today, too."

"Yeah? What did Jamal want? Did he need you to sneak him into the presser?"

"You know him. That's not really his scene."

"What is his scene exactly?"

"European soccer, jazz, cordial liquors, stamp collecting and African artifacts."

"Eh…What did he want, then?"

The Trilogy: Murder by Munchausen

"Well…"

I could feel her body tense against mine.

"Evidently, my victim was patronizing one of your victims. Number Two, to be exact."

Maddie turned around to face me and scowled. "Arrrggghhh. Great. Just great."

"Yeah. I know."

"How does he know?"

"Say what you want about Jamal, he's got a genuine bloodhound's nose on him."

"And I'm sure he's keeping it under his hat—for now, anyway." She took another sip of wine. Definitely not humming now. "And what does the weasel want?"

"What do you think? He wants a scoop. Just like everybody else in the biz."

"Vultures."

"Well, at least we know—thanks to Jamal—and maybe we can get out in front of this thing."

"Do you think our cases are linked?"

I thought for a moment. Of course, they were linked but only coincidentally—At least that's what I hoped. "Just in a *Strangers on a Train* or ships in the night kind of way. Look, I don't want in on the spotlight. No way. I've had my share. But since when did facts ever matter to a reporter?"

"That's what I'm afraid of. And God forbid they find out about us off-duty. It will be a damned soap opera."

I sighed. She was right. Jamal was right. But it's like getting stuck in the middle of a corn field in a hail storm: There's nothing you can do, really, but stand there and take the beating. Even so, I had to try. "But we can at least stay ahead of the storm."

"Do you think I should tell Sands?"

"Maybe I should talk to him. You know, *unofficial* like. That at least gives him an out for not telling the Captain. He's the one that I'd be worried about."

Maddie nodded. She sipped, then furrowed her brow. "Corporate definitely won't be happy."

"Hey, we're not partners anymore—not on the job—you know what I mean. We don't even work in the same squad."

"But when it comes to facts, Corporate is even worse than journalists. Then, of course, there's city hall."

"Yeah. Rock, meet Hard Place. Hard Place, Rock."

"Damn it." Maddie launched herself off the couch. The wave in her wine crested the glass and sloshed on the floor. "Damn it, Jake."

"Hey. It wasn't me. At least we got a heads up from Jamal before it hit the wire."

"Damn."

I sighed. I nodded.

Complications. I took a gulp of wine and asked myself, *There's always complications, aren't there?*

"Damn it, Jake," Maddie half scolded, half whined, more defeated than angry.

"I know. I know." After a long gap of dead air between us, I asked, "Are you staying?"

"You know I am," Maddie sighed.

Outside, the rumbles of a storm out over the lake bowled their way inland.

~~~

The West Bank

With Jamal's information, EC and I worked the late tour, prowling the West Bank. We parked down by the Powerhouse and took the boardwalk along the river north towards the lake. Mid-week, the place was quiet, which somehow made the dark a little bit deeper, a little more ominous. It sucked up sound like a sponge, dulling the occasional traffic noise of a car or truck crossing into or out of the city on the bridges high above.

The West Bank decor was still brick and steel. Lots of old buildings long ago converted from their industrial utility to low rent liquid havens for those looking to escape the daily grind of their working lives, mostly blue collar folks who work with their hands doing the inglorious dirty jobs that society still needs which take a human touch—plumbing, landscaping, putting up new walls or tearing old ones down—or a younger crowd not yet accepting their slavery to a paycheck at jobs they tell themselves are only a stepping stone to something better. Their delusion breeds an angst that seeks out baser pleasures like rainwater following a watershed. The Tiffany tease of the East Bank lights on the ripples of the river only stokes those feelings of class envy. Sometimes into ambition. Sometimes towards something darker.

Hell, it's a paycheck for EC and me.

"I read the interviews on Maddie's case," EC said with a

heavy sigh. "Had to have Q hack the servers downtown. Corporate has things buttoned up pretty tight."

"Yeah. It figures. I'm glad he's on our side."

"He's not on *our* side. He just likes putting it to *The Man.*"

I glanced sideways at EC. "And we're *not* on the same side?"

"I don't want to take sides. I just want to do my job."

"Fair enough." I looked across the river to Dr. Mullaney's high-rise and its tall wall of picture window views of the dark side EC and I prowled. "But good luck with that."

EC grunted.

"At least it's not raining." Nothing worse than doing a foot canvas in the rain. "So what's our play?"

"Swing down to the *Crystal Palace* to talk with the girls, then work our way back up river."

I sighed heavily. Strip clubs were never my cup of tea. You just can't ever scrape all the pheromones off the souls of your shoes. "To the crime scene?"

"It's on the way."

"Hmmm…" We stopped and leaned on the rail to watch an ore boat thrust its way into the river. "Kind of phallic, huh."

EC grunted. The ore boat passed by us so close we could practically touch it. A sailor, silhouetted against the rail by the deck lights, stared down over the side from fifty feet above.

"So, how is Maddie taking all this?" EC asked cautiously.

"About like I am."

"Am I going to need a jumbo-sized bottle of aspirin?"

"Just might. By the time this all shakes out, you just might."

The Trilogy: Murder by Munchausen

The ship made the ninety degree turn up the crooked river towards the steel mill. We watched it disappear around the bend, then headed across the parking lot to the *Crystal Palace*.

We flashed our badges to the bouncer and went to the bar to wait for the owner, Fast Eddie, to come out of his office. His nickname wasn't complimentary, having more to do with his staying power than his mental acuity. Fast Eddie is a sprinter, not a marathon man. If desperation has a smell, it is found in the heavy, smoky air of strip clubs—even well-maintained ones like the *Palace* that like to put on an upscale air. Onstage a heavily tattooed blonde worked a meager weekday crowd, mostly foreign sailors who were almost as bored as she was, mechanically going through the motions like a first generation droid. Funny how some vices never leave the human realm. Nobody ties up robots for fun.

"Good evening, gentlemen," Fast Eddie oozed out as he approached us. "Business or pleasure? After all, pleasure is our business."

EC ignored him and held up his phone with a picture of Maddie's second victim on the screen.

"One of the dead ones," Eddie said breezily. "I already talked to a lady cop about her and gave up everything I know—which is nothing really. She didn't work here—on the inside anyway."

"What about this guy?" EC swiped a picture of our victim onto the screen.

Fast Eddie looked at the picture and smiled. "Of course, the judge's son. He's dead, too. Such a shame. There's a lot of that going around these days."

"Good customer?" I asked.

"He hosted a few soirées…mostly for out-of-town business associates, I'm guessing. Though it is our strict policy not to care about whether our receipts find their way onto an IRS form or not."

"On account?" EC asked.

"He was always good for it," Fast Eddie answered with a shrug.

"And dear old dad?" I asked.

"It was a chip I had not yet called in. No need. I run a clean operation…for the most part, anyway. But you know what they say: *'If you're not breaking some law, sometime, you're not drawing breath.'* Damn politicians."

"And the judge's son with the girl?"

"All of our entertainment is on stage—as far as I know and care to. But if a good client wants to bring a magic act in for his private party, who are we to say no?"

"She ever perform her magic tricks for his business associates?"

"Like, *'watch me pull a rabbit out of my hat'* kind of act?" Fast Eddie grinned a toothy smile. "I think she might have done a hat trick or two…or three for the boys. But certainly not here in our establishment."

"And all the party goers were from out of town?"

"Did *you* have to sign in? We don't keep a guest register."

I smiled. "Of course not."

Fast Eddie smiled back. "You understand, then. We uphold the constitutional right to privacy."

"There is no such right," EC muttered.

"Well, I'll have to update our employee handbook, then."

"Do you think there was anything going on between her and the judge's son?" I pressed.

"Not in my job description. That's yours."

"Did the parties stay on this side of the river?"

"There are a few places one can go in the apartment buildings up the hill. But surely you know already that some, ahem, *gentlemen* are known to keep a vacation home there."

"Which one?"

"The Bridge Apartment building, I believe."

"So much for the right to privacy," EC snickered.

"Correct me if I'm wrong, but like doctor-patient confidentiality, I don't believe that right survives death."

"You must have a good lawyer," I noted.

"Did. We *did* have a good lawyer."

I should have known.

The music died and the tattooed blonde marched off the stage.

"Well, thank you for your time, Mr. Duvola," I said.

"Come again, anytime, fellas. Next time, I'll comp you a drink."

EC and I grinned, nodded and then exited the *Crystal Palace* back into the dark, a little more enlightened.

"Always something, ain't it?" EC muttered more to himself than as a legitimate inquiry.

We cut across the parking lot and into a ravine of brick between old warehouse buildings. EC drifted to the opposite sidewalk as we swept the block for any signs of commerce. There were a couple of working girls outside of *McCarthy's,* but their claims of ignorance were confirmed by EC's scan of Maddie's canvas interviews.

We hit the river and crossed the swing bridge to the east side. Upriver a mile or so from the lake, the East Bank quickly shed its ritzy glitter. Seagulls swirled in a cloud behind the ore boat, feasting on the chum whipped, grated and pureed by the ship's prop blade. Their screeching haunted the night air as we approached the alleyway where Ms. Demont met her demise.

EC swept the alley with his flashlight. The crime scene tape was long gone. Rain and industrial grime had washed away or covered the evidence not needed to be collected by Forensics. There were enough casual graffiti doodles to indicate that the alley saw regular foot traffic.

EC sighed. "Not exactly the Poconos."

"No heart-shaped beds, I take it." I surveyed the facades of the neighborhood: a welding shop, a janitorial supplies distributor and, across the street, an empty building available for lease or sale. "Not likely she came all the way here from the *Palace*. Maybe *Mickey's* up the block."

"Yeah. *Mickey's.*" EC said sadly. "That was in the reports. Zero. Zip. Nada."

I looked down the alley. You get a feel that doesn't come through on the crime scene pics. It was a perfect place for delivery on a cheap sexual transaction…or for dispatching a human life. We had been there for ten minutes and not a soul nor a vehicle had passed by. That was plenty of time for the crime—and the gratuitous evisceration.

At the end of the street, a man turned the corner and stopped short at the sight of us by the alley. He turned on his heels and went back the way he came. EC and I swapped a look and followed after him.

At the end of the block, we saw him disappear into *Mickey's*.

"Dumbass shouldn't be wearing a jersey," EC chuckled, as we headed down the block to the bar. "Fifty-seven. Who's that?"

"Can't tell the players without a scorecard." I stopped following professional sports a long time ago.

The Trilogy: Murder by Munchausen

We pushed into *Mickey's*. The place was barely open for business. Number 57 was sitting at the far end of the bar staring hard into a pint of lager.

EC and I went down and pulled up stools on either side of the man in the jersey.

He looked right towards EC, then left at me. Then back into the head on his draft.

"You come here often?" I asked, all friendly-like.

He shrugged. "Once in a while."

"After work?" EC asked.

"Yeah. After work. Never before, though."

"So, why did you turn tail and run?"

"Uh, two guys hanging around a dark alleyway where a murder took place? What do you think?"

"Fair enough. Did you know the girl?"

"Cops, right?"

EC showed his shield.

Number 57 sighed heavily. "I'd seen her around."

"Ever make use of her services?"

Jersey guy just shrugged.

"We ain't vice," EC noted.

"Yeah. She discounted on slow nights."

"Red-light specials?"

"Something like that."

"Did you see her the night she died?" EC asked.

"Like I told the other cops—*but hey,* what happened to the lady cop from the TV?"

"We're working a case on the East Bank," I said with just the right amount of disinterest. "Might be related. Might not."

"So, did you see her the night she died?" EC asked again.

"Like I told the other cops, I didn't see anything."

"But you were there, right?"

"I was coming back from the other side to meet some of my buddies. But I didn't see anything."

"Right." I rolled my eyes.

"The file says you saw her and her john duck into the alley," EC asked.

"I was coming back from the *Harbor Inn* and I saw her follow somebody into the alley. I stopped short cause I didn't want to interrupt. The sailors off the boats are usually pretty quick, but they get a bit testy when their shore leave is interrupted. So, I thought I'd wait it out and have a smoke."

"That's it?"

"She was breathing heavy and moaning. Getting all hot and bothered, then suddenly it stopped."

"What stopped?"

"Her breathing heavy. It was, like, totally quiet. Then I heard some sounds. Clinking sounds, like metal on concrete or brick. And some wet sounds. Sloshing like."

"Then what?"

"Then what what?"

"What did you do then?" I enunciated each syllable slowly.

"You read the file. I beat feet back across the river. To heck with my buddies waiting at *Mickey's*. I got pals on the other side, too, you know."

"That's it? You turned tail and ran…*again?*" EC asked, barely masking his disdain.

"I don't need any grief from those foreigners who work the boats. And I don't need any grief from you. I told you the same thing I told the other cops: *I didn't see anything.* I don't know anything and I didn't want to then—*or now.* Are we done?"

EC shook his head in disgust. He looked across at me. "Weasel."

I gave him a nod, but something was gnawing at my gray matter. "Totally quiet?"

"Huh?"

"You said she was breathing heavy and moaning, then it went totally quiet."

"Yeah. You could hear a pin drop."

"What about him?"

"Him who?"

"Sailor boy."

"I didn't see him."

"Did you hear him?"

"Hear him what?"

"Moan or groan or breath heavy or even grunt. It takes two to tango, you know."

As Number 57 thought for a moment, a puzzled look came over his face. "You know, come to think of it, no. I didn't hear him at all."

EC's eyes widened. "Nothing at all?"

"No…Nothing. Nothing at all. He was one quiet dude…whatever he was doing."

"Dude, huh?" I looked at EC and shook my head. "Maybe not so much."

EC squeezed his eyelids shut and massaged the bridge of his nose with his thumb and index finger.

"What do you mean?" Number 57 asked.

"Totally quiet?" I asked again.

"Like church."

"Right. When was the last time you came to Jesus."

"Hey, it's not like you really have to be reminded. Once would be enough to know. My mama took me all the time when I was a kid. Over on Fulton."

"Like church?"

"Like a silent prayer to the baby Jesus himself."

"Damn," was all that EC said.

And I agreed.

EC and I called it a night.

~~~

Lt. Sands

After a long walk back to the car and a quiet ride up out of the Flats, EC dropped me off at home. It was four in the morning. I was too wired to sleep and Maddie was at her place, so there was no sense in going to bed—for business or pleasure. After a bird bath in the sink and dragging a brush across my teeth, I went down to the precinct to park myself on the couch in Lt. Sands' office to wait for him to show up. I wanted to get to him first thing. I must have drifted off trying to figure out exactly what to say to him and how to say it, like I promised Maddie I would do.

When I roused myself from a rather lewd dream about Amy at *John's Diner,* my hand was cramped in a death grip on my phone and my nose was filled with the smell of fresh coffee. Lt. Sands was at his desk swiping his way furiously through the overnight arrest reports, like he did every morning. It pays to know what's going on in your own sandbox, even if it's not part of your caseload. Nothing happens in a vacuum—as I was just about to inform the brass. He might be on the bottom rung, but Lt. Sands was still management.

"Morning, sunshine," Lt. Sands said cheerfully followed by a long, loud sip of coffee. He didn't look away from the arrest reports. "Late night?"

"You can't really keep regular hours when you're chasing bad guys. After all, they don't."

"So, did you catch any *bad guys?*"

"Eh…not so much." I sat up.

"You take yours black, right?" Sands pointed at the end table where a cup of coffee steamed to my right.

"Thanks."

"Yeah, well, I had to leave for a moment while you finished your dream about one of my detectives—at least that's what I assumed, but then again you didn't actually call out her name in the throes of your passion."

I sat up and pulled my cup of coffee in front of my face. I breathed in the vapors deeply and sighed them back out again.

"Better exercise your Miranda rights, Jake."

I nodded and sipped.

"I don't mean to appear unhappy to see you…but why were you sleeping in my office?"

"I need to talk to you about Maddie's case."

"Did you talk to her about talking to me?"

"I kind of did."

"Do you really want to get involved?"

"No. But I don't really have a choice."

Lt. Sands finally looked up from the arrest reports at me. I got his attention.

"My vic and one of her vics crossed paths. Number two, to be precise."

"Casually, socially or professionally."

"Professionally, it appears."

He sighed heavily, impatiently. "Out with it."

"Do you want all the gory details? Or just the headlines."

Lt. Sands thought for a moment. "Is it relevant to either case?"

"Could be. Don't know for sure yet. Was there any DNA on number two?"

"There was all kinds of DNA in that alleyway, if I recall. It was a Darwinian cesspool."

"What about on the vic?"

Lt. Sands paused for a beat. "There was…"

"Huh. I'm surprised. Of course, maybe it wasn't the AnSub—I mean, the perp."

"Why is that?"

"Just trying to make sense of a couple of things."

Lt. Sands looked back at his screen and pulled up a report. "We were surprised, too, 'cause it matched out to a dead guy—like a really, really, *really* dead guy. Like a hundred years ago dead."

"What the—"

"Exactly. Collected in an unsolved case back in prehistoric times when the technology was new."

"Where? Here?"

Sands scrolled down. "Nah. Boston. A murder case, too—how's that for a coincidence?"

I shrugged, but in my mind I was paging through my stack of books back at the apartment.

"The original allele panel was pretty fractured, but tech went with the theory that it might actually be a residual transfer of familial material, but the genealogy trace dead ended in the last millennium. It was probably just a bad sample collection in the original case."

"Yeah. Okay. That's probably it." Though I really didn't believe it. Inside the box thinking.

"So, about the connection with your case." Sands folded

his hands in front of me and looked me dead in the eye. He was a good cop and knew there was something more.

There was, but I hadn't even told Maddie yet. I met his stare and held it.

"Jake…?"

I shook my head slightly.

"Right." He looked away to straighten items on his desktop.

"I just wanted to give you a heads up on the vics. I'm not crashing Maddie's case, but it's out there."

"In the press?"

I nodded.

"Great."

"Just one guy has it and it's under wraps for now, but I can't keep a lid on it forever. I got promises to keep."

"Do I want to know?"

I thought for a moment and shook my head. "Honestly? Probably not. Not yet."

"Great."

"You tell me how you want to handle this and I'll do it."

Lt. Sands just nodded. "Let me think about it."

I got up to go.

"And maybe you can check your wet dreams at the door next time."

I felt my face flush, so I chopped out a quick Boy Scout salute, then left.

~~~

Exit Alley

I walked down the alley—"Exit Alley" as it was known in the House. The regular precinct guys called it that because it leads to the "Geek Squad" offices, which they viewed as a revolving door out of a career in public service for any "real" cop. Maybe it was, but that would be a slow turning door for me. I wasn't going anywhere fast or soon—personally or professionally. I've got nothing else better to do. So in my mind, I went all Sartre on the situation during idle moments of the day—like just then as I waited for EC to show up for our tour—pondering its ramifications as "Existential Alley," a contested frontier borderline between humanity with all its messy mental and emotional implications and the creepy shadow world of…Robantiy? Binarykind? Digi Sapiens? A cold, bloodless and soulless man-made species untouched by the finger of God walking upright amongst us.

Robots were great when they were securely locked behind their safety cages in automated factories, picking and placing, welding and painting, doing all the mindlessly repetitive and hazardous labors that previously led to injury, death, labor unions and civil lawsuits. Nobody gets sued when a machine wears out its bearings. Nobody strikes when new technology threatens the job description of last generation AI. No unemployment benefits are paid out when a one-trick robot is no longer needed to satisfy the material needs of fickle human beings in a free market economy.

Everybody sneers at what I do: solving crimes they've convinced themselves aren't real crimes, because they're not real living, breathing perps. But the vics are real enough. Oh, sure, the judge's son's homicide made lead story headlines, but that was because of the victim and who he was—or more correctly who his father was—not because of any human interest in the perpetrator. Robotic criminals have no personalities. No Jack the Ripper. No Charlie Manson. No Ted Bundy. Just a cold, hard machine, with means but no motive; no behavioral profiles; no evil smiles; no dark empathetic links to the hidden urges in our own psyches that draws us to them with an unseen force like metal to a magnet. Nobody goes out to get a beer with the paint robot in a car factory. The public doesn't hungrily follow news feeds about malfunctioning machines, like they do Maddie's case. *No simpatico.* No 'there but for the grace of God go I,' as victim…*or killer.*

But I knew. The hundred-year-old DNA in Maddie's case was a real clue. So was the statement of Number 57 from *Mickey's* about hearing the physiological grunts, moans and heavy breathing of Maddie's victim but not her perp. And, especially, the stylized staging of internal organs that hearkened back to the very first serial murderer ever in London during the late 1800s and an unsolved copycat spree a hundred years ago in New England. I'll bet the *"real"* police up at the other end of *Exit Alley* didn't even look into that hundred-year-old case file.

Murder by Munchausen stories in the press were regarded like messy car accidents: the fleeting horror of mangled metal and flesh, not the cold shadow of evil showing its ugly face that great narratives are made of. Maybe not so much anymore.

I knew things were about to change. It would make Jamal happy…and wealthy.

I pondered my aimless doodles of arrows, cubes and fighter planes on the pad of paper. Just then EC waltzed in. I knew he would not be happy about my theory—but inconvenienced unhappy, not mad unhappy like Maddie and the brass will be.

EC saw my face and abruptly stopped at my desk.

"Jake?"

I shook my head and sighed.

"Crap."

~~~

No Anchovies

EC and I sat at Cutty's waiting for our "pizza with no anchovies" to be delivered. Even though it was nine in the morning, the lingering dredges of the night tour made the place almost half full. It was about the quietest time of the day for the deli—just what we needed for our meet.

It doesn't matter how dressed down a Fed gets for casual Friday, they still reek of arrogance, like PGA Tour pros smacking balls at a local hacker's driving range. He marched up to our table, his back ram-rod straight, and peered down at us with a look of disdain that had been long ago practiced into the standard DC default resting bitch face.

"Men."

EC and I looked up at the *federale* towering over us.

"Have a seat," I offered.

EC just stared up at the Secret Service man dripping with superciliousness for us, for Cutty, and for citizenry at large.

"No time. No need." He dropped a thick envelope onto the table between EC and me.

"Actually, I'm surprised to see you here—out here in *public*."

"Yeah, well, you start asking the wrong questions, you draw attention to yourself, the wrong kind of attention."

"Our spook friends?"

He nodded. "I was warned. Now you are, too."

"Another black mark on my permanent record."

"You owe me."

"For what? The black mark?" I tapped the envelope. "Or this?"

"For the warning." He turned to leave.

"Hey, what about your *quid pro quo?*"

"I'll take an I.O.U. on that, Jake. I wouldn't touch anything you've got right now with a level A hazmat suit. I have a pension to consider."

We watched the door ooze shut behind the Secret Service agent. The ego level of the deli retreated from the red line on the dial.

EC looked at the envelope, then up at me. "Great. Now, we've got the Feds mad at us."

"They are always mad at someone. It might as well be us."

I reached for the envelope, but EC grabbed my hand. "Not here."

"Where?"

"Your place?"

I nodded.

"What are you doing bringing his kind in here?" Cutty stood over us and barked out his question. "I run a respectable establishment."

"Sorry, Cutty," EC said in sing-song fashion, like a four-year-old busted by his dad for stealing cookies.

Cutty growled. "I hate those guys. They tip lousy and generally piss off the staff with their demands."

"How did you ever know?"

"Well, for starters, do they have those Ray-Bans surgically implanted or did he inherit his momma's eyes?"

The Trilogy: Murder by Munchausen

"So, Cutty, can we get a couple of pastrami Reuben's to go with no anchovies?"

"Anchovies? There ain't no anchovies on a Reuben."

"Exactly."

We got our sandwiches and left.

~~~

Federal Code

Back at my place, we tore into the envelope. Lots of pages with lots of words and lots of trademark Federale black magic marker redaction. Reading it was like a ride in an antique manual clutch-type car driven by a novice—jerky stop-and-go. I let EC plow through it and went to get the stack of books piled away in the corner.

I sorted through the first few, discarding them to the side, until I came to a yearbook-looking tome of Twentieth Century crimes. I turned to the page I had already bookmarked about a serial killer case from the late Twentieth Century in Boston. Unsolved, all the victims were working girls who were strangled then gutted in back alleys down by the bay. There were only five, so the case never caught on nationally—not at a time when Bundy and the Green River killer were running rampant. Besides, the killings stopped abruptly, so without any fresh blood the news media flamed out and quickly lost interest in a story going nowhere. I guess not much has changed. There was some initial rumble about it being a copycat crime for Jack the Ripper, but that didn't seem to get much traction with John Q. Public outside of Boston. Beantown was hyped up about it for a few months, but pretty soon the lack of empathetic victims, a single-digit body count, and a perp that suddenly went Rip Van Winkle, just like the original, wasn't shiny enough to distract people from their daily lives.

The thing was, though, that the killer's signature wasn't just a ripoff of old Jack from 1880s London. He went one better and looped the intestines around the victim's neck and made it look like a half-Windsor knot—*just like Maddie's vics,* who were also all working girls, who were also killed down by a waterfront—just not in Boston. Great. A copycat of a copycat. I read through the case, looking to see if there was any DNA evidence. Back then, the science was there, but there was a pretty limited database to match against, so it ended up being merely confirming or exclusionary evidence. The detectives back then actually had to detect. There was DNA. Unmatched, therefore unsolved.

"Great," I blurted out to myself.

"What's that?" EC looked up from the government file.

"Looks like Maddie's case has some strings attached—back a couple of centuries or so."

"Huh? What does that have to do with our case? Sure, our guy may have patronized her establishment, but he was dead when she hit the pavement. And that's her headache. There ain't enough aspirin in a Drug Mart to get me to want to share that pain."

"Yeah, but I got a gut feel it's a Geek Squad deal."

"Come on, Jake. She's got a perp with a blood thirst. Androids don't got blood, so they don't get a thirst for it. They're just machines."

"Yeah, but they are machines programmed by warm-blooded creatures."

"What are you saying?"

"You saw her crime scene and her vics?"

EC nodded. "So?"

The Trilogy: Murder by Munchausen

I spun the book around and slid it towards EC's end of the couch.

He looked at the pics and nodded, then turned the pages. "Crap."

"Sands told me they have DNA—DNA that doesn't ping anyone still drawing breath or ever has since it started becoming part of birth records."

"How can that be?"

"Right. How can that be."

"But it gets a forensics hit off the old CODIS system?"

"To an unsolved case in Boston." I tapped my index finger on the crime scene photos in the open book between us. "But that guy's been six feet under for a long, long time."

"Exactly, so why would that DNA show up now and show up here…*and how?*"

I shrugged my shoulders.

"Man, nobody's gonna want to hear this."

"Think about what the guy at Mickey's said about what went down in the alley that night. What if somebody—maybe some medical spook type—reverse engineered biological material off the alleles from CODIS to plant at a crime scene? Alleles that match a crime from, say, Boston, from, say, the last century?"

"And then programmed a droid to re-enact the crime."

I nodded. "And where does our victim's wife work?"

"The Clinic."

"In Genetics."

"Damn." EC shook his head wearily. "Got any aspirin?"

"I don't believe in headaches. Like luck and leprechauns." I got up and headed to the kitchen. "But I've got beer."

"That'll do."

I came back with a couple of cold ones and handed a long neck to EC. "So, what did my friend at the Secret Service dig up for us?"

"I think we're going to have to have Q take a look, but from what I can tell, it looks like the code was used to ghost the AnSub on the Atlas Grid by tapping into it and swapping out metadata. Not exactly something that's easily done—spook level stuff for sure. Only someone with an NSA tie-in or back door could pull it off. But that way, the droid could move undetected throughout the city—or the country for that matter, a Class B felony for starters. You just can't have machines out there unidentified and untracked, but this guy did it."

"I wonder if Maddie even thought to pull the Atlas metadata for the Flats."

"Why would she?"

"Yeah. Why. Nobody's thinking Munchhausen for her crimes." I took a long pull of Shiner Bock. "But maybe they should."

"I don't want any part of it."

"Me neither, partner. Me neither, too."

"But we don't really have a choice, do we?"

I shook my head. "Let's go roust Q."

~~~

Mad Scientists

Back at Exit Alley, Q poured over the stack of papers from the Feds. He looked up and shook his head. "Damn it, I really wish we had gotten the original digital files on these, 'cause the back channel data would be a tapioca treat for sure. But, if they came from where I think they did…"

"Spook Central?" I queried.

Q just looked at me, speechless for once, without a smart-aleck come back. His face was dead serious, a look not often seen.

"So, this isn't going to help?" EC asked impatiently.

"I didn't say that." Q cracked a mad scientist grin. "I'm just going to have to get creative."

"How's that?"

"Why don't you just leave that to me. It's like Chinese takeout: you might not want to see the kitchen if you want to enjoy the meal."

"Like if you're a cat lover?" I asked.

"Tastes just like chicken," Q smirked. "What I can tell you right now is that this is a very clever fellow. He's found a way to create digital shadows in Atlas and move through them. That's not a huge deal. It can be done, eh, easy enough for a mad genius like me, but usually, it causes disturbances in the metadata that can be observed, like little digital ripples in the Grid's space-time continuum. You can't see the fish, but you can see him move beneath the water—if you know where to look and what to look for. The beauty of this fellow's hack is not the shadows but the backfill. He's not only figured out a way to move without being seen but to digitally brush the sand back over the footprints of his mechanical minion."

"So, not your typical chop-shopper."

"I should say not."

EC pinched his eyes shut and massaged the bridge of his nose.

"From the pizza our delivery boy gave us, do you think the spooks are on to him?"

Q scoffed out loud. "Come on, Jake, you're talking about guys that fish with hand grenades. This is eloquent and subtle…*and beautiful.*"

I looked at EC, who shook his head in mild disbelief at Q's reverie of rapture over machine code.

"But not *too* subtle for you, right?"

Q smiled his mad scientist grin. "This craftsmanship is definitely not bureaucratically inspired. It's art—it's not only art, it's Picasso. A game changer."

"Can you find him?"

"Honestly? I don't know. This is *primo,* major league stuff."

"So what do we do?"

"Do you know how gulls and terns fish? They loiter on high and scan the surface, waiting for a flash of light, a reflection of the sun off the shiny scales of their prey."

"And how are you going to do that without help from the Feds."

Q rolled his eyes. "I don't need their help. The grid is like Swiss cheese—full of holes."

"So what then?" asked EC curtly. Even he was losing patience.

"I need to do my trolling without them seeing and knowing."

"Good luck with that, then."

"Huh." Q was suddenly distracted.

"What is it?"

"Well, it seems like such a…I don't know, such an incongruity. This is truly Mensa mad scientist quality stuff."

"Yeah? So?"

"To kill a spouse in a bitter divorce? You don't hire Michelangelo to whitewash a fence."

"The Pope did."

"Yeah, well, in our day and age, that's what they make droids for."

"What? To kill spouses? Or to paint?"

"To paint. But killing spouses is chop shop level stuff. Not museum quality art."

"Well, you did say that he's a *mad* scientist."

"I did. Quite mad. Mad like me. After all, I'm a scientist, too."

"Takes one to catch one?"

"Give me a few days to dig into this."

"And while you're at it…" I wrote down the dates and times of Maddie's murders and passed the scrap of paper to Q. "No footprints or breadcrumbs on this."

"Your case?"

I shook my head. "You don't want to know. Corporate is all over this, so don't even look for it. Just see if you see any flashes in the grid."

"Maddie's—"

"Don't ask. Don't think about it. Just let me know."

Q nodded, read the dates, then got up and fed the paper into a shredder. "That's the beauty of the old analog ways—you can actually destroy things and make them go away for good."

"Yeah. Kind of like murder."

"Yeah. Kind of."

~~~

Infinite Will

Machines might have infinite will and patience but zero passion. Without any will to break nor passion to succeed, I never found synthoid sports of much interest. No glory in victory or grace in defeat, just battle bot mayhem. The sports world had devolved into sterile weekly contests of grinding gears and Herculean hydraulic strength, devoid of any creativity and lacking in the pleasures of the unsuspected and unexpected. After all, the "coaches" were just programmers relying on statistical analysis for their play calling, so the games and competition had become merely mechanical logic contests played out in modern day coliseums. No doubt that is why the leagues reached back into their hall of fames to resurrect personalities to graft onto their atheledroids, but, even still, sports is about as engaging as computer models of the weather. At least for me.

Maddie's case made me realize that, like synthoid sports, I had been just going through the motions in the Geek Squad. Android crime was more puzzle than pursuit of perps, *real* perps. Maybe the cops up the alley were right. Maybe that was really why Maddie's case piqued my interest.

Sure, we had our victims and all, but even a petty criminal has some passion driving him to try to rob a C-store or break into someone's suburban castle—even if it is a pharmaceutically induced passion. They are still driven creatures, not logic executing machines that look eerily human-like. Solving the crimes that found their way down Exit Alley to me and EC was mostly mechanical and formulaic. The machines had their grid logs and they had their flash memories that Q and the boys pulled and decoded for us. Then, the hunt was on to go out to find them and pick them up like a repo man, not a detective. Even the murders by Munchausen. Most times…

Something was definitely different now. I didn't so much know it as I sensed it. I couldn't sort it out at my desk in the sterile cubicles of Exit Alley, so I bolted to wander the streets and let my feet do my thinking. I eventually ended up in Public Square in time to sit like a rock in the rapids of rush hour as the city drained of its drones…*and droids.*

I sat and picked the synthoids out of the crowd like spotting four-leaf clovers in an unkempt lawn. They are there, but most people can never find them. I let the ones that are different catch my eye. Same with droids. You can't really search for them. You have to *let* yourself see them. Unlike four-leaf clovers, though, there are far, far more of them in the crowd. Suddenly, I felt the oppressive invasion of our lives by machines. Of course, technology was everywhere scraping away always on our humanity, making us more and more dependent on it, addicted to it really. I imagine the empty vacuum of all your data going dark is like the junkie's crash as he comes down off his high. We have to have our data fix, just like he's got to have his chemicals.

The industry has its statistics about market penetration for their PSAs. They also have their "heartwarming" anecdotes of all that they do for mankind, for the sick, the needy and, especially, the children. All the dirty work. All the dangerous work. All the jobs that were once done by the poor souls in some dark corner of the world colonized and enslaved—physically in the ancient times, economically and culturally over the last century—whose lives were infinitely more wretched than the "civilized" folks who exploited them for their own comforts. I briefly wondered whatever happened to those less fortunate citizens of the world, but then I went back to visually picking digital fleas out of the rush hour crowd. Even though humans still far outnumbered synthoids, they seemed a malevolent presence, like cancer cells waiting, perhaps multiplying with the bad habits of their host.

But now, instead of just mindless agents of harm driven by hacker code at the behest of a calculating spouse, I sensed the manifestation of a passion to do evil. In the cases that Maddie and I were working a glint of that passion, of that evil beneath the surface, caught my eye—like Q described about the way gulls and terns fish. I had seen the flash in our crimes and now looked in vain for it again in the legions of machines that moved among us.

The hacker or bureaucrat or spook who was pulling the strings on these droids that killed a judge's son and the sex workers on the West Bank was doing more than providing a service, more than just automating murder. He was chasing his own internal demons through these machines. I wondered if there was true satisfaction by proxy. There would have to be. Droids malfunction and droids can be programmed to execute a crime, but to become a serial killer, there has to be a driving human passion that comes from somewhere deep and dark within a disturbed human psyche.

I waited for Maddie to meet me and witnessed the infection of society, wondering if the good doctor who had her husband killed knew who she was working with…or was wrestling with her own demons.

Love is a Battlefield

Maddie came at me out of the sun like an ancient Japanese Zero pilot from some World War a long, long time ago. "So…you come here often, sailor?"

She knew I did. We spent a lot of time together sitting on the bench by the Soldiers and Sailors monument, observing the foot traffic in Public Square when we were partners on the job. Sometimes to decompress. Sometimes to talk out a case. Most times just to people watch and have a few chuckles at humanity's expense. I still came quite a bit, though mostly alone anymore. I shaded my eyes and tried to look up into her face. It had been a while—a week, maybe? Or more, since we connected. It happened, though usually for a day or two, when we both got caught up in cases that were intensifying towards an arrest.

"I got your favorite." She held out a bag of warm cashews and a red delicious apple like we used to get inside the Rapid Transit station. "Angelo says 'hey' by the way."

"Thanks." I took a bite of apple and tossed back a couple nuts. "Pull up a bench."

She sat down beside me. "Boy, it's been a while since we hung out here. What's up?"

I munched and thought. Everything is a negotiation with Maddie, a mini-battle. She was definitely feisty and always testing boundaries. Not like Amy at *John's Diner*. That was simple. Maddie always took forethought and planning and maneuvering.

"How's your case going?"

Maddie sighed heavily. She stroked the top of my thigh as she scanned the crowd in the Square. "Kind of all consuming…but I guess I'm not telling you anything you don't already know. Sorry, Jake."

"Comes with the turf."

Maddie nodded and sighed. "How's yours?"

"Looking seriously at the wife. Gonna follow up at the Clinic campus tomorrow."

"What I wouldn't give to have an angle to chase. We're buried in leads from John Q. Public."

"Yeah, the press will do that for you. Any of them any good?"

"Not yet. At least Sands has thrown out some overtime for patrol guys to help on the phones. Still…"

"He told me about the DNA."

"Yeah, a dead end."

"Yeah…or maybe not." I offered Maddie some cashews, but she declined, like a pitcher shaking off a catcher's signal.

"What are you talking about? There's no database match."

"Did you check the case file for that DNA?"

"It was a murder in Boston—from ages ago. Unsolved."

"Did you check out the crime scene photos?"

Maddie shook her head. "They weren't online. Never scanned in, probably, but I browsed the murder book."

"Curious about the DNA match."

"It's not a great sample. They didn't get a complete panel,

so it wasn't really a true match. You know how the science was back then."

I looked at Maddie. "You know it's a copycat, right?"

She held my stare, then looked away. "I doubt it, Jake. Too obscure. Just your ADHD imagination working overtime."

We watched a wave of pedestrians flood the crosswalk, then drain until the last drip of humanity hit the curb as the light went green and traffic started into the intersection.

I took a loud bite of apple. She was too good an investigator to believe what she had just said.

Maddie swiveled her head back and forth taking a last quick look at the Square, then patted my thigh. "I gotta get back. I'd love to stay and just hang out. Really, I would, but…"

"But duty calls."

"Maybe this weekend?" She grabbed my hand and took a bite of apple.

"You bet."

She smiled and planted a wet sticky kiss on my forehead, then left.

I watched her go and wondered if Q had gotten a glimpse of our Munchhacker as he moved through the clouds.

I didn't want Maddie's case, but it was coming at me. She'd see that too, eventually—if she didn't already.

I ignored EC's texts and calls. Once the rush hour finished draining the city, I went back home alone for the night.

~~~

The Clinic

EC moped the whole way over to the East side where the Clinic campus sprawled out over fifty city blocks with towering monuments to Neurology, Cardiology, Ophthalmology, Cancer and the good doctor's specialty, Genetics.

Only when the cruiser pulled into the parking lot did he say anything. "So, what gives?"

"I know. I know. I should have answered, but I…but I tried to talk to Maddie yesterday."

"No go?"

"She ain't buying it—at least not consciously. I think some small suspicion might be gnawing at the back of her mind, though."

EC sighed heavily. "I don't want any part of her serial killer party."

"Hmmm…" I kept my thoughts to myself.

"So, what do you hope to find here?"

"Well, there's no money trail. And *Doctor* Mullaney doesn't seem to have much of a social life at all, so there's got to be something going on at work. Not to mention the hundred-year-old DNA in Maddie's case."

EC grunted. "Well, Q's hack into her patient files came up empty handed."

"So, we see what we see. Good old fashion police work."

"I hate stakeouts."

"Come on, man, it's why we make the big bucks."

"And I hate hospitals."

I just nodded, remembering the vigil over Patty's last hours. I raised my fist. "On three?"

EC mirrored me. On three, my paper covered his rock, so I got to wander the halls while he parked himself in a far corner of the huge waiting area outside our person of interest's office. I got back to spell him at eleven.

"Got to get some serious air," my partner said over his shoulder as he beat feet for the nearest exit.

I settled in for my shift of watching paint dry. Genetics is definitely white collar health care. No bloody lab coats or body parts being hauled away in plastic bags emblazed with the old Dow Chemical biohazard symbol. Dr. Mullaney was actually something of a modern day witch doctor who brewed up genetically modified *flora* and *fauna* extracts based on patient genome modeling to treat infectious diseases and molecular disorders. It was all voodoo to me, but her intimacy with DNA gave me pause.

Unlike the ER, the foot traffic in and out of her office was leisurely, mostly patients with the occasional lab-coated colleague, scrub-suited nurse, polo-shirted administrative type or latex-gloved housekeepers with their cleaning carts coming and going—much more quickly than the time required for a consultation. Synthoids passed by, but never entered her suite of exam rooms. I passed the time browsing online for dead trees stained with ink and watching the ebb and flow of her clients in search of a cure.

At eleven-thirty sharp, Dr. Mullaney emerged from her office and headed towards the cafeteria. I blended into a clot of patients and loved ones headed in that general direction and followed her. Finally, a change of scenery.

Her heels clicked on the tile floor of the corridor with the hypnotic regularity of a metronome. My mind drifted and I didn't take notice of the man in the jumpsuit pushing a maintenance cart towards us until the *ritardando* in Dr. Mullaney's pace closed the gap between us and I thought she might notice me. Instead, their eyes met and locked, pulling their heads towards each other as they passed until she shook her head ever so slightly and picked her pace back up to *andantino*.

Pretending to consult a building directory, I watched the man follow Dr. Mullaney's retreat over his shoulder. When he looked back, I read disappointment and frustration scrawled in his furrowed brow. My spidey sense tingled.

I quickly texted EC to hand off the tail of Dr. Mullaney and waited for the maintenance man and his cart to pass by. The patch on his jumpsuit declared his name to be Jeffrey. I inventoried him quickly: Caucasian; late twenties or early thirties; approximately six foot tall; lean, maybe a hundred eighty pounds—*maybe;* sandy hair; dark eyes. It was the eyes. They were not only dark in color but harbored a human darkness behind them.

Reeling Jeffrey out enough to be discreet, I followed his long and winding path through the maze of Clinic corridors. Just as doubt began to percolate in my mind, he parked his cart next to a synthoid that had broken down outside the Radiology Department and was twitching like it had Tourette's Syndrome.

As I passed by, Jeffrey tapped the droid's diagnostic port and stared at the screen of his *iSlate*.

~~~

The Baron

The alley cam was off. Q, EC and I huddled close to the door to keep from getting rained on. Even though we were outside the building, the discussion unfolded in hushed tones.

"M.I.T.?" Q asked.

"Full ride," EC answered. "Never finished, though."

"I knew *the Baron* was top shelf in the gray matter department. Gotta be to worm-hole the NSA servers."

"Jeffery also had some issues with anger and small animals in his youth. He never really did play well with others."

"And you're sure this is the guy?"

"Yeah, he really hits the sweet spot on a BAU profile," I added.

EC scowled, then asked Q, "You think you can do it?"

"I can. But 'should I' is the question." Q's eyes darted my way without turning his head. "You got paperwork on this?"

EC groaned a little under his breath.

"Ah, so suddenly you're a bureaucratic purist?" I teased.

Q turned and sneered in my direction. "Only when it's *my* ass on the line."

"Come on, man. You do this kind of stuff all the time for shits and giggles."

"Corporations are paranoid patsies. Trolling their waters is like cruising PTA meetings for MILFs. If you get lucky, nobody's going to say anything afterwards for the sake of the kids."

"Kids?" EC wondered.

"Customers—whatever." Q sighed. "This is different. They play for keeps. I kind of like having my life…unperturbed by big brother's intrusions."

"Look, we're not asking you to go out and attack the ramparts—"

"What's a rampart?"

I rolled my eyes. "Don't be a wuss."

"Hey, I'm the one playing tunnel rat and going in after him. Not you."

"We're not asking you to steal state secrets," EC blurted out in frustration. "Just follow his footprints."

"Yeah, into the creepy spook house at the end of the street. It's one thing to play peeping Tom and look into the place over the fence or through a window. Another thing altogether to go in the front door, wander around and come out the back way."

"Well, how is he doing it?" I narrowed my eyes at Q. *"Mister Super Genius…"*

"This guy is pushing code through the Atlas grid structure to commit murder—"

"So you say," Q cut EC off.

"No. So *you* say. That's what you told us," EC snapped impatiently back at Q. "This guy has figured out a way to drop and pull command libraries into droids to commit crimes. That data traffic has to move on the grid, in and out of the cloud, right?"

Q finally, reluctantly nodded. "I told you he's ghosting the grid and not leaving any breadcrumbs. I didn't know he's worm-holing through the NSA servers in Utah."

"You've seen the Baron going in, but you can't trace when or where or how he comes back out. We just want to know when and where that code is hitting the grid on the download."

Q blew a long, wispy exhale. "But you know where this is going to lead. Corporate is going to come down on us like a ton of bricks, especially if we lay a big stink bomb on their high profile case."

We all looked down the alley at the precinct house.

"But we might just save a life," I said softly.

"Damn." Q beat his fist against the wall. "You always go all Superman righteous and moral on me."

EC Smiled.

Q turned on his heels and pulled open the door. "I'll set up the bloodhound code. But I *have* to put a self-destruct into my algorithms, just in case the NSA starts knocking on our—on *my* door. So, I'm not making any guarantees."

"How soon?" I asked.

"It'll be up tonight." As Q went inside, he called over his shoulder. "Good luck."

"Yeah. Right." I looked at EC. "If it wasn't for bad luck…"

"I wouldn't have no luck at all…"

The security camera light came back on.

And so we waited.

~~~

Waiting Games

Waiting is always the worst part. Waiting for Mechanical. Waiting for Q. Waiting for the Baron to come out of his wormhole again.

I passed the time nursing a plate of ravioli and a half carafe of Chianti at *Maria's*.

"Hey, sailor…buy me a drink?" Jamal flopped himself down across from me in the back booth that over the years had come to have my name on it.

I grunted. *Why does everybody call me 'sailor?'*

He took out his phone and snapped a pic of me shoveling down a ravioli. "I hear this place serves great paparazzi."

"For your editor?"

"He insists. Otherwise, my expense report gets kicked back—unpaid, of course." Jamal filled the wine glass at his place setting from my carafe. He took a sip and scowled. "House wine."

"Snob."

"Yeah, but you're paying and I'm not proud."

When Maria's daughter, Gina, came by our table, Jamal ordered a plate of *Carbonara*. I nodded when she drained the last bit of Chianti into my glass and held up the empty carafe.

"Why is it you always show up around meal time?"

"Do I?" Jamal asked, acting innocent.

"Like a buzzard on road kill."

"Hey, I pride myself on being a professional. So, *detective*, how goes the war on crime?"

"You know. Hurry up and wait. Our Clinic guy moonlights at the VA and EC is connecting the dots between hardware serial numbers from their spares inventory and our droid perp. Thank God I've got a partner who likes doing puzzles."

"So, Maddie's gonna cross the finish line first, then, eh?"

"What do you mean?"

Jamal sat back with a silly smile on his face as Gina delivered his dinner. "You really should make more of an effort to stay informed on current events."

I watched the reporter dig into his pasta.

"In fact, I'm just fueling up on my way to the big press conference to announce an arrest."

"You know it's bull crap."

"Now, now. No sour grapes, Jakie."

"You don't arrest synthoids. And I'm here to tell you this one just won't stick on a human."

"Your DNA copycat theory?"

I nodded.

"I like your story better, but they must have something good to assemble the media."

"Don't buy it, man."

Jamal just smiled around a mouthful of garlic bread. "I never do. Just like dinner. Hey, you don't mind if I take a copy of the receipt, do you?"

"Double dipping?"

"It helps pay the bills."

"In our business, it's called fraud."

"Come on, Jake, neither of us wants the IRS looking over our shoulder."

I shrugged.

Jamal slurped up the last piece of fettuccine off his plate and wiped the sauce from his chin. "Gotta bolt. Don't want to be late for the *really* big news."

"Don't buy it."

"Hey, you know me. Just keep me in the loop on the truth."

Gina came up to the booth. "One check or two?"

I looked at Jamal. "Put it on my tab."

"You're a prince, Jake." Jamal grinned and diner-dashed to the front door before I could change my mind.

I finished my wine, stewing in the news about Maddie's case. Then, I wandered back to the building and fired up my *iSlate*.

Maddie got her pretty face plastered all over the local news feeds. Watching the stream of the press conference, I hadn't seen so much brass in one place since the last time I was at the range. The Commissioner stood at the podium claiming victory over evil with the precinct Captain so close his bad breath might have been fogging the Commissioner's cuff links. Maddie hung back with her partner, Lieutenant Sands and the rest of the task force at the back of the dais.

While the Commissioner prattled on about the greatness of *his* department, I scanned the arrest reports. Responding to a call to roust the city's dreck from the posh East Bank and herd them back to the other side of the river, a patrol unit found a bloody knife in possession of one of the homeless interlopers. Well, maybe possession is a bit of a stretch. Let's just say they both occupied the same pile of trash out back of *Sammy's* restaurant. The blade was the right size and shape to have been handy in eviscerating a corpse—or carving medallions of beef tenderloin. The homeless man was correctly aged and Caucasian to fit the F.B.I. Behavior Analysis Unit profile, with the requisite history of mental issues and a sketchy track record of taking his prescribed medications. As for an alibi, well, he didn't really seem to know where he was in the present moment, let alone weeks and months ago at the time of the crimes.

Once the Commissioner and the Captain were done boasting about their leadership, Maddie stepped forward to take questions. The camera definitely loves her. Most of the questions were pretty routine and she handled them with ease, though the attractive info babe from *Action News 5* got a scratch from Maddie's claws when she asked a particularly stupid question about lab results. Of course, the blood work wouldn't be back from the lab yet.

I was about to click off when Jamal stood to ask whether the suspect had any medical training in his background. Her hesitation in answering was so slight that unless you knew Maddie and could read her expressions like I could, the assembled reporters all missed that the question had snagged on a lingering doubt in her mind.

"We are still working to assure ourselves that all the blanks on Mr. Steinmauer are filled in accurately," she stonewalled.

Before she could move on, Jamal called out, "And is all of the DNA accounted for?"

"Oh, man…" I moaned out loud. The old Boston DNA information had never been released by the police. I swore that

Maddie's glare bored right through the cameras directly into my chest.

"As I told Channel Five, we are still waiting on lab results," she replied curtly.

After the exchange, I clicked off. Even if the blood on the knife came back as a match to any one of Maddie's victims, that wouldn't close the deal for me. My gut feeling on seeing their guy's mug shot was that this perp wouldn't make the grade for the murders. There was confusion in his eyes, not evil.

Out back on the fire escape, I turned a lawn chair towards the west and parked myself in it with my feet up on the hand rails to watch the sunset, hoping Q's bloodhound code would pick up the Baron's scent.

Between sips of Cabernet, I pondered how the ancient Greek mythological aether eventually turned out to be real: the invisible radio waves that filled the space between me and the horizon were literally the breaths of the government gods that lorded over all of us. We were all tethered to the Atlas grid with our *iNodes* or *Alpha-Bits*, trading the immediate gratification of human whims for the unseen manipulation of our Gamma waves by the malicious winds that blow only that information and those options across the face of our gaze that some AI algorithm has determined for the sake of society or commerce is best for the greater good. We're just digital fish swimming in a sea of data, not realizing how wet we are.

I ignored an incoming call from Maddie. Even though the presser had ended, her tour was far from over. There was paperwork to be done, no doubt, and I didn't want to take away her adrenalin high. On a more selfish note, not being up for an emotional scrum at the moment, I didn't want to face her wrath for sharing confidential info with Jamal.

Out there in the aether, everything human floated above and around us like a binary shadow of our world. Moving through it all the time was the natural evil of men, though typically it was merely a reflection of corporeal. A few used that shadow world to move their ill intents out and beyond themselves.

The sun went down. I refilled my glass, waiting for the ping that meant Q's digital hunt had flushed our quarry.

Perchance to Dream

I nodded off and slept fitfully on the couch, alternating between a recurring dream of Amy—the same one I had in Lt. Sands' office—and a new nightmare I'd never had before. Some people's dreams are surreal like a classic Tim Burton movie, but mine are usually hyper-realistic, almost flashbacks, especially when they're work related. So much so I'd kid Maddie there should be overtime on my pay stub for them.

I should have been reliving the warehouse takedown of the bodega AnSub with EC, but I didn't know where I was and my partner was nowhere to be found. Outside, I prowled down an empty city street through the cones of light thrown down by street lamps, in and out of blinding light followed by a hood of total darkness. I couldn't tell if I was headed somewhere or just going in circles. The storefronts were dark and unmarked. Animal sounds like out of a jungle bounced off the brick and concrete, hauntingly human at times, but only compounding my disorientation. Gripping so hard on my Glock the checkering dug painfully into my palms. No glass. No comm. No partner. No backup. No choice but to keep moving forward, but not knowing why. Sweating, but not hot. Gulping air, but not winded. Every muscle taut, then wound tighter yet as a door to my right creaked open, spilling a dim light into my path. Back to the entryway wall, I followed my Glock through the doorway and slid right into my recurring dream of Amy. She lay naked on my bed, but was melting into a pool of red on the floor like a Salvador Dali clock, flowing lazily toward a rear door that I could see led back to the street I had just left—

Until the *iCore* notification from Q hit my phone in 911 mode.

As I came back up to break the surface of reality, grabbing at the air with my lungs, my mind's eye glimpsed a blurry silhouette disappearing into the darkness between the street lights.

I peered squintily at the screen for Q's message, but it was blank except for the record of his call and the time: two-forty in the morning. As I scratched away the sleep from my face and groin, trying to figure out why there was no message or data, the phone 911ed me again. Heart and respiration rates back to near normal, I dialed the Alley offices.

"Jesus, Q, don't you ever sleep?"

"I'm an avid napper, Jake." Q's voice was void of his usual surliness and disdain. "The Baron's come back out of his lair."

"Great," I growled with sleep still caught in my throat. "Where?"

"Right where you thought it would be. The West Bank near Columbus and River."

"You got an A-VIN on the synthoid?"

"Yes. I do."

"Great send me the coordinates."

"No. Get a pen and write them down so they can't be hacked."

"Right. Good thinking." I reached into the nightstand and pulled out paper and pen. Old school.

Q dictated the synthoid's chassis identification number and the GPS latitude and longitude.

I confirmed the information in a read back and started shifting gears to spur myself into action and get down to the Flats with EC.

"Hey, Jake…"

"What?"

"I was actually able to decode some of the data payload…"

Q usually wasn't so dramatic, but there was something in his voice I had never heard before: fear. "Q, what is it? I gotta get going."

"I did an extraction on the facial recognition targeting mask. I'm sending that to you now. Look at it."

My phone dinged. I looked at the screen. "Are you sure?"

"Bytes don't lie, Jake. It's her. Maddie's the next vic."

Q was right. The composite image on the screen was a dead ringer for her. "Where is she right now?"

"The I/O board and the grid show her up at her desk in Robbery/Homicide."

"No doubt still doing paperwork on that homeless guy they nabbed." I was painfully alert. "Who else knows? Did you tell EC?"

"Nobody else. I didn't want this leaking out of the messaging servers."

"You get down the alley to the House and keep her there. No matter what. And message EC to get his ass into the Flats. I'm not going to wait to meet up with him."

"Right, Jake, but what should I tell her?"

"I don't know. She definitely won't want to hear any of this."

"You know I won't be able to make her stay."

"Tell her you found something suspicious with her kid sister's credit activity or something. Do a quick search and pull something out of your ass. Just keep her there in the House. If she knows what's really going on, she'll want to jump into the deep end."

"I…Okay, Jake. I'll figure something out."

"Just keep her safe in the House."

"Right."

After a quick birdbath, I strapped up and grabbed my "Go" bag. I'd take the Department sedan. I could put it into chauf mode to enter the data Q gave me as it navigated me to the West Bank.

Halfway there, I got a call from EC. "Jake."

"What?"

"Q said she's not there."

"What do you mean she's not there?"

"He said her *iNode* has been hacked and ghosted. According to the desk sergeant, she left sometime after midnight."

"Get there. Get there now."

"Right, Jake."

I killed Rochester, went cherry top and hit eighty down the Shoreway towards the Flats.

~~~

Off the Grid

I killed the lights and siren after I blasted through the West 25th Street exit and hit the hill down the Superior Viaduct, descending into the Flats, descending into my own personal hell, praying I would find a serial killer synthoid before he found my girlfriend.

I slammed on the brakes at Center Street to take the corner without squealing the tires, then crept towards the swing bridge to the East Bank. I manually turned off the headlights. The hybrid went all electric and I silently prowled into the dark blocks like a cat hunting in the night.

"Damn," I exhaled and slammed on the brakes. *The EMI from the traction motors.*

The synthoid's sensors were no doubt tuned to detect intruders across all bandwidths—heat, light, auditory and radio frequency. If I spooked him, he might bolt into the night…or he might hurry to finish the job.

Q's ping coordinates blinked on the dash map at Lockwood and Columbus, on the other side of the river. I'd have to go the rest of the way on foot.

The street was lined with junkers and delivery trucks parked for the night. I slid the *Interceptor* in behind a step van in the space next to a fire hydrant. Before I powered down, I glassed up and pinned the locations of Maddie's crime scenes to its map. EC's techie ways would have been helpful just then, but I didn't have time to wait for the cavalry to show up. I powered down my *iNode* and tossed it on the passenger seat, along with my shield with its RFID chip. To hunt the hunter, I'd have to go completely off the grid, too.

My mind thrashed with unpleasant scenarios, wondering if Maddie was really in the Flats—but she'd have to be or why else would the data payload for her assassination hit the AnSub down here? And just blocks away from her crime scenes. Why did she come back? An arrest had been made. The city was made safe again—or so it had been told by the brass at the press conference. Some doubt must have struck a nerve in Maddie like a cavity gone bad to bring her down into the Flats in the middle of the night to revisit her victims' murders. And I knew exactly the crime scene where she'd be: the alley where her case and mine crossed paths.

It wasn't until I got to the river and reflexively checked my six that I saw the pools of light cast by the street lamps. I was living the nightmare that Q's call woke me from less than an hour ago.

I stepped out on the swing bridge, its ironwork casting shadows in the moonlight like a holographic spider web as I crossed the river.

On the East Bank, I pressed myself to the facade of an empty storefront and scanned the street ahead. There was no sign of a department sedan anywhere around the entrance to the alleyway two blocks down.

I unholstered my *eM&P* and slid forward in the shadows.

A rodent rustled down the sidewalk, hugging close to the building, unseen like me, I hoped. Second thoughts scurried like rats in my mind. I should have tried to warn Maddie by text—but no; since the Baron had clipped and cloaked her data stream, it would have only alerted him that we were on to him and nearby to help. Maybe I should wait for EC. Maybe…

Shoe leather shuffling softly on pavement scratched the quiet night from the alley up ahead. I stopped and squatted down behind the back fender of a grimy Chevy *Volt* with historic plates on the opposite side of the street. I watched the alley entrance, enhanced in eerie thermal black and white detail on my *Google Glass*.

Maddie emerged from the alley and leaned against the wall looking in, contemplating the crime scene. Her curvy body was still a half silhouette.

I unconsciously grit my teeth, gnawing the dilemma I faced. I could warn her now and save her in this moment. But the Baron's drone would still be out there, loitering in the crowd, waiting with cold and infinite machine patience to execute the implanted code, when I wouldn't be there—when no one would be there to stop it. Or I could bait the trap with Maddie.

I stayed behind the fender and watched. She'd hold it against me but wouldn't hesitate to do the same…maybe.

I manually opened up the pulse bandwidth on my *eM&P*—there'd be no time to scan for the optimal frequency—then waited.

Time just stopped. It could have been sixty seconds. It could have been an hour. Sirens from up above spilled down from the city into the Flats. Maddie looked up over her shoulder at the lighted skyscrapers. It could have been an armed robbery in progress—or any number of other crimes that warrant a Code 3 response.

Somehow I knew, though, it was EC riding to the rescue but sure to foil my ambush in the process.

Maddie surveyed the murder scene again and pushed her shoulder off the wall. She took a step back into the alley. My glass suddenly flared up with a sharp glint, a street light caught on mirrored metal at just the right angle to explode off my lenses. When the blossom of light faded like a firework, I caught the thermal shadows of Maddie being pushed hard into the alley.

I bolted from behind the Chevy and dashed across the street.

The angle was right to keep me out of the synthoid's rearward vision, but I could see him grab her jacket and lift her off the ground, feet frantically, futilely trying to find traction in the air.

The synthoid twisted Maddie like a baton and tossed her ahead, arms and legs flailing as she tumbled deeper into the alley, followed relentlessly by the Personal Services Assistant now programmed to be her murderer.

I took a deep breath, exhaled halfway, then spun around the corner to the alleyway. I double tapped the droid with my Smith and Wesson. In the interminable wait for the chamber charging sequence, I could only observe the synthoid was merely slowed in his advance on Maddie, who was crabwalking back from one mechanical fist raised above to strike down and crush her skull and the other clutching a large butcher knife to finish the inherited killer's signature.

I watched helplessly as the gap between human and machine closed, fighting the instinct to pull the trigger again too soon and send weakened EMP rounds that wouldn't stop the assault.

The Trilogy: Murder by Munchausen

The synthoid's fist began to fall.

My *eM&P* shuddered against my palm and flashed green in my glass.

I pulled the trigger once, then again.

The cumulative effect finally locked the fist in midfall.

The alley was a frozen film *noir* scene in my glass. A panicked *femme fatal.* A serial killer. Sirens growing louder in the background.

The synthoid began thrashing spastically. The butcher knife clattered to the pavement. The droid finally collapsed in a heap.

Maddie's hyperventilating swelled slowly in my ears.

I let out the last of my own held breath, then inhaled deeply.

The acrid odor of ozone told me the synthoid's circuitry had been fried, so there would be nothing for Bob or Puff or Q to find.

I went to Maddie and held her in my arms as the street outside the alley filled with the noise of police cars arriving at the scene of a crime, after the fact, as usual.

~~~

Crash and Burn

"Idiot!" Puff erupted like an angry Vesuvius, spewing a hot lava flow of obscenities until he sputtered into insensibility and dove back into the synthoid's innards.

I just stood there and took it…deservedly, but Maddie was safe. Scraped, scratched and bruised a bit, but alive. Also, unfortunately, just as livid with me as Puff. About telling Jamal things I shouldn't have. About throwing a huge monkey wrench into her case. About using her like I did to be Munchausen bait. About…

"Yup, yup, yup," Bob muttered, shaking his head. It's a fish fry inside there. "Nothin' left but ash and bones. Ash and bones…"

"We'll tell Q," EC said with a heavy sigh, giving me a sympathetic sideways glance.

We pushed out a side exit on the House into the alley—Exit Alley—and slowly walked back to our offices.

"Wow. I think it's official now. You've got the whole world mad at you."

"The *whole* world?"

"Well, not me…*yet.*" EC grinned a bit. "But I'm sure I could come up with a reason or two. *If* you want to do a thorough job of it."

"Yeah…Well…"

Up ahead, Q waited for us under the unblinking surveillance camera, watching us approach like a wary alley cat.

"There was nothing," EC sighed wearily. "Zero. Zip. Nada."

"I wouldn't exactly say nothing," Q replied cryptically. "Hey, Jake, sorry about Maddie."

I shrugged. "Collateral damage. Comes with the turf sometimes."

"I mean—I couldn't help it. You know how she is. She made me show her."

"Show her what?" I asked.

"And what do you mean you wouldn't say exactly nothing?" EC growled.

Q tapped the screen of his phone and turned it towards us so we could watch a synthoid-eye video of Maddie's attack. "She made me show her. I—I…"

I shuddered at the panic on Maddie's face and the brute terror in her screaming which never registered in my ears that night. And in just how close I'd come to really losing Maddie—to the morgue.

"Jesus. What the—"

"My bloodhound code caught the stream before Jake zapped it."

"Well, I guess that explains a thing or two." I looked away from the video.

"We'll get this guy, Jake. We'll get him." EC's voice dripped with anger.

"Funny thing about the feed." Q pocketed his phone. "It split. One terminated into the Baron's *iNode* so he could watch it live—"

"That'll close the deal on a warrant," EC interrupted. "That and the money trail."

"What money trail?" Q asked.

"I finally found how Dr. Mullaney paid for the hit on her hubby. She laundered it through the Clinic with purchase orders for lab supplies to an LLC the guy owned," EC explained. "Can you put a BOLO lock on Atlas for him? We don't want him to get away."

"Sure."

I hit pause on the video replay of Maddie's attack running in my mind. "What was funny about the feed?"

"It split. Like I said, one feed went to the Baron's phone. The other disappeared into the darknet."

"What does that mean?"

"I don't know for sure," Q said with concern.

"Was he archiving it?" EC asked.

"Maybe…" Q looked directly at me. "Or someone else was watching."

"Who?"

"It's the darknet, Jake. Nobody good."

"Don't lose this guy," EC warned.

"I won't." Q looked at me one last time and muttered over his shoulder as he went inside, "Sorry about Maddie."

Yeah. Me, too.

~~~

Paperwork

Sometimes the wheels of justice move slowly…and sometimes not so much. While EC and I waited on the paperwork mill in the prosecutor's office, Maddie's perp was quickly deemed legally incompetent, which officially closed her serial killer case without the inconvenience of a trial. At least the poor sap who took the fall in the media got the mental health services he needed. Our off-the-books shadow investigation stayed in the shadows and off the books. The brass tidied up by declaring the assault on Maddie to be a PSA malfunction, not malware. And without any evidence to the contrary from Puff, Bob or Q, it stuck.

Deep down, though, she knew. She was too good of a detective. It was just another one of those situations that bureaucracies don't handle very well: too messy with too many loose ends and too much potential for radioactive media fall out—the kind that causes career cancer. Maddie knew the game. But that didn't help heal things between us.

Anyway, the city was officially deemed safe from a serial killer and everyone moved on…except for me, EC and the Baron.

Of course, Jeffery stopped showing up for work at the Clinic and the VA, but Q had a DDB—Digital Denver Boot—on him, so he wasn't going anywhere while we waited on the paperwork. Neither was Dr. Mullaney.

~~~

The Darknet

Maddie's call came through at three AM. Of course, I had changed her ringtone.

"Jesus. Why does crime always have to happen in the middle of the night," Amy complained hoarsely, then rolled over away from me and hugged her pillow.

"Yeah?" I answered, trying to be as discreet as possible.

"You're going to want to see this," Maddie said matter-of-factly. "I'll send you the details while you drag yourself out of…when you're on the way."

"Right."

Maddie was on familiar turf: The Flats.

I crossed beneath the crime scene tape and walked towards her standing guard over the covered body, holding the bunny suit crew at bay from their forensic harvest.

She nodded to the Medical Examiner to pull back the sheet from the body. "Looks like your case is closed, too."

Jeffery's corpse lay on the pavement. "But…he didn't do that to himself."

Maddie peered up into the dark night sky. "You don't have to say it, but you will, won't you? You can't help yourself."

I didn't answer. I just stared at the eviscerated body that was the object of our arrest warrant with his intestines wrapped around his neck like a fine silk tie. The only thought

that floated up in my mind was the darknet.
"What did you call him? The Baron?"
I nodded.
"I guess he's still out there."
The darknet...

~~~

The Darknet
Murder by Munchausen #2
A NOVEL BY M.T. BASS

For Karen

*Our technology, our machines, is part of our humanity.
We created them to extend ourselves, and that is what
is unique about human beings.*

~Ray Kurzweil

The Baron

Jake crossed beneath the crime scene tape and walked towards me as I stood guard over the covered body holding the bunny suit crew at bay from their forensic harvest. He does have the best poker face of anyone I know, but—ugh! I could practically smell it on him: the blonde waitress from John's.

I nodded to the Medical Examiner to pull back the sheet from the body. "Looks like your case is closed, too."

Jake peered down at Jeffery's corpse on the pavement. "But…he didn't do that to himself."

I gazed up overhead at the fat, heavy clouds glowing gray from the city lights. "You don't have to say it, but you will, won't you. You can't help yourself."

He stared at the eviscerated body that was the subject of an arrest warrant in his Munchausen murder with its intestines wrapped around the neck like a fine silk tie.

"What did you call him? The Baron?"

Jake just nodded.

"I guess he's still out there."

"Yeah…in the Darknet."

"Huh?"

Just then Lt. Sands came up behind us. "Well, this looks like nothing but trouble."

I had called him, too.

"What? Me or the dead body?" Jake asked with a smirk.

"Dead bodies are easy." Sands put his hand on Jake's shoulder. "They don't break any regs, and they don't smart off."

"Hi, Lieu. I thought you should know, too."

"But he got here before me." He squeezed Jake's shoulder hard.

"Well, maybe he didn't have anything better to do at the moment," I said, staring Jake down. Still, the best poker face ever.

"You know how it is." Jake gave Lt. Sands a fake wince, then winked. "Most people call 911. I *am* 911."

Lt. Sands rolled his eyes and shook his head. "So, what am I looking at, Maddie?"

"No doubt, a big fat 'I told you so' coming our way, courtesy of the Geek Squad here," I said.

"We need to get started," whined one of the Bunny Suit Boys behind us. "Before it rains again or we'll lose evidence."

We backed off, and I waved them forward to process the crime scene.

"You know what this means, right?" Lt. Sands asked us as we huddled apart from the crowd of technicians.

I looked at Jake.

He smiled that crooked, knowing smile of his. "Partners again, huh."

I clenched my eyes shut and shook my head. *Damn it.*

"Well, you kids have fun. I'm going back to bed." Lt. Sands could barely suppress his chuckling. He turned to leave. "Tomorrow afternoon. In my office. We'll talk. You detectives have a good night—well, morning, now."

I opened my eyes and caught Jake laughing.

"Come on. It won't be that bad, will it?"

I pushed past Jake to supervise *my* crime scene.

Of course, it wasn't that Jake was a bad cop or difficult to work with. When we were *professional* partners, we made a good team. Just now…

I suddenly caught movement out of the side of my eye. Rapid footsteps hit the wet pavement. Jake ran by me, and before I even thought about it, I instinctively took off after him like a partner would.

In the dim glow of tired, old street lamps, a short figure fled up the sidewalk ahead of Jake. I slipped between two parked cars to cross the street so I could cut him off if he veered to the left.

No thinking. Just running.

Another block and our runner instinctively paused as if to look both ways for traffic at the deserted intersection. Jake closed the gap between them quickly.

The perp looked over his shoulder and bolted quickly my way, caught sight of me, and zig-zagged back the other way right into Jake's path.

Instead of tackling, Jake grabbed his collar like the scruff of a dog's neck, and they twirled in a weird, contorted ballroom dance kind of way around and around and around until they tumbled into a heap on the pavement.

I crossed back over and drew down with my Glock…*on a kid.* So young I couldn't tell at first if it was a boy or a girl, especially dressed street-person style in layers of grimy tattered clothes.

Jake scrambled to his feet and held the kid by the collar like a trophy-sized walleye. He panted, "I think we just might have a witness."

I shot him a look, holstered my weapon and knelt down to eye-level just out of a pre-teen's arm reach. I saw by the eyes and soft facial features it was a young girl. "Are you okay?"

The kid shrugged and wriggled futilely in Jake's grasp.

"Hey, settle down," Jake commanded, with a shake of the girl's collar.

Our eyes met again. I always liked how he and I were on the same wavelength. Almost like ESP, we were instinctively working the kid Good Cop/Bad Cop. I missed it. It wasn't there with Walker, who took Jake's place when he got suspended for shooting the Councilman's son or now with Sanchez who was still back at the crime scene. I couldn't even begin to imagine her chasing a perp down the street. And what would the point be? She's a good cop and all but probably runs a four-hour mile—or maybe "waddles" would be more accurate.

"Hungry?"

No response, except in the eyes.

"Yeah. Let's see what we've got."

We led the kid back towards the crime scene but stayed well outside the tape. Jake took her to my unmarked car and sat her in the back seat—Sanchez would be sure to gripe about the body odor.

"Don't make me cuff you." Jake made his point with a poke to the shoulder but stood blocking her escape path.

"I'll be right back." I smiled, looked towards Jake, and rolled my eyes for the kid's benefit.

On my way to the food and coffee, I instructed a patrolman to discretely circle around and stand guard down the street and out of sight from the sedan in case the kid tried to take off again.

I grabbed a couple of donuts and a bottled water.

"Whatcha got going on over there?" Sanchez asked, slapping her notepad against her ample thigh like an impatient meter maid.

"I don't know. Some kid who bolted out of the alley, there. Might have seen something. Maybe."

"I'll call Protective Services."

"Yeah, but maybe give me a few minutes head start with her to see if there's any there, there."

"I wouldn't worry about that. I haven't met a social worker yet who likes coming out in the middle of the night."

"Thanks."

"Good thing you called him."

"Huh?"

"Jake." Sanchez smiled. "Foot races ain't my thing. I don't think I've actually run since the academy."

"Yeah. At least he's good for something." I smiled back.

"Whatever you say, honey." Sanchez laughed out loud. "I'll see if I can light a fire under Forensics so we can get out of here before morning rush hour."

When I got back, Jake drifted away from the sedan to give us some space. Kneeling again, I offered up the donuts. The kid grabbed them both and ate the first one with a fierce animal intensity, then seemed to remember her manners and took a dainty bite out of the second one.

"Thanks."

I nodded. "You know the drill, right? We have to call them."

The kid gave a heavy sigh and washed a bite down with a sip of water.

"You have to?" she whispered.

I nodded. "What name will you give them?"

"Um, Amy, I guess."

I had to grit my teeth hard to keep from screaming. "Anywhere close to your real name?"

She shook her head. "Why?"

"In case I want to check in on you."

"I won't be there long. Never am. And they never come after me."

"Did you see what happened?" I motioned towards the taped off crime scene with my head, then looked at Jake who hovered just out of ear shot over on the sidewalk. "Trust me, he won't let it rest and can make life miserable if you let him."

Amy looked at Jake, then back to me. "It was one of them."

"Them?"

"You know. A robot."

"How could you tell?" I had a hard time picking them out myself.

"Not many of 'em down here under the bridges. They kind of stick out."

I sighed. *The Baron.*

"Yeah. I hate them, too," Amy said, then finished off the second donut.

~~~

Throwing Lead

It can be therapeutic, especially early in the morning when the Department range is typically a ghost town. SWAT won't mob the place until at least mid-morning, and most guys worried about qualifications don't come in until later in the afternoon—before or after their tour. There are only a few of us who come regularly to hone our shooting skills, something ingrained in me by my dad.

From outside, I heard the familiar rhythm of his drill as he drew, fired, and holstered his gun, then drew again: *Tap-Tap…Tap………Tap-tap…Tap………*

Unfortunately, one of the us's is Jake.

He was in a far stall, so I took one near the door, put up a target and went to work. I don't know how long it had been because I cleared my mind and tuned out the world as bullets shredded cardboard, but suddenly the range was empty except for me. Pushing cartridges into empty magazines, my skin began to tingle like spiders were crawling all over me. He was still there. Outside, watching me through the window. But I didn't turn around. I reloaded and focused on the silhouette of a man fifty feet away. The chill went away as I threw lead downrange.

When I got upstairs, Jake was there making small talk with Lt. Sands in his office. While they joked and laughed, I went through my morning nesting routine at my desk, then filled a cup with coffee.

Boys, they're all the same. They get that sheepish, hand-in-the-cookie-jar look whenever we interrupt them, no matter who they are or what they're doing.

"Maddie, come on in." Lt. Sands motioned me into his office at my knock.

Jake turned and smiled. "Mornin', Mads."

I acknowledged with a tip of my cup and a sip of coffee, then Jake and I sat down in the chairs in front of Lt. Sands' desk like two kids called down to the principal's office.

"Where's Sanchez?" I asked. "Shouldn't she be here, too?"

"Haven't seen her yet," Sands said, scanning the squad room over our shoulders. He called down to the desk sergeant.

I felt Jake staring at me but wouldn't give him the satisfaction.

"Saw you down on the range this morning," he finally said.

I turned and smiled slyly. "You want me to keep sharp, don't you? We wouldn't want an errant round causing a blue-on-blue incident."

Jake smiled. "Yeah. Think of the paperwork."

"Detective. Come on in," Sands greeted Sanchez. He gave me and Jake the hairy eyeball. "Maddie and Jake were just catching up on old times."

Sanchez looked at us like scolded children and shook her head. She sat down on the sofa behind us. "So…why the pow-wow?"

Sands rubbed his temples. "Seems as though we have a bit of a situation."

"Yeah. I figured. Last night's mess in the Flats. Am I right?" Sanchez asked wearily. "So, what's the play?"

"Well, first of all, we need to keep this under wraps until

the investigation is down the road a bit and we have at least half a clue of what's going on."

"The big cheeses?" Jake asked with a smirk.

"Some of us still have careers to think about," Sands answered curtly.

Jake nodded and looked away.

"So, no talking to the press, right?" I asked, looking directly at Jake and thinking specifically about his reporter pal, Jamal.

"Right. And for now, Maddie, you go down the alley and get up to speed on Jake's case."

"Great," I muttered under my breath.

Jake just smiled.

"But Lieu," Sanchez said, "the perp we like in the armed robbery case has a court date this afternoon—if he shows."

"Okay. Tomorrow, then. First thing."

Now I know how it feels for death row to get a call from the governor.

Lt. Sands stood up. So did the rest of us.

"So…tomorrow, then," Jake whispered touching my elbow. "I'm looking forward to it."

"Say hi to EC for me."

I was the first one out the door.

~~~

Protective Services

The social worker was parked at my desk when I came out of Lt. Sands' office. She looked like she wanted to be there about as much as I wanted to go down to Exit Alley. She was digging through her stuff in a disheveled search for something or other, first in her purse, then the briefcase, then in a huge Naugahyde bag stuffed with papers spilling out of manila file folders. I swear, most of them are one cat away from being a shopping cart lady. As I stepped over to my desk, she pulled her phone out of her coat pocket with a look of surprise, as if she had just accidentally performed a magic trick.

"You wanted to see me, detective?" the woman asked flatly without looking away from the screen. "It's been a long night."

"Yeah, well, welcome to our world. Murder doesn't always keep regular office hours."

"Murder?" She finally looked up at me.

I shook my head and went to get more coffee. Her eyes followed the steam rising from my mug like an oracle as I sat down at my desk. I didn't offer her any. I took a sip. "Yup. Murder."

"I didn't know."

"Huh," I said casually without putting on my shocked face. My inside voice said, *Imagine that—a clueless civil servant.* "How is Amy handling it?"

"Who?"

"Amy. The young woman you came for last night."

"Is she a suspect?"

I sighed. "If she was, she'd be here. She's a witness."

"Really?"

"Yes. *Really.* So, we need to make sure we keep tabs on her."

"We will find a good home for her." Her voice took on a snarky, *don't-tell-us-our-job* tone.

"What was wrong with the last six? I pulled up her sheet."

"Do you know how many files I have in my caseload?"

"Do you realize a child was found at a murder scene at three AM?"

"I don't have to sit here and take this."

"No, but you will if something happens to Amy."

The social worker stood and gathered up her worldly belongings. "I don't know what you mean."

"Yeah. You do."

She turned in a huff and shuffled out. I imagined her pushing a grocery cart with a shimmying wheel.

~~~

Sanchez

Sanchez took the social worker's place in the chair by my desk. She looked around the squad room, overtly nonchalant, then met and held my eye. "So…you want to fill me in?"

"Seems like there's an ugly wrinkle in my last case," I sighed. "Jake tried to warn me, but I ignored him. Everybody did."

"Ah, *El Toro.*" Sanchez patted the top of my hand. "If we didn't need the calves, they'd all be steers in my book."

I hung my head and chuckled to myself. She really had no use at all for men.

"And if he's not careful, he'll find himself between a couple of sesame seed buns."

"Well, I got a stay of execution for a day before I have to go down the alley to Artificial Crimes. Should we get something productive done?"

"Sure."

Sanchez came to the force by way of the municipal court where she was a bailiff, so she was plugged into the inner workings of the halls of justice. The perp I liked in one of my moldier cases, one she inherited when she was assigned to be my partner, had proved to be particularly slippery. Sanchez found his name on the docket for traffic court today, so we had planned on heading down to Part B to see if he showed up for his court date. If so, it'd be an easy collar.

From the time we hit the metal detectors at the entrance of the Justice Center until we got upstairs to traffic court, it was old home week for Sanchez. I learned more about kids, moms, and lovers than I ever could have imagined as she ran a gauntlet of gossip, providing a running narrative to me between the spurts of dialog. By the time we made it through I knew more about the workers in the Justice Center than I did about myself. At least I got a new recipe for mole sauce. We slipped into the courtroom as the clerk started calling out names to line up the defendants down the center aisle for their turn in the meat grinder of justice.

I sat down on the back bench as Sanchez went up to see if our perp's name had been called. As a deformed Catholic, I immediately began to squirm. The gallery benches were too much like pews. The front was like the chancel with blue-uniformed acolytes. And, of course, the judge's robes—not to mention the law's propensity for Latin—brought back too many Sunday morning memories of boredom at the hands of the Pope's minions. I guess I have PCSD: Post Church Stress Disorder. For a long, long time, I couldn't eat fish either. Still can't handle fish sticks.

Sanchez shook her head as she walked down the side aisle and slid in beside me. She whispered, "So, now we wait."

We witnessed the full menagerie of moving violations committed in our city as each defendant got to the head of the queue to take their turn in front of the judge, who dispensed justice in seven to ten-minute spurts, assessing fines, levying court costs, and assigning trial dates, depending on the severity of the infraction and whether an accident was involved. If only our cases could be tried so expeditiously, but felony murder tends to make for more lengthy and messy proceedings. Testifying was never one of my favorite duties.

Sanchez watched the proceedings like a mama grizzly fishing for salmon in a river. I had my doubts when we got partnered up after Walker decided to cash in his chips and retire on a high note once we rid the city of a serial killer. Can't blame him. At this point, with Jeffery's mutilated body in the Flats, I almost wished I had my twenty in to collect a pension, too. Despite her meter maid physique, Sanchez was a good cop. Nothing got by her. And though we were close to the same age, she was protective of me like a mama bear. We watched the proceedings in respectful silence, both passing our own judgments on the crowd even though we weren't wearing robes.

A long pause before the next case was called drew our eyes forward. The judge listened to a bailiff whisper in her ear and kept a careful sideways glare on the next defendant in line. Another bailiff sauntered down the center aisle with a stack of legal-sized manila folders calling out names to keep the queue loaded. She passed the end of the line and gave Sanchez a nod. I got up and slowly walked down the center. Sanchez slid to the outside and crept forward.

I worked my way up the line, shuffling defendants back until I was right behind our perp, who was growing impatient with the on-going discussion at the judge's bench. I glanced to see Sanchez flanking us to the left at the side of the room, then sidled up alongside him and leaned lightly against him.

My stalking must have worked because he instinctively jerked back and stiffened his spine. The angry look he shot my way melted when I gave him a coy, flirty smile. Downshifting into a cool, gangster slouch, he leered back up into my eyes and, nodding his head slightly as if approving of my looks, cracked a sneering half-smile exposing some custom gold grill work. I could only imagine there might be a woman somewhere who would find it alluring.

"Marcus Williams," the clerk called out.

It was our guy.

He glanced forward to notice two large male bailiffs coming towards him. When he turned back to me, I slid open my jacket to expose my badge and pulled the arrest warrant out of my breast pocket. The confusion on his face morphed into malice. The bailiffs were still ten feet away, but before he could raise his arms to lay hands on me, Sanchez had her vice-grip on his elbow and his left wrist already in cuffs.

I grabbed his right arm as he turned to resist. "Don't. Don't do it. Walk out like a man or all us girls will giggle at you when those guys drag your ass out of here."

"You bitch."

I twisted his arm back for Sanchez to cuff it. "You don't know the half of it."

"Come on, *Ferdinand,*" Sanchez teased. "Let's get you into your pen."

Each bailiff took an arm and hustled Williams out of the front of the courtroom.

"Thanks," I said to Sanchez. "That was easy."

"No sense in breaking a sweat," she answered. "One last good one before you go into exile, huh?"

As we followed our collar out, the clerk called the next case. "Victor Stanislov — Disobedience to a stop sign; speeding sixty-three in a thirty-five mile an hour zone; failure to wear a seatbelt. How do you plead?"

Sounds like Jake, I thought to myself.
"No contest, your honor," I heard behind me as we left.

~~~

Exit Alley

I woke up bug-eyed at four-thirty in the morning and stared at my bedroom ceiling for at least an hour. Going "down the alley" was definitely the wrong direction for any career in law enforcement to be headed. On top of that, I would be paired up with Jake again. How could such a great thing have gone so sideways? Sure, he saved my life, but…Munchausen bait?

And the business with Jamal. I should have listened to Jake, but it was the mother of all cases. And it was mine. I'm guessing the gratitude of the city will be fleeting when the truth is known.

Then, of course, there was waitress Amy. Jake certainly didn't take his time about it.

When I hit that wall, I got up and dressed for a run. There'd be no shoppers that early, so I could run the streets, then hit the greenbelt to the Metropark. I didn't have to look at my watch to know I was taking longer than I should, passing my usual two-and-a-half-mile turn around mark. I just kept going deeper into the woods, mesmerized by the slap of sole against asphalt until my mind finally cleared of the troublesome thoughts that woke me.

Back again at Crocker Park, customers were just starting to gather at Starbucks like lint in the dryer trap. I got a *Venti* dark roast and blew that pop stand quick before the temptation of the pastry counter won out.

I purposely took my sweet time over a container of yogurt, reading deeper than usual into the morning news stories and stopping uncharacteristically to listen to entire segments on the *Today* show that usually passed for background noise. Thoughts of Jake were countered at the bathroom mirror by contemplating whether I should cut my hair. Then, of course, *What should I wear?* became a debate worthy of even Socrates, Aristotle, and Sartre. *Sartre?* And there was Jake invading my thoughts again through the back door.

Being in no hurry for my new assignment with the Geek Squad—even if it was only temporary—*and it would be temporary*—I by-passed I90 and took the scenic route to work down Lake Road knowing I'd be fashionably late.

And late I was. When the mousy little nerd showed me into the darkened conference room in Exit Alley, the briefing was already underway. No one—not even Jake—said anything, so I took a seat in the back of the room and surveyed the audience. Besides Jake and his partner, EC, there were a half dozen obvious keyboard jockeys in attendance, along with a bored Mutt-and-Jeff pair dressed in coveralls parked at the back of the room with me. At least Lt. Sands wasn't there to see I was late. I actually wished I was back in the House doing paperwork with Sanchez on yesterday's collar. Everyone but Jake followed along on their *iSlates*. He stared at the presentation slide projected behind the guy he called "Q"—at least I assumed it was Q from his descriptions of the head-hacker-what's-in-charge. The slide showed a map of the metropolitan area splattered with red dots, which were the locations of unsolved murders. I wondered if the victims in my last case were up there, too, but downtown and the Flats were covered by one big indistinct puddle of red.

As Q gave an eye-glazing recitation of the city's crime statistics, I wondered why every unsolved homicide had suddenly become our concern.

"You can gray out all the cases prior to 2030," EC instructed Q. "That's when the FTA approved and released synthoid PSAs for licensing and commercial deployment."

"Yeah, well, you know, there were government-approved trial runs going on before that," said the shorter, rounder, and balder of my coverall companions in the back row.

Huh. I would not have guessed they were actually paying attention.

"Twenty twenty-three," barked his companion, Puff, which I knew from the script in the embroidered oval over his heart.

"Could have been. Yup. Maybe," answered his partner as he adjusted his wire-rimmed glasses. "But the early trials were restricted to academic and industrial campuses, mostly in Silicon Valley and Boston."

"Q, can you do a split screen with EC's filter on the right, using what, 2025?" Jake turned and asked EC beside him.

"That's good," EC answered.

"And on the left put up twentieth century-only cold cases along with suspected serials and sprees from, ah, just put 1850 in for drill, and let's see what we get."

"Eighteen fifty? Seriously?" one of the nerds asked in a smarmy tone. "I don't get what these data points will demonstrate."

I didn't either, but I found there were a lot of times that Jake's way of thinking was like taking the scenic route—certainly not the most direct path, but you go with it because it always took you someplace interesting.

Q gave the gangly questioner the hairy eyeball, then went ahead and split the screen. Dots faded, and new ones bloomed as the filters were applied.

"Well, well, well…Looky there." Jake smiled at the Digital Doubting Thomas. "A *ruby* necklace."

Even Q was clearly confused by what Jake meant. I wasn't. A long strand of parks ringed the metropolitan area from Huntington Beach in the western suburbs south to the turnpike, then around north again to the lake at the easternmost edge of the county. It was called the "Emerald Necklace" from how the Metroparks system looks on a map of the city. I was guessing the pale, nerdy kids in Exit Alley didn't get out of doors much. Red dots on both halves of the screen formed a blood trail through the park system.

"Q, pull all these case files and have your team start looking for links," Jake said standing up and walking to the front of the conference room. He pointed to a red dot in Bay Village on the new side of the screen. I noticed it was mirrored on the map of historical cases. "Get me this one right away."

"Why's that?" Q asked.

"Maddie and I are going to take a ride."

Like I said, *the scenic route.*

*****~~~*****

The Crime of the Century

"You've got your slab, right?" Jake asked as we headed towards the parking lot. "I forgot mine."

"Of course," I sighed shaking my head. Typical Jake move. His techno-fossil attitude must really drive the digital tribe down the alley insane. I'm surprised one of them hasn't tried to bash his head in with a keyboard. Of course, that'd be the fast track to becoming a binary zero. "You want me to drive?"

"Nah. I got this." Jake veered away from the squad cars towards the employee lot.

A warm dread spilled down through my chest as I caught sight of Jake's car. *That bastard.* He knew. Of course he did.

I was an automotive agnostic before Jake—just a tool to get me from here to there—and as perplexed as the rest of my half of the species as to the passions that welled up out of testosterone for fossil-fueled vehicles. But Jake had restored a convertible-top car from the last century that he was kind of prissy about. If I was still going to church, I'd have to include in confession that I really enjoyed our Sunday afternoon drives through the park, down the lakeshore or busting every speed limit on the winding back roads of Amish country. It was fun just going, not having a destination in mind but always finding one.

I split off from Jake and rounded the trunk to the

passenger side. "Jesus. Where do you even find gasoline for this thing?"

"Race tracks, marinas, and airports mainly."

"Shouldn't we call Bay Village PD and let them know we're coming?"

"Nah, it's just a day at the beach for a dashing young couple," Jake answered over the ragtop of his shiny black *Mustang.*

"A dashing young couple carrying badges and packing heat."

"Packing heat?" Jake tossed a lecherous smile my way.

"Glocks, you moron."

"Yeah…right…"

We got in, and Jake put the top down. He pulled out of the lot, zipped down to Lakeside, then merged onto the Main Avenue Bridge over the Flats where the river spilled into the lake. The highway would have been faster, but I enjoyed the ride along the shoreline. And Jake let me enjoy it by not trying to make small talk. He knew, *that bastard.*

When we got to the westernmost link in the Metroparks "Emerald Necklace," Jake passed by the entrance. I had learned not to point out the obvious with him and said nothing. Just past the park, he slowed to eyeball the houses built on the lake. After trolling past four or five of them, he sped up, then turned around in a church parking lot.

"So, whatcha looking for?"

"The crime of the century—well, last century…one of them anyway," Jake said looking back over his shoulder. He squealed the tires pulling out of the lot.

"And which crime of the century is that?"

He took his eyes off the road to stare my way. I could read

his eyes even behind the sunglasses and knew what he was going to say: "Those who cannot remember the past—"

"Yeah, yeah yeah—are condemned to repeat it. You've told me that a million times."

"...*condemned to repeat it.*" Jake muttered it more to himself than to me.

"What is it?"

Jake pulled the *Mustang* into Huntington Beach and parked. "Let's take a walk on the beach and when we're done, maybe I'll buy you an ice cream cone. Don't forget your slab."

I grabbed my *iSlate.* Parallel concrete stairways led down the fifty-foot cliff to the beach. We stopped on the landing halfway down that formed a long sight seeing balcony. Jake leaned on the rail and looked east towards downtown. I braced myself for "the talk" we probably should have had when we broke up but never did.

"Down there. By the big tree." Jake pointed to a huge, solitary oak tree growing at the water's edge. "That's where they found her, right?"

"Huh? What?" My mind scrambled to get back into cop mode.

"Q sent you the case file, didn't he?"

"Let me look." I quickly lit up my *iSlate* and swiped until I found it.

"Brunette. Shoulder-length hair," Jake recited. "About thirty-one or so. Bludgeoned to death. Found in a nightgown with her legs dangling into the water."

I scanned the police report. There was a picture of the body that matched his description. "Yeah. So, you've already read the case file?"

"Nope." Jake shook his head. "No murder weapon?"

"Doesn't look like one was found."

"Check the autopsy report. Pregnant?"

I swiped through the murder book. Right again. "What are we doing here? Parlor tricks? You're clairvoyant now?"

Jake stood up from the rail. He paused to give me a serious look, then scaled down the rest of the steps to the beach. I followed him out to the tree, but stood back behind him ten feet or so to give him some space as he stared at the concrete block pier where the murder took place. It was part of his process to tune himself into the crime scene. We all do it different. Jake taught me that—and that you don't mess with another person's style. It wasn't *déjà vu,* but it felt damn familiar. And it should have after all the cases we worked. He'd come out of his meditation soon enough, so I watched the waves roll off the lake onto the beach. The water was deep blue. The sun was warm, but the wind had a bite of chill in it.

"A Munchausen." Jake finally said into the wind.

"Huh? You talking to me or yourself?"

Jake looked back at me.

"A robot? But Jake, her head was bashed in pretty badly. That's a crime of passion."

"It might have been. A hundred years ago. It's what I've thought all along though…and feared."

"But you haven't even read the case."

"Didn't have to really. I read the other one."

"What other one?"

"The crime of the century. For Cleveland anyway."

"What are you talking about?"

Jake started walking west. I fell in beside him, and we

pushed slowly through the loose sand. "Nineteen fifty-four. The Sam Sheppard case. His pregnant wife, Marilyn, was bludgeoned to death. There." Jake pointed to the houses up on the bluff we had trolled by earlier. "The house is long gone. But this is where it happened."

"But, that's ancient history."

"Yup. But those who cannot remember—"

"—the past are condemned to repeat it…Copycat crimes?"

"More like digital replications."

"By synthoids? How many more?"

"Your last, for one."

"The hookers in the Flats?"

"Jack the Ripper."

I felt my shoulders slump. I should have listened to him. "I don't like this. I don't like this at all."

"No one will." Jake put his arm around my waist and pulled me to head back towards the stairs up the bluff. "How about that ice cream cone, little girl?"

~~~

In the Wind

Sanchez bolted up from her desk and met me at the door to the squad room. "She's in the wind."

"Huh? Who's in the wind?"

"Amy."

"Amy? Why the hell should I care—" Then I noticed the CPS social worker making a hasty exit out the back. *Oh, that Amy.* "You! Cat Lady. Hold it—"

Sanchez sidestepped in front of me, blocking my path. "Cool it, *la roja*. Let her go. I got all the info and talked to the sarge about stepping up patrols under the bridges."

I stood and fumed.

"So, what's with the new look? You set your hair dryer on turbo?"

I tuned back into the moment and smiled wearily at Sanchez. "Jake's convertible."

"Those things aren't really safe, you know. Especially not if he's behind the wheel." Then she read something in the look on my face. "What's wrong?"

"Amy. She saw what happened. They'll come for her."

"Yeah, well, it's not like the kid shops at Amazon or anything, so without digital footprints, they can't cybertrack her either. We'll have the advantage with the number of eyeballs actually out on the street looking for the kid."

"We've got to find her before they do."

"And who's they? Do the Brainiacs down the alley have any clue?"

I shook my head.

"And what were you and Jake doing all morning? Joyriding in his rat rod?"

"Have you had lunch?"

"Nope. You buying?"

"Better yet. We'll make Jake pay."

"Then I'm in. I am definitely in."

I fixed my hair, and we walked over to Cutty's Delicatessen. Jake and EC were sitting on opposite sides of a booth in the back.

"What is this? Some kind of half-assed double date?" Sanchez threw a stern look back and forth between Jake and EC, then, thankfully, slid in beside Jake. "And you keep your hands to yourself, Mr. Jake."

"Hi, EC," I said smiling his way. I sat down catty-corner from Jake. "How've you been?"

"Good, Maddie. Nice to see you again."

I nudged EC with my elbow and leaned in to whisper, "Maybe we can shake these losers and take in a film or something."

EC smiled.

"Hey, hey, hey—everybody, hands on the table," Jake scolded. "No monkey business."

I blew gently into EC's ear with a sideways glance at Jake.

EC blushed.

Jake smirked back.

"Seriously? It's like a high school lunchroom in here."

Sanchez scowled. "Hand me a damn menu. What's good here?"

"Well, hey there, missy Madeline," Cutty said ambling up to the table, emphasizing the "line" in my name. "It's been a while. How's your Pop?"

"Hi, Officer Cutler," I gushed feigning childhood innocence. He leered at me like he always did, like an uncle you never wanted to get too close to at holiday family get-togethers. He had been my Dad's partner for a while. Jake's, too, when he just got out of the academy. "He's doing well. Thank you."

Cutty took a long, loud slurp of scotch out of the department mug "liberated" from the House when he retired. He cocked his head at Jake and then back at me. "Hmmm."

I just smiled. "I'll have the usual."

"A salad? Aw, you're killing me, Madeline."

"Pastrami Reuben," Jake piped in.

"Ditto," said EC.

Cutty stared down at Sanchez as she studied the menu like a crime scene photo. *"Detective…"*

"The chicken salad. Fresh?"

"Of course."

"Fresh today?"

"Well…"

"Uh-huh. I thought so."

"Sheesh. Tough customer." Cutty looked at me, then Jake.

"You better just bring me that meatloaf—and make sure there's extra gravy on it." Sanchez snapped her menu shut and handed it to Cutty. "In case it's too dry."

"Yes, ma'am. Right away, ma'am."

"That's more like it. And bring me a Pepsi-Cola."

Cutty shook his head as he retreated with his marching orders.

"So, what did Q come up with?" Jake asked EC. "What dots did they connect between the cases?"

"Nothing yet. They were still involved in an animated debate over programming algorithms when I gave up and started pulling files manually. There's a lot, Jake. A lot."

"What the what." Jake looked at Sanchez. "See what I have to put up with?"

"You made that bed you're lyin' in, mister." Of course, Sanchez knew the score on Jake and me. "I never shot no councilman's son. Maddie neither."

Well, maybe she didn't really know *everything*.

"Means, motive, victim, scene, time of day." Jake counted them off on his fingers. "It's simple, but no. They've always got to reinvent what Gates and Jobs figured out nearly a hundred years ago."

"Who?"

Jake slapped his hand over his eyes and shook his head wearily.

"Sounds like a kid's game: Gates and Jobs…Jobs and Gates." Sanchez poked her thumb in Jake's direction, then asked me, "You and…*him?*"

I just shrugged my shoulders.

With no police business to discuss, the lunch degenerated into a session of good-natured juvenile banter and teasing until EC got a call. Sanchez and I watched seriousness melt the merriment off his face as he listened. Jake finished his Reuben.

"That was Q. There's been a fresh one," EC explained with a heavy sigh. "In District Four."

"Let me guess." Jake licked the Thousand Island salad dressing off his fingers, then wiped them clean with his napkin. "No head. And the balls were cut off."

EC slowly started to nod.

"What the—how'd you—" Sanchez stuttered.

"*Voodoo.*" Jake gave Sanchez a long sideways stare.

"I'm Hispanic, not Haitian."

"Whatever."

"He thinks he's psychic now," I explained. "Right?"

Jake shrugged. "So, ladies, would you care to join us for a sunny afternoon jaunt to a crime scene?"

As we left, Jake told Cutty to put lunch on his tab.

~~~

Kingsbury Run

We got there about the same time as the CSI van. There is a certain reverence about a murder scene. It's busy, sure, but busy like communion at church. Lots of purposeful, muted movements. Hushed conversations. Footsteps like Iroquois stalking through the woods in moccasins. A death at center stage. Sanchez actually crossed herself as we paused at the crime scene tape, which wrapped off an urban wooded area just south of the Red Line Rapid Transit tracks off Grand Avenue.

"Whatcha got?" Jake asked a detective who approached us on the opposite side of the tape.

"Murder most foul," he answered and extended his hand. "Wally."

"So I heard. Jake." They shook hands, and Jake made a quick round of introductions. "Mind if I—we take a look." He threw a thumb in my direction.

Wally shrugged and held up the yellow tape for us to duck under. He motioned EC and Sanchez to follow, too. "Not really going to disturb anything. The vic's been here long enough for the coyotes to find him. So, what's Artificial Crimes doing out here? Kind of off your regular beat, isn't it?"

"Looking for patterns."

"You got another dead headless horseman out there?"

"Not really. The location threw up a red flag from our tech guys."

Wally shook his head. "How many flags you guys got? It's a dumping grounds along here."

"Has been for a long time."

Wally stopped about ten feet from the body. He sighed heavily and scratched the back of his neck. Discolored with bloated limbs, the headless torso had been ripped open and hollowed out by hungry scavengers.

"Hey, thanks. Good luck," Jake said and abruptly turned to head back to the car.

Wally gave us a quizzical look.

"That's it?" Sanchez asked me.

EC and I smiled. I reached out to shake the detective's hand. "Thanks, Wally. Looks like the forensics team is ready to go. We'll get out of your way."

"What is it with him?" Sanchez asked as we trailed behind Jake.

"He saw what he needed to see," EC explained. "No need to hang around and make a career out of it."

"And what did he see?"

"I'm sure we'll get a lecture on it in due time."

I just smiled.

Jake was leaning against the car scanning the area up and down the tracks.

"So, Sherlock, what have you got?" EC teased.

"They used to call it Kingsbury Run after the dude who settled here eons ago. Became a shanty town in the depression before World War II last century. Starts by the river up in the Flats and basically follows the tracks out to Shaker."

"Yeah…so?" Sanchez asked impatiently.

Jake looked up the tracks towards downtown. "It's where the Torso Murderer's victims ended up. A serial killer who cut off the victim's heads. The men usually lost their other brain, too."

EC's chuckle drew a scowl from Sanchez. She looked back at Jake. "Like I said, yeah…so?"

"You should check out the CPD museum sometime."

Sanchez shot me a "what the hell" expression. I nodded. "Been there. Done that. Got the t-shirt."

"Thirteen documented. But, really, probably thirty or more—at least around here. They say the killer was also active in Pittsburgh. And they even tried to pin a murder in LA on him. The Black Dahlia. Never caught the perp. It killed the career of the original *Untouchable.*"

"Elliot Ness," EC explained.

I'm sure EC's been to the museum, too. A few times.

Jake nodded and smiled.

"You solving crimes hundreds of years old?" Sanchez asked incredulously. "I figure we got our hands full in the here and now, don't you?"

Sanchez looked my way. I shrugged.

"That body wasn't a hundred years old." Jake pointed to where Wally stood watching the Bunny Suit Boys process his crime scene. Jake looked skyward. "In fact, I'm surprised we don't have buzzards overhead."

"Yup. And that's District Four's headache."

Jake smiled down at Sanchez. "Yeah. You'd think."

~~~

The Muni Lot

As I came down the alley to Artificial Crimes the next
morning, Q was outside slouched against the wall with a pouty
look on his face, swiping furiously at his *iSlate*. "Shouldn't you
be inside getting ready for the briefing?"

Q grunted. "A little change in agenda. Some synthoid's run
amuck down in the Muni Lot. Smashing windshields, I guess.
Jake and EC caught the call and went to bring it to heel."

I shuddered. The Muni Lot parking garage at the west end
was where Jake shot the councilman's son. "How long ago?"

"Just left a few minutes ago. You can probably still catch
the show." Q never looked up from his *iSlate,* so I doubt he
even noticed I had already started off in that direction.

It was maybe a ten-minute walk and a fifteen-minute drive
by the time I checked out a car and waited on traffic lights, so I
decided to head down there on foot. About halfway, the
adrenalin pumping through my veins reached my feet, and I
found myself jogging down Lakeside towards East Ninth. It was
a good thing I didn't have Sanchez in tow.

When I turned the corner towards the lake, the East Ninth
garage entrance was cordoned off. Jake and EC were at the tac
van suiting up to go in. I flashed my badge to patrol and crossed
over.

"What's going on?" I asked breathlessly. I guess I had been

running harder than I thought.

Jake shot me a look like he caught the nervousness in my voice.

"Q said you were down here."

"One of the city sweepers went off the rails, grabbed a hammer, and started smashing headlights and windshields down by the Rock Hall. Then it ducked into the garage," EC explained. "They're old units, and the city stopped ponying up for the OS updates a while back, so they get cranky sometimes. This shouldn't take long."

"Yeah. We'll get in, get out…" Jake said, strapping up his vest.

EC finished Jake's thought with a chuckle. "And nobody'll get hurt…*we hope.*"

"A walk in the park." Jake winked at me, then put on his *Google Glass* and his helmet.

A dark memory sucked the breath out of my lungs. It was the same thing he said after he swapped out his magazine and put mine—with one less cartridge in it—into his Glock, then followed the wounded councilman's son into the parking garage.

The piercing squeal of Jake's *eM&P* pistol as it armed and charged made me grimace. I hated that sound ever since the alley in the Flats. It was the one thing I actually remembered from the synthoid attack on me and, even though it saved my life, it brought back a very bad moment. Now there were two bad memories floating in my head as I watched Jake and EC get swallowed up by the mouth of the garage.

I went over to the Command Vehicle and rapped on the side.

"Hey, Maddie. Come on in." Sergeant Kovacic, the SWAT

team leader, motioned me into the back of the step van. "Welcome to the show."

I stood behind him and scanned the bank of monitors. On the right was the feed from Jake's *Google Glass*. EC was on the left. Center stage was the tap into the garage security system and up top was the feed from the ePD scanning app on EC's *iSlate*. Kovacic scouted ahead of them, paging and panning through the camera feeds floor-by-floor to locate the city's wayward synthoid. Along the inside row of cars, tailgate and rear windows were pocked with what looked like giant bullet holes from where they were struck with the hammer.

I looked over my shoulder outside the van and saw that SWAT had taken up positions at the garage entrance, just in case.

"No joy," EC said over the comm channel. "Moving to level two."

"Sweep is clear to two so far," Kovacic answered. "Watch the blind spots at the ends."

I found my eyes drawn to Jake's visual feed and couldn't help but let my thoughts be pulled back to that night when Sara Ann's murder case went sideways and shuffled Jake out of Robbery/Homicide and down the alley to chase robots. I was green and got too anxious and careless and let myself get jumped. I guess the councilman's son didn't realize he was being tailed by detectives who suspected him of murder when he ducked into the parking garage at two AM and ambushed me with other ideas in mind. Jake saw and bolted across East Ninth Street, but my instincts just kicked in. Since the perps's hands were full grabbing my private parts, I was able to get my weapon out and fired a round into his leg. He dazed me by throwing me hard into the back end of a sedan, drew on me, but saw Jake coming at him and bolted up the ramp. As I shook the cobwebs from my head, four more shots echoed down from above—one smaller caliber and three from Jake's Glock. It wasn't until the shooting team checked my weapon that I realized that my gun was fully loaded. Jake gave me a look and took the whole shooting on himself. Politics being what it is, he got demoted to the Artificial Crimes Unit. Work partners no more, during his suspension, we became…well, *involved.*

Jake's view through the monitor panned methodically left, then right. Then left again. They turned the corner, and Jake's eyes paused on the big "Level 3" painted on a pillar. That's where he shot the councilman's son. He turned his head back over his shoulder like he was looking directly at me through the monitor, then moved on, eyes forward again. Up ahead, silhouetted against the outside light at the end of the aisle, was a human-like figure holding a raised hammer. I shuddered at the sight.

"Halt! Police!" EC's command echoed back thinly through the comm channel.

Kovacic quickly paged back and forth through the security camera feeds until he found the best angle and zoomed it to take in the scene over Jake's and EC's shoulders.

The synthoid froze, hammer poised above its head. Jake's monitor was filled with his sight view down the barrel of his *eM&P.*

I could see from the ePD scanning app screen remoted into the monitor bank that EC was trying to establish a channel link to the synthoid's operating system.

Jake's *Glass* status flashed green. He had a confirmed frequency lock on the droid with his EMP pistol.

The synthoid remained frozen like a statue. Kovacic zoomed in on it.

I could only imagine in the static, flat screen images before me that electrons and digital signals were flying furiously through the air between EC, Jake, and the AnSub.

"What the hell?" EC looked up from his *iSlate* screen at the synthoid as it let the hammer drop from its hand, fell to its knees, and put its hands behind its head.

It was too far away for the words to be audible, but the simultaneous text message that appeared on the ePD app screen, as well as the *Google Glass* feeds was clear: "I SURRENDER, JAKE."

~~~

Would You Know My Name

We sat around the conference table on Q's side of Exit Alley waiting for Jake: EC, Q and me. Q's *iSlate* lay flat and dark on the table in front of him. I can't ever recall him being so…unfidgety. It was eerie. He just stared off into space.

EC doodled aimlessly on a yellow legal pad.

I couldn't fathom why everyone was so moody. The takedown of the synthoid in the parking garage seemed to me to have gone off without a hitch or even much drama, but obviously, something happened that I missed to put everyone in a funk. Jake had gone down to the Captain's office to explain the facts of life to the civil servant from the Division of Streets about why they weren't going to get their robot garbage picker-upper back. So, we waited, and I caught up on my real case load with Sanchez.

Marcus Williams didn't make bail, and a prelim was scheduled for the eighteenth. It was an open-and-shut case, but when you've got a public defender and the bill for legal fees doesn't come to your house, you milk the system and get your money's worth—I mean the taxpayer's money's worth. Still no sighting of Amy by patrol yet. I sighed loud enough that Q and EC both looked my way.

Just then, Jake appeared at the door to the conference room and rolled his eyes up into the back of his head. He tossed his *iNode* into the middle of the table and motioned toward the exit with his head. The boys anted up their electronics into the pot and slid out past Jake.

"Come on, Mads. You in or out?" He looked down the hall towards the exit. "Eyes and ears only."

I unclipped my *iNode* and slid it forward.

"Phone, too."

"Sounds serious," I said, pushing my phone forward.

"Eh…"

Jake chivalrously stepped back to let me out the door. Down at the end of the hall, Q tapped away at what I presumed was a burner phone. When we went outside, they all looked up at the security camera above the door to make sure the power light was off. Nobody said anything.

"*What?*" I finally asked impatiently.

"My name," Jake mumbled. "It said my name."

I still didn't get it.

"I surrender…*Jake.*"

"So?"

"It's personal," explained EC. "Like people, droids don't get personal with strangers they've never met. How could it know Jake's name?"

"Maybe it read it off the chip in your badge," I offered. "You know, like when we swipe it to log in."

Q shook his head. "That info is pretty deeply encrypted in the system. For tactical reasons. Too risky to broadcast in the clear to John Q."

"Facial recognition?"

EC exhaled loudly through his pursed lips and shook his head slowly. "RSHA…and, of course, the ACLU."

"Huh?"

"Robotic Safety and Health Administration," Q said clearing his throat.

"I know what RSHA stands for."

"Fourth Amendment, right to privacy, yada yada yada," Jake said dismissively. "Damn lawyers."

Q saw from the look on my face that I didn't get it. "Early on, there were a bunch of lawsuits, so the Justice Department and the industry came up with a consent decree for intelligence gathering on citizens by socially embedded entities. While they can passively record, synthoids can't actively catalog individualized metadata on citizens."

"What's that mean?"

"It means that while synthoids certainly have facial recognition capabilities, legally their software must be structured to be task specific with limited access only to appropriate database libraries. A security guard synthoid would be programmed to do facial matching against the database of a company or agency employee roster, just like a human guard would know the people who came in and out of the building every day. A low-level municipal street sweeper would probably have Department of Streets employees resident in its memory banks and maybe access to the U.S. Marshal's fugitive database, but not much more. Not even law enforcement units have unrestricted access to AFFRIS."

"So, for this thing to call Jake by name…"

"Means that someone hacked it and planted my name there."

"Munchausen? The Baron?"

Q shrugged his shoulders. "We'll have to see what we get out of the synthoid when Mechanical is done."

"I guess this time it's personal." Jake opened up the door to Exit Alley. "Come on, let's get our electronic leashes and go see Bob and Puff."

*****~~~*****

Bob and Puff

"Puff?" I asked Jake. "As in Puff the Magic Dragon?"

He stopped in the middle of the hallway on our way to Mechanical and stared at me with a bemused smirk growing on his face.

"What?"

Jake shook his head. "Wow. That's a cultural reference out of the antiquities."

"And you say I never pay attention when you talk."

"Well, then, I stand corrected," Jake chuckled. "As for the origins of his name, ah, let's just say that Mr. Puff is not really the sharing type. Nobody knows. Not even Bob."

"Great. Yet another victim of testosterone poisoning."

"We're all damaged goods in our own way." Jake shrugged and continued on down the hall.

I picked up my pace to catch up with him. "Is that a confession or just more bragging?"

Jake stopped at the door labeled "Technical Forensic Lab" and paused. "Look, just don't ask any dumb questions."

"Hey—"

"Puff does not suffer fools lightly and, as entertaining as it is sometimes, I'm not in the mood for one of his lectures."

We pushed into the Lab. I hadn't been there before, and it was kind of creepy just like Jake described it to me in the past:

a strange mix of a robot morgue—the street cleaning synthoid was laid out on a table with its guts exposed—but also an electronics junkyard lined with shelves crammed with circuit boards, wires, motorized actuators, and who knows what else in overflowing Tupperware bins. Heads and various other body parts hung from the ceiling off to the sides of the room. There was a vague whiff of machine shop oil in the air. A Mutt-and-Jeff pair from central casting stood over the synthoid, and I immediately recognized the shorter, chunkier, and friendlier bespectacled Bob and his cohort, the tall, lean-and-mean nearsighted Puff.

"Hey, Jakie." Bob looked up from the abdomen of the synthoid and beamed a huge smile. He pushed his way around Puff to get to our side of the table. Wiping his hands on a soiled cloth and adjusting the wire-rimmed glasses on his face, Bob gave me a not too subtle once over with his eyes. "Wow. Traveling in style I see. A bit out of your league, wouldn't you say?"

"I'm Maddie," I said and extended my hand before Jake could make some wisecrack. We shook hands. His felt slick with oil even though he had just wiped it off.

"Hi, Maddie. Pleased to meet you." Bob held onto the handshake a bit too long. "You know Jake, here, used to talk about you a lot. Not so much anymore."

"Well, ah…" I could feel myself blushing, and Bob obviously saw it.

"Boy, I can't even imagine if one of these things went beserkoid on me in some dark alley in the middle of the night." Bob smiled and looked from me to Jake, then back to me. "That last case was, well, a doozie. Sorry it was such a close call for you. Anyway, it's his loss for sure." Bob pointed at Jake with his thumb.

Puff groaned loudly behind Bob. "Jesus, cheese and jam on a cracker already. Are we done with the tea and crumpets yet?"

"And good day to you, too, eh, Puff?" Jake said sweetly.

"Don't try to make Canadian nice-nice with me. I got no use for 'em or for you neither."

Jake looked at me. "I told you."

"Don't mind ol' Puff here," Bob chuckled. "He's more bark than bite."

Puff growled just loud enough to be heard and bared his teeth.

Bob stepped back in mock fear. "Down, boy. Down."

"Boys, boys, boys…let's not make a fuss over the lady," Jake said, wagging a finger at them. "I don't think any of us here are her type…anymore anyway."

I put my hand on Bob's shoulder and rubbed lightly. "Oh, I don't know. This one is kind of cute."

This time it was Bob's turn to blush.

"Tea and crumpets," Puff mumbled. "Can we help you with something? If not, get along then."

"Anything on the street sweeper?" Jake asked, meeting Puff's squinty-eyed stare.

"Should have been put out to pasture a long time ago," Bob said to Jake but looked at me and smiled. "Gen two. Early rev level. Haven't seen any evidence of it being chopped."

Bob read the quizzical look on my face.

"Unauthorized physical modifications," Bob explained to me with a big toothy grin. "Any repairs, parts replacements, or upgrades have to be logged and verified at the biennial inspection before recertification. Got a clean bill of health on the paperwork."

"Gen twos were solid machines," Puff said, looking down into the android's abdomen and poking around with his finger as if he had dropped a coin in it. "Nothing really fancy. But damned reliable. Vertically integrated manufacturing helped. There's still a lot of them out there. More than you'd think."

"Yeah. I can't see the city springing for the latest and greatest just to pick up litter in the Muni Lot," Jake said.

Puffed glanced sideways at Jake. "Gets the job done. What else do you need?"

"So, nothing mechanical?" I asked.

"Highly unlikely," said Bob. "I'd have Q take a close look at the security patches. It's been a problem keeping them current with so many and, oh, I don't know, maybe the Streets Department's IT guys haven't been diligent about updates—if you know what I mean."

"I do," Jake answered. "I do."

"We'll have the memory modules over to him to dump by tomorrow."

"Thanks, Bob."

"So, what are you hanging around bugging us for?" Puff straightened up and stared at Jake. "Leave already."

"Aw, Puff…Didn't we brighten your day even just a tad?"

For the first time, Puff looked at me. "Her, maybe. You? Not so much."

~~~

Phantom Evil

So, there was nothing to do but wait. No sense in doing it down in Exit Alley. I don't really belong. Normally, I would have at least stopped by my desk in Robbery/Homicide, but with my reassignment, I was even feeling a bit of a square peg in a round hole there as well. Plus, if Sanchez was still around—besides her personality taking a heavy toll in and of itself—she'd make me go through every moment of my exile with Jake. I didn't need a grilling.

I was tempted to take a leisurely ride home along the lake, but that was the way Jake took to the Sheppard crime scene and re-enactment at Huntington Beach. So, I allowed myself to be grid locked on the highway out of downtown. In the quiet corpuscle of my car, time stopped and passed simultaneously as I amoebaed my way home. No radio. No thoughts. Just floating along in the four-lane blood red flow of brake lights until the car parked itself.

Usually, the commute home serves to purge the workday and its worries from my mind, but as I walked along the sidewalk crowded with shoppers, diners, drinkers, and movie goers, I started searching for *them*. Jake explained it a hundred times—or so it seemed—and I never got it. But now I cared like I never did before—straining to see, trying to find a constellation in a field of stars. But if you don't know already, all you see are points of light. The images don't come and nothing in the sky makes sense like it does to others who know.

I got a bowl of lobster bisque to go from the deli around the corner, but it cooled on the counter as I poured a big glass of cab and stood at the window watching the foot traffic down below.

In all of my crime-fighting experience, evil was always incarnate in the man. Now evil, unmoored, floated free among us. And I could not see it.

In the morning, I dumped the cold bisque and went back to work.

~~~

Old News

I got to my desk early. Like just before six, well before the day tour officially started. I still can't really believe it, but in some ways, I was turning into my dad. He was always up hours before the rest of us. He'd be on his way out the door before me and my brothers dragged ourselves out of bed for school. I never really got it, until my day got crammed full of the demands of others, too. A half-hour or so alone at my desk with a cup of coffee centered me for the day and let me get one up on it. Unfortunately…

"Hey, Detective." Jake's reporter buddy, Jamal—aka E.J. Quick in print—was parked next to my desk, as out of place in the House as a rat rod in the Pepper Pike Country Club valet lot. "Top of the morning to you."

"We are not all Irish, you know." I cruised on by to the coffee machine, pulled down my *Wizard of Oz* cup and inspected the pot.

"I just made that about twenty minutes ago," Jamal called out, raising a department mug. "Elliot said to go ahead."

I shrugged and poured a cup. I took a sip and was momentarily thankful to at least start my day with a fresh brew rather than graveyard sludge. I walked back to my desk and sat down. "So, how are you here and why are you here?"

"Not stalking. Not stalking." Jamal raised his hands in mock surrender.

"Did Jake put you up to this?"

The reporter slowly shook his head. Jake trusted Jamal. I didn't. I didn't trust any of them. And when I found out the two of them were swapping inside information on my last case, I hit the roof, convinced that was what almost got me killed by the synthoid in that alley. Jake tried and tried to explain how it was a two-way street, but in my mind, he crossed a serious line. Terminally serious. That's me: stubborn, like my dad.

"No. Jake doesn't know I'm here."

"So, why?"

Jamal took a measured sip of his coffee. "Business."

"Of course. 'Cause we're not friends."

"Look, we both have our roles. We both have our *jobs* to do. We both have to scratch out a living and make it home at night. It doesn't mean we have to gouge each other's eyes out."

"What? Are you actually calling for a truce?"

"*Realpolitik*. We may not wear the same uniform, but that doesn't mean we're not on the same side. Jake gets it—"

"Don't. Don't even go there."

"No problem. I get it. Old news. Old wounds. But a pain that lingers is not always the next injury."

"What do you mean?"

"Do you want to end up in Exit Alley? Permanently like Jake?"

Inside, I could feel my chest tighten, reflexively answering Jamal's question.

"Your last case was a stink bomb. Not your fault, but, still, you got blue dye splattered on you."

"No thanks to Jake."

"No. Thanks to Jake you still get vertical every day." Jamal took a sip of coffee and let it sink in. "Besides, when you have all that department brass inertia behind you…well, it gets to be a bureaucratic runaway train sometimes."

He had a point. The case ended up going exactly the way Management wanted it to go. And I'm the one that got reassigned.

"Here's how it works. I can get places—I can talk to people—I can ask questions that might get certain folks with, you know, official public duties into a heap of constitutional trouble."

I nodded.

"I don't need—or want—official file information that's off limits. Sometimes a little space helps. Time is good, too. A wink. A nod…a point in the right direction."

"If you already have this understanding with Jake, what do you need me for? I'm just on temporary duty in his world."

Jamal sighed, sat up straight, and leaned in towards me. "He's on a bad path and, frankly, I'm worried."

"Bad path? How? What does that mean? Him and me?"

"No. No, professionally. This case is starting to lead down some dark rabbit holes, and the feel is, well, it feels like it's getting personal."

"You think Jake has too much invested in this one?"

"No. The Baron does."

The street sweeper android in the Muni Lot garage came to mind. Jamal was right. I found myself slowly nodding, and we came to have an understanding.

~~~

Windtalkers

After Jamal left, I lingered over a second cup of coffee and pondered. Some unnecessary filing was in order along with the straightening up of my desk. Then a third cup. I was in no hurry to get down the alley for Q's briefing, and by the time I got to the ACU conference room, no time was left for idle chit-chat with the gang—just the way I planned it.

I sat at the far end of the table from Q at the front of the room. Jake was up and across from me. EC was on my side, talking up a twenty-something female I hadn't seen before. Another androgynous analyst entered the room and reluctantly took the empty seat next to Jake.

Q got started with the same slide of unsolved area crimes from last time, reciting the basic facts of the cases, only this time connecting them to past crimes highlighting similarities in means, motives, and victim profiles. EC and the two analysts followed along on their *iSlates*. Jake and I focused on Q and the slides projected on the stark white wall behind him. Funny…you gotta look up every once in a while to see what's actually going on around you—especially if you want to be the kind of detective that closes cases.

Q droned on, reviewing my Ripper killings of prostitutes, the Torso Murders and, of course, the Sheppard case in Bay Village. I noticed Jake's gaze drifting off. Q talked about

Nightstalkers, Zodiacs, and the Son of Sam. I'm sure Jake knew all about them. Most of it was news to the rest of us.

"What's he like?" Jake suddenly asked out of nowhere, derailing Q's presentation.

"Who? Berkowitz?"

"Nah. Our guy."

Q was obviously stumped but didn't actually sputter out loud. EC and the analysts looked up from their *iSlates* at Jake.

"Really, how should I know?" Q finally asked.

Jake cracked a sly smile. *"Sympatico…*No?"

Q winced.

"Come on. The Baron isn't just some garden variety hacker. Neither are you." Jake watched Q try to shrug him off. "Code within a code within a code. A *Windtalker.*"

"Windtalker?" EC asked.

Q blushed. He looked at Jake. "So, cruising the Darknet, eh?"

"Everyone needs a hobby. So, where does he come from? Gaming? Tech? AI? VR? Spook Central?"

"Bored rich kid?" Q asked, staring down Jake.

"Yeah. Or bored rich kid." Jake nodded and met Q's stare.

"Anybody's guess."

"No. Actually, it is our guess to make. That's how we find this guy."

"He's kind of like an inverted profiler," said the analyst next to EC, drawing all the eyes in the room to her. She took a moment to absorb everyone's gaze. "I mean, no matter where he hangs, he's sponging up the lives of these killers and slowly squeezing them back out, drip-by-drip. Right?"

Nods around the table.

After a long pause, Jake asked, "A cop?"

"Uh…maybe?"

Jake sat back, clasped his hands together, and looked up at the ceiling tapping his index fingers against his chiseled profile.

"I-I don't mean—I don't really know. I'm not—*Not you, of course,* or…" She looked nervously at EC next to her.

EC laughed out loud. "Jake? Write code? Only with a number two pencil and an Agent Zero secret cypher wheel."

"Samantha's right," Jake said, leaning back into the table. "One way or another, it's an inside job. No reason law enforcement is off the table."

"Every family has its black sheep, huh," I said.

"Every serial killer had a mom and dad," Jake answered.

"Behavioral Sciences?" EC asked.

"Hell, no." Jake punctuated his objection on the table with his fingers. "The Feds got their share of geeks, too, in VICAP and White-Collar Crimes—No offense, Q."

Q shrugged it off.

"We need to keep this in-house—in this room, as a matter of fact. We don't get anyone else involved." Jake looked my way. "Sands will be good with that, right?"

"As long as we solve the case and he doesn't get ambushed with a ton of bricks falling on his head, he'll back our play—for as long as he can anyway."

And with that, I could feel the ice break beneath my feet and I fell into the investigation. I was now fully part of it.

~~~

Animal Farm

"So, you're in." Jake blocked my path down the hall outside the conference room after the briefing broke up. "Really in."

A shrug.

He squinted and gave no ground. "I can tell. I saw it in there. Partners, again. I'm glad."

"What about EC?" Though, truth be told, waitress Amy involuntarily came to mind first.

"He's good. But he's not you. He doesn't have the old bloodline from guys like your dad and Cutty. That's what it's gonna take. You know that."

"He seemed quite smitten with Samantha in there."

"It ain't smit. It's love." Jake drew out the word "love."

"Good. Good for him. He deserves it."

"Yeah, he does. We all do." Poker-faced Jake.

"I gotta—"

"There's my long-lost partner." Sanchez's voice called out from behind Jake. "I'm beginning to think you might like it down the alley here."

Jake turned and watched her amble up, missing the wave of relief that no doubt washed over my face. But Sanchez caught it. I could tell by the way the corners of her eyes crinkled, suppressing a smile.

"Welcome to our little corner of paradise, detective," Jake

said. "This is a pleasant surprise."

"For you, maybe. Me—not so much."

"Can I buy you girls a drink? I can make some fresh joe."

Sanchez looked over Jake's shoulder at me. I rolled my eyes and gave my head a shake. "Thanks, but no. I need to borrow Ms. Madeline, here, for a few hours or so."

"What's up?" I asked, pushing past Jake.

"The ninth floor called us down about the Williams case. The search warrant came through."

"Really?"

Sanchez winked. "Yeah. Funny. The wheels of justice and all. Maybe we'll find the weapon."

"Sounds like fun," Jake said, but there was no mistaking the disappointment in his voice.

"Come on, *la roja*. I've got a patrol unit sitting on the place waiting for us. And we don't want SWAT to get all prickly on us because we left them biting their chain for so long."

I looked at Jake. "I'll call…I guess."

"Sure."

Outside in the alley, Sanchez smirked, "*El novillo* in there seemed a little sad. Poor Ferdinand."

"Thank you."

"For what? Doing my job?"

"Yeah. That."

Up on the ninth floor of the Justice Center, Sanchez and I watched the suits come and go as we waited outside Assistant Prosecutor McGinty's office. You can dress them up, but the same animal instincts are there beneath the tailoring—the ones that when misdirected cause predators to cross my path. He waved us into his office.

"Detectives." McGinty greeted us but did not get up. He surveyed the sea of manila on his desktop, looking for our warrant. "Nicely done, snagging our friend in traffic court."

"We caught a break," Sanchez answered modestly. "Guess he didn't want to lose his wheels."

"Yeah, well, it obviously doesn't take brain power to rise to the top of the felony hit parade," McGinty effortlessly snatched back his compliment. He found our warrant and held it out. I reached over and grabbed it, but he didn't let go right away, cracking a sly smile and a one-eyed squint that treaded perilously close to being a leering wink. Our history was thankfully brief and pre-Jake. "Here you go, *Detective…*"

I smiled as innocently as I knew how.

McGinty released the warrant. "I really want that nine millimeter to seal the deal."

"Yes, sir." Sanchez quickly answered for me and grabbed my arm to lead me out, before any blood was shed. She shook her head after we got out of his office, muttering under her breath, *"El puerco."*

I had to smile: Sanchez's *Animal Farm.*

Outside Marcus Williams' apartment building just off Detroit Avenue on the near west side, we put on our vests as the SWAT team huddled to draw their Xs and Os in the dirt before bashing their way in. Ten minutes later, Sanchez and I followed their conga line into the second-floor apartment once the battering ram took down the door. The rooms were quickly cleared, and Forensics was invited up to the party.

Gloved up in latex, Sanchez went through the dresser drawers while I mined the bedroom closet looking for the pistol McGinty wanted so badly for trial. Digging through dirty laundry was never my cup of tea, whether in a sparkling clean suburban split-level or a Section Eight hovel—and from the stench in the closet, it had been a long, long time since Williams had been to the laundromat. I started stripping coats, shirts, and pants from hangers, carefully squeezing down all the pockets before tossing them into the middle of the bedroom floor.

"Well, well, well. One step closer," Sanchez said holding up a couple of boxes of ammunition pulled from the underwear drawer. "Federal, nine mil—just like the casings we picked up."

I nodded, turned back to the closet, took a deep breath, and dug into the clothes piled two feet high on the floor. I prayed, *Dear God, please let there be no rats.*

Nearly gagging on the stench of sweat socks and Nikes at the bottom of the pile, I came up empty-handed. *I'll bet synthoid feet don't stink.*

With an assist from a kitchen chair, I cleared the shelf up top. A shoe box held several ziplock bags of pills. Underneath was jewelry, probably loot still too hot to fence. I bagged it, tagged it and took it out to be logged by Bunny Suit Boys and added to the bin.

A couple of other boxes up on the shelf had mostly knick-knacks—lighters, reading glasses, photos, pipes, papers, paraphernalia, and a junkie kit—but also a couple of knives which were obviously weapons—three-inch blades or longer, one of them spring assist opening. There was a prison shiv fashioned from an Oral-B and cheap flatware, obviously a memento of his alma mater, Trumbull Correctional University. Bagged and tagged.

I added some t-shirts to the pile on the floor and, underneath, there it was, wrapped in a Cavaliers jersey: A Glock 17.

"Bingo." I held it out for Sanchez to see.

She nodded. *"El puerco* will be happy."

It felt good to find it. But it still took two more hours to finish searching the apartment. Snapping off my gloves, I couldn't wait to get home and scrub myself clean.

~~~

Scene of the Crime

A scorching hot shower helped scour one crime scene off me physically. Despite a big glass of Petite Sirah, another lingered mentally.

I nested into my sofa and swiped through the Baron's case files, pulling pics out of the murder book galleries to tile on the screen for comparisons. I don't know how long it was, but I was on my second glass of wine without getting anywhere when one of Jake's crazy theories came to mind. He was always making dubious claims so that half the time you wondered if he was just making stuff up to punk you. He swore there was some academic psych study done decades ago that demonstrated temporary Alzheimer's whenever a person walks through a doorway, thus explaining that sudden amnesiac feeling when you step into a room and end up wondering what you went in there to get.

He insisted the same thing happened with browser windows, but I always thought it was just a lame excuse for him to avoid technology. Truth be told, though, switching from window to window to window was inducing vapor lock in my brain. I soon found myself printing out pictures and shuffling them around me like big puzzle pieces, like Jake would do. I started to sense something connecting in the photos, but, try as I might, I couldn't force it into a coherent thought.

Coming back from the kitchen with a third glass of wine, I lost the hunch I felt, proving Jake's crazy theory. *Damn it.* All that was left was a feeling of *déjà vu*. But I *had* witnessed this scene before—dozens of times—coming home to Jake's apartment to find open books, photos, and official reports scattered about his living room like evidential tea leaves he tried to read to crack a case.

With a heavy sigh, I gave up and put on my favorite playlist of old crooners—Bennett, Cole, Krall, Jones, Sinatra—that Jake had hooked me on and watched the setting sun melt the night over the foot traffic on the street below my apartment.

I shouldn't have skipped dinner. I was out before ten and up an hour earlier than usual. Surveying the explosion of wood pulp in my apartment, I fought the urge to gather it all up into neat piles, hoping my hunch might return.

After jogging the throbbing ache out from between my temples, I showered, dressed, and headed downtown, but not to the House.

I parked down the block until the street lights went out before I revisited the crime scene—*my* crime scene, as both investigator and victim.

It was this alley in the Flats where Jake saved me…and lost me. *Literally.*

I stood back on the curb, staring down the alleyway into the lingering stains of nighttime darkness. I wish I could say I remembered what happened, but my memories of the attack are synthetic, just replays of the video Q had found on the Darknet, showing the assault on me through the eyes of my synthoid attacker. Maybe it was better that my point-of-view was lost.

The Trilogy: The Darknet

My footsteps followed those I planted months ago. The body had been found by a Republic driver pulling in to empty a dumpster at four in the morning. At least he was paying attention and didn't run her over. I guess there are some sights that will disturb even a garbage man, though—and gruesome it was.

White female. Twenty-eight. Split open like a watermelon at a Fourth of July picnic. With her intestines pulled from her abdomen and wrapped around her neck—just like the other two…and, later, Jeffery, the perp in the case Jake was working at the time. He had started connecting dots that drew different conclusions than had been sketched out in my case.

Management liked the crazy, lone wolf angle and prefabbed a house of cards for the press around it. They didn't want to hear about a serial killer from two hundred years ago and a madman breathing life back into him with modern technology. I was beginning to have second thoughts—and not just because of my relationship with Jake—and those seeds of doubt brought me back down to this alley in the middle of the night to be attacked by the robotic puppet master we called "The Baron." Jamal was right. Jake is the only reason I'm still alive.

I stepped to the back of the alley where the dumpster sat askew to accept human waste. All evidence of Alice's murder was long gone, but I could see the outline of her body as it was preserved in the murder book gallery. What I didn't see, nor believed later, was the connection to Whitechapel in London. At least not until it was bruised into me by a synthoid when I came back to the scene of the crime at two AM for answers. Answers that didn't fit Management's party line. By then, though, I had drunk the Kool-Aid.

I looked back towards the street, and a memory flashed—my memory, not a mental screen cap of Q's video—of one hand raised…of the glint off a large knife blade…of a synthetic smile placed there by a fiendish programmer, *the Baron*.

I shuddered, then left quickly to swap this alley for *Exit Alley*.

~~~

Waffles and Death

I tracked down Q on his side of the Exit Alley building. Funny how environment mimics its inhabitants. Jake's bullpen was messy and gritty—dirty cups, crumbs, and crumpled up paperwork and food wrappers strewn about—like real life on the streets. The analysts lived in an antiseptic cubicle farm. No danger of reality with its pungent bouquet of odors intruding here. Q's office was in a far corner. He saw me heading his way through the glass front wall and met me at the door. The eyes always give them away. I didn't know what he was guilty of, but he was.

"Detective…?" Half greeting, half question.

I smiled. It's the most useful weapon of choice we have with men.

"This is an unexpected—though pleasant—surprise. How, ah, can I help you."

"How does it work? Can you explain it to me?"

"What? Explain what?"

"You know, how is this all happening? I deal in flesh and blood evil. There are mysteries, of course, but the templates are as old as the Bible."

"Sure. Come in." Q stepped back to let me enter his office.

Behind me, I sensed the attention of testosterone drawn my way, like metal filings to a magnet. I looked back over my shoulder, and all the male prairie dogs disappeared back down into their cubicle holes. I imagined Q's scowl their way when he closed the door. Still, it makes a girl feel good and brought a smile to my face, which I quickly suppressed.

"Coffee? Tea? Bottled water or anything?"

"I'm fine, thank you." Sitting down, I surveyed: a pathologically neat desk; a coaster beneath his sports water bottle—*seriously, a coaster?*—and Andy Warhol's Marilyn Monroe hung on the wall behind his desk. An abstract print of red, blue and yellow squares outlined in black hung off to the side drew my eye.

Q turned and looked at the print. *"De Stijl."*

"Hmmm?"

"The style. Neoplasticism. Mondrian. He's very spiritual."

I smiled. *If you say so.* "Is that you?"

"Yeah." He handed me the framed picture I had pointed at on the credenza behind his desk. It was a not-that-much-younger Q, padded and helmeted up, flipping a BMX bike. "I used to compete."

"Used to?"

Q shrugged. "Weekender now. Skateboarding. Parkour. Just for fun."

I handed back the photo and wondered why anyone needed three phones. They were all neatly lined up on the credenza. One was more than enough for me. I smiled weakly with an ever so subtle sigh. "How does he do it? How does he get to them?"

"You mean, how did he get to you?" Q echoed my question softly. It had pained him to show me the video of my attack that he found on the Darknet. But I had made him.

"The victims."

Q pulled his *Alphabit* from his belt and contemplated it, turning the module left, then right one hundred and eighty degrees in front of his face. He set it down gently on the desk between us. "People think the Atlas Grid is like a fine wire mesh—and compared to the old cell technology it is. Instead of a grid measured out in miles, we're literally down to a square meter, and that's fine enough to locate a specific human or a human-sized entity. Without triangulation."

"Like a synthoid?"

"Like a synthoid."

"So?"

"So, everybody thinks of it mainly as a one-way street: up. For tracking. For navigation. For the efficient delivery of XG comsigs. But Atlas is not really a fine, two-dimensional virtual mesh. It's more like a waffle than a window screen. It has depth, depth in bandwidth. Not much, but enough for the Baron to use it as a delivery system, too. That is what's new. And pretty scary."

"New?"

"Munchausen hacks have always taken place at the machine level. The hardware and firmware were chopped to override the RSHA laws, and code was embedded into the OS to execute—literally—the murder. Sometimes the code is memory-resident and the synthoid actively hunts the target. Sometimes it's a sleeper that gets triggered by algorithms in the BLC logic ladder—"

"BLC?"

"Biology Logic Control. It's what makes the synthoid artificially human. It synthesizes sensor inputs, location coordinates, and library functions, like facial recognition and emotional response protocols."

"So, the AnSub waits until it finds itself in the right place at the right time with the right human in front of it, then kills?"

"That usually works if the droid is a direct plant into the vic's environment. First generation hacks. Crude, but effective. That was Jeffrey's MO on the Councilman's son. Nowadays, they hack into the target's digital shadow and employ predictive algorithms, to make sure the Munchausen shows up at the right place at the right time. You know, like a pop-up ad for an item you had searched for or a restaurant you liked and once reviewed—when you just happen to be in the neighborhood. Nothing left to chance, really."

"And that's *not* the scary part?"

Q grimaced and contemplated the irregular grid of the Mondrian.

"Is that how the Baron found me?"

He turned back to me with such a serious look on his face that it literally aged him in an instant. His brown eyes pooled into darkness. He picked up his *Alphabit* with his left hand and gestured with his right for me to hand over my *iNode*. I did. He set them in the middle of his desk, grabbed one of the cell phones from the credenza and motioned for me to follow him.

At the fire exit at the end of the hall, Q tapped out some code on his phone and opened the door without the alarm going off. We stepped outside into the alley, and he slid his ID between the latch and the door frame.

"Why the cloak and dagger?"

"Eyes and ears everywhere. You know that, Detective, don't you?"

I nodded.

"You have to create your own confessional booths." He pointed towards the surveillance camera above us. "And it helps to know where the on-off switches are."

"Catholic school?"

"Saint Eds."

"Magnificat."

Q nodded.

"So, the scary part?"

"The street sweeper."

"Huh?"

"The one Jake took down in the Muni Lot garage. It was a freelance."

"So?"

"Remember, I told you that a Munchausen had to be created hands-on by modifying the hardware and firmware."

"Uh-huh."

"The Baron has developed a push technology to plant malware in any synthoid he wants to. That's what the street sweeper was. Bob and Puff didn't find any mechanical mods. Samantha didn't find any unauthorized firmware patches in the chipset. He somehow knew the exact Atlas coordinates and mainlined his code into the OS to have the droid start smashing headlights and windows in the parking garage. He never had to touch it."

"Is that how he attacked me?"

Q sighed. "I think so."

"But it's still using a machine to commit a crime, right?"

Q nodded slowly. "But do you know what the PSA population is?"

"No."

"Millions."

"So?"

"He never had to physically touch it. So now instead of each Munchausen being a one-off creation, specifically chopped for a target, they are all potential weapons—any of them. *All of them.*"

"Millions?"

Q nodded slowly. "And that one was a city droid, not a civilian."

"Which means?"

"Not all synthoids are created equal. There are the Three Laws for John Q. Public. And then there are other laws."

I could feel a knot tightening in the pit of my stomach.

"So, who called this meeting," Jake interrupted as he came down the alley towards us from the precinct house. The tone of his voice had a hard, sharp edge. I could tell he was working too hard to hold his poker face.

Q and I watched as Jake walked by and tossed me a set of car keys. "A fresh one. You drive."

I started after Jake, but Q held me back by the arm. "We need to be careful. *All* of us. Very careful."

I looked him directly in the eyes. Maybe it wasn't guilt, but a dark knowledge. I gave a curt nod. Q released me, and I followed Jake to the parking lot.

~~~

A Hillside Dump

The ride to the crime scene was deathly silent. Nothing personal. That was just Jake's usual way, an angry meditation to prep for facing down the grim reaper's handy work. I could have let the *Crown Vic* chauffeur us but driving gave me something to do. It was a short trip down the Shoreway towards Battery Park. We got off at West 49th Street, near the Parkview Nite Club, a blues club Jake used to haunt in his youth until it went too upscale for his taste. The collection of official vehicles with flashing lights on Herman Avenue made GPS unnecessary.

As usual, Jake jumped out and went right for the body before the engine was even off. I tracked down the patrol unit that was first on the scene to get briefed. The guys were responding to a call from Animal Control which got a call from an elderly dog walker who noticed a growing circle of buzzards overhead and called to get a presumed carcass removed from the neighborhood before it drew coyotes which surely, she feared, would have eventually turned their hunger towards her beloved Bichon. I spotted her easily, cradling her pet in her arms among the gaggle of gawkers pooling outside the crime scene tape. Even though patrol had taken her statement, I went to speak with her. I didn't expect to get much more from her—and I didn't—but sometimes it's more about "customer relations" than police work, and witnesses feel slighted if they don't get to speak with a detective. Something Jake had no patience for.

I checked in with the body snatchers from the morgue to confirm the body had not been touched. Funny how Jake's reputation still held sway. Everybody knew to stay well back until he was done with his preliminary survey of the scene. He always was pretty amazing at seeing things everybody missed—even me—like some Native American tracker reading broken twigs and shuffled leaves, following a trail in the forest invisible to us palefaces.

When I got to the top of the embankment leading down to the Shoreway, I was glad to be wearing slacks. Jake was already halfway down by the body. I paused to take in the view: the city back to the east, the lake, the crib five miles out, ore boats unloading, the empty Soapbox Derby track across the highway, the Whiskey Island Marina, the old Westinghouse building to the west where centuries ago they actually made batteries. Then I carefully scaled down the hillside to Jake. The coroner and a photographer followed me down, figuring it was safe or at least that I'd shield them from his wrath.

"Hey, Jake. Long time no see."

"Hey, Elvis," Jake answered the coroner. Not his real name, which was Woodrow, but because—as it was explained to me—he dressed in white and always announced his departure by saying, "The body has left the crime scene." An inside joke between the two. I still didn't get it.

"Pretty."

"Was."

The victim was a female with dirty blonde hair fanned out around her head like a halo. Maybe late teens, but I was betting twenty-something. She was on her back, naked except for modest teal panties—nothing fancy, probably from Kohl's or Walmart—with legs spread out. Her arms were up with the elbows out and her hands together above her head, kind of diamond shaped. Behind and between us, the photographer quietly worked the scene.

"Patrol guys said she was dumped here, but…"

"Obviously not," Jake finished Woody's sentence.

The embankment was steep enough that if the body had been tossed over the guardrail in a hurry, she would have rolled all the way down to the shoulder of the Shoreway. Instead, her body had been deliberately placed vertically against the hillside and carefully arranged.

"Strangled, huh." All eyes were drawn to the ligature marks on the neck. "Wrists and ankles, too."

"Maybe." Jake knelt down beside the body and pointed to the crook of the right arm. "Puncture wound. The only one I saw and too healthy-looking to be a junk hound. Make sure you test that blue ooze around the injection site. I'll bet it's some kind of detergent or cleaning fluid."

"Seriously? Like, what, *Cheer* or *Windex?*"

Jake just nodded. Squinting, he looked up at me. "This has got Bianchi and Buono written all over it."

"Who's that?" asked Woody.

"Serial killers from LA, in what? The nineteen seventies?" I answered, vaguely starting to recall details of the case from Q's briefing slides.

"Seventy-seven to seventy-eight."

"The Hillside Strangler in the media. But there were two. Cousins," I explained.

"They taunted the police by pointing the victim's bodies at City Hall." Jake leaned over the body and looked out between the ankles. He stood up slowly. *"Damn."*

We all looked that way. There, on the other side of the highway, in the deserted stands of the Soapbox Derby track sat a solitary figure, watching us. Too far away to tell any distinguishing features. After a few moments, he—*or it*...stood up, turned, and walked away.

"Damn."

~~~

"Well, well, well, if it isn't the vaunted fourth estate," Jake said when we got back up to the top of the hill by the *Crown Vic.* He pointed out Jamal standing on the other side of the crime scene tape.

"Wait—let me get my shocked-face out of the trunk and put it on," I answered. We ambled over his way. He met Jake's eyes, then mine, and gave me a wink..

"Detectives…" Jamal fingered the yellow plastic tape like he was testing the fabric of a fine suit. Unlike the concerned citizens gathered in worry over the evidence of danger in their neighborhood, he smiled broadly and had the casual air of a man out for a walk in the park. "And what, pray tell, has caused so many civil servants to congregate together here this fine morning?"

"And he fancies himself a *crime* reporter," Jake taunted.

"It keeps me on the streets and in as much trouble as I can handle," Jamal answered. "But, I'm guessing, oh let's see, a one-eighty-seven?"

"Lucky guess." Jake shrugged his shoulders.

I just folded my arms across my chest and watched the two of them play their little game.

"Hows about a little look-see?" Jamal asked.

Jake shook his head slowly. "Mmm. Or not."

Jamal threw out his lower lip in a classic sitcom pout. "But all the other kids…"

"All the other kids what?"

"They get to see." Jamal held up his *iSlate* and tapped the screen to play a video. We squinted out the sun and saw ourselves skitter awkwardly down the hillside followed by Elvis and the photographer to the body. It was a *déjà vu* moment.

"What the hell?" I blurted out.

"Meanwhile, out on the net…"

"Where's that at?" Jake asked angrily.

"Over on the dark side, I'm afraid."

Jake and I simultaneously turned to look at the now empty bleachers at the Soap Box Derby track. "Damn it."

"You think?"

"Had to be."

"Had to be who?" asked Jamal.

"Where's the host?" Jake demanded.

"A DI-7 channel chat labeled 'JtR-Overlords.'"

"What is that?" I asked.

"The seventh circle of hell, for the violent. You gotta admit, at least there's some sense of culture on the Darknet." Jamal smirked. "Not sure about the 'JtR' part."

"I am. *The Ripper.*"

"Well, whoever they are, they've got eyes on you, Jake." Jamal shot me a look.

Jake noticed, then asked, "What are you doing prowling the dark side anyway?"

"You think my only sources are *official* sources?"

Jake just shook his head wearily.

"So, what's on this channel?" I asked.

"It ain't *I Love Lucy*."

"Lucy who?"

Jamal heaved a heavy sigh. "I'm trying to relate to the Neanderthals among us." He jerked his head towards Jake.

"Huh?"

"Another redhead in his life. The channel is mostly rants, manifestos, and homages to, shall we say, the homicidal elite."

"Serial killers," said Jake.

"Let's face it, they are the cream of the creative crop when it comes to the criminal element. Hence, the public's enduring fascination, I suppose."

"You suppose…"

"Eyeballs, Jake. Eyeballs. Clicks and page hits still rule in my corner of the world, dude." Jamal looked from Jake to me, then back to Jake. "But, as far as I can tell, the real business gets done there behind closed doors and through secret passages."

"Can Q help?"

"He could try, but I'm thinking the secret handshake is a pretty closely guarded secret. By taunting you with this video, they've got to be expecting that the *authorities* would bring them under excruciatingly close scrutiny. But, hey, tell him to knock himself out. Meanwhile, I know a guy or two who might know a guy or two who aren't afraid of the dark."

"Black gamers?"

"Yeah, shadow warriors. They're always up for a challenge that goes off the board."

"Great," Jake grunted, looking over Jamal's shoulder at the herd of media vans lumbering onto the scene like wildebeests coming to a watering hole. "You want to stick around for my 'no comment' comment?"

"Nah. If it's mainstream, it ain't Quick. I follow my own angles." Jamal slid along the crime scene tape away from the techs setting up their tripods. Before he was absorbed into the neighborhood crowd drawn towards the camera lenses like pigeons to popcorn, he warned, "Be careful out there."

It took a moment to feel the heat of Jake's glare.

"What?" I turned to face him.

"You…*and Jamal?*"

"God, no. And you got some nerve—"

Jake laughed out loud and shook his head.

"What?"

"You and Jamal? *That way?* No way."

"What then?"

Jake stepped in close, into my space, but I stood my ground. He spoke in a soft voice so only I could hear. "Just be careful around him. Hell, I'm careful around Jamal. Snake handling one-oh-one. He can be a good guy, but he's still one of *them.*"

I followed Jake's eyes to the reporters heading our way from the news vans.

"And trust me, he has fangs…and they shoot venom when need be."

I nodded, and my inside voice said, *Thanks.*

Jake held up the crime scene tape for me and to the cameras said, "No comment. *No comment.*"

~~~

Amy

On the drive back to the House, Sanchez must have pinged me a half-dozen times. I ignored them and rode out the silence with Jake. He bolted for Q's office when we parked, and I went up the alley and found my way home to Robbery/Homicide.

"You've got a visitor," Sanchez said when I got upstairs, meeting me at the coffee pot before I got to my desk.

I looked over and saw Amy sitting in the chair beside my desk. Though her clothes were newish, she was layered up like a homeless person. I didn't have to ask.

"Patrol found her down in the Flats. Near *our* crime scene. Remember?"

I took a sip of coffee, then sighed.

"Are those jokers in ACU going to be of any help at all to us?" Sanchez asked.

"It's getting complicated."

"Complicated don't really help us, does it?"

I just shrugged. "What was Amy doing down there?"

"Didn't say. Didn't ask. Just got her a couple of donuts and figured I'd wait, since she took such a shine to you."

"Thanks."

I took a long sip of coffee and observed. Amy sat nonchalantly picking donut crumbs off herself, yet still attuned to her surroundings. The occasional odd sound or new voice caught her attention and a dismissive gaze, like a wary cat, then she returned to grooming herself. I caught myself smiling, thinking of Jake's semi-feral cat, Frank. I shook it off and went over to my desk.

"Didn't expect to see you here," I said, even though I did—eventually.

Amy shrugged.

"You didn't have problems with the foster family, did you?"

She shook her head. "No. They were nice—okay, I guess."

"Looks like they bought you some new clothes."

"Yeah."

"I'll bet the food was better, too."

"I guess."

I shuffled through the in-basket on my desk. "So…"

"There's more."

"More what?"

"Of them."

"Them who?"

"You know. The machines."

Amy got my attention. "What do you mean?"

"Down there. I know where they come from, too."

"Show me?"

Amy hesitated, then nodded quickly.

"Sanchez," I called out. "I'm gonna get Amy a hot meal and take her back."

"You want I should call her social worker to do that?"

Amy shook her head quickly.

I rolled my eyes. "Nah, I'll take care of it."

We left and rode down to the Flats. I crossed over the river and went down off Detroit. We slowly prowled the West Bank.

"There's one." Amy pointed to a homeless man shuffling along.

"How do you know?"

"I know. I don't know how, but I know. It's not one of us."

I cruised by and looked closely but could not tell. And why would they turn a PSA into a vagrant? "Where do they come from?"

"The other side."

I turned on Sycamore to loop around on Winslow to Center Avenue. We crossed the swing bridge to the East Bank.

"So, how come you bolted?"

"It's not my kind of neighborhood. You know, picket fences, cutesy dogs, husky suburban kids."

I nodded.

"Where do you live?"

"Out in the 'burbs."

"Oh." Amy sighed heavily, as if she were a mother disappointed in her child's grades. "Turn down there."

I took a right. The flesh on my shoulders and back began to tingle. We were near the alley where I was attacked by the synthoid. Where Jake saved my life.

Amy watched me closely. "What's wrong?"

I tried to smile. "A bad night a little while back."

"Must have been really bad."

"Yeah. Yeah, it was. I'm lucky to be alive."

Amy reached over and gently put her hand on my shoulder. I didn't realize I had started shaking, even though it wasn't chilly.

"I had a case—cases, actually, where women were being murdered down here in the Flats."

"I remember. I knew one of them. Helena was always nice to me. Helped me with spare change whenever I saw her. Did you catch them?"

I bit my lip at the thought of the fiasco the case had become, putting me in my present situation with Jake. Then, it struck me. "Them? What do you mean *them?*"

"Stop. Pull over here."

I did.

"There." Amy pointed through the windshield to a three-story abandoned building down the street a ways. "They come and go out of there."

We were less than three blocks from the alley. I pulled out my *iSlate* and mapped our exact location: Ox Bow Bend, a particularly dark corner of the Flats, a graveyard of gritty businesses. I pulled the building's address and pinged it to Sanchez for a utilities check.

"Tell me."

"I sometimes come down to that old park under the tracks. You know, away from the bars and the sailors and what goes on over there. It's mostly quiet. And there's spots I know where it's safe, but you can see well enough to still keep a lookout. People are always going in and out of that place at weird times. And not like they have, you know, regular jobs or anything."

"Different people?"

"Um, yeah. A few different people. Sometimes it's hard to tell from so far away. I don't ever get close. Different vehicles for sure."

"Cars? Vans? Trucks?"

Amy nodded.

"The robots?"

"Yeah. You mostly see them come out and leave."

Sanchez answered: Minimal gas and some water usage, but a whole lot of electric going into the building. *Why for?* She texted.

Later, I answered.

Amy and I watched the building as dusk fell. No one came or went. The lights inside never came on.

"Come on. Let's get something to eat and get you back."

Amy sighed, then slowly nodded.

"What did you mean, did I catch *them?*"

"I really liked Helena," Amy sniffed.

"I know, hon. I know."

I put the car in gear, and we headed out of the Flats to the 'burbs.

~~~

Exit Alley

I went straight home after I dropped Amy off in the cookie cutter housing development in the Heights. The foster folks were nice enough, but she was right: it was a fish-out-of-water situation compared to living on the streets in the Flats. Of course, if Amy stuck it out, she would no doubt be running the neighborhood yard apes like some middle school *mafioso* don.

I was looking forward to an adult beverage before turning in when I remembered Sanchez and I were scheduled to testify at the Marcus Williams preliminary hearing the next day. So, I skipped the glass of wine and reviewed our reports. The case was pretty fresh in my mind, but if you slip up on even the stupidest little detail, the defense jumps all over it, and the grief rolls quickly downhill from the prosecutor's office through the command structure to Lt. Sands, who dutifully does his management obligation and delivers the corporate lecture on professionalism, case closures, and conviction rates. Besides that indignation, I just hate getting bested by the suits—especially by the off-the-rack guys in the public defender's office.

I met Sanchez the next morning at eight-thirty outside the Part B Felony Courtrooms.

A couple minutes later, McGinty strolled up. "Good morning ladies. Ready for this morning's show?"

"Mmm-hmm," answered Sanchez, dismissively looking down the corridor.

"Who wants to go first?" When neither of us answered, he went into playground mode. "Eeny, meeny, miny, moe—"

Sanchez's head snapped around so hard to deliver an angry scowl that McGinty actually took a step back.

"Right, then. Maddie it is." He turned on his heels and quickly entered the courtroom.

"I don't like that guy." I swear I could hear Sanchez's teeth grinding. She handed me the casebook with all our reports and paperwork. Although everything is digitized, of course, we still use a binder full of paper when we testify, so judges and jurors can see that there are real reports, real pictures, and, hence, real evidence against the perp. McGinty's right: it is a show.

"Yeah. Me neither. Let's start a club."

"I'm sure recruiting members won't be a problem."

"On either side of the blue line."

Sanchez answered with an angry huff and parked herself on the bench beside the courtroom door. She pulled out her phone and started swiping furiously at the screen. I sat down beside her and held the casebook on my lap, working to clear my mind to testify.

"So, what was up with the utilities on that place in the Flats? They use a lot of juice."

"Yeah, especially for a place that gives all appearances of being abandoned."

"What gives?"

"Amy said there's irregular activity—trucks, people, and synthoids coming and going at odd hours. Well, the synthoids mainly go."

Sanchez groaned. "Oh no, not Jake stuff. I don't like it. I don't like them. Don't know why anyone wants one of those creepy machines hanging around their house."

I nodded.

"Is this going to help our case?"

Treading lightly, I sighed and said, "Maybe. You can't ignore the coincidences. And, after all, the vic was a Munchausen guy himself. Killed the lawyer in Jake's last case."

"Yeah, I read the DD-5s on that one."

"What the reports didn't say is that Jake thought all along he might have been involved in the Steinmauer murders."

"Your big case." Sanchez shook her head. "So, you think they turned on one of their own?"

"Who knew those guys were organized?"

"Maybe they get better benefits, being unionized."

The bailiff pushed out the courtroom doors and motioned me in. *"Showtime."*

"Knock 'em dead."

The bailiff stepped out and held open the door for me. I walked down the center aisle, got sworn in, and took the stand. McGinty made me wait while he went through the show of shuffling folders on the prosecution table. I never look at the perp. No sense in starting a staring contest, which sends the wrong impressions, like I'm out to get them personally. I'm just there to do my job. Like Jake says: Just the facts, ma'am. Just the facts. So, I scanned the gallery with a purposely disinterested look on my face, and something caught my eye, but—

"Could you state your name and badge number for the record, please?" McGinty finally got the ball rolling, and I turned my attention to him. His questions walked me step-by-step through the elements of the robbery and assault, taking the victim's statement at the hospital, canvassing friends and neighbors, and the arrest at traffic court. Pretty dry stuff, but again, no outrage, no hatred, no emotion. Just facts. "Was a search conducted of Mr. Williams' apartment?"

"Yes. Detective Sanchez and I executed a search warrant after his apprehension."

"Did you find any items related to the crime?"

"Yes. We found a Glock 17, Gen X, and boxes of nine-millimeter jacketed hollow point ammunition. Federal brand."

McGinty walked back to his table to retrieve the firearm. As he attended to the process of showing it to the defense and having the court enter it into evidence, I rescanned the gallery. Again, my eye was caught. A man in the back, wearing a Tribe baseball cap and lightly tinted glasses, sat watching me intently. I reflexively began to catalog his features and vitals, but it was too vague. Caucasian. Male. Age was, what? Twenty-ish? Thirty-ish? He pulled at his ear, and in that programmed motion I realized: he wasn't human. It took off the glasses. Even across the courtroom, the eyes appeared cold and reptilian. I shivered.

"Is this the weapon you and Detective Sanchez found at the defendant's apartment?" McGinty resumed his questions, holding the gun out towards me.

"Huh?" I took the pistol but looked over McGinty's shoulder. The synthoid rose, put the tinted glasses back on, and left the courtroom.

"Detective?"

I looked down at the Glock, cold and dark like the synthoid's eyes. "Ah, yes, well, this is a Glock 17."

"Detective…"

"Excuse me." I set down the pistol, grabbed my phone, and pinged Sanchez: *Follow him. B-ball cap & dark glasses.*

"Detective!" the judge barked at me.

The defense attorney sat up and suddenly started paying attention.

"Sorry, your honor." I picked up the Glock again. "Is this…"

McGinty approached the witness stand and stared me down. "Is this the weapon you and Detective Sanchez found at the defendant's apartment?"

"Let me be sure." I paged through the case binder and found the inventory sheet. I checked the gun, then the sheet. "Yes, it is. The serial numbers match."

The defense attorney sighed and shook his head.

I looked down the aisle at the doors leading out of the courtroom and wondered if Sanchez got my message in time.

McGinty's questions continued to lay out the details of the state's case against Marcus Williams, but my thoughts were outside the courtroom. McGinty, taking note of my distraction, silently questioned the judge with open palms and a raised eyebrow. The judge gave a single sharp nod of his head. "No more questions."

"Defense?" asked the judge.

"No questions, your honor."

"The witness is excused."

I quickly gathered my things up.

"Mr. McGinty?" the judge asked.

As I quickly made my way out of the courtroom, McGinty and the judge went through the script of binding the defendant over for trial.

Sanchez was gone. I called her but got no answer. I called the desk sergeant to check her Atlas Grid location. Sanchez was down in the Flats. The sergeant sent me her track. I ran to the car and followed her down. By the time I got to the alley where I had been attacked by the synthoid, her dot on the map had not moved for twenty minutes.

I took a deep breath and approached the entrance to the alley. Peering around the corner, I—she was there on the ground, lifeless. I drew my weapon and entered the alley.

"Oh, Rosa." Her body was clearly broken, but she was barely breathing, so I made the call. "Officer down. Officer needs assistance."

I gave my location and moments later I heard sirens.

~~~

Whitechapel

I stayed glued to Sanchez's side, holding her hand, until the EMTs rolled her away. Then, Jake ushered me out of the alley. I didn't even realize he was there but should have known. It would be an ACU case.

"It should have been me. It was there—in court. They're stalking me…or maybe all of us. Who are these guys?"

Jake didn't answer. He just kept his arm around my shoulders as we walked down the dirty sidewalk in the Flats, away from the crime scene.

I stopped and turned to him. "Who are these guys?"

"Not here." He pulled me along. "We've got to be careful."

"Why? What's wrong?"

He leaned into me and whispered, "They're unlatched. *Free range,* Q called it. They're not on Atlas—and yet, they are. Black data pipes or something."

"Waffles."

"Huh?"

"It's how he described it to me."

Jake nodded.

"Come on." I led him away from the crime scene, further into the Flats, heading towards Ox Bow Bend, the park, and the abandoned building Amy showed me. We cut through the park and followed the curve of the river until we got to the train tracks overhead. I pulled Jake behind one of bridge supports and pointed. "That one."

"Yeah?"

"Sanchez said it's sucking in more electricity than the lights at an Indians night game."

"What's inside?"

"Vacant. Records show it's owned by White Chapel Associates, LLC."

Jake gave me a quizzical look.

"What?"

"Whitechapel?"

"Yeah. So?"

He shook his head. "It's them. Right under our damn noses." I nodded.

"Is that why Sanchez was down here?"

"No. I was in court, and I saw a droid in the gallery. When he left, I had her tail it—" I bit my lip. "Maybe…"

"Don't go there. It's not on you." Jake stroked my cheek, then squeezed my shoulder. "Let's get out of here before we attract anyone's attention. I'm sure they're camera-ed up."

"I should head over to Metro to check on Sanchez."

"I'll collect EC, and we'll come back down here to put eyes and ears on that place."

Once back at the crime scene, we went our separate ways, again. Jake sought out his partner, and I went to check on mine at the hospital.

~∼~

Metro ER

The automatic doors whooshed closed behind me. I scanned across the sea of human pain of those awaiting triage and absorbed the salty odor of sweat and fear and antiseptic. I got to the ER too late. Sanchez's family—her sisters and mother—were sobbing with quiet dignity in an out-of-the-way corner of the crowded waiting area. A uniformed officer stood guard to protect their privacy until Management could get there. The pained look on the officer's face read out like one of Q's PowerPoint slides. I couldn't help but understand: Sanchez was gone. The muscles in my shoulders tightened. I closed my eyes.

The firm grasp on my arm sent a wave of relief over me; I was grateful that Jake had come. I slumped back into the arm around my back, but when I opened my eyes, it was Jamal. I stiffened reflexively, but he just smiled and nodded.

"Come on. Over here." He led me away from the Sanchez family to an empty corner of the waiting area.

"I should…" I looked back over my shoulder.

"In a minute. The doctor just left them."

We sat down side-by-side. I took a few deep breaths. Grief and anger mingled as I struggled to bring my thoughts into some kind of order. But all that came together was a question: *Where is Jake?* I really needed him there.

"Can I get you something?"

Jamal's question brought me back to the moment. I must have looked at him like he was talking at me in Mandarin. It made him chuckle. "Coffee. Please."

"Black, right?"

I nodded quickly. I just wanted him away for a moment.

"Be right back."

Jamal left. I stared across the ER, wanting to go to them, but unable to stand. My hand found my shield on my belt, grabbed it, and held onto it hard. I don't know how much time passed before the aroma of freshly brewed coffee drew my eyes to Jamal standing before me. I took the cup, blew over it, then sipped carefully.

"Thanks."

He sat down again beside me.

"It was the same alley," I said.

"I know. That's why I came." Jamal leaned forward and rested his elbows on his knees. He looked straight ahead. "It was one of them, right?"

I nodded, then sipped to mask my guilt.

"What was she doing there?"

"She followed it from the courthouse."

"Huh?"

"We were there for a hearing on one of our cases. I was testifying and noticed a synthoid in the gallery. When it left she followed it and…"

"In the gallery?"

I nodded.

Jamal sat up and looked at me. "That's strange."

"Why?"

"How did it get through security?"

I frowned.

"They don't let civilian PSAs into the Justice Center."

"Oh, no…" My hands began to shake, sloshing coffee on the floor. Jamal grabbed the cup out of my hands. "Excuse me."

I got up and bolted towards the entrance doors with such urgency faces turned my way like the wake of a speedboat cutting through water. Outside, I ran to the far end of the parking lot. Leaning on a stranger's car, I caught my breath and called Jake. He didn't answer, so I called Q and told him to get down to the Justice Center and inventory all the synthoids there. I don't know how many they had, but I was sure one was missing.

Across the lot, I saw Lt. Sands, Captain Caldwell, and a Public Relations guy pull up and enter the ER.

When I went back in, Jamal was gone.

~ ~ ~

Media Glare

We were in an empty patient room, standing on opposite sides of the unmade hospital bed. I briefed the PR guy, and he left with his notes. Wordlessly, Lt. Sands asked the Captain for the room.

"You've got three minutes," Caldwell muttered, checking his watch. "I want to go live at the top of the hour."

Lt. Sands nodded, then sighed.

I stared at the middle of the bare mattress.

"What's going on, Maddie? What's really going on?"

"They're coming after us."

"They who? What us?"

I shrugged. I wouldn't have believed it either a week or so ago.

"Maddie…" His voice was calm, friendly—not his briefing room command voice or his scolding Management tone. "You know this is going to go ugly…fast—like three minutes fast."

I nodded. "We don't know who, exactly, but we do know where. In the Flats. At least it's a good lead."

"Jake?"

"He's down there now. With EC. Setting up surveillance." I could feel my breathing quicken. "They're sick, serial killer wannabes."

"You keep saying *they*. Munchausens?"

I looked up and slowly nodded. "Only worse. It's like a dark gaming cult or something—I don't know exactly."

"And they came after you?"

I nodded.

"And Sanchez?"

I bowed my head and couldn't stop myself from letting out a muffled sob. *"Damn it."*

Lt. Sands reached over and squeezed my arm.

The door opened, and the PR guy stuck his head in. "You guys have got to get out there. *Now.*"

Lt. Sands looked over his shoulder, and the suit disappeared like a groundhog seeing his shadow. He turned back to me. "You want out?"

I shook my head.

"Didn't think so. Come on."

I walked around the bed.

Lt. Sands put his arm around my shoulders and walked me to the door. "Let's get through this. Then get those SOBs."

He held the door open for me, and we slid along the wall down the hallway crowded with media types to join the Captain and the PR guy facing a bank of video cameras and outstretched cell phones. Sanchez's sister, Lorena, stood next to the Captain. She shot an unfriendly look my way. I couldn't blame her. If I had been with my partner, Rosa wouldn't be dead. I hung back a bit, just behind Lt. Sands' right shoulder.

It hadn't been that long since I had been in the center ring of the media circus when I solved the Steinmauer serial killer case—or thought I had. Everybody did. Except Jake—and he was right. I was the hero back then, but that screw was sure to turn. Reporters have long memories.

The Trilogy: The Darknet

"Good afternoon, everyone," the PR suit greeted the reporters. He went through the "who, what, when and where" of what happened to Sanchez. Then he gave a brief summary of her service and turned the stage over to Caldwell. I tried not to squint at the glare of the lights, but I wasn't as practiced at it as the Captain. He consoled Lorena and expressed an appropriately measured rage at the loss of one of his own. I know it played well. I had seen it before, only now, for the first time, I was on the wrong side of the news, especially when they can knock someone down a notch or two.

Lt. Sands stepped forward and vowed to find the killer or killers, then asked for the public's assistance. When he finished, questions erupted from the crowded reporters. Off to the side, in the back, I noticed Jamal. He wasn't taking notes, just watching.

"Detective, where were you when your partner was murdered?" It was Kirstie from Action News 5, claws exposed.

I tried to step forward—I couldn't let silence be my answer, but Lt. Sands held me back. Thankfully, the PR suit ended the press conference.

Jamal shook his head and quickly left.

~~~

Uncle Cutty

I wanted badly to use my lights and siren to plow through all the traffic to get back to the House ASAP but didn't. When I got there, I went straight to the ACU in Exit Alley. The detective's bullpen was empty. On the other side, Q's office was dark. The techs all stayed hunkered down in their cubicles. The tapping of keyboards slowed to a weak, erratic trickle, like the spooky ticks of an abandoned old house. Scared little rodents, waiting for the cat to move on.

I went back out in the alley and took a deep breath polluted by a nearby dumpster. I couldn't bring myself to go up to Robbery/Homicide, so I cut through the back lot and headed for the Justice Center with a vague idea of finding Q.

Halfway there, my determination began melting away inside. I veered off course to Cutty's Deli. Though it was close to dinner time, the place was less than half full. Breakfast, lunch, and shift changes were his busy times. Even still, the din ebbed as I cut through the tables towards an empty booth in the back where I could hide out. Word about the loss of my partner traveled fast. I slid into the booth with my back to the room and hid my face in my hands.

Eventually, the scrape of ceramic sliding across the tabletop made me look up into Cutty's craggy face.

"Here, Mads. It won't fix anything," he said, pushing a

coffee mug my way half filled with Scots Whisky. "But it don't hurt, neither."

I wrapped my hands around the mug and shivered.

He sat down across from me and slurped from his own mug. "Go on. Take your medicine."

I sipped tentatively as if it were piping hot. It went down harshly, then warmed me. Hoarse from the whisky, I whispered, "Thanks."

He answered with a curt nod. "It's not really a happy club you've joined. And it's not very big."

I looked down into the amber liquid. Both Cutty and my Dad had lost partners before they rode together.

"You should at least take the day."

I gave a one shouldered shrug. "But I—"

"Don't. Some just don't make it to the end of watch. Not for us to second guess. Or pretend things could be different."

I sipped.

"Go see your Dad. Family's good at these times."

I nodded but knew I wouldn't have to go there. He'd be at my place waiting. "Thanks."

Cutty raised his mug. We clinked and drank. My coughing made him grin. "You'll be all right, Mads. It'll be all right."

I smiled weakly.

Cutty stood up. "Take as much time as you need."

He took a loud slurp and headed back behind the counter. I sat. I sipped. When my mug was empty, I sneaked out the back and wandered up Ontario Street to sit in Public Square until the sun went down. I wanted the night to give me cover when I got my car out of the employee lot. I found the bench by the Soldiers and Sailors Monument where Jake and I used to people watch when we were partners—official partners—and waited.

Later, sitting in the dark in my car, I was tempted to go down into the Flats, but didn't. Instead, I stayed up top and drove across on the Lorain-Carnegie Bridge. I cruised by the West Side Market, then down to the Shoreway past Edgewater Park. I cut back up to Detroit Avenue. I didn't think I had any route in mind, but I ended up parked across the street from Jake's building. The lights were on in his apartment upstairs, and I wanted so badly to go up and let myself in like before—like nothing had changed.

But I didn't. I couldn't.

After a while, I pulled away and drove home to meet up with my Dad at my place.

Uncle Cutty was right. Family is good.

~~~

Heat Signature

Pounding on my door woke me the next morning. Late. After my dad left, I decided to get up early and run but didn't set the alarm 'cause I usually don't need it. It was after nine, though. I guess events and exhaustion caught up with me. I wiped my eyes to peer through the peephole. Jake stood outside, so I swung the door open. He grinned at me. I let him in.

"Shut up," I said, trying not to sound groggy.

"Sorry. Didn't mean to roust you out of bed before the crack of noon." He came close.

"Shut up." I didn't mean to, but I wearily leaned into him. He put his arms around me and held me. It hadn't been that long, but it had been too long. I closed my eyes and slowly squeezed him close to me. He let me. "Just shut up."

After a while, he kicked the front door closed with his foot. "Come on. Let's get some coffee in you."

Jake led me to the kitchen. I sat at the breakfast bar while he loaded up the coffee maker. He didn't have to ask. He knew where everything was, and it wasn't long before I had a steaming mug in front of me. The Colombian dark roast smelled great.

"I came by last night but saw Mac's car. I figured…"

"Yeah. He left about two." Dad liked Jake but hated that I got involved with another cop. "He was going to crash on the couch, but I talked him out of it."

"Good call. It's a killer on the back."

I smiled. Jake might have spent one night on the couch, the first night he ever stayed over when he came to me after his suspension. "What did you and EC find down in the Flats?"

Jake held up his hand and shook his head. "Um…maybe you should get dressed, and we can take a walk. Go down by the pool."

I could feel myself blushing. All I had on was my Forty-Niners jersey. "Yeah. I'll, ah, be right back."

"No hurry." Jake tossed a leer my way. "Finish your coffee."

"I'll be right back." I hopped down off the stool, grabbed my mug, and marched back to my bedroom. I slammed the door closed for effect. I dressed in shorts and a tank top to torment him, then quickly dragged a brush across my teeth and, not wanting to deal with it, I just put my hair up. He said, "Go down by the pool," so I slid on flip-flops. Padding back out to the kitchen, I called out "What's going on at the pool?"

"A little privacy. No electronics." Jake took the *iNode* off his belt and set it on the counter with his phone. "And, you know, synthoids don't swim."

It brought me up short. I never thought about that. "So, you came by on official business."

"I came by last night—*unofficially.*"

I remembered parking outside his building the night before. "Thanks. I appreciate it. I really do."

We filled our mugs and headed down to the pool. What were they going to do? Arrest a pair of cops for using glass poolside? Most of the early morning lap swimmers were gone to work, and it was still too early for the tanning crowd, so the only other person there was an older gentleman slapping the water as he crawled up and down the length of the pool. We grabbed a table on the opposite side of the pool and watched him finish a lap, then turn.

"Tough about Sanchez. I'm sorry, Mads."

"Cutty helped. I stopped by the deli. Dad, too."

"Good." Jake reached over and squeezed my arm. "Anything you need."

"Did you and EC catch her case?"

He nodded.

"Good. What did Q find out at the Justice Center?"

"Would you be shocked to learn that confusion reigns supreme down there? At least six PSAs are totally unaccounted for. Their shop is a mess, so they could be piled up in pieces parts or wandering aimlessly about the city panhandling—or worse. Of course, they don't keep any tracking logs on their movements, since it's a closed environment. So, basically, the whole herd is unaccounted for, except possibly on Atlas—presuming their firmware settings were up to code. And that's doubtful."

"So, it was…an inside job?"

"Yeah, well, you'd think so with security screening to keep weapons and civilian PSAs out of the Justice Center. But then again, droids have gotten through TSA at the airport, too."

I shook my head. "What about that vacant building?"

"Not so vacant. We put a FLIR gun on it, and it lit up like a four-alarm fire, confirming the huge electrical load. Q is pretty sure they have a serious server farm, but without an industrial strength cooling system, the plumbing probably can't keep up with it, so it throws off a pretty intense bloom."

"What's it for?"

"Well, the working theory was that Jeffery worm-holed NSA servers to download the Munchausen data packs into synthoids for his hits and keep them off the Atlas Grid. But Q could never figure out how he got in or out. And, you know, the spooks weren't going to be of any help—especially if you're pointing out vulnerabilities in their system. So, he developed an algorithm to see what he called 'free radical' metadata ripples in the grid."

I shook my head. "Techno mumbo-jumbo to my ears."

"Yeah. I still don't speak it fluently, but I've picked up some of the lingo. I mostly nod my head while Q prattles on out of my depth and get the English translation from EC later."

"So, what's the bottom line?"

"Are you kidding? The tech dweebs are always taking it to a next level, even when there isn't one, like it's all some big game."

"I think it is—to everyone but us…and the victims."

Jake nodded. "Well, this week's big idea is that they've found white space in the Atlas Grid bandwidth that they're using to push apps and libraries through, so there's got to be some serious computing horsepower behind it."

"Q's waffle theory?"

"Something like that. But me and EC are skeptical. Why would they go to all that trouble to stay off the grid, but be tied down to a physical location with a server farm that's going to tag them on smart meters? Plus, Q hasn't found any net port in or out of the place."

"What does any of this mean for what happened to Sanchez? And me?"

"I always thought that the attack on you was payback by Jeffrey. Now, I'm not so sure. And Sanchez…I don't know. It just can't be a case of being in the wrong place at the wrong time."

"Is this one guy? The Baron?"

"Unfortunately, the video on comings and goings at the building indicate it's a team effort. But there's got to be a leader of the pack. It's too organized. I'm beginning to think Jeffrey was a minion who went off the reservation when we got too close, so he became a loose end to be clipped—as well as a message sent to us. Q's been trying to infiltrate the DI-7 group, but hasn't been able to get past the gatekeepers."

"Have you told Sands?"

Jake shook his head. "Not yet."

"Anybody?" I stared Jake down. "Jamal?"

"No," he answered firmly. Jake started to say something else but stopped himself. He sighed.

"What?"

He shook his head. "Anyway, it's looking like our only move is to take down the server farm. If we do, we'll have no choice but to brief Management…and SWAT, of course."

"You really think tactical is the way to go?"

"The techies are coming up dry. Maybe we can get our hands on some real-world evidence before they get wise and close up shop."

We sat and watched the swimmer crawl through another lap.

"Take the day, Maddie. I can wait before I talk to Sands."

"Stay with me, please." My plea came out before the thought had even formed in my head.

Jake took my hand and squeezed. "You know I can't. The first forty-eight."

I nodded. The sun was warm, but the heat I felt came from inside.

~~~

Running Scared

I went for my run after Jake left to investigate Sanchez's murder. I prefer the cool of early morning. The day was heating up, but I thought it would still make me feel better, clear my head. Usually does, but it didn't this time.

Jogging up towards the entrance to the Metropark, a feeling of dread came over me. And maybe fear. I wasn't even halfway, but I stopped. Panting, I stared down the lane into the woods, shoulders tingling with a primordial, animal warning mankind never lost even after we crawled out of the evolutionary muck.

I tried to tell myself it was only an echo of the fears wrapped up in my initial reaction from the night before that it should have been me instead of Sanchez dead in the alley. My gut knotted hard, though—to a present danger, not a recollection.

Shuffling back away from the woods, I reached into my fanny pack and found a grip on my Glock 26. I pirouetted to scan all around me, then turned and ran back towards suburban safety, looking back over my shoulder every few paces until I reached the condo development. I slowed to a brisk walk, breathing hard, not so much from exertion as emotion. When I got to Crocker Park, there was comfort in the mid-day crowds of shoppers and workers breaking for lunch. I finally released the grip on my pistol and slowed my steps to blend in with the foot traffic. Still, it took a conscious effort of breathing deep to bring my heart rate down.

My feet found their way to the storefront bakery where I occasionally allow myself indulgence, as if they knew that returning to my empty apartment was the wrong thing to do just then. The clerk's unspoken impatience as I stared blankly at the pastries in the counter and the customers lining up behind me nudged me into getting a brownie and a cup of coffee, though I really had a taste for neither.

An empty bistro table on the sidewalk out front beckoned. Sitting down with my back to the shop, I could see up and down the street. Eventually, I took a bite of brownie. It made me realize how dry my mouth was. A sip of coffee did not help much.

"Detective…"

Though familiar, the voice startled me. Jamal had sneaked up on me as I stared into my coffee and stood on the other side of the wrought iron fence beside my table.

"Are you alone?"

I arrested my instinctive answer. A deep breath. "Just a little me time…and a sweet reward for sweating it out."

"May I join you?"

I glanced at the empty chair on the other side of the table and shrugged a shoulder. "Sure. Why not."

"Let me grab some java."

I had never encountered Jamal out this way, in the 'burbs. According to Jake, he hung out in grittier neighborhoods, closer to downtown, often in the Flats.

"Are you sure it's okay?" He stood behind the empty chair with coffee in hand.

I nodded.

"My condolences on your partner." He sat.

I nodded, but wondered at the comment, since we had spoken at the ER. I took a sip and peered over the rim of my cup. "So, are we talking on the record? Or are you stalking me on your personal time?"

He smiled. "Like rust, news never sleeps either."

I sighed. "I wasn't there. I can't tell you anything. You should probably talk with Jake. He caught the case."

"Um…definitely another Munchausen episode, then."

I involuntarily grit my teeth.

"First you…then Sanchez…"

The unasked question hung in the humid air between us.

"It's kind of hard to figure out what's going on, huh."

"We usually don't know until the very end. That's why they call it an investigation. And answers don't always come as easy in the real world as they do in Hollywood scripts."

"Still, for you to be on the receiving end of things. That's, well, highly unusual. Especially in ACU cases."

I kept my thoughts to myself.

"Anyway, Jake will get to the bottom of it, I'm sure. He's got a nose for it, even though he hates Exit Alley."

"He gives a hundred percent in whatever he does."

"I know. But he's got a blindside, too."

"What does that mean?"

"Careful, Maddie. Just be careful. It's a dangerous world out there." He took a long, loud sip of coffee.

"Out where?"

Jamal just smiled. "Sometimes it doesn't matter where, exactly, where is. Danger finds you."

Heat pulsed through me like a wave lapping the shore,

followed by a cold shiver. "Do you know something, Mr. Reporterman?"

Jamal cracked a smile. He casually looked up and down the sidewalk. "No. Not really. It's just the way it is. You should know that."

"She was my partner," I hissed.

"I know. I get it." Jamal sipped his coffee. "But I've got a job to do, too. You have your leads. I have mine."

"And…"

"*And*…when this is all over, I'll definitely have a story to tell."

"This isn't just a story. This is real. I'm real. And Sanchez is…was real."

"Oh, I know. Believe me, *I know*."

Another heatwave.

Jamal stood up. "You be careful out there—Jake, too."

I watched the reporter saunter off, stricken again by the shivers.

~~~

Psycho

The next morning, I sneaked up the back way to Robbery/Homicide early—before shift change, when it was still quiet. I really didn't want to cope with the steady stream of condolences from everyone and anyone I might pass by on the way to my desk. I hate funeral receiving lines and have ever since my favorite cousin died in a sledding accident when we were thirteen. No doubt they would all be sincere and mean well, but…honestly, *déjà vu* twenty or thirty times over loses its charm and novelty quickly.

When I got upstairs, she was sitting at my desk—the woman from CPS. "May I help you?"

"Oh…Detective…I, ah, didn't expect to see you back at work." She stared blankly at me.

"And?"

"And, ah, I heard about Detective Sanchez. Sorry." Okay, not all of them sincere. She stood up abruptly. "I was just leaving a copy of the missing persons report."

"Who's missing? Amy?"

"Yes. She's been gone forty-eight hours. And I did file a report with the local police." She picked up a piece of paper off my desk and waved it at me. "I was just leaving you a copy."

I nodded. "Did they issue an Amber Alert?"

"Oh, well, I wouldn't know about that. I can only do what I can do."

"I guess as long as the paperwork is in order."

"I can only do…*What I can do.*" She gathered up her over-sized Naugahyde file cabinet stuffed with manila folders, her briefcase, and her purse. "You have the report. Good day."

I watched her trundle down the aisle between the empty desks. It was true magic that a mere eight-and-a-half by eleven piece of paper could cover that ass. I started to sit down at my desk, but my eye caught a glimpse of Sanchez's trinkets and family photos on her desk across from mine. I got a cup of coffee and sought refuge in Lt. Sands' office—for how long, I really couldn't say. I kind of blanked.

"Can I get you a warm up?" Sands asked.

Startled, I hopped to my feet, looked into my empty cup, and was relieved. I would have been wearing coffee otherwise. "No—I can—I can get it."

"At ease, Maddie. At ease. I'm going that way."

I surrendered my cup.

"You know you don't have to be here, yet," Sands said when he returned, handing my cup back.

"I know." I moved from the sofa to one of the hardwood chairs in front of his desk.

He sat down behind his desk and immediately began shuffling papers around. "You want in on the ops?"

I nodded.

"Yeah. I figured. The judge should be signing off on the warrant today. We meet with SWAT this afternoon, so they can do their mission planning thing. So, likely tomorrow. The earlier the better."

"And Sanchez?"

"Commissioner's office is handling the arrangements with

the family. It'll be a few days to put everything together. Line-of-duty death and all. It'll be a big deal."

"Should I…"

Sands shook his head. "Just lay low for now. Emotions are still running high. In fact, do yourself a favor and get down to Public Square. See the department shrink if you can. At least, get an appointment set up for your mandatory session."

"But I'm fine."

"Come on, Maddie. It's policy. You know that. Don't make it hard for me—or you."

I nodded. "Does Jake have anything?"

He shook his head. "It's early. But him and EC are dogging it."

I sighed heavily.

"Go on over to Public Square. Maybe you can put that behind you." Lt. Sands tapped a pencil impatiently on his desktop. I got the hint and stood up. "Besides, maybe hanging around the squad room might not be the best thing right now."

"I'll go." I threw out my lower lip. "But I won't like it."

"No one does." He shooed me out of his office. "Now, go on. I've got important police work to do."

Sands was right on all accounts. I went out of the House the way I came in and avoided well-wishers. Jake's car or his motorcycle weren't in the employee lot, so there was no point in putting off the department shrink by hanging out at Exit Alley. I thought about stopping by Cutty's on the way, but it would be jammed with the breakfast crowd. No reason to put a damper on that party, so I headed over to Headquarters.

Still too early for the bureaucrats in blue, I found a hole-in-the-wall coffee shop, grabbed a cup, and made my way up to the third floor where the medical staff was housed. Before I finished my coffee, the department psychologist showed up—even before the secretary.

He recognized me right away. "Detective…I wasn't aware the notification had gone out yet."

"Probably didn't. My CO recommended I come over." I stood up. "So, do I need an appointment, or do you guys take walk ins?"

His beard parted as he cracked a smile. "Sure, come on in. Though I have to say, usually it's like pulling teeth."

I flashed back my pearly whites.

So, I had a fairly pleasant conversation with the guy in his fairly pleasant, but bland, windowless office with the nondescript decor and framed family photos of a wife and a couple of kids that I swear were really characters from central casting. Or maybe they came with the frame. Mostly we talked about the job. Touched on following in my dad's and his dad's footsteps in joining the force. Talked about Sanchez, of course, but also Walker and Jake.

"Kind of unusual to have so many different partners in such a short a time."

"Yeah, um, I guess." I pondered. He had a point. "But, you know, Jake got punished for what he did—for what happened to the Councilman's son. Walker retired. And Sanchez…"

"Still…"

"But, you know, there's nothing I could have done about it."

"Still…"

I didn't know what to say.

"Do you want to stay in Robbery/Homicide?"

"I do." And I did.

"Even after what happened to Sanchez? After all, it's an ACU case."

"They'll take care of it."

"Jake?"

I nodded. He seemed to know too much about things. Involuntarily, I let out a sigh.

"I have to ask." The psychologist took a deep breath. "Any significant changes in your personal life recently?"

How did he know? I asked myself. Then I realized that he already knew all about me and Jake—on duty and *off*. In fact, our entire conversation suddenly had a creepy, scripted feel to it. I nodded.

"Intimate?"

I nodded again.

"Male or female?"

I shot him a scowl.

"Okay. I get it. What happened? Was there someone else involved?"

I thought about waitress Amy and Jake being together. But that was before us, then after us again. I shook my head.

"What happened?"

I shrugged my shoulders. "I guess we drifted apart."

He stared at me, then finally said, "But he saved your life."

"You know about Jake."

He nodded. "So, what happened?"

I looked away, but there was nothing interesting in the office to look at really. "I guess I screwed up."

"How's that?"

Just then the phone rang. "Saved by the bell, eh." He got up reluctantly and went around his desk to answer it.

I listened to him listen and uh-huh his way through the call.

"I'll send her over." He listened. "Yeah. That would be best for now."

I sat up straight. "Me?"

"Your lieutenant. There's a briefing scheduled with SWAT in an hour or so down at…*Exit Alley?*"

"It's the Artificial Crimes Unit. It's literally a building down the alley from the House."

He smiled. "Huh. That's an…interesting allusion."

"It's filled with innn-teresting characters."

"Jake?"

I nodded.

"I'll fill out the paperwork, and you'll be cleared to return to duty after Detective Sanchez's funeral. It will take that long for my report to get processed. You'll get an official notification mailed to you. Modified desk duty until then, but I agreed with Lt. Sands that you can be there tomorrow—but only to observe, then assist after the scene is secured. Okay?"

I nodded and headed for the door.

"Maddie…"

I stopped and felt my grip tighten on the knob. *There's always more, damn it.* I looked back over my shoulder.

"Don't let it consume you."

"What? Sanchez?"

"No. The job. Don't let it suck all the oxygen out of your life, your off-duty life."

I paused, nodded, then left.

~~~

War Plans

Everybody was milling about the big conference room when I got there, sipping refreshments and chit-chatting in clutches of threes and fours: Sergeant Kovacic and his SWAT team in their battle fatigues; Captain Caldwell, Lt. Sands, and a couple of civil servant types in suits and ties; McGinty, his secretary, and one of his Assistant Prosecutors; Jake and EC in street clothes; Q, Samantha, and a couple of other techs, dressed like skateboarders. I hung back at the fringes and watched like a distant relative at a wedding reception.

Jake and EC eyeballed the SWAT team trading asides, no doubt cracking wise over their Hoo-rah attitude like they always did. Most of the SWAT Team were ex-military, of course, still craving that adrenalin surge from overseas. *Muscle memories,* Jake called it, for muscle heads. He saw them as a necessary evil, like his Glock. Glad to have handy when needed but kind of annoying to just be hanging around. I was tempted to join him and EC but, instead, drifted discreetly to the back of the room and sat down to lower my profile. Sands saw me, though, and gave a quick wink and a nod. EC gravitated over towards Samantha. She was younger but not by that much. I hadn't seen him smile like that for a while, not since he lost his wife. She smiled back a lot. *Good. Good for him.*

Jake followed EC over and punched Q in the arm. Jake

looked my way. and our eyes met. He smiled. Then, just as he started towards me, the Captain called the briefing to order, and everyone drifted into seats, pooling together in their respective tribes.

"Okay. Looks like the judge signed off on our warrant." The Captain looked at EC and nodded when he waved the search warrant in the air. "ACU will brief on the perps and what we're looking for. SWAT on tactical. And then we'll wrap up with CSI and Prosecutor McGinty. Okay…Jake, you're up."

When he got to the front of the room, we made eye contact. I felt myself smile a little. His face rippled with a pained expression, then went "snake eyes."

"You are all familiar with the so-called Munchausen murder-for-hire crimes. What we are investigating in this case is a series of pattern, or copycat, crimes that are being executed—so to speak—by way of synthoids."

The screen flashed on behind Jake with the crime scene photo of the victim from Huntington Beach, mirrored side-by-side with a black-and-white photo of a woman's bludgeoned and bloodied dead body sprawled on a bed.

"The Marilyn Sheppard murder case from 1954."

A series of paired crime scene photos appeared behind Jake as he spoke.

"The Torso Murders from the 1930s. The Los Angeles Hillside Strangler case in 1977."

Jake paused to look directly at me. He took a deep breath.

"We now suspect that the recent series of prostitute killings in the Flats is actually the first one."

I cringed at the montage of my victims on the screen. A few people turned in their chairs and looked directly at me. I felt myself blush.

"And that was a copycat crime, too?" Lt. Sands asked.

I knew that he knew the answer to his own question. My inside voice silently thanked him for pulling me back out of the spotlight.

"The very first serial killer: Jack the Ripper. 1888," Jake answered.

"But wasn't there DNA in that case?" The Captain asked earnestly. He turned to look at Lt. Sands. Evidently, he was not yet up to speed on how my last case had gone seriously sideways after it was supposedly closed. "Droids don't have DNA."

"It was synthetic," Sands answered. "Created in a genetics lab at the Clinic by the doc who had her husband Munchausened."

"But that case was closed when the hacker was found dead in the Flats." Suddenly aware that his ignorance was showing in public, the Captain gave the Lieutenant that 'you just wait till your father gets home' look. "See me after."

I was not looking forward to getting an invite to that meeting.

"So…Jake…" The SWAT team leader's usual stone-faced visage cracked with a broad grin, obviously relishing Management making a fool of itself. "Who's the perp—what do you guys call him, *Baron Von Munchausen?*"

The SWAT team giggled like a Girl Scout troop.

A slide of Jeffery's eviscerated body on the street quieted the room again.

"A synthoid technician at the Clinic was the prime suspect in the Mullaney murder. We started to like him for the Ripper murders, but, alas…" Jake looked at the slide of Jeffery's body behind him to make his point. "Anyway, the *Baron* actually appears to be more of a murder club that meets up on the Darknet. We haven't gotten into the chatroom, but evidence we've developed IDs the warrant address as a likely part of their infrastructure for pushing Munchausen code out through the Atlas Grid."

"Darknet, *schmarknet*. We operate out here in Meatspace, you know, the real world. You can't cuff up an avatar. Or have you forgotten, Jake?"

Jake stared down Kovacic. "You know, if you don't like the answers, maybe you should think twice about asking the question—*Oh wait…*" Jake put his hands to his cheeks and looked around the room. "Did I actually use the word 'think'?"

Laughs and chuckles percolated on the non-SWAT side of the room.

"Careful, pal. Remember who's got your back."

"Ooooo…"

"Youch."

"Careful Jake."

"Burn—Major burn."

The room quieted back down. EC took Jake's place and briefed on the building in the Flats that Amy had led us to. Then, Q did his best imitation of a shuffling, swayback perp-walk to the front of the room.

"Nerd alert," sneered the SWAT team leader.

Q put his hand into his pocket. A moment later a phone dinged, and Kovacic pulled his out of his pocket.

"What the hell! Overdrawn? How the hell can that be?"

Q cracked a smile.

"Oh, Lester…Don't stop, please." A woman's voice with a sultry Asian accent came out of the commander's phone. "Don't…stop…Les. More. More, Les, More. *Oh, Lester…*"

Out and out guffaws from the group.

"Enough!" The Captain silenced the room. "Bunch of damn five years olds."

"So, from a tech perspective," Q began, "we are looking at a significant server installation within the building that we suspect is being used to create a shadow network in the white space of the Atlas Grid to connect to free-range synthoids."

"White space?" asked one of the suits with the Captain.

"Unused bandwidth within the spectrum allocated for grid operations. In the zettahertz range, to be precise." Q stared at the suit.

"Uh, okay. Thanks."

"Free-range synthoids?" asked McGinty.

"In the past, hacking a droid required physical access to the unit in order to both modify hardware—required to override the RSHA Three Laws—and to implant firmware, software, and code libraries to program the droid for the specific crime to be committed." Q looked back over his shoulder at the slide of the dead hacker's body. "Jeffery, here—bless his heart—found a way to plant his code remotely once he chopped the synthoid by worm-holing through NSA servers, which all have various plug-in points in the Grid. And after the Munchausen crime, he could purge it of incriminating lines of code. A novel approach, which keeps the unit itself clean of any evidence of hacking. But the process left metadata breadcrumbs, which we were able to use to track him down. And if we could do it, surely the spooks in Utah could as well. So, Jeffery ended up with his insides on the outside."

"You mean CIA wetworks?" asked a CSI tech.

"No, more likely by the Baron's group. No doubt to hinder our investigation, as well as send a message. At that point, we thought this guy was a lone wolf, but…" Q looked at the SWAT team leader. "The bottom line is that the most critical objective here is to preserve and secure the server hardware *intact*—you know, without any bullet holes—so these guys can be identified and apprehended—and more importantly so ACU can find and repo the synthoids they've hacked."

"Collateral damage happens," said Kovacic.

"Well, it better not happen to those servers," said Lt. Sands.

Sergeant Kovacic took his turn, going through the Xs and Os of the SWAT deployment, the timeline, radio calls, and color of the day. The CSI supervisor echoed Q's call for preserving the scene for evidence gathering. Prosecutor McGinty's canned "by-the-book" speech was like a legal disclaimer tacked on at the end of a TV pharmaceutical commercial and closed out the meeting.

I saw Jake looking for me, but gave him the sign and sneaked out quickly to avoid getting sucked into the Captain's conversation with Lt. Sands about my last case.

He knew where I'd be: Cutty's.

~~~

Jake and Me

Cutty brought a cup of coffee to me at the back booth. He didn't say anything. Just put a hand on my shoulder and squeezed gently, then went back behind the counter.

Jake came in a sip or two later and worked the room a bit on his way back to me, hitting a couple of beat cops and a suit I didn't recognize. He stopped at the coffee machine, poured himself a cup, chatted up a waitress, then joined me.

"You made the right move." Jake slid into the booth opposite me. "Sands hadn't dropped the big one on Caldwell yet. *You gots some 'splainin' to do, Lucy.*"

I nodded. "Yeah. But not now. Not yet."

"Uh-huh. Better to deal with it when there's some good news—like after tomorrow."

"Yeah. Tomorrow." I took a deep breath. "Jake, I need—"

"So, you heard about Amy, right?"

The first thing that came to mind was stupid, blonde waitress Amy that Jake was sleeping with. "Oh, Christ. Really?"

He gave me a one-eyed squint. "The kid. She went missing again from the foster family. I saw the Amber Alert."

"Uh…yeah…Her social worker stopped by this morning and told me. Left a copy of the report."

"Oh, you thought…"

"It doesn't matter what I thought."

"Mads, it does. It does matter."

The conversation had gotten clumsy—not at all like I imagined it in my head as I walked back to the House from the department shrink. I knew what I felt, but I didn't really know what I wanted anymore.

"I was hasty, you know, after the attack in the Flats and all. I went off on you and shouldn't have."

"You are a firecracker." Jake smiled, then suddenly reached over and grabbed my forearm. "Wait—wait a minute. Are you, like…making amends?"

My skin tingled at his touch and I gulped a breath.

"You saw the head shrinker, didn't you?"

I could feel heat rising up my neck. Damn it. *He knew me too well.*

"You got nothing to apologize for, Maddie. Nothing at all."

"You always stuck by me. Always."

"It's what partners do."

"I should have…"

"I didn't like it. But I understood."

"You didn't?"

"Still don't."

"But Amy?"

Jake sighed. "I shouldn't have left you hanging out there like that. But I didn't know what else to do or how else to stop it from coming down on you, you know? He would have kept coming and coming. I had to keep you safe."

"Yeah. Maybe you're right." But I wasn't so sure.

"He's still coming—or they are. We're still not safe. You know that, right?"

"I guess." But I was still thinking about waitress Amy, not

the case. And thinking what a huge mistake I had maybe made.

"We'll get these guys, Maddie. We will."

"I guess," I said, but didn't know if I believed it. "We'll see tomorrow."

"Yeah. You look tired. Go home and get some sleep. O-dark-thirty comes awful early."

"I guess you're right."

Jake stood up. "I've got to go iron my dress for the ball...You okay?"

I just nodded.

Jake leaned over, kissed the top of my head, and was gone.

~~~

The Bomb Squad

After the two AM final briefing, I rode down to the Flats with Lt. Sands. SWAT was already down there clearing the perimeter, setting up the command post, and taking up their tactical positions.

"Sorry I bolted yesterday."

Lt. Sands looked over at me and smiled.

"I mean, you know, leaving you high and dry with the Captain. He didn't seem happy."

"Eh, he never is. It's my job to run interference sometimes."

"Thanks."

"Oh, don't thank me yet. I'm not a magician who can make it all just disappear. We are going to have to have that conversation eventually. But maybe we'll have some mitigating good news after today."

"Maybe, but…"

"Hope for the best, but expect the worst."

"Yeah. Something like that. Anyway, thank you."

We descended down into the Flats on the East Bank and followed the river upstream to Ox Bow Bend, turning on Columbus Road where the SWAT command center van was set up.

"What's the Bomb Squad doing here?" I asked Lt. Sands,

pointing to their step van up ahead. "I don't remember them in the briefings."

"Don't know. Probably SWAT pulled them in. Just in case." Lt. Sands parked. We got out, put on our vests, and hiked towards the command center. We passed a couple of SWAT guys all dressed up in their battle gear. "I sure am glad these guys are on our side."

It's funny how darkness can cover so much activity. They went about their business in a deadly silent way. Kind of creepy. I slowed down as we passed the Bomb Squad van. "I'll be along in a sec."

"Don't be too long." Lt. Sands tapped the face of his wristwatch.

I went around the back of the step van. The doors were open, and an eerie red glow oozed out from within. Inside, a couple of bomb techs were gathering equipment to suit up. "Hi, guys."

I startled them, then they saw my vest and badge. "Oh, geeze, ah, hi, uh…"

Kind of jumpy for bomb techs, I thought. "I'm Maddie."

"Hi, Maddie." They both grinned that stupid boy grin.

"Missed you guys at the briefings."

"Yeah, last minute call," said one of the techs as he lumbered down out of the van carrying his "fat" suit.

It was my turn to be startled at the sight behind him of three powered-down synthoids stored along the side of the van. "Huh."

"Be nice to know what the hell's going on."

"Yeah. Yeah, it would." I backed away from the van. "Hope you guys aren't needed."

"That's what everybody says."

"Don't take it personal, boys." I smiled coyly and hurried to catch up with Lt. Sands.

I drew all the eyes my way as I slipped into the SWAT van and pulled the door shut behind me.

"Detective," said the SWAT commander as he turned back to the bank of monitor screens along the wall above the console. "Make yourself comfortable. The show's about to start—sorry there's no popcorn."

Of course, there was no place to sit and make myself comfortable, so I sidled up next to Lt. Sands and surveyed the monitors. Along the top row was a grainy feed from a drone angled off and zoomed in to avoid detection. The video from the three snipers' nests was much clearer, one being eerie green night vision imaging.

On the second row were the glass feeds from Jake and EC, next to the SWAT entry team's body cams. Each one was labeled by name with magic marker on masking tape. On the third row were street-level views of the building. It was dark, but then again, the windows were probably blacked out. Thermal imaging showed a couple of warm bodies on the first floor and what could have been pizza ovens at full blast on the second floor. In all of the briefings and meetings down in Exit Alley, I was never able to ever really get what it was that Jake and Q and EC and everybody called the Darknet, where the Baron and his minions met and plotted and played out their sick homages to the sickest of individuals in history. But there it was on the monitor, dark…foreboding…real—and filled with nothing but the evil intents of evil, evil men. Hidden down here in a dark, forgotten corner of the city known as the

Flats, ignored by citizens crossing over high above on bridges during their daily commutes.

I gasped at the hand suddenly on my shoulder. I looked. Lt. Sands must have seen the fear and worry on my face and read my mind. "They're not going in alone this time."

I covered his hand and gently squeezed. He was right. I was glad Jake wasn't going it on his own.

It was going to be what SWAT called a "shock and awe" raid to gain control of the premises as quickly as possible in order to preserve the server farm inside from sabotage. As I scanned all the monitors, a creepy feeling came over me that something wasn't quite right. I didn't know what. Suddenly, the camera view from one of the sniper's nest zoomed in and drew my eye. The familiar conga line of heavily armed men shuffled rapidly through the shadows along the front of the building, barely visible against its dark facade. The infrared view on the other monitor made them look like a glow worm. It stopped midway. A moment later, the thermal image exploded, and every other screen strobed as the first flash-bang grenade went off.

"GO-GO-GO-GO-GO," crackled across the TAC channel. The body cams fed dizzying flurries of activity. All I could see on Jake's monitor was the back of the SWAT team guy he was following.

A hot flash broke over me. More flash-bang grenades went off. Suddenly, the command trailer walls closed in and I felt myself starting to hyperventilate. I had to escape the claustrophobic feeling gripping my chest tighter and tighter like a boa constrictor.

Focused on the unfolding raid, no one noticed when I stepped outside. The cool air slowly sponged the panic away. I caught my breath, but unsettled at being alone, I gravitated back over to the Bomb Squad van. The techs would still be there, waiting to be called in, if needed, after the building was secured.

I saw in the back of the van that two of the three synthoids had been unloaded. I walked around front, where the techs had staged their gear and waited, watching the front of the building intently and listening to the radio chatter through their earbuds. They both looked my way when I came up beside them. They smiled at me with a lingering gaze, then focused again on the building.

It was much more peaceful watching from outside. Rifle-mounted flashlights flickered occasionally in the building windows like fireflies on a dark summer night as rooms were cleared. Intermittently, a dull thump was heard as another flash-bang was set off.

I took a deep breath and peered up into the night sky. Getting outside, getting out of the face of the raid, had a calming effect. The dread I felt inside the command center dissipated like mist in the dawn.

When I looked back down, I reflexively began inventorying my surroundings, scanning the Bomb Squads gear. Ruck sacks and tool boxes sat in a small mound next to a small tracked rover with cameras, sensors, and mechanical arms sticking out the top. Next to the rover was one of the synthoids in idle mode.

"Where's your other synthoid?" I asked.

"They're back in the van," answered one of the techs, not taking his eyes off the building. "You only need one. The other two are backups in case the first one gets blowed up good."

I had to find Jake; one of the bomb squad droids was M.I.A.

Without thinking, I bolted towards the dark building, drawing my Glock as I ran.

~~~

Hunted Hunter

I burst through the main entrance into a lobby dimly lit with backup emergency lighting. It smelled like explosives and body odor—the extreme body odor typical of the homeless who counted the time between baths in months. A small group of SWAT guys rounded up vagrants from the first floor and lined them up against a side wall.

"Jake—where's Jake? Where are they?" I asked one of the SWAT guys.

He pointed up. I ran down the hall to the stairway at the end of the building and took them in twos to the second floor. The stairwell door opened out into a huge room filled with racks and racks of computer equipment. Cables snaked every which way across the floor. Smoke from the flash-bang grenades hung in the air, and flashlights cut through the misty half darkness.

Suddenly, the overhead florescent lights came on. The room spanned the entire second floor. I moved into the room, scanning frantically for Jake in rows of equipment racks and at the indiscriminately placed desks and cubicles. The walls were a combination of whiteboard scribblings and layers of printouts, pictures, clippings, maps, and pages from books and magazines taped up in some kind of haphazard montage, meaningful only to whoever put them up there. A half-dozen guys who looked like they could have been on Q's team sat around a conference table with their hands zip-tied behind their backs. I took a second look to see if I recognized the bomb squad's synthoid.

Jake was at the far end of the room chatting with EC as they surveyed SWAT securing the room. I sighed in relief, holstered my pistol, and walked his way. Halfway there, I saw him pull out his phone. Whatever he saw made him draw his pistol and bolt towards the stairwell in the corner, catching even EC by surprise.

"Jake! Wait!" But he was already gone.

"Maddie?" EC asked as I ran by.

"Come on."

I drew my Glock and entered the stairway quietly. I listened. Jake's footsteps were above me.

"What's going on?" EC said slipping through the door behind me.

"One of the bomb squad droids went rogue," I whispered and pointed up.

The door on the third floor creaked open and slammed shut. I hurried up the stairs along the outside rail, following the sight line of my pistol. EC followed with his shotgun at the ready, pressed against his shoulder.

In the moments it took us to climb the flight of stairs, crashing and clattering erupted from behind the door. We burst through to see Jake being manhandled by a synthoid dressed in green-gray coveralls with the yellow letters "BDU" on the the back. The droid swung Jake into a row of filing cabinets with a loud metal crash. It thrashed him about like a rag doll.

EC aimed, but didn't fire. The shotgun blast would have hit Jake, too.

I aimed carefully and shuffled slowly forward, waiting for some separation between them, trying to ignore Jake's bloodied, blank expression. He had obviously lost consciousness. I couldn't wait any longer and fired. It was risky—head shots always are—but Jake always said a synthoid's center mass is invulnerable to standard service weapons.

The impact of five shots pushed the droid's head around and maybe shattered an eye socket. Five more to its knees swept it off its feet and into a tangle with Jake on the floor. In human form, droids have human vulnerabilities.

EC ran forward to pull Jake's lifeless body away.

I came up behind the bomb squad synthoid and emptied my clip into its face at point-blank range, flinging synthetic skin and composite bone fragments off like shrapnel.

EC came back and blasted off its legs at the knees with his shotgun.

We backed off and watched the robot writhe on the floor, blinded and crippled, reaching out mindlessly for Jake to finish the job.

Hearing our shots, SWAT spilled out of the stairway door behind us, pushing us out of the way and surrounding the synthoid, though they didn't seem to know what to do with the mechanical perp.

"Call for medical," EC ordered. *"Now!"*

I silently prayed as I went over to Jake's body. On the way, I picked up his phone and looked at the screen.

Behind the cracked glass a video loop played of Amy—street urchin Amy—sitting on Jamal's lap. Behind them was the city, lit up through a window of the building. The fear on her face was obvious as Jamal stroked her hair with one hand and rested a pistol in the other on her shoulder, a grin of pure evil on his face.

"Come on, Jake. Come on up and get me," Jamal's voice looped over and over and over

~~~

Exit Alley

It was a cruel irony that machines now kept Jake alive.

I rode with him in the ambulance. Sat by him in the ER. Waited out the hours during the surgery. Then stood outside the ICU and watched waitress Amy weep at his bedside. I went home and finally slept for the first time in days.

Two days later, I went back to the House but not to my desk in Robbery/Homicide. I found myself at the ACU offices down the alley…*Exit Alley*. Jake's exit.

The bullpen where the detectives had their cubicles was a ghost town. Jake's desk was like a crime scene that no one had taped off. Not even the cleaning crew moved his chair to sweep the carpet underneath. I just stared at it frozen in time—both me and the desk. For how long, I don't know, until EC came up behind me.

"Maddie."

I just sighed.

"Day-by-day…day-by-day…" EC's voice trailed off. "Come on. The meeting's about to start."

The scheduling bots had simply put the debriefing on my calendar, no invite to accept or decline. Just show up. Otherwise, I would have still been in bed, or in front of the tube in my bathrobe eating ice cream, or down at the bakery by my condo yielding helplessly to temptation.

I thought we'd be in the briefing room, but EC led me to a

small conference room on the tech side of the building. All the usual suspects were there: Bob and Puff and Q. EC sat down at the end of the table in the back of the room. I took the chair between him and Q, facing Bob and Puff. A moment later, Lt. Sands came in, closed the door, and sat down at the head of the table. I said a thankful prayer with my inside voice that the Captain wasn't going to be in the meeting.

"EC, how's Jake doing?" Sands asked, opening up his leather portfolio and pulling out some papers.

"He's still on the ventilator. His vitals are good. The docs hope to start bringing him out of the coma in the next couple of days." EC paused to wrestle his emotions back under control. I read the pain etched on his face, no doubt from the memories of his vigil at Patty's bedside and the battle lost after his wife's accident eighteen months ago. "Then, they'll get him moved to a step-down unit. Won't really know much more until he's conscious again."

"Good. Please keep me posted daily if you wouldn't mind."

"Will do."

Sands looked around the room at each of us. He pulled out his phone and showed us the screen as he powered it down. "No transcript here. We'll have *that* meeting in a day or two. Right now, I want to sort out exactly what we know; what we think we know; and what the hell is going on, before any, ah, upper echelon types start sticking their noses into our business. Everybody off now, please."

We all powered down our phones and put them in the center of the table.

Sands looked at Bob and Puff. "So, what do we know

about the bomb squad synthoid that went off the rails and attacked Jake?"

"Well, boy, I'll tell you, it's really something about that one," Bob said, adjusting his glasses. "Most of the chassis was intact and in good working order—though ten slugs in the cranium did some damage. Those BDU guys take really good care of their equipment, you know—not like the Streets Department and that sweeper in the garage—'cause, after all, their life depends on it. Firmware and software library updates and upgrades were up to snuff and properly logged. None of the hardware had been tampered with, so it was a completely remote takeover—and that's a real problem."

"Why's that?" Sands looked up from a note he was making.

"The Three Laws. They're for civilian units. Embedded on the boards in the BLC module." Puff's gravelly voice caught everyone by surprise. He rarely spoke more than a word or two during meetings. "Gotta be a hands-on job to hijack one of them. Gotta physically change out chip sets. Not so with government-issued units."

"Why not?"

"Well, see, use of force protocols are allowed in law enforcement and military droids," answered Bob. "Got to have 'em so they can do their jobs. Which means, if these guys figured out how to remote access one of our units…Well, that ain't good for nobody."

"How would they do it?"

"We got nothing. Nope, nothing at all out of the teardown. Nothing out of the ordinary in the droid's libraries or memory banks. Whatever was downloaded is vaporware now, or evaporated back up into the cloud."

Sands nodded his head and made a note. "I'll let you guys get back to the lab. Thanks."

"Okie-dokie."

Puff squinted at Lt. Sands. "This is serious bad mojo. *Serious.*"

Bob and Puff got up and left, closing the door behind them.

Lt. Sands looked at Q beside me. "Now, what about the server farm?"

"We got most of it intact. The bad guys tried but only managed to power down a couple of the units in the database tier, but it doesn't look like we lost any hardware and minimal data. I've got a half-dozen techs going through the millions upon millions of lines of code—and it keeps generating more on its own. Kind of crazy."

"The servers are still running?" EC asked. "What-the-what?"

"Observation is the best way to figure this thing out. Can't tell much about the habits of nocturnal creatures from staring at roadkill."

"So, how did they do this remote penetration of the droid that Puff was talking about?" Sands asked.

"Don't know yet. We didn't find any portal, either direct into the Grid via a secondary data link or into a transmission array to push into the white space." Q looked from Lt. Sands to EC and back to Sands. "Not to worry, guys. We've ensured that the thing is air gapped, so it's basically quarantined."

"So, you don't have anything yet, either." Sands looked at me and raised an eyebrow.

Q started to say something but thought the better of it. He shrugged his shoulders. Finally, he sighed, "We're working it. I mean it. The techs are putting in overtime."

"Then get back to it and let me know when you've made some progress."

Q sat back, stunned at being summarily dismissed from the meeting. He grabbed his phone and left, closing the door hard, but nowhere near what a hormonal teenage girl would.

"So, what's up, Lieu?" I asked.

"A little compartmentalization." Lt. Sands closed his portfolio, stood up, and walked down to our end of the table.

"You mean like a sinking ship?" EC asked.

"Eh…you guys know the interview drill. Divide and conquer."

"You don't think…" I didn't want to finish my thought.

Lt. Sands sat down across from me, folded his arms on the table, and leaned forward. "Look, Maddie, I have to ask: Do you want in on this? Sanchez and Jake and the whole 'Baron' thing—it's not a Robbery/Homicide gig. You know that, right? You'd have to be officially assigned to Artificial Crimes."

"A permanent transfer?" I asked.

"Doesn't have to be. A fill-in for Jake with EC, until…Or, if you'd rather, we could get you back into the rotation at your old desk upstairs pretty quick with a new partner and let ACU pursue the case. Your call. No harm, no foul, either way."

I didn't answer. I knew what Lt. Sands wanted to hear. And I knew what I would end up doing. I just didn't know if it was the right thing or not. I watched myself trace imaginary shapes on the tabletop in front of me, avoiding EC's stare. Jake would know the right thing to do, but he wasn't around to help me. "However long this takes, to see it through. To get these guys. I'll do it."

Lt. Sands sat back and smiled. "Good. 'Cause you two are the only ones I trust right now."

"Thanks, Maddie," EC whispered.

"Now, who is this Jamal guy and why did he kidnap that girl?"

Oh, my God. Amy! The pit of my stomach leapt and fell from somewhere high—I don't know where, but it was a long way down. I buried my head in my arms on the table. "How could I? How? Does he still have her?"

"Hard to tell, since she was already missing from the foster family," Lt. Sand said. "I saw the Amber Alert and your notes. I've got extra patrols cruising the Flats, keeping an eye out. Nothing so far."

"Q looked at the video loop on Jake's phone and thinks it was green screened with composite of the third floor and a live feed of the raid through the window," EC said. "Obviously, to draw Jake up into the ambush."

"And it worked. So, is this Jamal guy the Baron? Who the hell is he? And is he really a friend of Jake's?"

"He's an independent reporter who writes under the byline E.J. Quick," EC said. "Specializes in tech crimes—mostly white-collar stuff—so, of course, he's been a long-time fixture at the ACU. Latched on to Jake when he was first sent down. Don't know as I'd call them friends. They had a more of a *quid pro quo* kind of relationship, I'd say. Q has Samantha digging into his background."

"And why did he take this Amy girl? Who is she to him?"

"Jake and I grabbed her up at Jeffery's murder scene after you left. As a witness," I said. "Homeless kid who camps in the Flats. She eventually led us to the server farm building. I guess she came back home after she ran away from the foster family. I tried to tell that damn social worker—"

"Do you think he still has her now?"

I thought for a moment. "I hope not, but my heart tells me he does. It's leverage for him—over Jake…and me. I don't think he'd give that up. I don't think he's done with us."

"That's what I'm afraid of." Lt. Sand closed his portfolio. "Did we collar anyone of value the other night?"

"Some low level techie babysitters. And a bunch of homeless guys they let squat on the first floor as human camouflage. In case anyone came snooping around the building," EC answered. "The smell alone is enough to drive anyone off."

"Damn." Lt. Sands stood up. "Effective immediately, Maddie, you're working ACU. Don't wait for the paperwork. Just get after this guy and bring him down. Please get ahead of this before there's any talk of a task force—or calling in the Feds. Please."

I nodded.

"You." Lt. Sands pointed at EC, then at me as he said, "You take care of her."

"Will do."

With that, Lt. Sands left.

"Thanks, Maddie," EC whispered, even though we were the only ones left in the room.

This wasn't the career or the life or the future I had ever wanted…or even imagined.

I just buried my face in my hands, wishing I was home in my bathrobe eating ice cream.

~~~

The Invisible Mind

Criminals aren't the only ones who return to the scene of a crime.

The patrol officer posted at the building in the Flats recognized me and let me in without asking to see my badge. I went to the third floor first, unconsciously walking the path I had taken the morning of the raid in a much bigger hurry. Jake's blood was still on the floor and the filing cabinets. It gave me a chill. I saw small fragments of synthoid scattered around the spot where EC and I had put the robot down. Most of the big pieces had been taken into evidence for Bob and Puff. The floor was pock-marked where EC's shotgun blasts had shattered and severed the knee joints. There was a clean bullet hole up where its head had been. I guess I missed with one of my shots.

You bastard. I never did like that Jamal.

"Detective?" Q had come up close behind me while I was lost in thought.

"Jesus, Mother Mary. Don't do that. *Please.*"

"Sorry." Q stood beside me. "Is that Jake's blood?"

I nodded.

"I hate that guy."

I sighed. "Yeah, me too."

After an awkward silence, Q asked, "If I tell you something, you won't get mad, will you?"

Oh, God. Now what?

"I didn't really give Sands the full download on those servers in here—I mean, I did about what I know for sure, but maybe not what I suspect."

"And…"

"This guy Jamal? He's good. Damn good. Spooky good."

"Meaning?"

"This isn't just a server farm like typical infrastructure stuff for data storage, info access, automation, backbone or even pumping nefarious code through the Atlas Grid to the droids like we thought. Remember how I said it keeps generating code on its own?"

I nodded. There was something in Q's eyes as he spoke. Glassy and darting, they betrayed an admiring nervousness.

"You know, on the outer fringes of AI metaphysics—and mostly in the Darknet—there's talk of what it would take to control things, really control everything, like a system that not only moves information but creates it—No, more like creates a collective unconsciousness. An id, a digital id that moves people and events and societies in ways that no one knows is happening. You just wake up one day and the world is different, you are different—sometimes a little and sometimes a lot—because, well, you don't know why, just because. Because there's some, like, *invisible mind* at work. The possibilities, well, they're limitless."

"And that's what's downstairs? An invisible mind?"

"A serious attempt at it."

"And the murders?"

"Just a scratch on the surface."

~~~

The Baron

He savored the delectable irony of it all as he watched through the observation window in the Intensive Care Unit: Jake, the synthoid hunter, was being kept alive by machines.

Jamal, dressed in green surgical scrubs, pulled his phone out and tapped on the screen. Waitress Amy's head jerked around to the bed next to Jake's as the alarms on that patient's medical monitoring equipment began to flash and bleat.

"Code Blue to ICU bed nine," an emotionless automated voice announced over the public address system. Soon after the bed was swarmed by nurses and doctors.

Jamal did not wait to watch the patient die…

~~~

The Invisible Mind

Murder by Munchausen #3

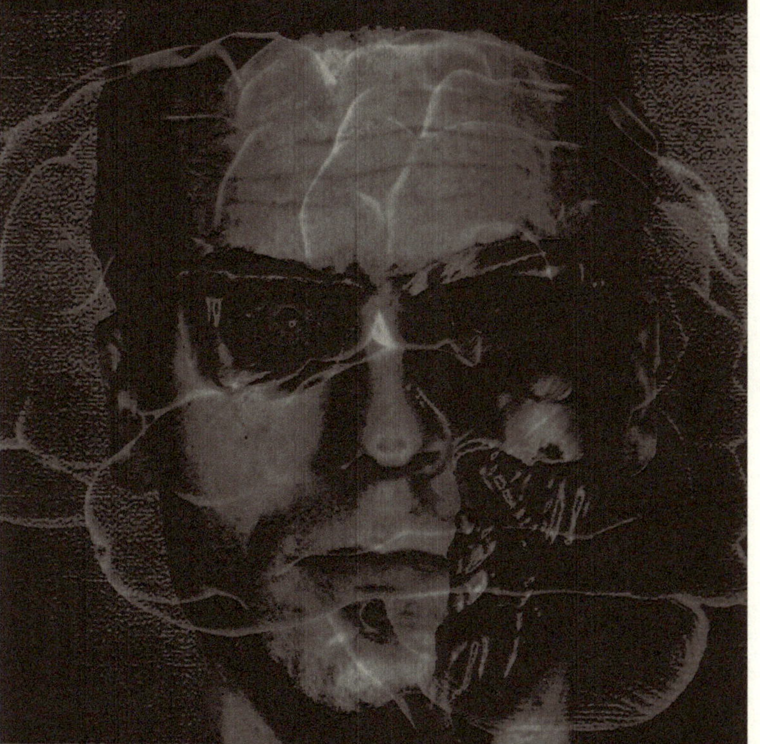

A NOVEL BY M.T. BASS

*For Dave and all my fellow scribblers at
the Cleveland Writers Group.*

Thank you.

"...he intends only his own gain, and he is in this, as in many other cases, led by an invisible hand to promote an end which was no part of his intention."

~Adam Smith, 1776

"When wireless is perfectly applied the whole earth will be converted into a huge brain, which in fact it is, all things being particles of a real and rhythmic whole."

~Nikola Tesla, 1926

"...so, too, the psyche possesses a common substratum transcending all differences in culture and consciousness. I have called this substratum the collective unconscious."

~Carl Jung, 1931

The Baron

He savored the cruel irony of it all as he watched through the observation window in the Intensive Care Unit: Jake, the synthoid hunter, was being kept alive by machines.

Jamal, dressed in green surgical scrubs, pulled his phone out and tapped on the screen. Waitress Amy's head jerked around to the bed next to Jake's as the alarms on that patient's medical monitoring equipment began to flash and bleat.

"Code Blue to ICU bed nine," an emotionless automated voice announced over the public-address system. Soon after nurses and doctors swarmed the bed.

Jamal did not wait to watch the patient die.

In his glass-walled office in Exit Alley, one of the three cell phones neatly lined up on the credenza behind his desk dinged out Morse Code for the letter 'V', causing him to look away from the lines of computer programming language filling his laptop screen. He pulled a fourth burner phone from his shirt pocket and called the IT department at MetroHealth Medical Center, then called EC with his police issued *iPhone*.

"Just now. In bed nine, next to Jake." Q listened, then hung up.

Maddie looked around Cutty's Deli as EC, sitting across from her at a back booth, took a call. It was one of the few places where she felt safe anymore. To her, it was like home—her childhood home—warm with fond memories: of lunching with her dad once a week ever since she was twelve years old; of "Uncle" Cutty's career counseling that tipped the scales in her decision to go to the police academy instead of law school—an act of defiance to her father's urgings, but one that warmed his heart nonetheless; of endless debates on so many arcane subjects with Jake over coffee when they were partners in Robbery/Homicide. She knew it was a false sense of security; nevertheless, Maddie felt safe at Cutty's.

"That was Q," EC said, setting his phone down on the table. "He's been monitoring the data traffic in ICU. There was an inbound spike, and the patient next to Jake died."

"The Baron? Is he there?"

"Even if he was, I doubt he stuck around." EC sighed. "We should probably check it out, though."

"In a minute. Okay?" Maddie fingered the rim of her nearly empty coffee mug. "Let me, ah, finish my coffee."

"No hurry." EC wanted to say more but couldn't find the words.

Shackled to the metal bed frame, a child sat stoically staring at the door, almost as hungry for freedom as she was for food. Amy hoped someone missed her, but doubted it—after all, she was homeless and had no real family. Even if anyone did miss her, who of them would come to her rescue? Her social worker? That thought brought a wry smile to her young face. Maybe the female detective…

Though medically shackled to his hospital bed by a chemically induced coma, Jake's mind floated freely through his own subconscious, like a Freudian derelict riding the waves of swelling and ebbing dreams and memories. He was aware of waitress Amy's presence there beside him and commotion at the next bed over and even, vaguely, briefly of some malevolent presence nearby, but Jake seemed to stir or blink only when Maddie came to visit.

.

~~~

Richard Speck

It sat on a bench outside the dormitory of nursing students, waiting with its kind's infinite patience. Originally acquired and programmed for landscaping at the Cleveland Clinic, the synthoid was one of a brigade of units which had been hacked and Munchausened, then returned to their menial daily services to mankind to await the Baron's call.

There was no adrenalin surge behind the extremely life-like facade of humanity when that call came. Data packets, sent scatter-shot through the Atlas Grid, coalesced at the location outside the Cole Eye Institute where the synthoid methodically trimmed and shaped the immaculate shrubbery around the building. To avoid Q's metadata sniffing algorithms from detecting a download spike in the grid, the information came in digital sprinkles over the course of its human handler's work shift, slowly building a malevolent intent to be executed that night. In the middle of the afternoon, the synthoid left the unfinished topiary to melt into the hospital shift change and disappeared.

Personality modules were a Gen-3 feature upgrade, which is why the earlier models were initially preferred. Swapping out a few IC chips and uploading hacked firmware was a relatively easy way to turn a quick buck with an automated contract killing. But evil innovates, too, and the same features that made synthoids even more human-like in their behavior also helped create robotic assassins which could better camouflage their malicious intents and evade the reach of the Artificial Crimes Unit by melting into and moving undetected through the humanity that surrounded them. For the Baron, it allowed for a greater measure of artistic expression in programming the synthoid's behavior to not only recreate infamous crimes of the past but to mimic the behavior of their perpetrators, which intensified the thrill of watching the video feed through the eyes of Jack the Ripper, Ted Bundy or, this particular evening, Richard Speck. Jake wasn't the only history buff, and it amused Jamal that London police had photographed the eyes of Jack the Ripper's victims, hoping to capture the last thing they ever saw: their killer's face. *If only Scotland Yard could have imagined the future.*

The Gen-3 personality modules also supported the ANSI Adaptive Artificial Intelligence Protocol #9 to enhance the artificial human experience of real men and women who interacted with synthoids. The constant writing and rewriting of code in the personality/experience loop formed unique individual synthoid consciousnesses, which manufacturers uploaded to their servers for product improvement teams to study. In Munchausened units, that feed was hijacked and routed to another portal in the Darknet to build a collective id of evil.

At eleven PM, it rose from the bench and entered the dormitory. The bodies of nine women would be found the next day, having been strangled and stabbed to death. Unlike 1966, no eyewitness was left alive, though the phrase "Born to Raise Hell" was written on the wall in blood.

~~~

Slaughterhouse Five

While EC interviewed the ICU staff about the death in bed nine, Maddie sat beside Jake and read to him. EC was visibly uncomfortable whenever they came to visit. His wife never came out of her coma after the car accident just a year ago. Maddie understood how the replay with his ACU—Artificial Crimes Unit—partner bore down hard on him. She knew what he was afraid of. She feared it, too. But during her visits, the muted expressions that passed across Jake's face like a light breeze etched upon the surface of a calm pond gave her hope, and she clung desperately to it.

When they were partners and, later, lovers, Jake would teasingly give Maddie reading assignments, then quiz her relentlessly on them. Kurt Vonnegut was one of his favorite authors, so she held his hand and read him the story of Billy Pilgrim becoming unstuck in time. She knew in her heart that Jake was awake inside his lifeless body and, no doubt, bored to tears by the soap operas and game shows on the TV screens in the ward during the day for the conscious patients.

Maddie stopped in mid-sentence when she felt Jake's hand tighten around her finger. His eyes danced behind their closed lids. Maddie fearfully searched up and down the row of beds for a nurse, then felt a gentle squeeze on her finger and another. Slowly she became aware of the local news anchor interrupting

The Days of Our Lives on the screen up and across from Jake's bed. Nine women had been found murdered in a dormitory near University Circle. Behind the reporter at the scene, the entry to the building had been cordoned off with yellow tape and was guarded by uniformed patrolmen. Jake squeezed her hand again.

Maddie rose, kissed Jake on the forehead, then went to find EC.

"You know what Jake would want, right?" EC asked as they sat in their unmarked *Crown Vic,* watching the media jockey for camera angles and story angles among the spectators outside the yellow crime scene tape. "Eyes on the scene."

Maddie nodded. She hung her badge around her neck. "Let me go in. That way, we can keep ACU under the radar. As far as anybody knows, I'm still in Robbery/Homicide. I'll tell them Cutty asked me to check it out—worried about one of his nieces. He'll back our play."

"It won't be long before the Captain's down here."

"We've got time. He won't want to face the cameras without a full report. Besides, we've got three hours before the six o'clock news comes on." Maddie opened her car door. "Don't worry. I'm in. I'm out. Nobody gets hurt."

Once inside the crime scene tape, Maddie noticed a gray-uniformed man cut from the herd and pacing frantically. She looked back at EC and motioned him to follow her. When he caught up with Maddie, she pointed out the upset policeman, then went into the dormitory.

"Hey, son." EC held up his badge as he slowly approached the young man in his twenties. He noted the "Campus Police" patch on his sleeve.

The man spun around to face EC. His eyes darted erratically about like a caged sparrow. He wiped his mouth with his sleeve, fighting back a little spasm of dry heaves. "I-I already told the other guy everything."

"No, no. That's okay, Paul," EC said calmly, reading the name tag pinned above his shirt pocket. "It's okay."

"It was a slaughterhouse inside there. Blood everywhere. The bodies—those girls…"

"That's okay." EC slowly closed the gap between them. He put his hand on Paul's shoulder and slowly turned him away from the crime scene. He gently guided him towards the cordoned off parking lot around the side of the building, where the vans from the forensics unit and the coroner's office were parked along with several patrol cars. He spoke softly, which made Paul listen closely to hear. "We see bad things sometimes in our line of work."

Paul wiped his mouth again and nodded.

EC shook off the image of Jake's bloodied and broken body on the floor of the warehouse in the Flats. "And it's never like on a movie screen or gaming headset. It's just not."

"But those poor girls. I-I…"

"I know." EC led Paul around the back of a patrol car. They leaned against the trunk side-by-side with the dormitory behind them and looked away, towards the downtown skyline. "Did you know any of them?"

Paul shrugged. "Not really. But you see them regular like. They're familiar, you know?"

EC nodded. "How long have you been on the campus force?"

"Eighteen months. I'm finishing up my Master's in

Criminology. Hoping I can get into Quantico. But now…I don't know."

"The first one is always the hardest. You'll be fine."

"Really?"

"It doesn't get easier, but you learn to carry the weight."

"It just seems so senseless."

"How's that?"

"Why them? It was like they were picked at random."

"No recent incidents of assaults on campus?"

Paul shook his head. "He didn't even try to hide it."

"He?"

"I only saw one set of footprints between the two suites and hand prints on the hallway wall. Whoever it was didn't even try to wipe the blood off of himself."

"When did you find them?"

"It was about six-thirty or so. I was the closest one. Wish I hadn't been."

EC nodded.

They silently studied the skyline.

On the fifth floor, Maddie found the lead detective inside one of the dormitory suites, hovering over the medical examiner tech checking the liver temperature of one of the victims. She grabbed a pair of blue, disposable booties from a Bunny Suit Boy, donned them, and went into the dorm room.

"I'm going to have to get more probes," the tech from the Medical Examiner's office said. "Too many bodies."

"Do it then, *damn it.*"

Maddie did not recognize the detective. She knew all the grizzled veterans, the ones who were around when her father was still on the force. This guy was young—Maddie's age—and new to plain clothes as his suit was too fresh off the rack to have weathered many crime scenes.

He turned and ran his dark, cold, reptile-like eyes over Maddie. The tension on his face relaxed. He reflexively groomed himself by running his hand through his black, combed-back hair and checking his tie.

"I'm Maddie." She fingered the gold shield hanging at her chest. She smiled coyly.

"Derek." Her badge held his gaze, then he looked up and smiled back.

"I'm from Downtown Services—"

His smile evaporated. "Oh, great. Corporate is big-footing me already?"

"No. No. I'm here for a friend. Cutty asked me to check out the vics."

"Deli-man Cutty?"

"Yeah. He's got a niece in nursing school."

Derek relaxed again and his smile returned. He stepped up close to Maddie and scrutinized her face. "I know you, right? I never forget a redhead. The academy? No, TV. You were lead on that serial killer case, right?"

Maddie fought back a familiar wince, a reflex response whenever anyone mentioned her biggest case and, though it was not yet public knowledge, her biggest professional failure—the one that landed her in ACU. She nodded her head.

"I thought that was solved."

"Like I said. I'm just here as a favor for Cutty. What have you got?"

Derek took a step back. "What you see is what you get. A

slaughter factory. Nine all together. Four from this suite and five more from across the hall." He walked Maddie through the crime scene, carefully circumnavigating bodies and bloodstains. "We've got four out here in the living room area."

Maddie carefully eyed the victims. Three sprawled on the floor, one half-naked. The fourth sat upright on the sofa facing the dark TV screen with duct tape across her mouth and around her wrists and ankles. A huge red bib covered her chest and abdomen from a slash in the throat. "Born to Raise Hell" was written in blood on the wall over her head.

"There's two in this bedroom. One's still tucked into bed. She's probably the first." Derek looked through the doorway on the right, then stepped back for Maddie to lean in and view the student bedroom furnished with matching twin beds, dressers, and desks. A pair of MacBooks gave the room an eerie glow. "And there's three more over in this bedroom."

They walked across the living room to the other bedroom in the suite.

Maddie looked in. The room was still being photographed. "I only see two."

"One is stuffed under the bed. Weird."

They stepped back into the living room. Maddie's eyes were drawn back to the student with the slit throat watching TV. "Have you got IDs?"

"Got this list from the university." Derek offered up a piece of paper. "Of course, we'll have to verify it."

Maddie took the list, scanned it, then gave it back. "I don't see Cutty's niece."

"Good."

"Born to raise hell," Maddie read the bloody graffiti again.

Although red streams ran down the wall like excess wet paint, the handwriting caught her eye. It was too neat, too…mechanical. "What do you suppose that means?"

"Kind of obvious, don't you think?"

"Yeah, well…" Maddie took a breath. "Were any sexually assaulted?"

"Looks like it. Panties torn off three of them."

"DNA?"

"Nothing blatant. But there's tons of blood. And he might have been a…you know, non-performer. We'll have to wait for the autopsy reports."

"Just one guy?"

Derek looked around. "There's just one set of size twelve bloody footprints leading out of the apartment and down the hall."

"Just one for nine girls."

"He must have been one bad ass dude."

"No witnesses, I presume."

Derek shook his head.

"Surveillance footage coming in or out?"

"Should have been, but no such luck."

Maddie nodded as she surveyed the scene again, trying to burn every detail into her mind for Jake. "Thanks. Good luck."

"Anytime." Derek's eyes lingered on Maddie as she walked out of the apartment.

The Baron surveyed the same scene in his virtual reality headset, then skipped back to watch the nine murders again from the beginning, streamed through synthoid eyes and ears.

"Can I have more, *please?* I'm still hungry."

Jamal did not hear Amy's plea from the bedroom as the sobbing, pleading, and dying of young women filled his headset.

Outside the Cole Eye Institute, the Munchausened AnSub—Android Subject—trimmed shrubbery. Its Dermaloy skin, impervious to bleach, was blood free. Its internal silicon was also scrubbed free of malignant code and dynamic link libraries. And, of course, the last twenty-four hours of the on-board data and location recorders had been replaced with its normal daily routine.

~~~

Exit Alley

EC waved his badge over the blinking pad to unlock the door to the Artificial Crimes Unit offices, which were down an alley and apart from the downtown district police station in a separate building. Cops in the House called it "Exit Alley" due to its reputation of being a dumping grounds for incompetents and mavericks, a last stop on the way out the door to retirement or a new career outside law enforcement. EC had requested a transfer from Robbery/Homicide after his wife's death. He mistakenly thought that chasing robots would be less stressful for a change. Jake fell into the maverick category.

Maddie hesitated as EC held the door open for her. Like EC, she had "volunteered" but, really, had no choice. Accepting the temporary assignment was the only way to clean up the mess her career had become after it turned out the perp in her series of prostitute killings in the Flats was really Jamal, recreating Jack the Ripper's crimes with Munchausened droids—and not the homeless man she had arrested and convicted to much media acclaim. And, of course, she had to do it for Jake.

"Come on, Maddie. You'll get used to it."

She shook her head. "I'm going back to Robbery/Homicide after we get him." She waved her badge over the pad and the embedded near-field communications chip logged her in. She went inside.

EC nodded, then followed her into Exit Alley.

Four rows of partitioned desks lined opposite walls of the bullpen for the detectives. The room was quiet and lifeless, like any regular office after 5 PM. Maddie's eyes gravitated to Jake's desk, which he hated with a passion—he called it a "cubicle-let," because it looked like a partitioned office cubicle that got shrunk in the wash. It was still exactly as he had left it his last day on duty, a rubbish heap of papers, food wrappers, and to-go coffee cups, a stark contrast to EC's orderly desktop beside it.

Maddie went to the far end of the bull pen where she had commandeered a small conference table for her temporary workspace. She called the Middleburg Heights PD and asked for Missing Persons to check on Amy, the missing homeless child. While waiting, she watched Samantha from the Tech Group on the other side of the building interrupt EC's concentration as he stared at his computer screen. Maddie noted that since Samantha and EC had begun dating, her appearance had become markedly less androgynous with a new, more stylish haircut, some subtle makeup and a bit more feminine cut to her wardrobe. Their involvement was one of the worst kept secrets in the building, but a subject that was never broached on duty due to department policy.

"No. Nothing yet," the Middleburg Heights detective said when he came on the line. "You know how it is. Without parents calling and constantly posting emotional pleas for their kid's return, it doesn't get much media play and fades into the pile of runaway reports. I'm sorry."

"I know. I know."

"The case is still open. I'll call if something comes up."

"Thanks." Maddie hung up and briefly considered calling the child's social worker but decided it would be a pointless exercise.

"Q's looking for us," EC said as he walked up to Maddie's table.

She nodded, and they followed Samantha to the other side of the building where the cubicle farm for the analysts and programmers was located. Q waved them into his glass-fronted corner office. He pointed at Samantha and motioned for her to join them.

Q's office furnishings were very modern, almost abstract, mainly black metal framing and glass-topped furniture. Maddie and EC sat down in webbed chairs. Everything was polished clean to the point of sterility. Severe white walls held a few colorful art prints, a Mondrian and Warhol's "Marilyn Monroe." The only personal picture sat on the credenza behind his desk, one of Q padded up and helmeted on a BMX bike. A skateboard leaned against the corner. It was an on-going source of speculation how someone not yet thirty had come to head the ACU tech group. The theory that nepotism was involved was partially true, though no family ties were ever identified or revealed by Q. It was also true his job was part community service arranged to atone for a youthful streak of hacking corporate IT departments, which made him imminently qualified to chase criminal hackers.

"This guy, the Baron—what's his name—Quick? Jamal?" Q asked, looking at Samantha. He tapped nervously on his glass desktop with the pad of his index finger.

"E.J. Quick is an online persona for his blog and tech reporting." Samantha hesitated and looked at Maddie. "Jake called him Jamal, but there's nothing that comes up in data searches that makes any connections."

"Whoever he is—if he's really the Baron—this guy is damn good." The rhythm of Q's tapping increased. "We're still deconstructing the code we seized at the warehouse. It's intense."

"The invisible—" Maddie started to say.

Q's hand froze in mid-tap, and he quickly cut her off. "I'm not ready to, ah, publicly advance that theory."

Maddie frowned at Q.

He slowly shook his head and scanned around the room with his eyes while tugging his ear.

EC looked from Maddie to Q, then back to Maddie. Jake was the only one who ever seemed to connect with Q in a way that went beyond the departmental roles spelled out in official job descriptions. EC took note that Maddie seemed to have filled that void but didn't press. He'd find out soon enough, just like with Jake. EC preferred not expending his patience on stroking—or teasing—*prima donnas.*

"What about physical evidence from the warehouse?" Q turned and asked EC.

"There were a dozen synthoids in the place in various stages of teardown and rebuild."

"A serious chop-shop?"

"Definitely a production line operation. Bob and Puff are working through the ones we took into evidence. Not much there." EC shook his head. "No telling how many they had run through there and released back into the wild, but it almost looks like they were trying to create their own little army or something."

"And we haven't gotten anything from the warm bodies we rounded up." Maddie sighed. "The homeless camped out on the first floor were truly clueless, and the hackers upstairs have all lawyered up with some high-priced downtown suits."

"Who's paying for that?" Q asked.

"Good question. They all made bail, too."

"County auditor's records show the building was owned free and clear by an LLC called White Chapel, which, of course, was also Jack the Ripper's London stomping grounds," EC said. "Without a mortgage, though, we're going to have to pull tax and utility records to dig up some banking records. McGinty's office is working on the subpoenas."

"What about corporate records?"

"The incorporation papers list a rogue's gallery of serial killers for the company officers: Henry Lee Lucas, Albert DeSalvo, Ed Gein, John Gacy."

"Where's the corporate offices?" Q asked.

"The East Ninth Street address on file is about three blocks into Lake Erie," Maddie answered.

"So, what now?"

EC looked around the room and pulled his *iNode* off his belt and put in on Q's desk.

Q nodded and put his *AlphaBit* on the desk. He looked at Samantha and shook his head.

Maddie anted up her *iNode* and the three of them went down the hall and out an emergency exit into the alley. Q went through the motions of disabling the security camera with a burner phone.

"You heard about the murders in University Circle?" Maddie asked.

Q nodded. "The Baron?"

"We think so. We're just trying to figure out the copycat

connection. The only thing we've got is that 'Born to Raise Hell' was written on the wall in blood."

"And all I've come up with on that so far are links to a heavy metal song and a two-star Steven Seagal movie from decades ago," EC said. "Take a look at the case file and run the MO through your magic algorithm for a match up."

"Can do." Q scratched the back of his head. "Under the radar, right?"

"We're not out here in the alley for the ambiance." EC looked at Maddie. "A real wizard of smart, eh?"

Q scowled and went back into the ACU offices.

"What do you think?" EC asked Maddie as they followed Q into the building. "Want to get some carry-out from King Wah's?"

"You know, it's been a long day," Maddie said wearily. "And I think I need to put some distance between me and that bloody dorm room scene."

"Sure. Understood."

"I'll take a stack of documents home and go through them later."

Maddie and EC retrieved their *iNodes* from Q's empty office. Then Maddie went home, and EC went in search of Samantha.

*****~~~*****

So It Goes...

Maddie woke at four-thirty the next morning. The file folders, pictures, and documents seized in the warehouse raid were still stacked neatly on the breakfast bar of her condo where she put them the night before. An empty wine glass was parked next to the kitchen sink. She avoided eye contact with the pile of evidence as she passed by on the way to the refrigerator to pour a glass of orange juice, gulping it down as she walked back to her bedroom to get dressed in running shorts, Nikes, and a gray F.B.I. Quantico hoody. On the way out the door, she grabbed her Glock 26 off-duty pistol and put it into the fanny pack around her waist with her keys.

Crocker Park was still a suburban petri dish of shops, apartments, restaurants, cluster homes, and businesses, all artfully arranged by architects to mimic that damn Bedford Falls in the movie Jake used to make her watch every Christmas, *It's a Wonderful Life*—in black-and-white no less. But, it was easy. You could buy your way into a cozy small-town, Mayberry-like existence with mere mortgage approval from the bank. She eventually learned to ignore Jake's teasing.

The streets were still dark and deserted when Maddie started her run. She liked that she could serpentine through the streets without having to jink and zig-zag around pedestrians and traffic. The slap of her running shoes echoed softly down the canyons of glass storefronts until she got to the greenbelt where commerce stopped and the Metroparks started. She steeled herself to continue on the trail through the woods. It still took some effort to venture forth alone, even in familiar places, after being ambushed and assaulted by the synthoid down in the Flats. By the time she got back, Sysco food and Orlando bakery trucks were making their early morning deliveries to the restaurants; the smell of fresh brewed coffee wafted from Starbucks, bagel shops, and bakeries; and the early-rising corporate ladder-climbers marched zombie-like towards their offices.

Maddie skipped her usual post-run dark roast and scone to shower, dress, and get on the road so she could stop by the old Glick Building Jake owned on Detroit Avenue which used to be his parents' flower shop. He lived in the second-floor apartment and turned the storefront downstairs into a huge mancave in the front and a workshop garage in the back. She knew Jake would have never given waitress Amy a key to his place, so Maddie had been checking his mail and tending to Frank the Feral Cat—if he was around. Sometimes it was not clear whether Jake adopted Frank or vice versa.

Maddie lingered upstairs, wandering from room to room, remembering better times. She grabbed Jake's hardback copy of *Huckleberry Finn* off the bookshelf in his living room, then drove to MetroHealth Medical Center, passing by John's Diner down the street to make sure that waitress Amy's car was in the lot.

A swell of hot panic crested in Maddie's neck when she got to the ICU and found Jake's bed empty.

"He came around late yesterday," Kindra, one of the R.N.s who had taken care of Jake, smiled and said as Maddie approached the nurse's station. "Isn't it great? They transferred him upstairs just a bit ago. He's in room seven-thirty-four."

Upstairs, Maddie hung back in the hallway and watched Jake leisurely savor cubes of red Jell-O. She smiled. He still had his typical, tousled morning hair after waking up from the coma. Though his face was scruffy, thin, and a bit haggard from the lack of real food, his blue eyes were clear and sharp, intently staring a hole into the wall across from his bed as he ate.

Maddie took a deep breath, exhaled slowly, then entered the room. "I thought you hated that stuff."

"I hate hospitals, too, but here I am." Jake slurped another Jell-O cube and smiled. He winked at Maddie. "So it goes…"

He *knew*. Maddie felt tears roll down her cheeks. "You heard me?"

"Vonnegut is always a good choice."

She quickly wiped her cheek. Stepping next to the bed, she took Jake's hand and squeezed tightly. She smiled broadly. "Uh, yeah, but…you know, Jell-O?"

"Oh, it hurts going down from the tubes. But at the same time feels good. Kind of like life."

"We'll have to get a real, home-cooked meal in you." She kissed the back of his hand. Their personal relationship began after she consoled Jake with food when their professional relationship ended with his suspension—until their personal relationship ended when Jake used Maddie for Munchausen bait in the Flats that got her attacked by the synthoid.

"Just promise me, no Jell-O."

"No Jell-O. I promise." She smiled and shook her head. "EC will be glad to hear you're vertical again."

"How's he doing?"

"Good. We're, ah, kind of working together."

"Don't tell me you got booted to ACU."

"I volunteered…sort of. Kind of had to do it to clean up the mess with the Steinmauer case."

"Not permanent, though. Right?" Jake asked.

"Sands assured me I could go back to Robbery/Homicide."

"I don't know. You might get hooked on it."

"Doubtful. Very doubtful."

Jake looked away and stared off into space. He had no choice when he got sent to Exit Alley. It was either take the transfer or lose his job. You can't shoot and kill a Councilman's son without consequences. He sighed and asked, "What's going on with the murder of those nurses? Not much on the news."

"A District Three guy named Derek caught the case. I think he's new in plain clothes."

"Not ACU?"

"The Baron's not really public knowledge…so far. Sands wants to keep it that way until we make up some ground on him."

"And Jamal?"

"In the wind."

"He did it," Jake said. "He did those nurses. You know that."

Maddie nodded her head. "But we can't figure out the angle. EC and I went down there and checked out the scene. Bad, bloody bad. 'Born to Raise Hell' was written on the wall in it. But, the handwriting—too, ah, font-like, if you know what I mean."

"Born to raise hell? That was Richard Speck. He stabbed and strangled eight nursing students back in the Sixties."

"Yeah? But we've got nine vics."

Jake thought for a moment. "Was one of the bodies stuffed under a bed?"

Maddie nodded.

"Yeah…right."

"What?"

"It is Speck. That *son-of-a-bitch.*"

"What? Jamal?"

"Uh-huh. The Chicago cops caught Speck because a ninth student hid under a bed. She watched him kill the others and saw a tattoo on his arm."

"What was it?"

Jake gave Maddie an impatient look.

"Born to raise hell."

Jake nodded. "That's how they found him. From the eyewitness who survived. So, the Baron wasn't just doing another copycat. He's fixing history."

Maddie shook her head.

"I've got to get out of here."

"No. You can't."

"I know Jamal. I can stop him." Jake started to get up.

Maddie pushed him back down into bed. "But not if you check out AMA, before you've regained your strength. You'll just crash again."

"But I can help."

"I know. I know."

Jake pushed back against Maddie, but she held him down, too easily.

"I've got half a stack of evidence from the warehouse raid in my car. I'll sign it over to you and get the other half from EC."

Jake eased back into the bed.

"I'm not even sure what I should be looking for, so go through it while you recoup. Rest and get your body right. When the docs green-light you, come help us."

Jake nodded.

"And I'll make that home-cooked meal I promised. Chicken Parm sound good?"

Jake smiled. "Deal."

Jamal stood by the "Please Seat Yourself" sign next to the cash register at John's Diner and watched the choreography of the waitresses serving the tail end of the breakfast rush. When she went back into the kitchen, he took an empty booth in waitress Amy's section and perused a menu.

"Hey…you're Jake's reporter buddy, right?" Amy asked, sliding onto the bench across from Jamal.

He lowered the menu and smiled. "And you are Amy, correct? Jake's a lucky guy. A very lucky guy."

Amy lowered her eyes and smiled, tucking an errant strand of blonde hair back behind her ear.

Jamal stared hungrily.

"Have you decided, yet?"

"Mmmm…not exactly."

"Coffee, then?"

"Sure."

⁕⁕~~~⁕⁕⁕

The Black Tier

Nothing Q ever saw in cyberspace scared him, until now. Behind the depravity found in the Darknet, it was still intensely logical, because, after all, that's what programming is: logic. And that made it understandable intellectually, emotionally disengageable and, therefore, at least somewhat manageable ethically. At least that was what he always told himself.

In the dead of night, Q sat on the second floor of the warehouse in the Flats admiring and fearing the racks of servers humming, blinking, and internally generating malignant code on its own. While he was safe from outside intruders by the patrol unit parked out front guarding the building downstairs, Q was vulnerable to the illogic of the Baron's evil inhabiting the millions of silicon circuits surrounding him.

He had not been completely forthcoming with Maddie, EC, and Lt. Sands in telling them the server farm was "air-gapped"—completely cut off from the outside world with no physical or wireless connections to any other network. He could have done it that way, but to stop the Baron's experiment would mean sacrificing crucial evidence…and leaving his own curiosity unsatisfied—a curiosity that often led him into trouble. Now, though, he had a bigger problem. His tracking algorithms had not caught the metadata push through the Atlas Grid into the AnSub like before; but, here, Q had observed the inbound "eyes and ears" feed from the Speck copycat murders at the University Circle dormitory in real time. The video was disturbing enough, but the flurry of encrypted I/O activity in a "black" tier of the data center he had not yet been able to penetrate haunted him.

Jake was right: true horror is not in eye of the beholder but in his imagination. And while Jake was a techno-fossil, his instincts were like something out of Harry Potter. The detective could also read people like they were billboards, which made him a somewhat dangerous ally for Q—but an ally he wished at that moment was there to help him.

Q got up and turned off the overhead florescent lights. The room took on an eerie neon glow of blue and green from the cabinet lights, annunciator panels, and monitor screens. He wandered up and down the rows of eight-foot tall racks filled with server blades, RAID storage drive modules, and patch bays sprouting Cat5e cables like ivy vines entwining themselves on the sacred halls of learning at the colleges he had been expelled from. He could feel his skin moisten with sweat from the heat thrown off by the electronics. A musty hint of ozone floated in the air.

Q stopped at a shelf sticking out with a keyboard and monitor in a row deep inside the Baron's server farm. He split the screen into two windows, one to monitor the traffic activity into and out of the impenetrable Black Tier. In the other window, he called up the synthoid's video stream of the brutal slayings of the nine student nurses. As it played, the graphs and data streams spiked and ebbed with each killing and stalking. He played the video again, this time monitoring his own reactions as he forced himself not to look away—revulsion at the slashing, choking brutality; ratcheting dread of anticipation; bottomless sorrow at the broken and lifeless evidence of inhumanity as the synthoid panned at the end to survey his handiwork—Richard Speck's programmed handiwork.

Q closed his eyes. He bent over the keyboard and drew deep breaths until he felt his heart rate slow again, then turned his eyes back to the monitor screen.

As the video played again, he watched the window with the graphs and data streams, realizing that deep within the Black Tier, the machine was reacting emotionally…just as he had.

~~~

Broken Dreams

Maddie slept fitfully. When she woke, vague reverberations of dread haunted her. Not knowing if it was her dreams or a premonition, she called down to MetroHealth Medical Center and checked with the nurses on the seventh floor. Jake was resting comfortably.

Figures. She flopped back down on her pillow and stared at the ceiling. She hated the waiting: waiting for Q to crack the computer code enigma; waiting on Jake to review the evidence collected from warehouse; waiting for the investigation of the student nurses' murders to hit a dead end; waiting for a hit on the BOLO for Jamal; waiting for one of the Baron's minions to rise and attack; waiting for Jake to get out of the hospital.

She got up and ran, and the act of running pounded away the haunting thoughts. After, Maddie mindlessly went through her morning ritual and headed downtown. Normally, she would go to her desk in Robbery/Homicide and savor a cup of coffee in the quiet before the shift change began to fill the bull pen with fellow detectives. It wasn't the same in Exit Alley where the tech analysts seemed to have no sense of time, coming and going at all hours of the day. There was never any peace and quiet there. Besides, she had no home—no desk to call her own—just temporary squatter's rights on a conference table.

So, Maddie stopped at Cutty's deli, grabbing a cup of coffee and a bagel with a smear of cream cheese. She parked herself in the back booth she and Jake shared when they were work partners where they would watch the comings and goings in the deli. But she didn't, instead staring into her coffee mug and lamely skating the bagel around on her plate like a hockey puck.

"I figured I might find you here." Derek, the detective from District Three, sat down across from her in Jake's spot.

Maddie noted his wry smile and was immediately on guard. "You're kind of off the beaten path, no?"

Derek shrugged.

Cutty suddenly appeared beside the table. He eyeballed the stranger in his place with suspicion. "Hey, Madeline. Who's your friend?"

"This is Derek. He caught the case of the nine student nurses."

"Yeah…on the news. I seen it."

"How is your niece doing?" Derek turned his head up towards Cutty but kept his eyes on Maddie.

Cutty took a long, loud slurp of scotch out of his CPD coffee mug that drew Derek's eyes. He caught the quick furrow in Maddie's brow and the jerk of her head across the table. Cutty shook his head. *"Kids.* Glad I never had any. First, they eat you out of house and home, then suck up your pension to party on for four more years. But, hey, that's my sister's problem."

Derek nodded slowly, then looked over at Maddie. He smiled knowingly.

She smiled back.

"Can I get you anything, detective?" Cutty asked.

"No, thanks. I've been called down to the Director's palace to brief the powers that be."

"Suit yourself. Good luck with the case," Cutty said as he walked away.

"Great to be in the spotlight, eh?" Derek asked Maddie.

"Depends."

"On?"

Maddie thought for a moment. "Whether it's the glow of admiration or heat for getting roasted. They weren't too kind to one of my former partners."

"The one that shot the councilman's son?"

Maddie nodded.

"Well, from what I saw online, the camera likes you—a lot." Derek studied Maddie's face as if inventorying her features and counting the few freckles splashed on her cheeks. "I'll bet you've got a lovely off-duty smile."

She turned her head down and away to hide her blushing and a reflex smile. *That's Jake's line.*

Having hit his mark, Derek slid out of the booth and stood up. "Do me a favor, will you?"

"What's that?"

"The case—my case." Derek looked over at Cutty behind the counter, then back at Maddie with a serious expression. "If you know something—if you hear anything, please let me know. Don't let me get hung out to dry. Please."

Maddie looked up. Her smile slowly drooped away. She met his eyes and nodded.

"Thanks."

As Derek walked out, he passed by EC on his way in, who turned and watched him leave the deli.

"Do I know that guy?" EC asked as he came up to Maddie.

"He's the lead on the nurse murders. I met him when we were at the crime scene."

"Oh." EC sat down where Derek had been. "Old habits die hard, huh."

Maddie frowned.

"You know—Jake. You guys used to meet here, too, right? This booth should have his name on it."

She nodded, looking at the deli door.

"Man, that guy."

"Huh?"

"Jake."

"Yeah, Jake."

"So…Samantha thinks she found something as we were going through stuff from the warehouse last night."

"Last night?"

EC looked down as he wrung his hands. "I-I—we…"

Maddie grabbed his hands. "Let's just go see what she has."

EC nodded, and they got up to leave.

On the way out, Maddie stopped and leaned over the deli counter. "Thanks, Uncle Cutty."

"My niece, huh?" Cutty paused and looked up from the brisket of corned beef he was slicing. "My brother-in-law still has tuition nightmares. Better him than me."

"Just a little cover."

Cutty eyeballed Maddie with a squint. "You guys be careful out there. It's a mean old world."

"Thanks." Maddie started to follow EC out.

"And say hi to Jake for me."

She looked back, and Cutty was working on the brisket

again. Back at Exit Alley, Maddie waited in the conference room while EC fetched Samantha. "Where's Q?" she asked when they returned.

"I guess he's still down in the Flats at the server farm," Samantha said. "He's taken that on personally and has been spending most of his time down there."

"Making any progress?"

"Don't know. He's pretty tight lipped about it."

"And what have you got?"

Samantha sat down with her *iSlate* and began swiping across its screen.

Maddie watched a moment, then looked impatiently at EC, who sat down beside Samantha.

"I've been going through the evidence from the warehouse," EC said. "There's some creepy stuff in it, but I'm not seeing much of a pattern or anything."

"I hope Jake can come up with something." Maddie shook her head. "I don't see anything that's going to help us get Jamal."

"So…I went and pulled down as many of the E.J. Quick articles as I could find off of his blog and from news sites," Samantha said, eyes still locked on the screen of her *iSlate*. "And ran them through the Strunk-Skinner meat grinder—"

"What's that?" Maddie asked.

"It's an analytical tool that evaluates grammar, vocabulary, syntax, form, structure, allusions, figures of speech, and patterns of thematic development to construct a unique linguistic fingerprint." Samantha spun the tablet around towards Maddie to show her a screen tiled with graphs, numbers, and cryptic codes.

"And, since we already have his articles, this can help us, how? After all, we can just read what he wrote, right?"

"Well, some posit the theory that it goes deeper—metaphysically and ontologically—that it represents an individual's cognitive schematic—how he perceives and processes and structures the world in his head."

"Profiling? How is that going to help? We already know who the bad guy is."

"Yeah. Kind of. But there's more to it than that."

"More? I've read his stories. It's pretty straight forward reporting for the most part."

Samantha looked at EC for help. "The next step is to take Jamal's linguistic fingerprint and start looking for it across the web…and in the Darknet."

Maddie frowned. She looked at EC, too.

"He's out there networking with others, above ground and under," EC explained. "Social media, chat rooms—who knows where else—and who knows with what identities. But he's using words, mainly—maybe some pics, but mostly words. And with the S&S profile, we can find him under whatever rocks he and his cohorts are hiding."

"And once we start matching up posts to the profile," Samantha added, "we might be able to map his trail and find him."

"Find him in cyberspace? We need to find him in the real world and stop him," Maddie insisted. "And stop him quick."

"But that's just it," Samantha said. "He has to post from somewhere in the real world. This guy is extremely careful and uses a bit scatter masking protocol, even on his E.J. Quick stories. But they're not infallible. And not everybody he interacts with may be as disciplined as he is. We look for cracks in the castle wall."

Maddie sighed. *Techno mumbo-jumbo.* She looked at a complex abstract print on the wall of the conference room. It was an extreme closeup of a microchip circuit, a labyrinth carved in silicon. There was no clear way in or out of the maze.

"I think it will help find him," Samantha said.

Maddie looked at Samantha and smiled. *Whatever…*

"What have we got to lose?" EC asked.

"I don't know. Nothing I guess," Maddie answered. *Except my sanity.*

Amy woke with a start from her dream: a grim fairy tale of a young girl trapped in a castle tower. She closed her eyes quickly, confronted with her own imprisonment. In her self-imposed darkness, she stoked her anger with thoughts of revenge.

~~~

Homecoming

Jake stepped out of the Westlake Express cab in front of the Glick Building on Detroit Road carrying a plastic bag with the few possessions that came with him into the emergency room—except for his shield. Lt. Sands held his badge for safekeeping. Police evidence, discharge papers, and medication filled another bag with a matching blue-and-green MH logo. The sweat suit nurse Kindra bought for him at the Walmart by MetroHealth Medical Center aged him artificially by hanging loosely on his frame, an impression aided by his slow, shuffling gate. He couldn't wait to get into a hot shower to scrub the sick from the hospital off his skin. But when he got upstairs to his apartment, a wave of fatigue swelled over him and he sank into the sofa in his living room.

When he woke from the nap his body imposed on his mind, he was still weary. He smirked. *Must have taken more energy than I thought to convince the doctor I was good to go for discharge.*

At the door to the fire escape on the back of the building, Jake heard a familiar scratching. "Duty calls."

He got up to let Frank the Feral Cat in, twisting, stretching, and pulling his arms and legs as he went to wring the ache out of his muscles put there by the synthoid that manhandled him at the warehouse in the Flats. Frank led him back to the kitchen to be fed.

"Slim pickings, my man." Jake set down a bowl of dry cat food, which Frank sniffed, then walked away from.

Jake pulled down a box of *Cheerios* for himself. He went to the refrigerator and grabbed the gallon jug of milk, but it didn't pass the smell test, so he dumped it and tossed a handful of pulverized oats into his mouth.

"Yeah. I get it," Jake said to Frank, crunching on the dry cereal. "So, should we call for pizza or Chinese—oh, sorry about that, pal. Pizza it is."

As Jake finished texting his order to Angelo's, a knock drew their eyes towards the front door. Jake reached into the dishwasher and grabbed his Colt 1911.

"Come on in."

A moment later, Q walked into the kitchen. "Don't you think it would be a good idea to lock your door?"

"A lock is just a speed bump, not protection." Jake sat down at the kitchen table and laid the pistol in front of him. "Grab a beer."

"Jesus. You look like hell." Q opened the refrigerator and peered in. He pulled out a Shiner Bock long neck and twisted off the cap. "Are you sure you should be out yet?"

Jake grunted.

Q sat down across from Jake. "So, what's so important?"

"I want you to do something about this." Jake pulled up his left sleeve and rolled his arm palm up. He pointed to a dark shadow beneath the skin of his forearm. "This. Turn it off or spoof it or…*something.*"

"An implant for monitoring your vitals?"

"It was the only way they would release me."

"Big Doctor is watching, eh?"

"Yeah. Well, not me. 'Cause if they can, the Baron can."

"Right." Q's grin evaporated. "Get me your *iNode.*"

Jake pushed himself up from the table and went into the living room. "We're getting pizza. You in?"

"We?"

Jake pointed at Frank flopped down in the middle of the kitchen floor and slid his *iNode* across the table to Q.

"As long as there's no anchovies on it, I'm in." Q pulled out a phone and began tapping on the screen.

"Right. No anchovies." Jake watched Q work. "Have you found it yet?"

"What? This? Piece of cake. I'll patch it to a biorhythm routine in the cloud based on your medical records. By the time they figure it out, you'll be the picture of health."

"No. You know what I mean." Jake leaned in. "The server farm."

Q looked up. He nodded slowly. "I found it, but…you're not going to like it."

"Didn't think I would."

"There's a black tier in the configuration that's sucking in data, churning it, and spitting it back out. I haven't broken the encryption on the code yet, but it seems to be what they call curved logic."

"What's that?"

"Beyond straight-line *If—And—Or—Therefore* progressive machine think." Q chuckled to himself and shook his head. "Intuitional—like you."

"To what end?"

Q looked up with a serious look on his face. "I don't know."

Jake read Q's face. "Yeah. You do."

"I don't know for sure, but..." Q sighed. "It's reactionary, not just causal. You know, cause, effect—*reaction*. There's a working theory out there that AI can develop a consciousness. That it can become an invisible mind, competitive with human intellect. An unseen force that can bend the cultural evolutionary time line."

"You guys. Always have to try to rule the world."

"Yeah, but—I mean, but what if it wasn't just—wasn't strictly an intellectual force?"

"What other kind of force could there be inside the machine?"

"When I played the synthoid A/V stream of the nurse murders, there was a reaction to it—just like I reacted to it. Inside. I can't give you calibrated percentages or timeline overlays or anything, but just like my heart rate and respirations rose and fell, so did CPU usage, memory I/O, network streaming, like—like—"

"Like artificial emotions."

Q nodded.

"Great. Just what the world needs: hormonal technology." Jake gazed off into space. "I guess that explains that."

"What?"

"I've been going through the piles of physical evidence taken from the warehouse. Papers, pictures—out of the file cabinets and off the walls. There were the usual homages to Tesla, Turing, Jobs, and Musk—"

"Mount *Tech*more."

"Huh?"

"Mount Techmore. You know, there's North Dakota, South Dakota, and Geek Dakota."

Jake shook his head. "Whatever. But there were also shrines on the wall to Freud, Jung, and Skinner."

"Freud? What's that all about?"

"You know that consciousness is just one side of the coin."

"Coin?"

"Heads and tails. You've got the thinking side and the feeling side. The id. The entire history of AI has been on the ego and super ego side. Now…"

"How does that help control the world?"

"It doesn't. And maybe that's not what he wants."

"What does the Baron want?"

"Look at the personalities he is going id mining in. What do you think?"

The Angelo's delivery man arrived.

Jake, Q, and Frank ate the pizza in silence, lost in their own private thoughts.

When Maddie let herself into Jake's apartment the next morning, Frank greeted her at the door. After a perfunctory petting, he scurried out, leaving Maddie to wonder how he had gotten in. She listened to the apartment, then drew her Glock and slowly moved through the rooms. A pizza box and beer bottles were on the kitchen table. The living room was empty. Two MetroHealth Medical Center plastic bags were on the sofa. As she moved towards the bedrooms, she could hear a soft snoring. She peeked around the doorway and saw Jake sleeping in his bed. She was mad, then happy, then a bit irked. She holstered her Glock.

Maddie went into the kitchen and called EC to tell him she

would be late for work. After making a pot of coffee, she sat with Jake while he slept, reading *The Red Dragon* by Thomas Harris.

~~~

Murder Keep

Sometimes, he could feel the electro-magnetic fields of high-voltage power lines literally bruising his soul. So, one of the many renovations he made to his lair was to embed a Faraday cage behind the walls, ceiling, and the sub-floor of the windowless hideaway built off the second-floor master bedroom. There were no lights or electrical outlets in the room and all the copper wires had been stripped off the studs before the insulation and walls were put up. When the pressure of radio waves, which inexorably flooded the aether ever since the time of Marconi, grew unbearable, he retreated into its darkness to seek relief from his migraines. The extensive sound-proofing added throughout the old stone structure helped as well.

Jamal emerged refreshed and parked himself in the armchair by the turret windows of the master bedroom. He watched midnight traffic trickle this way and that on Franklin Avenue and West Forty-fourth Street. He checked his watch. The download to the next Munchausened synthoid would take well into tomorrow's swing shift to complete. Then, the murder clock would start ticking down. In the empty time, he could watch replays but decided against it, preferring to let the anticipation build within himself, like a Cedar Point roller coaster ratcheting up ever higher into the sky. In truth—and

Jamal prided himself on not being self-delusional—he realized his anticipation needed amping up even more lately.

His castle was quiet. He could sleep but knew he wouldn't.

I could eat. But why?

He felt no physical hunger.

A patrol car drifted by slowly on Franklin Avenue. Jamal briefly wondered how Jake was doing, then lit up his *iSlate,* using its encrypted Sawtooth wireless to connect into the web of security cameras, microphones, and sensors spread both outside and throughout the inside of the house. It was the only network he allowed in the entire building. No cell phones or connected devices like *iNodes* were permitted inside. Utility smart-meters had been spoofed with digital images of "normal" household activity. Behind that facade, the residence was a dark hole on the Atlas Grid. A brief scan around the perimeter revealed no movement. The front, back, and side doorways were closed. The green lights on the control panel indicated they were safely locked. The staircases, halls, and hidden passageways were empty.

Downstairs in the basement servant's quarters, devoted caretakers Bill and Stephanie slept soundly. On the main level, Carbon, an all-black cat, sat at his perch on the table in the parlor front window, directly below, watching the street scene out front as well.

The previous owners had sacrificed one of the six bedrooms on the second floor to create a completely hidden safe room that only he, Bill and Stephanie knew about. There, Amy slept peacefully.

Jamal broke the "fifth wall," a carefully maintained cyber firebreak between him and his synthoid minions, by taking the urchin off the street and bringing her there to taunt Jake. An impulsive move questioned less now, he found it stirred something new and darker still within him to have had, physically, "hands-on" an illicit act.

As he watched Amy sleep, the Baron marveled at these feelings and wondered what new mayhem they might bring.

~~~

The Au Pair

The mousy hair was cut short and styled simply with a part in the middle. A pair of softened blue-gray eyes belied a careful attentiveness to the activities on the lakeside playground where young preschoolers ran and swung and climbed and slid down timber, steel, and plastic structures designed for maximum childhood fun within the legal and bureaucratic strictures deemed necessary for public safety and risk aversion.

Feature set E-DC640827-JA-451010 Rev. C, based on an Anglo-Saxon female, was aged for twenty years, six months, and mounted on a five-foot, eight-inch, fifty-eight-kilogram chassis designed to evoke mild to low-scale moderate male attraction. The optimized occupational wardrobe set included knee-level skirts, jumpers, and loose-fitted slacks paired with cotton blouses and knit tops sleeved appropriate to the season, though ambient temperatures were rarely a functional consideration except in severe climate extremes when auxiliary heating or cooling was recommended, either with internal HVAC micro-units or with temperature-compensating outer garments.

"Julie" sat on a bench at her post near the entrance to the playground as part of a one-person, two-synthoid team to supervise the forty children of the daycare center out for afternoon recreation at the public park. Programmed for surveillance and child care assistance, she maintained a continuous scan of the activities in her sector like an air traffic controller monitoring the flow of flights into and out of a busy airport, ready to issue verbal instructions or to intervene physically if threat of harm appeared to her charges.

As a cost-cutting measure, the daycare center, like so many other businesses with a small synthoid head count, transported their units to a suburban service center for the mandated biennial inspection, rather than pay for a "house call" by a certified technician. From there, Julie's review was subcontracted to a company in a warehouse in the Flats where some special modifications were also made, including the unlocking of port 139 for remote access via the Atlas Grid.

Julie's wellness software failed to detect the snippets of malicious machine code slowly trickling into unused memory registers, piggy-backed on the routine hive monitoring traffic which would soon be ghosted to send false location and status information up to her manufacturer's customer service and tech support servers. The scattered puddles of data and malware agents would soon begin to pool, multiply, and migrate throughout the operating system, BIOS, and Biology Logic Controller modules, attaching themselves to host routines and supplanting datalink libraries. With her civilian "Three Laws" chip set critically crippled during her biennial inspection, Julie would soon be as deadly as any government "Specials Operations" synthoid.

As playtime for the children came to the end of its allotted time period, the daycare's certified human child and synthoid minder rose from her bench, shadowed by Julie and the other PSA unit. They shepherded the boys and girls together and walked them back to the nearby center. After the last parent retrieved their child at the end of the Friday work day, Julie was parked at her charging station for the weekend.

When the battery packs reached one-hundred percent shortly after two AM, Julie came out of sleep mode, assumed a new functional identity, and let herself out of the facility. As planned, she would not be discovered missing for two days. Her first task was to retrieve the pistol and ammunition cached for her back at the lakeside park.

Overkill

Maddie sat at the ten-foot-long wood conference table Q used as a workspace in the second-floor server room of the White Chapel LLC building in the Flats. Her phone and *iSlate* were dark. In the dim lighting, she waited for Jake and EC to come back from their guided stroll through the labyrinth of eight-foot-tall racks of blinking servers. She had seen it all before. She did not need to look at it again, so she stared out the window at an ore boat crawling its way up the river, doubting it was right for Jake to be there on his first day back to work.

Hundreds of small plastic cooling fans running in the back planes of various modules in the racks pumped the room full of warm air and raised the ambient noise level with a subtle hum which Maddie noticed most by its absence when she got back outside.

With all the hours Q spends down there, how can he not be stark raving mad himself?

As they U-turned around the end of an aisle, Jake's eyes were drawn to Maddie by the window cooling herself by fanning her blouse over her breasts with her head tilted back and her eyes closed. Q's voice up ahead faded away in his consciousness as Jake slowed and swiveled his head to keep her in his gaze. EC noticed, but said nothing.

The walk-through over, Q and EC sat down at the conference table across from Maddie. Jake went to the window and looked at the bend in the river, now empty as the ore boat had moved upriver. The hum of the cooling fans seemed to grow louder in their silence.

"Where are they on the Speck murders?" Jake finally asked.

"I've been monitoring the murder book through a server back channel," Q said. "No eye witnesses came out of the campus canvas. Lots of ugly pictures from the crime scene and lots of blood samples, but no forensics on a perp."

"There won't be any." Jake sighed.

"Most of what's going on now is background interviews—family, friends, faculty—and scavenging social media accounts. Probably trying to find a jilted lover of one of the girls or something."

"What else can they do," EC said.

"Should we tell them?" Maddie asked.

Jake turned from the window and looked at Q. "Anything?"

"We've gone through the metadata off the traffic logs and LUDs. All the university units are accounted for and the few other synthoids active that night were on the periphery of the sector and didn't get near the dorm."

"And this place?"

"There's nothing to bloodhound back to this location or to any of the NSA portals in the grid we've staked-out," Q answered. "Sorry."

Jake sat down next to Maddie. "What do we tell them?"

Maddie shrugged and shook her head.

"What about Jamal?" EC asked.

"A phantom," Q said. "Actually, a shadow of a phantom. Samantha's been trying to track his online activity linguistically.

He's a clever fellow. His reporting is highly stylized, and she's gotten some hits, but they're all phishing and fraud cases from over a decade ago, so she'll have to take a closer look. Nothing at all in the Darknet chat rooms and social media we're monitoring. What is unusual is that some of those postings seem machine generated. They're almost generic. Pretty unusual for such fringe personalities."

"Is he using an AI composition bot to hide behind?" EC asked.

"Could be. That or there are apps that run what you've written through a series of translations—Portuguese to Mandarin to Hebrew to Russian then back to English—which scrubs out language identity markers. She's checking those posts to see if there are any hits in the headers and routing that match up. It's a long shot, since even on his signed blog posts, the guy uses a high-level Tor onion services protocol."

"Which means?" Jake asked impatiently.

"Which means the paths of his online activity get whipped, grated, and pureed through an IP blender and can't be tracked."

"Figures." EC shook his head. "Could be anywhere, then. Right?"

"That's the idea. But sometimes you get lucky."

"Well, skill never won the lottery," Jake said. "Have her keep at it."

Q's phone dinged with an alert. He swiped the screen and read. "Looks like a synthoid went MIA. On the west side. Jesus, from a daycare center."

"When?" EC asked, lighting up his *iSlate*.

"Not sure exactly. Reported missing yesterday, so it could have been anytime over the weekend."

"What shows up on the blotter?" Jake asked EC, watching him swipe the screen of his tablet.

"The usual mayhem. Nothing on the west side—wait a minute. Metropark Rangers found a body in the valley. But that's a shooting. Droids can't have guns."

"*Shouldn't* have guns."

"Right…Get this, the vic was naked except for a baseball cap."

Jake thought a moment then asked, "Shot six times in the chest?"

"Yup. Overkill, too. Not a likely Munchausen."

"But likely the Baron," Jake said.

"How's that?" Maddie asked.

"Search Aileen Wuornos W-U-O-R-N-O-S."

EC did, then read, "Aileen Carol Wuornos Pralle was an American serial killer who murdered seven men in Florida between 1989 and 1990 by shooting them at point-blank range."

"Victim number two."

"David Spears, age forty-three. Construction worker in Winter Garden. On June 1, 1990, his nude body was found along Florida State Road 19 in Citrus County, wearing only a baseball cap. He had been shot six times."

"Ah, you should probably know," Q said, "the missing unit from the daycare center…it was female."

Maddie whispered, "Welcome back, Jake."

~~~

Into the Valley of Death

"Coffee?" Q asked after Maddie and EC left for the daycare center to investigate the missing synthoid. "Black, right?"

Jake nodded, then rested his forehead on his arms crossed on the conference table in front of him.

"You okay?"

"No. I ache like hell. Everywhere."

"Didn't they give you any meds for that?"

Jake gave Q a harsh scowl. "Junkies are junkies with junkie thoughts, whether you get it off the street or from Drug Mart."

Q nodded. He left to make two cups of coffee. He returned and slid a regular brew across the table to Jake, then sat down and sipped his own espresso. "At least these jamokes had a decent rig for their java."

"You know what hurts most?" Jake sat up again. "He's been right there within arm's reach the whole time."

"The guy's good."

"Yeah, but so am I. And nothing. No Spidey sense. Not a tingle. Man, he is one stone cold reptile."

"Unfortunately, he's so good, he knows how to go off-the-grid—really *off-the-grid*. Like I said, he might as well be pixels on moonbeams. And it seems like he's got the discipline to stay off, too."

Jake sipped his coffee. "Not bad, Marge."

"I'll bet you say that to all the geeks."

"Now, how are we going to get him?"

Q shrugged his shoulders. "I know there's something rattling around in all that silicon over there. But…"

"But?"

"But getting it out—intact…I don't want a nuclear meltdown."

"Well, we've got to get out in front of this parade. Fast. Playing catch-up is leaving too many dead bodies everywhere."

"But how?"

Jake pondered. "Dots. We're not seeing all the dots."

"Dots? What's *that* mean?"

"You didn't have a normal childhood, did you. Didn't your parents ever take you to a place with a kid's menu?"

"Like what? A *Cracker Barrel?* Yeah, right. In your dreams—and my nightmares."

Jake shook his head. He closed his eyes, leaned back, and rested his head on the back of the chair. "Maybe Kovacic's right."

"Come on, Jake. The SWAT guy? He's a meathead. What does he know?"

"Yeah…but if we can't get ahead of Jamal in cyberspace, we might have to do it the old-fashion way."

"How's that?"

Jake sat up and looked Q in the eye. "Out here. In meatspace."

"Yeah, well, just remember, I'm the guy with no kid's menu or crayon experience. You're on your own."

Jake sipped his coffee and stared into space.

Some called it the "Emerald Canyon." The Rocky River cut a deep gorge through the near west suburbs on its way to Lake Erie. After interviewing the owner, manager, and minder at the daycare center without getting much new information, Maddie and EC headed to the Metroparks Ranger headquarters, turning off Detroit Road and descending a hundred feet down to the Valley Parkway which followed the winding river upstream. Five miles in, the gorge opened up at a flood plain large enough for three golf courses. They pulled into the ranger station parking lot across from the Big Met clubhouse.

"Should we read this guy into our case or not?" EC asked before they got out of the car.

A pained expression crossed Maddie's face. "I don't like this."

"Like what?"

"Keeping these guys—and Derek—in the dark. I wouldn't like it. Neither would you. My dad always hated being treated like a mushroom." She sighed. "But I'm thinking not. Jake's right. At least not until we've got more than just a gut feeling to tie them together. I hate to do it, but maybe we should dump it all on Lt. Sands' desk."

"Fine by me. I didn't transfer into ACU for the politics." EC opened his car door and got out. "Besides, that's why he gets the office and the big bucks."

Maddie got out, and they headed towards the entrance. Two uniformed rangers and a husky middle-aged man in khakis and a sports jacket came out of the building and met them halfway.

"You the guys from downtown?" asked the man in street clothes.

"Detective Morgan?" Maddie asked.

"Yeah. Call me Wil."

"I'm Maddie. And this is EC." They showed Morgan their badges. "What's up?"

"Hiker just called in. Found a body out by Wallace Lake." Morgan took a long look at Maddie, then glanced at EC, and put his eyes back on Maddie again. He smiled. "Why don't you ride with me and we can talk. Your partner can follow us."

EC rolled his eyes and turned back towards their car.

Maddie fell in step beside Morgan. They got into an unmarked Ford *Explorer*. The two uniformed rangers pulled out of the parking lot with the roof lights on their patrol SUV flashing, heading south. Morgan pulled out behind them with EC in trail.

"So, what makes downtown so interested in our little murder in the park. Don't you guys have your hands full with big-city crime?" Morgan asked.

Maddie watched the trees flash by in a blur as the gorge narrowed and the bluff walls closed in again on the Parkway. "Wil, I'm going to level with you. Have you ever heard of Ailene Wuornos?"

"Nope."

"Neither had I until a few days ago. Wish I hadn't, but here I am. My lieutenant pulled me off my Robbery/Homicide cases and stuck me in with EC and his partner, because they have this idea that there's a copycat murderer loose in the city."

"And my case fits the pattern?"

"A couple of cases, actually. The naked guy in the ball cap and a woman's murder in Huntington Park."

Morgan looked over at Maddie. "That one's a few years old. One of our cold cases."

"EC's partner swears it's a knock-off of the Sam Sheppard case from the 1950s."

"That's a reach. Who even remembers that far back?"

"I don't know," Maddie sighed. "That's their working theory, anyway."

"Same guy?"

Maddie shrugged her shoulders.

"And your lieutenant is buying it?"

"That's what he wants me to figure out."

"Well…two bodies in one week is not exactly run-of-the-mill for us." Morgan looked at Maddie and smiled weakly.

"I don't want to get in your way. Just need to check out their theory. Satisfy the brass."

"You help us clear these cases, and I'll be grateful. Then I can go home at night and sleep again."

"No problem."

They drove in silence for a half-mile or so.

"So…how did you come to being on the job?" Morgan asked.

"Family business. My dad put in his twenty on patrol and retired a sergeant. My grandpa, too. I was supposed to go to law school, but…didn't," Maddie said. "I was always kind of headstrong that way. You?"

"After three tours in the sandbox, I thought a job as a park ranger would be good for my PTSD. You know, nice and mellow. Telling folks not to feed the bears and to make sure to put out their campfires."

"Marines? My dad was in the Corps."

"Army. Rangers."

"So, how's that plan working out for you?"

"Not so good…this week." Wil pulled into a parking lot by Wallace Lake in Berea and drove around to the three ranger SUVs with their lights flashing by a pavilion. He killed the engine. Staring through the windshield at the crime scene, he said sincerely, "I'll take any help I can get."

Maddie just nodded.

"Thanks."

EC parked behind them and came around to the passenger door. Maddie and Morgan got out and the three walked to the pavilion.

"What have we got?" Morgan asked the uniformed ranger who met them at the crime scene tape wrapped around the pavilion pillars.

"Hey, Wil." The ranger looked over Maddie and EC.

"They're Homicide from downtown," Morgan answered the unasked question. "Might be a connection to some of their cases."

"Got a male. Late thirties, early forties. No ID. Shot eight or nine times. Looks like a twenty-two. Maybe a three-eighty."

Wil shook his head and looked at Maddie. "Hell hath no fury?"

"It fits Wuornos," Maddie said.

"You might want to have the patrol guys start checking for abandoned cars throughout the park," EC said. "She totaled out at seven."

"Great," Morgan growled through his gritted teeth.

Each lost in their own thoughts, the three silently watched the Bunny Suit Boys process the crime scene for evidence. When the medical examiner's van took the body away, Maddie and EC went back to the city.

The Trilogy: The Invisible Mind

The bodies of four more men, all shot to death, would be found by the park rangers over the next week.

On the way home, Maddie stopped at the lakeside park playground used by the rogue robot's daycare center. She waited in her car until dusk swept away the last of the parents and children, then meandered around the slides and swings and jungle gyms, trying to see the world through synthoid eyes. Her thoughts inevitably drifted to orphan Amy.

A piece of paper flapping lazily on a posted warning sign caught Maddie's eye. A welcome distraction from disturbing thoughts, she walked over to see what it was. Her hand went immediately to the grip of her Glock, and she pirouetted to scan the park for danger. The area cleared, she turned back to study the paper, which held a collage of photos: Maddie coming and going at work…at home…at Jake's building…at the University Circle dormitory…at the Metroparks Ranger station…sitting at a patio bistro table at a Crocker Park bakery…standing outside the alley in the Flats where she had been attacked by the synthoid and saved by Jake. *Jamal…*

She went to the edge of the bluff and stared out to sea until night fell, fear and anger rooting deep within her subconscious.

~~~

Stakeout

Exit Alley was deserted by the time Maddie finished her paperwork. EC and Samantha left together at six-thirty to get dinner. Q never came back from the Flats and his minions had cleared out at 5:01 PM like a migrating herd for happy hour at a virtual reality tech bar in the Warehouse District.

Maddie quickly tidied up her workspace on the conference table and left when the cleaning crew made their appearance. Instead of going home, she drove down the Shoreway to Lake Road, cut up by John's Diner, then cruised the alley behind the Glick Building before parking in one of the metered spots across Detroit Road from the dark storefront. She stared at the building like she had stared out across the lake at the park, haunted by the stalking of a serial killer. Jake's silhouette momentarily broke the steady glow from the second-floor windows, then moved away. Maddie rested her forehead on the steering wheel and closed her eyes. It didn't help.

She watched for another half-hour—maybe more—then drove around the building again. The tenant spots in the rear lot were empty, so she took one and went in the back way with the key she had from before. Frank scurried in between her legs. She followed him up the stairs to the second floor, took a deep breath, and went into the apartment.

"I wondered how long you were going to sit out there,"

Jake said, greeting Maddie at the door with a glass of wine. "Your stakeout skills need a little polishing."

"I—I didn't want, you know…" She took the glass and sipped quickly. "In case you had…"

"Company?" Jake stepped up and kissed Maddie's forehead. He put his arm around her shoulders and led her into the apartment. The living room furniture was littered with open books and stacks of papers leaving nowhere to sit, so they went to the kitchen. "You eat? I'm betting not."

She shook her head. "Did EC call you?"

"He did. You know, technically, he's still *my* partner."

Maddie sighed. She sipped, glancing nervously around the kitchen. "What have you got for food?"

"Just so happens, I went to the market and got a couple of slabs of cow meat from Mel." Jake pulled a platter with a pair of Delmonico steaks on it from the refrigerator and headed towards the back fire escape. "Come on, the coals are ready. Leave your Glock. Bring the Zinfandel."

Maddie went to Jake's bedroom and dug through his dresser for a pair of gym shorts and a T-shirt. She changed clothes, then, barefooted, joined him on the fire escape. "You don't mind I got comfy, do you?"

Jake looked Maddie up and down and smiled his approval. He shook his head, moved the baked potatoes to the side of the Weber, then threw the steaks on the grill.

Maddie sat down on the aluminum lawn chair and gazed out towards the lake, sipping her wine. "What are we going to do, Jake?"

"Um…about what, exactly?"

Maddie did not answer.

"Food fixes everything. So, first we eat."

After they finished the steaks, then emptied the bottle of wine, Maddie and Jake made love, just like old times.

Shortly after seven the next morning, Jake's phone rang, dragging him into consciousness. Maddie, naked beside him in his bed, moaned and rolled away when he answered. The caller was John from John's Diner. Waitress Amy had missed her second shift in two days, and he was calling to see if Jake knew where she was.

Asylum Inmates

Without windows, Amy had long ago lost all sense of time, though through street-wise animal instinct could at least still tell when it was day and when it was night. So, she knew it was sometime in the middle of the night when the commotion of a struggle seeped through her prison walls. Muffled cries on the other side did not last long before they faded into whimpers, then silence.

She waited for what she reckoned was an hour before tapping lightly on the wall: Knock…knock-knock.

No response.

She tried again. Again, without reply.

She kept trying every hour until she sensed it was morning. Then stopped until night came again.

~~~

Every Breath You Take

Jake sat alone at a booth up front in John's Diner. His third mug of coffee was half gone. He mindlessly watched the traffic on Detroit Avenue until EC arrived and sat down across the table from him.

"Coffee, hon?" Jackie came over and asked EC. After he turned over his mug, she poured. She topped off Jake's mug and said to him, "She's a good kid, you know. You better find her."

Jake just nodded, looking out the window.

"Thanks." EC smiled up at Jackie, then she left. He studied Jake over the brim of his mug. Three sips later, he said, "You didn't tell Maddie, did you."

"I did not. I figured it really wasn't the best way to start the morning." Jake sighed and looked at EC. "You know?"

EC shook his head. "No. Not really."

"Well, it's complicated."

"Yeah. I imagine. And you're a complicated guy."

"So everybody says."

"So…what now, *Kemo Sahbee?*"

"Simple. We get this guy."

"Gosh. Why didn't I think of that." EC sipped his coffee. "And how is that, *Mr. Complicated?*"

Jake pointed out the window to the traffic light at the intersection.

EC looked. It took a moment, then he understood. "The traffic cam?"

"And shoe leather." Jake smiled. "We can't just sit and wait for Q and his merry band of techies."

"Good ol' fashioned police work, then."

"I went to her apartment after Maddie left. It's at the west end, in the Mayfair."

"Was that an official visit or personal?"

Jake shrugged. "Looks like that's where she got grabbed up. And I'm betting it wasn't a 'droid. She's blonde, but not stupid. She wouldn't have let a stranger in. Not after all the shop talk I've shared with her."

"The Baron's not a stranger?"

"She knows I know Jamal. Seen me here with him. Jackie says he's been in a few times lately. Always sat in Amy's section."

"Oh. Great."

"It's been forty-eight hours. I told John to call the Lakewood PD and put in a report. Once it pops up in the system, we'll have some cover to start collecting video footage."

"Until then?"

"Let's take a walk and see what other eyes are on the street between here and the Mayfair."

Maddie got back to her apartment, made coffee, and lingered for a long while over a cup at her breakfast bar. *What a mess.*

Then her body reminded her how much she enjoyed being with Jake. How much she missed him physically, too. She could not suppress a smile. And all the messy complications of work and crime and relationships and death dissipated like fog in the hot rays of dawn piercing a clear morning sky. She savored a sunbeam warmth within herself.

It was later in the shower that a creepy dread bore into her as hard memories pushed back against her feelings. All the times Jamal had randomly appeared flipped through her mind like playing cards slowly dealt out at a mental blackjack table…and no longer seemed so random.

At the hospital when Sanchez died.

But that was news, right? And he's supposedly a reporter…supposedly.

Then at the "Hillside Strangler" crime scene off the Shoreway.

News, again. And Jamal wasn't the only reporter there—but he was there before anyone else. And what about the video of her and Jake working the crime scene he showed them on the Darknet…

In the station house, there making fresh coffee when she came into work at five in the morning before the shift change.

Jamal and me…no one else around. He was there to talk about Jake. To warn me about Jake.

On the patio at the bakery just down the street, after a morning run.

Just down the street…

In the alley in the Flats where the synthoid attacked her.

I never saw him, but he was there…I know it…he was there…

Maddie shut the shower off and hurriedly wrapped a towel around her body. She rushed into the master bedroom and grabbed her Glock off the nightstand, dripping water onto the rug. She stalked through her own apartment, methodically clearing all the rooms, until she ended up at the front window looking down on the street, wondering if the Baron was out there, watching.

She turned back inside and surveyed her apartment.

Is he here…seeing her now?

Maddie called Jake. He promised to come right away with EC, Q, and the gear needed to sweep her apartment for bugs, cameras, and IoT taps into her appliances.

The Baron would watch the last footage to come out of Maddie's apartment later, aroused by her nearly naked body dripping wet, armed with a semi-automatic pistol. But especially from the look of fear on her face.

~~~

The War Room

Maddie, EC, and Jake waited downstairs while Q swept the Glick Building for cameras and microphones. No one spoke. Their phones, *iSlate*s and *iNodes* were in a shielded and hardened lock-box in the trunk of EC's unmarked car parked in the lot out back.

The two-story building was twenty-five feet wide and one hundred feet deep. Once home to his parent's flower shop, Jake had paid off his sister to take title of the property and began renovating. Upstairs was the three-bedroom apartment where he lived. Downstairs was hollowed out as one big room in the front sixty feet to be a huge mancave. Against the back wall was a complete kitchen, which featured a set of glass-fronted refrigerators from the old flower shop, now filled with beer and wine, and a twelve-foot long oak dining table. The rest of the room was filled with a plethora of distractions, including a pool table, baby grand piano, professional-grade surround sound audio equipment, kayaks stacked on a rack against the east wall, golf clubs, baseball bats, a well-stocked bar, and a huge sofa pit that faced a blank, white-washed portion of the wall for watching old movies. The rest of the exposed brick walls was covered with an eclectic collection of framed artwork, movie posters, and old concert handbills. The back third of the downstairs was a large workshop and garage area where Jake parked his classic black Ford *Mustang* convertible and his motorcycles.

Maddie and EC sat at the bar and watched Jake tape up a four-foot by three-foot detailed map of the city on the movie screen wall.

"Where in the world did you get that?" EC asked.

"Don't ask," Maddie sighed.

Jake turned and scowled at EC.

"Yeah, I know. I know. Radio silence." EC planted his chin in his palm and rolled his eyes.

Maddie silently shook her head.

Finished with the upstairs apartment and the back workshop, Q scanned the mancave under their watchful eye, then headed downstairs into the basement.

"You're clean," Q announced after another half an hour when he emerged from downstairs to declare the building clear of any unauthorized eavesdropping devices. "Now, we're going to have to keep it that way."

"How's that?" Jake asked.

"Really? You really want to know?"

"Humor me."

"We put a chastity belt on your meshnet authentication protocols and upgraded your encryptions with an Enigma XR module."

"Those are illegal, aren't they?" EC asked.

"The bane of national security and law enforcement agencies around the world." Q smiled broadly. "Thank you, Cartel IT department."

"You're right. I don't want to know," Jake said.

"All righty, then. Where's your router?"

Jake pointed towards the workshop.

Q disappeared into the back.

In the meantime, Jake joined Maddie and EC at the bar. "Once he's done, we can set up shop here. Just the four of us."

"Samantha, too," EC said. "She's been doing the heavy lifting on his profile."

Jake nodded. "But she keeps on working her end from Exit Alley. And Q will continue mining the server farm. We gotta keep chumming the digital river with activity to keep Jamal pre-occupied."

"Sands?" Maddie asked.

"Only if and when we have to. My guess is that he'd rather not know about it, so he doesn't have to lie to the Captain or Public Square."

Maddie and EC nodded.

"Now, the hard part."

"What's that?" Maddie asked.

Jake looked at her and grimaced. "We need cutouts."

"Huh?"

"It would be best if we can gather as much evidence and intel as possible without any of our fingerprints showing up on them. We need some fronts to put in the requests and pull that info for us."

"Who?"

"Maybe Wally. His Torso Murder case has gone cold. I'm thinking Derek from District Three. Mr. Ranger, Morgan."

"Why would they help us?" Maddie asked.

"Well, for one, how are the Speck and Wuornos cases going for those guys? From what I read in the media, about as well as Wally's."

"And?"

Jake looked at Maddie, then to EC. He rolled his eyes and nodded back towards Maddie.

"You dog," EC said to Jake.

"What?" Maddie asked.

Jake shrugged.

EC looked Maddie. "He thinks they may not be immune to your feminine charms and wiles."

Maddie scowled at Jake.

"It worked on me." Jake smiled.

"We're all buttoned up," Q announced as he came back from the workshop. He noted the staring contest at the bar. "What did I miss?"

Maddie got up and headed towards the rear exit. "Come on, *partner.*"

EC smiled at Jake, then followed Maddie out.

"Something I said?" Q asked.

"Fuhgeddaboudit!"

Jake went over to the map taped to the wall and began marking with a red Sharpie all the places he could remember being together with Jamal.

~~~

A Little Help from My Friends

Maddie sat at a back booth in Cutty's Deli nursing an iced tea, angry as she usually was when she came around to the conclusion that Jake was right. *Again. Damn it. 'Cause we're in a race against time: Jamal has Amy.*

Her hair was in off-duty mode, unleashed from the usual tight pony tail or from being piled up and pinned on top of her head. It cascaded down and flowed over her shoulders like a wavy red waterfall, framing her face which now carried a bit more mascara and subtle shadow to accent her dark green eyes, accompanied by a deeper shade of red lipstick around her pouting expression. The extra makeup was added when she went back to her condo to change into leg-hugging jeans and a tight, low-cut top revealing the faint splash of freckles on her chest.

Cutty sidled up to the booth and leered at her over a long sip of Scotch from his CPD mug. "Miss…*Madeline?*"

"I don't want to." Maddie pushed her lower lip out even further.

"*Mmmmm…*" Cutty took another long sip, then offered his mug her way. "You need something a bit more, um, fortified?"

Maddie shook her head.

"Where's Jake?"

If her dark green eyes were lasers, two holes would have appeared in Cutty's forehead.

"Whoa. I just thought—"

"Sorry." Maddie's scowl melted back into child-like innocence, then bounced back into a sly smile as she spied Derek, the detective from District Three, coming up behind Cutty.

"Officer Cutler." Derek put his hand on Cutty's shoulder. It was quickly withdrawn when greeted with a glare as if it were pigeon droppings. "Maddie."

Cutty took a sip, eyeballing his goddaughter down the length of his mug, then stepped back to let Derek slide into the booth across from Maddie. "What can I get you, *detective?*"

"I'm off duty, thankfully. How about a Great Lakes Dortmunder?"

Cutty went back to the deli counter and sent a waitress over with Derek's beer.

"You look better every time I see you," He smiled and drank out of the bottle, his eyes never leaving Maddie's face.

She smiled back.

Derek slid his back against the wall and sat sideways in the booth with his leg up on the bench. He surveyed the smattering of deli patrons in for an early dinner before the rush. "So, your dad and Cutty, huh?"

Maddie nodded and sipped her ice tea. "Partners. On patrol."

"And you?"

She quickly fought back a reflexive wince. "I'm between—working with EC on temporary assignment."

"Sanchez…"

Maddie nodded.

"Tough break." Derek took a pull of Dortmunder, then set the bottle down. He twirled it on its bottom rim like a top. "And off the job?"

Maddie blushed and looked away. *Damn it.*

"Yeah, I'll let you take the Fifth on that one...*for now.*" Derek plugged his smile with the bottle.

"So...downtown, again?"

"Yeah, getting to be a too regular thing. Wish it wasn't, but, then again, here *we* are." He cocked an eyebrow her way. "At least my case isn't the lead story *every...single...day* in the news any more. Six bodies down in the Metroparks helped—at least for a little while."

Maddie recalled her similar meeting with Detective Ranger Morgan earlier in the afternoon. It was a much more straightforward conversation.

"But the hungry jackals will be back gnawing on my flea-bit carcass again. Count on it."

"Reporters. They all have their own little agendas," Maddie commented staring off into space shaking her head, thinking about Jamal. "Turn up anything yet?"

"A lot of busy work. Trolling the vics' online activity and accounts. Interviewing the dreck that gets dredged up. Their parents would likely be horrified at some of it, but, really, nothing that called for the archangel of death to visit. I don't know if we're going to find any connection there. Seems almost like a random bolt out of the blue."

"Physical evidence?"

"Nothing. The guy was a ghost." Derek sighed.

The right corner of Maddie's lips turned up slowly in a grim half-smile.

"What?"

"Nobody—I mean nobody wants to hear it. Maybe you don't."

"Hear what?" Derek sat up straight and turned to face Maddie squarely.

Maddie dug in her purse for her notepad and pen. She wrote "Richard Speck" on a page, tore it out, then folded it over, creasing it hard with her fingernails, then folded it tightly again. She placed the paper on the table and held it down with her fingers in front of her.

"You got something?"

Maddie shrugged her shoulders and stared into Derek's eyes.

"What do you want?"

She thought for a long minute, then smiled. "I'm kind of hungry."

"Dinner? I'll get the waitress."

"Not here. Someplace nice."

"Sure…the *Chop House?*"

"Mmmm, yeah. Steer meat." Maddie chuckled to herself, recalling Sanchez's disdain for men: *If we didn't need the calves, they'd all be steers in my book.*

"Okay. Deal." Derek reached for the paper.

Maddie held it down tight. "This probably isn't the help you want."

"I'll take any assistance at all that comes my way at this point."

"And…you'll help me, too, if I come to you."

Derek smiled at the thought of Maddie needing him. "Absolutely."

"Put this away and read it later. Then do the research." Maddie pushed the paper across the table and released it. "And maybe we can help each other."

Derek picked it up and held it in front of his face, turning it, and considering it from every angle. "Thanks."

"Just don't hold it against me."

"Never." Derek reached to take hold of Maddie's hand, but she pulled back.

"Now, put that away, so we can go get something to eat."

Derek stashed the folded paper in his wallet and they got up from the booth.

Cutty tracked his goddaughter as she left the deli with Derek. He put the detective's beer on Jake's tab.

~~~

Suburbia

From behind dark-tinted safety glass, Jamal cast his eyes on the twenty-foot concrete wall along the interstate, allowing it to blur his passing and mask time ill spent as the self-driving car chauffeured him out to the suburbs. He much preferred walking. Sure, the fresh air was invigorating, but casually strolling through his near westside neighborhood or Gordon Square or Edgewater Park or even through the concrete and glass canyons downtown was, counter-intuitively, an active meditative state even better than his quiet time in the Faraday cage in his castle. Beta waves stilled themselves until his mind imitated a calm reflecting pool, opening the gateway to his subconscious to absorb sights, sounds, smells and even the contortions of the air all around from the mechanical turbulence of the wind or the microvariations of temperature due to both natural and man-made causes. He always came home filled with fresh ideas, the genesis of which he savored as a psychological mystery of religious proportions.

But exposing himself in public had become unacceptably risky as of late. He might briefly wander the backstreets and alleys around his lair in the middle of the night or disguise himself for an hour at eight AM or five PM to raft in the gushing ebbs and flows of distracted downtown workers swarming in and out of the Terminal Tower Rapid Transit station like ants. But the exhilaration at flirting with the danger of discovery polluted the calm pool of contemplation with adrenalin, leaving Jamal vaguely unsatisfied and somewhat irritable.

So now he rode out to the suburbs where he cruised the carefully planned subdivisions with their precise grids of residential streets named for all the trees clear-cut to create a middle-class utopia. He savored the illusion of order presented by the regularity of colonial, ranch, and split-level facades lined up along uncracked sidewalks cutting a proper border through unending meadows of closely cropped Kentucky bluegrass. He loved to imagine the chaos and mayhem bound and held captive deep in the closets, basements and attics of the prim and proper abodes. He smiled, because he knew murderers and serial killers were not unknown in this land, too.

But he was a quiet, God-fearing, lawn-cutting, family-loving, neighborly-waving fellow…just like me.

It tickled the dark heart of Jamal's soul.

But these regular joyrides also served a practical purpose, timed as they always were to slow-motion surf rush-hour traffic when the data load was highest on the highways due to the intense hive activity of Vehicle-to-Vehicle speed, direction and location streaming to maintain safe and orderly flow on the roadways. Due to the encryption hardening undertaken by automobile manufacturers to curb hackers from commandeering self-driving cars for "drone riding," it had taken nearly a decade for Jamal to crack the DOT transponder code protocols and develop the masking algorithms to use the shoaling commuters to hide his communications with the outside world via the Atlas Grid, necessary now that Jake and

The Trilogy: The Invisible Mind

Q had possession of the White Chapel facility and his own castle was connection-free.

He regularly pinged his embedded army of Munchausened synthoids to maintain an up-to-date census of serial killers-in-waiting. He checked in on Jake's investigation into *"The Baron"* through police department servers which, unsurprisingly, were as water-tight as the *Titanic* proved to be. He visited a closed DI-7 chat room in the seventh level of cyber-hell deep in the Darknet to read and post cryptic messages from and for the cabal of fans, supporters, and fellow travelers hunkered in the deep shadows of cyberspace.

Jamal was exceedingly pleased that Q had not yet taken the White Chapel server farm off-line so he could continue to pull down the re-gen code and park it in the NSA's online world where it could continue to propagate through the ecosystem of commercial data center service providers around the world.

Before he left suburbia and went off-line, Jamal confirmed the launch of data packets to activate his next murder by Munchausen.

~~~

Fly Fishing

He almost missed it. A water bug's lightning quick skate across a calm pond. The faint stir of dorsal fin momentarily etched in the mirror of water above. The briefest spark of sunlight struck on silver scales to catch a kingfisher's eye.

At two AM, Q still sat on a stool deep in the dim alleyways of silicon, steel, and glass at the White Chapel building, bathed in the neon glow of a server monitor and his laptop screen. He was mining the database tiers again to gain entry to the Baron's impermeable virtual lair buried deep in a dark neighborhood of microchips populating printed circuit boards neatly lined up within their metal enclosures.

Bleary-eyed from hours of watching lines of computer code stream across his screen like whitewater rapids, Q thought his eyes were playing tricks on him.

There it is again.

He hit the spacebar on his laptop to freeze the video screen cap recording of the server monitor. He went back in near time frame-by-frame, then saw it. He was not going crazy. The flow of database coding was interrupted by the insertion of neural networking commands:

```
# Dense Layer
pool2_flat = tf.reshape(pool2, [-1, 7 *7 * 64])
```

```
dense = tf.layers.dense(inputs=pool2_flat,
units=1024, activation=tf.nn.relu)
dropout = tf.layers.dropout(inputs=dense,
rate=0,4, training=mode == learn.modeKeys, TRAIN)
```

Q video-framed forward, and the code insertion disappeared. It reappeared when he went back a frame, then disappeared when he went back a second frame. He went forward to expose the code again.

"Damn." Q slowly smiled. He pulled at the short reddish-brown hairs of his closely-cropped goatee, staring at his laptop screen. "You are sly…but so am I."

The code was a fragment of Tensorflow implementation of standard Convolutional Neural Networking, often used in the vision realm of artificial intelligence. It was a breadcrumb to track the Baron's trail into the Black Tier.

Q spent the hours until dawn fishing for more breadcrumbs and cataloging their memory registers to find the gate to the Black Tier and decrypt the key to unlocking it.

~~~

The Epicenter

Jake sat back twenty feet in an old wooden wheeled office chair. He swiveled slightly to activate the squeak of ungreased bearings, staring at what had become a huge murder board in his mancave. The three-by-four-foot map speckled with red Sharpie dots held center stage on the white movie screening wall, a giant replica of a child's place mat with a connect-the-dots game. Laser printed pages of photographs surrounded the map like suburbs ringing the city. Each contained a gallery of victim portraits from past and present topped by a centered mugshot. Threads of blue sports yarn splayed out from the map connecting crime scene locations with each local victim's picture. At the far-left border of the whitewashed section of wall, copies of bygone hometown newspaper front page stories announcing the arrest of a serial killer terrorizing the community were plastered up next to a portrait of the lead detective. The far-right side displayed an anthology of the online local crime coverage of E.J. Quick. A step ladder stood nearby to reach the quickly vanishing white space left on the top half of the twelve-foot-high wall.

Jake heard the back door open, then close. He stopped swiveling to listen but did not look away from the murder wall. He recognized the ever so slight shuffle of Florsheim shoes on the oak plank floor. Footwear for the office, not the beat.

"Are we paying for all this?" Lt. Sands asked as he stepped up next to Jake and surveyed the wall filled with investigatory puzzle pieces.

"Just the yarn. I kleptoed Sharpies from the office," Jake answered.

Lt. Sands huffed a chuckle. He stepped up close to the wall to take a closer look at the photos. "So…you back up to full speed?"

"I'd say eighty…seventy to eighty percent."

"Good."

"You know, you and your fancy suit are standing in my way."

"Oh, gee, *sorry,*" Lt. Sands said, looking back at Jake over his shoulder. He turned to face the wall again and did not move away.

Jake sighed. He stood up and walked up next to Lt. Sands.

"What do you see?"

"Not what I need to—yet."

"And what's that?"

"The epicenter."

"Huh. Right. Interesting." Lt. Sands looked at Jake, then studied the portraits again. "I'm keeping my finger in the dike as best I can. But I've got this guy from District Three having a serious relationship with my voicemail."

"Derek."

"Yeah. Claims he talked to Maddie. He wants what you got—whatever it is. Bad."

"I don't think you want to do that yet. He's in the Director's office more than the shoe shine boy."

Lt. Sands nodded. "Who else?"

"A Metroparks Ranger," Jake said, tapping the mug shot of Aileen Wuornos. He pointed to the Kingsbury Run area on the map, where blue yarn led back to a picture of Eliot Ness above a series of gruesome crime scene photos of headless murder victims from the 1930s. "Wally in District Four. He's a good guy. He's been by, too. Knows the score and is all in. Haven't met Mr. Ranger or Derek, yet. I don't know. Might have to bring them in from the cold, huh."

"You know the score, Jake. We're out pretty far on this limb."

"Yeah. You keep saying."

"And if the bodies keep piling up…"

"You know the next one is out there, right? Even as we speak." Jake looked at Sands.

"Like I said, if the bodies keep piling up, we're going to have more help than we want. Whether we want it or not."

"More than we need. Nobody wants any suits from DC stomping around."

"Yeah. I know. But, seriously, where are we at on all this?" Lt. Sands waved his arm across the papers taped to the movie wall.

"You know about the kidnappings, right?"

"Kidnappings? Plural? Not just the kid?"

Jake nodded slowly.

"Great. You got something to drink around here?"

"There's some scotch behind the bar."

"Not the cheap stuff Cutty swills."

"Nah. Single malt Glenmorangie Signet."

"Thank you." Lt. Sands took off his suit jacket and hung it on the back of a bar stool. He loosened his tie as he went behind the bar. "You want one?"

"Nah." Jake sat back down in his squeaky chair and began swiveling—and squeaking—again.

Lt. Sands stopped mid-pour and threw a scowl Jake's way. "What, are you three years old? Cut it out."

"What?" Jake spun to look towards the bar.

Lt. Sands dragged a chair over next to Jake and sat. He sipped his scotch, pursing his lips as he savored the flavor. "How's Maddie doing?"

With a long drawn out squeal from the chair spring, Jake leaned way back in his chair. He put his hands behind his head and slowly shook his head.

"This isn't going to get even more complicated, is it?"

"This isn't complicated. It's evil—and that's pretty damn straight forward."

"It may be evil, but our day job is crime solving, not soul saving, and we got bodies stacking up as deep as snow in Buffalo."

"Those are just props—like the furniture on stage at the State Theater. They're in the play, but not part of the plot."

Lt. Sands groaned out loud. "Oh, man, don't ever be saying that to anyone outside this room, okay?"

A long silence hung between the two men.

"But it's true," Jake said softly.

"I know." Lt. Sands sipped his scotch. "But don't ever say that out loud, again. *Ever.* I won't be able to save you like last time and your career in law enforcement will definitely be over for good. As in roll credits. *Fin…*The End."

Jake just stared at the murder wall.

~~~

Breaking Bread

Bill brought them down one-by-one. First the street urchin.

He watched Bill seat her to his right, nearly halfway down the absurdly long dining room table, first cuffing the D-ring on the back of the thick, pad-locked leather belt to the slats in the back of the chair, then her ankles to the front legs. Her handcuffed hands were separated by enough chain, threaded through a D-ring on the front of the belt, to allow her to eat, yet without permitting enough wind-up to throw any cutlery or glassware—at least not very far or to any great effect. Jamal smiled ever so slightly at the heat of the glare Amy threw his way.

This was Amy's first opportunity to put eyes on Jamal since her abduction before the raid on the White Chapel building in the Flats. Once the video was made to taunt the police, he locked her away alone in the castle safe room. She studied her captor's face as he slouched back in his chair at the head of the table, his smile hidden behind the steeple of index fingers above clasped hands, pressed against his lips. A bland, yet eerily calm expression masked his thoughts, though his deep black eyes met, welcomed, and seemed even to embrace the hatred in Amy's glare. Amy did not comprehend what their staring contest was about, but she could feel herself losing.

Jamal felt no arousal but saw in Amy's finely sculpted features and rich brunette hair that she would one day mature into a strikingly exotic beauty…*if allowed.*

Bill brought the waitress, shuffling submissively, to her place setting on the left. Her blonde hair hung down about her bowed head, shrouding her face. After being shackled to her chair, waitress Amy stared down into her empty plate.

Amy unlocked from Jamal's eyes to look across the table at her fellow prisoner, whose half-closed eyes gazed into an abyss beyond her empty plate like a dazed junkie. She began to fear what she, too, might become.

The waitress was also pretty in a suburbanly girl-next-door kind of way, Jamal thought, *but not quite worthy of a pedestal like Maddie or the grown-up version of the young orphan.* He sat up straight in his chair and in a soft, smooth baritone voice greeted his guests, *"Ladies*…I trust you have brought your appetites."

He nodded to Bill, who went around the table filling their wine glasses with a blood-red Cabernet. He placed the bottle in front of Jamal, then retreated to the kitchen.

Jamal smiled warmly at the surprise on the young orphan's face. He nodded.

Amy hesitated halfway in her reach for the wine glass. She looked to head of the table, as if for permission.

Jamal lifted his own glass to encourage her on.

She brought the glass close to her lips. Sniffed, then gingerly sipped.

Jamal swirled his wine as he watched closely the youngster's exploration into adulthood, then tested the wine himself.

Waitress Amy aroused from her stupor with a jerk. She grabbed her glass and gulped, stopping only when she inhaled instead of swallowed. She coughed hard into her arm, nearly spilling her wine.

Jamal looked, then turned back to the youngster to his right and rolled his eyes. She responded with a hurried second sip.

Bill came out of the kitchen with a tray of lobster bisque. He served them and left.

"I trust you have been well taken care of by Bill and Stephanie," Jamal said.

"I don't know why I am here," waitress Amy said in a hoarse whisper.

"We are here to break bread and enjoy a special meal. Stephanie is quite the culinary artiste."

"No. *Why am I here?*" she whined.

"Life is suffering, my dear…" Jamal tested his bisque and smiled. "But there is no reason for it to be completely unbearable. Please. Try your soup. I hope neither of you are vegetarian. We're having medallions of beef tenderloin with peppercorn sauce, wild rice, and a lemon broccoli that is simply delicious. I do not know what her secret is, but it is amazing. And that is just the vegetable."

"What are you going to do with us?" orphan Amy asked softly.

"That, I am afraid, is a chapter that has not yet been written." He looked at the young girl. "Please. Eat. Do not let your bisque cool."

She set down her wine and tried the soup.

Jamal again savored the child's reaction to her first taste. He turned to waitress Amy. "You, too.

After they finished, Bill magically appeared to clear their bowls.

"You are aware, of course, of your…um, *utility,* shall we

say." The Baron sipped his wine, then asked orphan Amy, "Do you know our friend, Jake?"

She shrugged.

"Well, perhaps, you are not aware of his deep feelings for the red-headed detective who took you off the streets." Jamal turned to waitress Amy. "I am sorry. But you do know how he feels. Deep down. Right?"

Waitress Amy replied with only a heavy sigh. She stared at the empty space where her bisque had been.

"But what does that have to do with me?" orphan Amy asked.

"Well…"

"You can't just do this to people—to us," waitress Amy sobbed.

The Baron smiled. "Oh, but I can. In fact, I have."

Waitress Amy shrunk back into mute submission.

"But why?" asked orphan Amy.

Jamal smiled as he scratched at his new, closely-cropped beard, contemplating the question. "Why do you live on the streets when there is no reason to? After all, Miss Madeline saw to it you were placed safely, comfortably in a nice home in the suburbs."

"I dunno."

"Hmmm…I think perhaps you do, but you will not admit it."

Orphan Amy shrugged.

"It is hard—harder living that way. But…" The Baron leaned in to look directly into Amy's eyes like a stern father. "Tell me the truth. It is hard, yes? But it is more…*real.*"

Amy stared back, then gave a quick nod.

"Precisely. For quite some while now, our lives—everyone's lives have become increasingly *unreal*—broken down. Fragmented. Self-pixelated, if you will." Jamal sat back and smiled at his own allusion. "All fancy themselves as digital deities—avatars—it is Hindu, you know. One really must admire the utter *hubris* of even the most common of mankind. *They are worthless.* To themselves. To everyone. Can they look you in the eye? Can they even truly understand another anymore? Or do they even care to. I think not."

Waitress Amy looked up quizzically.

Jamal stood and picked up the bottle of wine. He went to her side and towered over her. "Do you understand what I am saying?"

The blonde slouched back in her chair, crossing her arms over her breasts. She shook her head and stared at the wine pouring into her glass.

"Mmmm. I did not think so." Jamal walked around the table to orphan Amy. As he refreshed her glass, he said softly, "But I believe you do. Deep down. Though you may not see it, yet. For, you know, we are quite alike. Much more than you think."

She reached for her wine as soon as he lifted the bottle away to mask herself with a sip.

Jamal emptied the bottle into his own glass and sat back down at the head of the table. He stared into his wine and spoke in a rising voice, with a harsher tone, "Their white picket fences will not—*cannot* hold back hell from the purgatory of their own making behind all the false facades of their petty, soulless profiles."

His anger reverberated back fear on their faces as both girls stared towards the head of the table.

The Baron sipped his wine, then in a calm, quiet voice said, "And so purgatory shall be purged."

"What do you mean?" asked orphan Amy meekly.

"If they refuse to seek, then you bring it to them." Jamal sighed. "As you well know, reality has great cleansing properties. So, you bring it to those who refuse to partake."

Bill entered the pause in conversation to serve their entrees.

"So, let us break bread, then," Jamal said in his soft, smooth baritone voice after Bill left the room. "Please, eat. Enjoy."

And the three ate dinner in silence.

~~~

M.I.A.

Maddie and EC waited in the sumptuous reception area of the Stein, Baylor & Stein law firm outside the elevators on the thirty-fourth floor of the Tower at Erieview. EC perused artwork valued in the millions in the huge gallery of a lobby, strolling and pausing in front of original oils and watercolors on the walls and pedestaled sculptures as if he were visiting the Cleveland Museum of Art.

Maddie found and sat in the lone stuffed leather chair positioned to allow a sliver of a view of Lake Erie through the glass walls of the lobby, down a long hall and through the open door of a much-coveted partner's office facing north. Storm clouds gathered over the water. Whitecaps pushed relentlessly toward shore. Maddie watched blankly, lost in that moment of time until the feel of a colony of ants on her calves presaged the tsunami of a hot flash that hit her like a breakwall. She closed her eyes and waited for the inevitable ebb. After, her mind backfilled with thoughts of the young girl she had tried and failed to save from the dangers of a life on the streets in the Flats. Fear for Amy in the hands of the Baron stirred the vortex of these internal storms.

Someone at Stein, Baylor & Stein called to report one of their Personal Services Assistants, used for file and document retrieval, had gone missing. Such a call was unusual—like citizens too embarrassed or guilt-ridden to report their handgun being stolen—even though it was required by federal law. Civilian owners and operators typically turned to private tech firms to trace and track their errant synthoids. Most times, the disappearance resulted from a programming glitch in the unit's location services algorithms. Annoying, but harmless. Less frequently, larceny was involved, which made it a matter for Robbery/Homicide. But truth be told, android bounty hunters gave those disappearances a much higher priority than detectives who were already swamped investigating crimes committed by and against humans, which Maddie knew first hand. Besides, the private sector more often produced results with the prompt return of the missing PSA before it was smuggled out of the country or run through a chop shop for its parts and precious metals. When a malware hit for ill intent was suspected—as Lt. Sands feared in this instance—the case was referred to ACU, which he did forthwith without the usual bureaucratic routing of intake paperwork, instead calling Maddie directly to send them there in person.

A tall blonde woman in a tailored business suit came to the door of the lobby to escort them in. "Come this way, please."

Her beauty made even Maddie stare.

Without introduction or chit-chat the woman led them to a small, darkly paneled and windowless conference room. "Donald will be with you shortly."

EC stared at the closed door and whistled.

Maddie cleared her throat. "And Samantha?"

EC shook his head as they sat on the side of the table facing the door. "I've still got a pulse, you know."

Men. Maddie just smiled.

Precisely three minutes later, Donald marched into the room. "Please, officers, don't get up."

Maddie, who made no move to stand up, deduced from the military-style cut of his sandy-colored hair, perfect posture, muscular build, and impeccably bland dark suit the firm had probably recruited Wilkinson from the Secret Service.

EC stood to shake his hand.

"Donald Wilkinson, Vice President of Security Services for the firm."

"Maddie." She shook his hand with a demur smile. "In the Corps?"

"No, ma'am. Navy. SEALs."

"And after?"

"The Department of Homeland Security."

I knew it.

Donald sat down across from EC and Maddie. He folded his hands on top of a manila folder. "So, to what does Stein, Baylor and Stein owe the pleasure of this visit?"

"The firm recently reported a missing Personal Services Assistant unit," EC explained.

Donald looked at EC. He looked at Maddie and smiled broadly. "So, to what does Stein, Baylor and Stein owe the pleasure of this visit?"

"Why would you ask?" Maddie reached out and tapped the top of the manila file folder. "I assume you are aware that a report was made."

"Of course. It is a federal regulation for any civilian owner and operator of synthetic humanoids to do so. And Stein, Baylor and Stein is a legal firm which, of course, holds itself to the highest standards of integrity. I am just curious as to why this particular report—unlike the two prior made by our firm and the dozens made by or handled on behalf of the firm's clients—has finally brought the police to our door. In the past, these matters were dealt with…directly, privately."

Maddie looked at EC, then sat up straight in her chair, arching her back and folding her hands together on the table in front of her. The smile left her face. "Mr. Wilkinson—"

"Please. Call me Donald."

*"Mr. Wilkinson…*We are not from Robbery/Homicide. We are not here concerning the possible theft of your PSA. We are from the Artificial Crimes Unit, which investigates felonies perpetrated through the illicit use of synthetic humanoids. And the report provided by Stein, Baylor and Stein was, let's say, perfunctory with very little investigatory information of value."

"Surely, you don't think the firm—"

"We do not." Maddie sighed heavily. "Can we be assured of the firm's cooperation in keeping our conversation completely confidential?"

EC whispered at his partner, *"Maddie…"*

Wilkinson looked from Maddie to EC, then back to Maddie.

"I can arrange for you to speak with our commanding officer, if you like. But…you should know, time is of the essence in our investigation. And lives are at stake."

"I am intrigued." Wilkinson sat back and smiled.

"Do we have your cooperation? And Stein, Baylor and Stein's?"

"Yes. Of course. How can we help you?"

"You are aware, of course, of the murders of nine nurses in University Circle and the six bodies found recently in the Metroparks."

The smile evaporated from Wilkinson's face. "I am."

"You are probably not aware that a child and young woman have been kidnapped."

The executive's face hardened into that of a former Secret Service agent whose character and personality had been razed and rebuilt by the Naval Special Warfare Command on the sandy beaches at Coronado, California.

"Have you employed the services of a recovery agent?"

"That is something we handle with in-house staff."

"Excellent. When can we meet with your team?"

"Wait here, and I'll arrange for it directly." Wilkinson got up and left the conference room.

"Maddie, do you think this is wise?" EC asked.

"I don't know. But we'd obviously be wasting our time otherwise." Maddie put her elbows on the table and rested her forehead against her fingers.

The door opened. EC's blossoming elation at the reappearance of the blonde who led them there quickly wilted as she was followed in by a waiter pushing a serving cart of coffee, soft drinks, and pastries. *What the hell…*"

The blonde was brought up short by the unexpected greeting.

Maddie looked up and stared the food service synthoid directly in its cold, artificial eyes as it stood at attention beside the cart, awaiting their beverage selection.

"Mr. Wilkinson said he would be a few more minutes yet before he returned. Would either of you care for refreshments?" She noticed Maddie staring at the PSA. "Right, then. I'll just leave the cart. Please, help yourself. Roland, come with me."

"Unbelievable," EC said after the pair left.

Maddie just shook her head.

EC got up and inspected the assortment of cookies, bite-sized brownies, and mini cannoli. "Do you want anything?"

"No, thank you."

The conference room door opened. Wilkinson held it open for a tall, thin, white-haired authority figure. He was followed in by a veritable black-haired clone of Wilkinson, then Wilkinson himself. The door was quickly pulled closed.

"Officers. Welcome. I am Lance Baylor, senior partner." He greeted Maddie and EC each with a nod in their direction, then went directly to the food cart and poured himself a cup of coffee. "Donald, here, has filled me in on your earlier discussion. The firm appreciates your forthrightness. I will see to it that you have the unfettered assistance of our firm to help resolve this unfortunate situation as quickly as possible."

"Thank you," Maddie said.

"However." Baylor sat down directly opposite Maddie, flanked by Wilkinson and his clone. "We need assurances of reciprocity with regards to confidentiality. Then, we can have the most productive conversation for the benefit of all."

"For a robot file clerk?" EC asked.

The question hung in the air as Baylor focused his full attention on Maddie, awaiting an answer to his proposition.

She slowly nodded. "Certainly."

"Very good." Baylor sipped his coffee.

"The missing PSA was no mere file clerk," Wilkinson explained. "As do other firms of our size, with our involvement with major corporate entities, we handle many confidential matters with regards to trade secrets, mergers and acquisitions, joint venture negotiations, and the like, so we must be sensitive to any and all attempts to breech attorney-client privilege. We are careful not only in implementing secure communications protocols, but often times we find it necessary to camouflage the movements and meetings of our client principals and our partners, so as not to leave breadcrumbs for others to map their activities and thereby draw conclusions about the intents of our clients. Sometimes, it involves masking the N numbers of corporate jets in flight plans, making safe house arrangements for face-to-face meetings, and…" Wilkinson looked at Baylor, who nodded, then continued. "And, in this case, using PSAs as secure couriers of legal documents."

"You can well imagine, then, our concern for confidentiality in this incident," Baylor said.

"Exactly what kind of documents?" Maddie asked Baylor. "And where were they being delivered?"

"It was the final, executed agreement for a, um, major business acquisition for one of our wealthier clients," Wilkinson said.

"Who is that?" EC asked.

"The who is not important," Baylor said curtly. "It is the *what* which has us most concerned. You see, the documents were being delivered with the private key for a cryptocurrency payment to complete the transaction."

"How much?" Maddie asked.

Baylor sighed heavily. "Four hundred and fifty million dollars."

"Holy cow." EC whistled.

"Quite."

"And you just sent this droid off into the world on its merry way with four hundred and fifty million dollars?" Maddie asked.

"First of all, fail-safe procedures were implemented in the event of a hostile act against the unit's will—I mean, of course, in violation of its preprogrammed mission profile—which purges the secured memory locations holding the data and keys and overwrites them seven times," Wilkinson explained defensively. "So, there is nothing physical to steal except the synthoid. And an act of theft would trigger the fail-safe protocol."

"And second?" asked EC.

"Of course, the delivery was monitored electronically from our operations center here, as well as being physically shadowed by human operatives."

Wait for it, Maddie told herself. She smiled. "But…"

"Somehow, the unit mistakenly got into the wrong *Uber* for the route segment to the airport Sheraton drop location and disappeared."

Wilkinson's dark-haired clone bowed his head, leaving no doubt who would take the fall for the breach in security.

"The wrong *Uber?*" Maddie looked at EC incredulously.

"We have a corporate contract with them for Level One secure livery services." Baylor said. "We've never had any issues in the past. Ever."

"I don't think that was the wrong *Uber,*" EC said.

"It was the wrong one according to our plan," Wilkinson argued.

"Yeah, well, Custer had a plan, too," Maddie mocked. "And so did Crazy Horse."

EC chuckled at her quoting one of Jake's more well-worn retorts.

"I think someone else had a plan, too. And that someone hacked and hijacked your unit. So, if this 'Plan B' was not sensed as a hostile act?" Maddie asked, looking at Baylor, then Wilkinson.

"Then the fail-safe protocols may not have triggered," Wilkinson revealed.

Baylor sighed. "So, the contract and crypto key would remain intact."

"And the Baron now has four hundred and fifty million dollars." Maddie closed her eyes. She felt the lava-like heat and pressure of another hot flash building toward eruption within her chest.

~~~

The Tears of a Clown

Jake met Lt. Sands at the crime scene. "This is no coincidence."

"No. No, it is not." Lt. Sands sighed. "One block further west, and it's out of our jurisdiction."

They stared at the sheet covering the victim's body which had been dumped beside the railroad tracks behind the GFS store on West 117th Street.

Jake looked down the tracks west, towards his apartment, then to the east.

"Don't worry. Norfolk and Southern is holding their freight traffic until we're done here," Sands said.

"Where's Maddie?"

"I want you on this one. You and me."

"Okay…"

Lt. Sands motioned over the Coroner's tech to pull back the sheet, revealing the naked body of a woman in her twenties.

The first thing that caught Jake's eye was the face garishly painted like a clown. He stepped over and leaned in to more closely examine her circus mask, then looked up at Lt. Sands.

Lt. Sands pointed to the victim's chest.

Jake looked down and saw that the left breast had been removed. "Oh."

"Yeah."

Jake took out his phone and snapped a picture of the victim's face. He did a photo search. "Huh."

"What is it?"

Jake stepped back over to show Lt. Sands the results. "Pretty close match.

Lt. Sands looked at the picture on the phone, then the victim. He looked at the phone and pointed to the face on the screen. "Who's that?"

"Pogo the Clown."

"Again, who's that?"

"Also known as John Wayne Gacy. More than thirty killings. In Chicago."

"Damn."

They looked back at the dead woman.

"But this is not his MO. And definitely not his preference in victim," Jake said.

"Men?"

Jake nodded.

"So, what does this mean?"

"I don't know." Jake shook his head. "I don't know."

A second body was found later that afternoon east along the railroad tracks on Whiskey Island. A third body was discovered near dusk on the other side of downtown where the railway passed Gordon Park. Both victims had been mutilated in the same way with their faces made up to look like Pogo the Clown.

~~~

Search and Recovery

Q couldn't quite believe it when he first saw the unencrypted incoming video stream at the server farm. Hands methodically folding and neatly stacking a coat, blouse, skirt, stockings, and shoes on a beach. Then, a semi-automatic pistol carefully placed on top. He saw the orange and white "crib"—the municipal water system intake station four miles out from shore—as the view panned the horizon from the deep darkness west to the soft pink glow of sunrise behind the downtown skyscrapers to the east. Waves lapped at the beach. A slow march towards Canada began. Sand gave way to nothing but water, rising step-by-step, until the splash from cresting waves blurred the lenses on artificial eyes. Then, a few murky moments before the feed went dark.

His gut knotted hard. Even an inanimate death is unsettling.

Q called Maddie.

She met EC at Edgewater Park. They called the Coast Guard, then bagged and tagged the pistol and each item of clothing. By the time all the evidence was collected, inventoried, boxed, and locked in the trunk of EC's *Crown Vic*, a medium response boat ringed in orange searched in close to the shoreline. Forty-five minutes later, an orange helicopter arrived from the Coast Guard Station in Detroit.

EC parked himself on a bench to watch the chopper fly an ever-expanding search grid over the lake.

Maddie went back to the beach to amble along its length and back, just beyond the reach of expiring waves.

Rush hour traffic on the Shoreway had dissipated when the helicopter began hovering over the east end of Whiskey Island. Maddie watched as the motorboat gunned its twin outboard engines and banked around in a tight U-turn to speed off to the east. Twenty minutes later, the helicopter headed north. EC got a phone call and waved Maddie back. She followed his *Crown Vic* to the Coast Guard station downtown between Burke Lakefront Airport and the Rock and Roll Hall of Fame to meet the search boat.

The female synthoid brought ashore strapped to the stretcher was still eerily life-like. It's Dermaloy skin had not wrinkled after all the hours in the water. The open eyes were unhazed, their blue-gray color still clear. There was no smell of death, just lake. A demur smile taunted the detectives.

EC called Puff and Bob from the Technical Forensic Lab to come retrieve the unit.

Maddie called Morgan at the Metroparks Ranger station. "It's over…at least for you."

"You sure?" he asked.

"We found a Bersa three-eighty with lavender grips with the body—I mean, the synthoid. Well, among the effects left behind. Anyway, I'm willing to give odds that the ballistics will match the park victims. I'll let you know for sure when I get the report."

"Thanks. What do you need from me?"

"A little more time to get our guy."

"You getting close?"

Maddie sighed. "Closer."

"Sure. I'll hold 'em off as long as I can. But you know how the powers-that-be are sometimes."

"Thanks. I appreciate it."

When they got back to Exit Alley, Derek from District Three was there in the parking lot, leaning against the front quarter panel of his car. As Maddie and EC approached, he called out, "You promised me, you know."

"Go on," Maddie said to EC.

"You sure?"

"I'll be there in a minute."

EC shrugged. He watched back over his shoulder as he walked to the entrance, then let himself into Exit Alley with the evidence from the beach.

"Hi, Derek." Maddie smiled. "What brings you downtown?"

"I thought we had, you know, *an understanding.*" Derek smiled back. "You haven't been returning my calls."

"Perhaps you *mis*-understood our understanding."

"A nice dinner. Fine wine. I even sprung for dessert. Then?" Derek wagged his finger at Maddie. "Crickets. What's a guy supposed to think?"

"Are we talking shop, here? Or…"

"Hey, Derek," Lt. Sands called out. He stood at the door to Exit Alley flanked by Jake and a linebacker-sized man with a crew cut. "Thanks for coming."

Saved by the bell. Maddie smiled and waved at the trio.

"To be continued?" Derek asked Maddie.

"Come on. Let's get started." Lt. Sands waved them over.

"Hi, Wally," Maddie said to the Detective from District Four who was investigating a Torso Murders copycat. "Find any new headless horsemen, lately?"

"No. Not lately." Wally chuckled. "Good to see you, too, though."

Lt. Sands held open the door.

"Hi, Jake," Maddie said as she breezed by, followed by Derek and Wally.

Jake sighed, then went into Exit Alley.

Lt. Sands squeezed, then roughly patted Jake's shoulder from behind as they walked to the small conference room.

Q, Samantha, and EC were already seated around the table. Maddie quickly grabbed the seat next to EC closest to the head of the table where Lt. Sands would conduct the meeting. Jake sat next to Q at the far end with Derek and Wally.

Lt. Sands held up his phone and powered it down, then pushed it towards the center of the table. "Ante up, everybody."

When everyone's phones were off on the table, Lt. Sands sat down.

"You didn't bring in Morgan from the Park Rangers?" EC asked.

"We're going to keep it in the family for now." Lt. Sands pointed down the table at Derek and Wally. "Jake's painted the broad strokes for you guys and the ACU tie-in to your cases. Right? Synthoid copycats of Speck and the Torso Murder case."

They nodded.

"Well, we've had three more victims show up within a twelve-hour period—one west side, one downtown, and one on the east side. Based on the coroner's estimated TODs, highly unlikely that there is only one AnSub. Probably three. Not even AI is smart enough to figure out how to be three places at once."

"But one of them could have done the nurses, though, huh?" Derek asked.

"Possibly, but…" Lt. Sands looked at Q.

"Possible, but not likely," Q said. "At least not without reprogramming. He's replacing the personality and occupational specialty libraries with the specifics to recreate past serial killers. First, he'd have to flush and refresh repeatedly, which is more likely to leave metadata markers in the Atlas Grid. Second, the only two synthoids reported missing so far are the au pair and the law firm's unit. I think he may be returning them after the crimes to keep them *on* the grid—hidden in plain sight."

"And the female droid washed up on Whiskey Island this morning," Maddie said. "The date-time stamp on the video stream puts her at Edgewater within twenty-four hours of the latest murders, so it's a possibility for the downtown victim, but unlikely. The au pair's spree in the park was with a gun. All men and no mutilations. Totally different M.O."

"What have you got on these latest ones, Jake?" Lt. Sands asked.

"The clown faces are definitely Gacy—John Wayne Gacy. A Cook County serial killer in the Seventies convicted of thirty-three killings." Jake passed a set of pictures around the table.

"What's the clown deal?" Wally asked, looking over the painted faces of the victims.

"Get this, the guy used to dress up like Bozo and do kids' birthday parties and fundraising events. He'd even march in holiday parades," Jake answered. "But Gacy's victims were all teenage boys."

"But these latest vics are all women," Lt. Sands said.

"So, what gives?" asked Derek.

"He's taunting us."

"Who?"

"The Baron. The amputation of the left breast is the signature of another series of Chicago killings by a gang of four Satan worshipers called the Ripper Crew. Suspected in the murders of eighteen women."

"And the Gacy connection?" Maddie asked.

"Gacy was in the construction business and the leader of the Ripper Crew, a guy named Gecht, did some painting or spackling or something for him as a subcontractor."

"So, we're three-deep into a series of eighteen," EC said.

"Yup. And like with Speck, the Ripper Crew only got caught 'cause one of their victims inadvertently survived and later IDed them." Jake shook his head. "The Baron's not going to let that happen again."

"And there are two, if not three, AnSubs on the loose out there," Lt. Sands said. "A major escalation—and this is on top of two abductions, which we still haven't figured out how they fit in with the Munchausen murders, right?"

Jake and Q both shook their heads.

"So, you two…" Lt. Sands pointed at Derek and Wally. "Are now part of our rag-tag task force. We gotta stop this guy. Fast."

"Does corporate know?" Jake asked.

"I've briefed the Chief one-on-one. Whether he's told the Director yet is his call, but I don't think he'll carry the weight on this for long, so we need to figure out a plan, cause I'm sure Reagan is going to have some hard questions on all this once he finds out. Q, what have you got?"

"The Baron has to still be communicating with the Munchausened units somehow to activate them. He used to wormhole through NSA servers, but there's nothing popping there, so he has to have found another channel."

"And the server farm in the flats?"

Q glanced quickly at Jake beside him. "Nothing, yet. There's something in there in a heavily firewalled and encrypted tier. I just haven't breeched it yet."

Lt. Sands looked at Jake, then back to Q. "Do it. Just get it done. Jake, what have you got off the wall?"

"Off-the-wall?" Jake grinned.

Lt. Sands replied with a no-nonsense look.

"Still connecting the dots. My gut says he's a westsider. Activities are slanted that way."

"Figure it out. Pronto. Okay, EC, you coordinate the tech side. Vet through what Samantha's come up with in her profiling and put a damn gun to Q's head—if you have to—to crack those servers. Wally, you're with Maddie on the au pair and Stein-Baylor angle." Lt. Sands looked down the table at Jake and smiled. "Jake…Derek here is going to help out with the Ripper Crew murders."

"Yes, sir." Jake saluted.

"Don't call me sir."

"Yes, sir."

"Remember, there's a woman and a young girl who need to be found, ASAP. Find the Baron and we'll find them—*before it's too late.*"

The room went silent.

"Well, what are you waiting for?"

The meeting quickly broke up and the teams went their separate ways.

~~~

Destroyer of Worlds

Amy's stomach growled with hunger. When the key hit the door, the youngster sat up eagerly at the edge of the bed, ready to receive her dinner wondering why it was so late. But when the door opened and Jamal came into the room dragging a bentwood chair behind him, she reflexively pushed herself back against the headboard and pulled her knees up to her chest.

The Baron set the chair at the end of the bed and sat. He smiled at Amy.

Bill came in behind him with a bottle of wine and two glasses on a serving tray. He poured a splash into one of the glasses and handed it to Jamal, who swirled, sniffed, sipped, then nodded his approval. Bill poured a glass and handed it to Amy. He filled Jamal's glass then left, closing the door behind him.

Jamal saluted by cocking his glass in Amy's direction.

Amy took a quick gulp of wine.

"Now, child…" Jamal's voice was soft and smooth. "You are young and still…petite. Sip and savor."

Amy nodded. She took a dainty sip.

Jamal drank. His steady gaze unnerved the child, and she drank again. "Have you heard of a man, a man named Oppenheimer? A scientist, actually."

Amy shook her head.

"Not surprising. No, I suppose not."

"What do you want with me?"

Jamal bounced with a slight laugh. "No. Not what I want of you. What is it *you* want?"

"To go home."

"Home? And where, exactly, is home?"

Amy cast her eyes into her wine and sipped.

"Precisely. You know, we are not so much unalike, you and I."

"Yeah? How's that?"

"In the end, it is of little matter. Except, for you to know that. And remember it."

"Okay."

They sat, only their sips scratching softly at the silence between them.

"So, this Oppenheimer. He fancied himself a destroyer of worlds. And though he did, indeed, terrorize an entire generation of human beings on this planet with his…discovery, he ultimately failed in his god-like pretensions. After all, here we are—still. No?"

"He sounds like a bad guy."

"Mmmm, no. Not really. You know how sometimes the smartest geniuses in the world are the dumbest people in the room? They have the world before their eyes—even in their grasp—and yet remain unconscious to its true meaning."

Amy shrugged. "Are you a bad guy?"

"I am sure there are many who most sincerely believe I am. But those who might also spend their lives denying pain and misbelieving evil to be an imperfection in the world their perfect God created. It is not."

"Are *you* a destroyer of worlds?"

"No. I am not a god. More like…a lowly agent of change."

"What change?"

"You have chosen, right? You return to the streets again and again to live a hard life—much harder than need be. Why?" Jamal sipped and waited, but Amy did not answer. "The story is as old as stories themselves. In suffering, there is redemption. The only real truth each and every one of us all see in complete clarity is pain. It is a primal truth. It is truth without words. The truth before words."

"Are you going to hurt me?"

The Baron smiled. "No. I'm here to save you…if I am allowed."

"I—but…"

He savored the chaos of Amy's thoughts etched in confusion on her face. Jamal stood and picked up his chair. "I'll send Stephanie in with your dinner."

~~~

The Floater

"You'll like these guys. They're a hoot," Maddie said to Wally as they got to the door of the Technical Forensics Lab.

"Colorful characters are they?"

"You could say so."

Wally held open the door for Maddie. "After you, darling."

Maddie smiled and entered. "Hi, boys."

"Well, well, well. Looky here, Puff. We got company." Bob abandoned his partner leaning over the female synthoid at the workbench. He extended out his hand to shake. "I'm Bob. That there is Puff."

Puff waved a Phillips-head screwdriver without looking up.

"Yeah. I'm Wally," he said, looking around warily at the robot heads, hands, and feet dangling from the ceiling against the walls and spilling out of plastic bins on the shelves. "So, Bob, how do you guys decorate for Halloween?"

Bob looked around. He chuckled. "Welcome to ghoul town, friend, where every day is Samhain."

"If it's not Scottish, *it's crrrap,*" Wally said with a heavy brogue. "I had a feeling about you guys."

"Criminy crackers, already." Puff looked up from the android torso. "We're on the clock here, people. Teatime ain't until four."

"Don't let him fool you," Maddie whispered to Wally. "He really missed me."

"I heard that, young lady. The only missing I'll be doing is all of you people at happy hour—*Not.*"

"Now, Puff. Where's your manners," scolded Bob. "He's just cranky that you called us out of the lab first thing this morning, before he had a chance to finish his coffee."

"Sorry, Puff. But what's a poor girl to do when she's in need of help?"

"Yeah, well, dang it all," Puff grumbled. He pointed down at the synthoid pulled out of the lake. "So, what's the deal with Mary Poppins, here?"

"Mary Poppins?" Wally asked. "Really?"

"Yup. Really," answered Bob. He looked up earnestly at Wally and adjusted the wire-rimmed glasses on his nose. "Funny thing most folks don't know is that when this whole deal was just getting off the ground, the android guys in the Valley secretly went to their Hollywood buddies down south and licensed up as many characters as they could—especially from beloved old G-rated classics. See, they figured that if the units resembled familiar faces from the big screen, that John and Jane Q. Public would subconsciously feel more comfortable having robots hanging around them all the time. We ran the feature set ID and this one was modeled on an actress named Andrews from the mid-nineteen hundreds."

"As in Julie?" Wally asked.

"The very one."

"Sure, sure. Makes perfect sense for daycare work."

"Oh, no. Don't tell me you're an old movie buff, too?" Maddie asked Wally. *Just like Jake.*

"You should see my collection. I've got a copy of the original *Mary Poppins.*"

Maddie shook her head in silence.

"Hey, *Professor*. You done with your damn lecture yet?"

"Cool your jets, there, Puff. Most folks like hearing a little inside info."

"I get my fill of shop. I don't need no talkin' about it—and yer yappin' ain't making my day go any faster."

Bob shook his head and rolled his eyes for Maddie and Wally. "See what I put up with."

"So, what have you found so far?" Maddie asked.

"This one ain't no mermaid," said Puff. "Droids and water definitely don't play nice together."

"Damaged bad?" asked Wally.

"Just lucky it wasn't salt water."

"Of course, first off, we pulled the Three Laws chip," Bob said. "Tested bad. Ran the manufacturer's serial number, and it's actually supposed to be installed in a unit registered to the Naperville Household Hazardous Waste Facility near Chicago."

"Don't tell me," Wally said. "That synthoid is present and accounted for."

"Yup, yup, yup. Pulled the cert records from the database for this A-VIN. Mandated inspection was done last September by NEOdroid Services in Brookpark. It all seemed to be in order, but then we ran the license number of the tech who signed off on it."

"And he's deader than this here floater," said Puff. "Hit by a bus and kilt, four years ago."

"Yup. So, we called and NEOdroid said they farmed the work out to—"

"White Chapel," Maddie said. "In the Flats."

"Yup."

"Should have known." Maddie looked at Wally. "The Baron's lair—or used to be—until SWAT took it down. That's where Jake was attacked."

"That's about all we know so far," Bob said. "It'll take us some time to dry things out and pull the data for Q's gang."

"And we'll know a whole lot more a whole lot quicker if you get out of our hair already," Puff stood upright and squinted at Maddie.

"I missed you, too, Puff," Maddie whispered.

Puff's scowl melted ever so slightly at the corners of his lips and eyes.

~~~

Partners

"Totally iced-out place," Derek said as he prowled around the perimeter surveying Jake's mancave. "So, do people ever wander in off the streets thinking they can buy stuff—what with the storefront and display windows and all?"

"Used to. Especially just after Mom and Pop's shop closed down," Jake answered. He tossed his keys on the bar. He went around and grabbed a couple of bottled waters out of the refrigerator. "Most of the locals know better. A few stop by for a beer instead. You know, in the summertime when the door's open. Most give the shield a wide berth."

"Lots of nefarious activity out on the streets?"

"No more than usual, particularly later in the evening around the bars. But, hey, live and let live. Even dog catchers get to clock out at the end of the day."

Derek circled back around and met Jake in front of the murder wall. He took the water Jake offered, cracked off the cap and drank. "So...you and red, huh."

Jake smiled. "Yeah. We were partners."

"Were?"

Jake just smiled.

"Her dad retired out of the uniform, right? Him and Cutty. Thick as thieves—or so I hear."

"You checking up on her?"

"Just doing my homework. You know, due diligence and all." Derek took a long pull off his water. "Wouldn't you?"

"Harry was my training officer."

"Oh, so you go way back with the family."

"I got…*history.*"

"Hmmm. Interesting choice of words." Derek winked at Jake. He stepped over to the wall and started reading the postings. "So, I take it the jumbo-sized murder board is here to keep the NSA and SVR from poaching and solving our cases right out from under our noses. A little paranoid, don't you think?"

"Q swept the joint and hardened my net connection. So, we're good." Jake parked himself in his old office chair and started rocking slightly to excite the spring's squeaky sweet spot.

Derek looked over his shoulder at Jake.

"It's not the spooks on the federal payroll who are worrisome. Or aren't nine dead nurses enough to give you pause?"

Derek turned back to look again at the wall. "And you and Sands and Q and all the merry little digital elves are convinced it was a 'bot?"

"It seems a safe bet. Fits the serial killer copycat angle we got going on."

"Spree killer. That's what Speck was. Technically, anyway."

Jake stopped rocking and the chair went silent. "That all you got so far in your investigation?"

Derek's shoulders slumped. *"Touché."*

"And, technically, the F.B.I. says you need more than one location for a spree killer. So, what you got there for yourself is what we in the trade call a *mass* murderer case."

Derek's head bowed.

Jake started rocking—and squeaking—again. He tried to scan the murder wall around Derek, who began shuffling back and forth to read the different pages taped around the map of the city.

Derek hummed an unfamiliar meandering melody as he read.

Jake gave up and swiveled away from the wall.

"Lots of windy city connections up here," Derek said.

"Huh?"

"Speck…Gacy…that Ripper Gang. How many serial killers were there in Chicago, anyway? Sounds like a pretty dangerous place."

"Chicago?"

"And sweet Jesus. Eliot Ness, too? I don't see Al Capone up here. What's the deal with Ness?"

Jake swiveled back to face the murder wall. "He was Safety Director here during the Torso Murders—Wally's copycat case."

"Gruesome stuff. Lucky him."

"The Ripper Gang…Jack the *Ripper*—of course."

"Of course, what?" Derek turned and looked at Jake.

"Mudgett. *Damn it.* Come on."

"Where are we going?"

"Cutty's. You drive."

On the way downtown, Jake called EC to meet them at Cutty's Deli, then stared out the window lost in thought.

EC was already there in the usual back booth. "Hey, Jake. What's up."

"Might have a break." Jake slid in across from EC. "Thanks to Derek."

"Me?" Derek stood at the end of the booth.

"Yeah?" EC slid in to let Derek sit next to him.

"It was right there. Right in front of my face. *Damn it.*"

"You're welcome, I guess," Derek said. "But what'd I do?"

"Is Samantha having any luck on her profile?" Jake asked EC.

"Slim pickings. The guy's like vaporware—not really there, you know? Or anywhere."

"Tell her to start scrubbing records in Chicagoland—you know, the city, Cook and Dupage Counties. Maybe even Gary, Indiana. But particularly the south side. Around Jackson Park."

"Okay…What's she looking for?"

"Holmes. Jamal Holmes. Especially juvie records, CPS and Family Services. Get Q to help crack them if they're sealed."

"That's his last name? Holmes?"

"And maybe some kind of Biblical 'E' name. Elijah, Ezra, Ezekiel, Emmanuel."

"E.J. I get it. But what's Sam going to find?"

"I don't know. But that's where she's going to find it. I'm sure of it."

"Why's that?" Derek asked.

"You caught it. Not me. Too many Chicago connections."

"Ness and all the serial killers?"

"And the infamous player-to-be-named-later," Jake said.

"Who's that?"

"Maddie's case. The hookers in the Flats. That was Jack the Ripper."

"He's not from Chicago," Derek smirked. "I still don't get it."

"Jack was the first serial killer ever. Our first—the American Ripper—was Herman Mudgett—"

"What the hell kind of name is Mudgett—especially for a serial killer?" Derek asked

Jake looked and sighed. "Also known as H.H. Holmes."

"Also, from Chicago," said EC.

"You got it."

"And you think there's a connection with the Baron?"

"I think he thinks there is. And that's what is important."

"I'll get Sam on it right away. Let me out."

Derek got up to let EC leave. He sat back down across from Jake.

"Thanks, Derek." Jake smiled.

"You're welcome…I guess."

"Now, buy your partner lunch," Jake said and waved Cutty over to the booth.

~~~

Parkour

Q laced his shoes tight. He slipped on a gray hoody with the Tampa Bay *Buccaneers* flag—his adopted hacker logo—then a Navy "Top Gun" baseball cap turned backwards and a pair of Ray-Ban brown-gradient Wayfarer sunglasses. He bounded down the stairwell from the second floor of the warehouse, bursting out the emergency exit at the end of the building in the Flats. Waving to the patrolmen in their black cruiser parked at the front entrance, Q loped off south to the river, taking the path of most resistance, vaulting retaining walls, climbing up and around and over iron bridge trestles and jumping completely up and down over stairways, sometimes using center handrails with his feet in a perfectly timed stride to extend his leap.

The late afternoon sun drew a stretched-out cartoon silhouette that flailed comically on the ground parallel to the trail Q blazed along the river around Oxbow Bend, back to the north. He crossed the Cuyahoga River and continued along the shoreline under the Main Avenue Bridge, down the boardwalk and through the malls and plazas of the upscale Flats East Bank, dodging pedestrians now as well as architects' esthetically pleasing exterior renderings made real out of brick and concrete. At the boardwalk's end, he easily scaled a security fence, crossed the railroad tracks at the lift bridge over the river, then sprinted out to the Lake Erie shoreline. He sat to catch his breath facing the gap in the breakwall where an ore boat hovered in the water pointed up stream like a Paul Bunyon-sized steelhead.

Q gazed at the northern horizon for a long while, his mind temporarily cleansed by the improvised urban obstacle course. His discovery, though, slowly swelled again like a mental boil, pressuring his thoughts painfully. To the west, the sun neared the water. He rose and began the long walk back to the warehouse.

In the sepia induced in the Flats by the sunset and his Wayfarer lenses, Q saw a figure leaning over the driver's side of the police cruiser, head bobbing in conversation with the patrolman behind the wheel. *Of course. But how? How did he know?*

"Get it out of your system?" Jake stood up and asked as Q approached.

"Eh, you know how it is." Q pulled off his Ray-Bans and gave Jake the once over. "You're looking better."

"Yeah. Funny how sometimes the best medicine is no medicine."

"You want to come upstairs?"

"I thought you'd never ask." Jake turned towards the cruiser, reached in and squeezed the driver's shoulder, a reflex habit to check that a fellow officer was wearing his bullet-proof vest. "Thanks. And you guys stay safe out here."

Q led Jake up to the second floor and NFCed them into the server room with his police ID. "I reprogrammed the locks after the door was fixed."

"Now you're thinking. Man, kind of…tropical in here." Jake took off his jacket.

"Yeah, the cooling and venting is totally inadequate for the thermal load."

"It's an old building. Like mine." Jake stepped over to the window. "These don't open, do they?"

Q shook his head.

"Okay. So, what are we *not* talking about, already?"

Q took a deep breath. "The Baron, he's left-handed, isn't he."

Jake looked out the window and thought for a long moment, remembering times spent with Jamal. He turned back to Q. "Yeah, he is…*So?*"

"That's what I thought. Artistic."

"Well, he's a writer, though I never found his pieces particularly arty."

"No, not really that. I mean left brain-right brain, stuff. Right-handed people are left brain dominant. That's the verbal, rational, orderly side. Lefties lean to the right hemisphere."

"Can we cut to the chase?"

"Since I can't read it directly, I've been mapping and modeling the Black Tier. You know, like unexplored territory. It's like satellite imagery, not like actually pounding the pavement. But…no, maybe more like an MRI."

"Enough with the similes. What's the map look like?"

"It's definitely a brain simulation."

"How good?"

"Damn good. Hellaciously good."

Jake stared at Q. "Who's brain? Jamal's?"

"Maybe mostly. To start. But, now it's also a little bit of Speck's and of Wuornos' and the Ripper gang guys. It's growing experientially. We're not dealing with just an outbound push to the synthoids. There's a sensory return loop, too."

"The videos."

Q nodded. "And…*it dreams.*"

"Dreams? Seriously?"

"I may not be able to see what it's doing, but I can watch how it's doing it. So, I've been tracking the server metrics for a while—power consumption; I/O; CPU, memory and graphic engine loadings; bandwidth consumption; RPS, ARTs and PRTs—"

"English, please."

"Requests per Second. Average Request Times. Peak Request Times—*But,* the point is, there is a circadian clock-thing going on. At night—which is actually during the daytime for us—"

"Right. Graveyard shift."

"You did not just say that."

Jake shrugged it off.

"Anyway, during the sleep cycle the left hemisphere is quiet, except for random internal pixel, video and audio waveform transfers from the right side. Like how we dream. Our unconscious sends over crazy video clips of ourselves in weird situations with people we know that leave us scratching our heads when we wake up in the morning—but they somehow make sense. You know, the whole Freud thing."

Jake reflexively looked to the left side of the server room.

Q chuffed. "There's no real spatial left or right…I mean, *I don't think there is.*"

"And during the day—I mean night. The machine's day, damn it, then what happens?"

"It starts…you know, thinking. Rationally. Increased thread counts, heightened CPU utilization, increased network packet transfers."

"Network transfers? Like to the Grid? I thought you said this thing was cut off from the outside world."

"Yeah…not so much, really. I lied to Sands."

"Well, that's gonna be between you and him. I'm not management. Does it help the case?"

Q nodded.

"Show me."

~~~

The Bar Maiden's Death

The synthoid waited in the dark, narrow space between the dumpster and the building behind the bar. Odor sources had been cataloged and dismissed as non-relevant to the downloaded mission profile. The distance from where it stood to the bartender's parked car had been measured to the millimeter by laser and the transit time had been calculated in milliseconds. CMOS optical sensors auto-calibrated themselves to the ambient light in the alleyway. The noise gate on audio input was reduced to -48 dB to maximize listening sensitivity.

The unit's day job was walking through and inspecting intercepts for the Northeast Ohio Sewer District, so it was already dressed in Tyvek coveralls to protect from blood splatter. The map of city sewer lines resident in its memory would guarantee an untraceable egress from the crime scene through the predesignated manhole nearby. It waited with infinite patience and absolutely no trace of anticipatory anxiety. At two AM, the synthoid's readiness state escalated to Condition Orange. One thousand, three hundred sixty-eight seconds later, the rear entrance to the bar opened.

Target confirmation by facial recognition. Blonde. Five-foot, five inches tall. One hundred, twenty-six pounds. And alone. The bar maiden never made it to her car.

The synthoid's hydraulic grip around the throat

immediately silenced her by crushing the windpipe. Lifted off the ground by the neck, arms and legs flailed futilely, then eventually went limp with the loss of consciousness. A series of weak tremors through her body preceded her death.

The synthoid threw the body over its shoulder and quickly, stealthily moved north to the Norfolk and Southern railroad tracks, then west. At the preprogrammed navigation waypoint, the course turned back south and terminated in the alleyway behind the Glick Building. There, the corpse was stripped naked and the left breast was removed with a boning knife to be discarded in the sewer where rats would make quick work of it.

Jake woke before dawn with crazed blue and red beacons from police vehicles dancing on the walls and ceiling of his apartment. Through the back window, he looked down and saw a pair of patrolmen reeling out yellow tape to establish a perimeter around what was obviously—against the black asphalt of the parking lot—a female Caucasian victim. He dressed and went downstairs.

"Morning, Jake," said the Lakewood Police sergeant supervising the scene when he walked up. "Sorry to wake you."

Jake stared at the blonde hair, then the wound where the left breast should have been. He inhaled slowly, deeply. He closed his eyes, looked up, and blew audibly between his pursed lips.

"You didn't happen to hear…or see anything did you?"

Jake looked back down at the victim. He shook his head.

"Hell of a thing. Poor girl."

"I'll leave you to it." Jake turned and went back inside.

~~~

Chicago

"Hey, Cutty, what time is it?" Jake asked after he stepped into the deli and surveyed the dining room.

"Almost ten." Cutty replied from behind the counter.

"How long has she been here?"

Cutty followed Jake's eye-line to his usual back booth. "Oh, almost a half-hour. Why? You late for a date?"

Jake smiled. "No. Actually, I'm right on time for a change."

"I'll be damned. Better get myself square with the Pope for the end of days."

"Yeah. You do that." Jake went over to the coffee service station and poured himself a mug. He watched Samantha's lips move as she read off the screen of her *iSlate*. She was rehearsing, but he didn't want a canned presentation. *She probably has a PowerPoint, for Christ's sake.* He smiled behind a sip of coffee and walked over. "Sorry I'm late."

Startled, Samantha looked up. She nervously checked the time on her screen. "Oh, no. You're right on time."

"Well…whaddaya know." Jake sat down in the booth. "Thanks for coming."

"Um…oh, sure." Samantha tucked her wavy brunette hair behind her ears. "You look tired."

"Just an early morning commotion in the neighborhood." Jake looked her over. "It's nice."

"Huh?"

"Your hair. You've had it done. Used to be straighter. Longer, too. No?"

Samantha nodded, looked down, and rearranged her silverware. "Thanks for noticing."

"EC like it?"

"Yeah. He does."

"Quite becoming." Jake took a sip of coffee. "You finished the profile, right? What does EC think about *that?*"

"He said it's good. Quantico quality he claims, but…I don't know. He's sweet."

"Yeah. He's like that. Could you please send it to me when you get a chance?"

"But—but don't you want to go over it?"

"Let's see, male…twenty-five to forty…highly intelligent…loner from a dysfunctional family…in and out of trouble as a *yute* with a minor juvenile record—sealed of course…probably dropped out of college, but has managed to establish and maintain a steady, if somewhat erratic, employment history—I think I'm really close on this one, no?"

Samantha, crestfallen, nodded her head. "Then, why—"

"Have you eaten? Cutty makes the most amazing blintzes."

"Oh, no, really. I'm fine. I should probably get back—"

"Nonsense." Jake waved over their waitress. "Hi, Emma. Breakfast still being served?"

"You know it is, Ace," Emma snapped back.

"Great. Come on, try them."

"No. I shouldn't. Maybe just a fruit cup."

"Nonsense. There's berries on them. That counts. Trust me. Get them."

Samantha caved and nodded. "Blintzes, please"

Emma wrote, then pointed her pen at Jake.

"And I'll have my usual: dry rye, a scoop of cottage cheese and a grapefruit—gotta watch my girlish figure, you know."

"Honey, don't trust this guy any further than you can throw him," Emma said to Samantha. "An order of blintzes and one kitchen sink omelet with extra crispy hash browns, whole wheat toast—extra butter--and a large OJ coming up. Cottage cheese and grapefruit, my ass."

After Emma left, Jake smiled at Samantha. "Trust me, you won't be sorry about the blintzes."

Samantha sighed heavily. "So, how did you know about Chicago?"

"It was Derek who connected those dots."

"And the fact that his real name is Holmes?"

"Now, *that* was me. I don't think Derek has a clue about who H.H. Holmes was. Not exactly the studious type, that guy."

"You know, I'm embarrassed to say it…but in a way I kind of feel a little sorry for him. Is that bad of me?"

Eureka, Jake thought. He looked Samantha in the eye and said softly, "For him, the kid? No. He was just a kid then. Not a monster yet. How could you not?"

"I mean, his mom getting killed in a drive-by gang shooting when he was only seven."

"And mom was on her own, right? Dad was M.I.A."

Samantha nodded. "It looks like he tried—tried really hard, but nothing ever seemed to work out for him. It's not clear why."

"The system is a hard place to be. Bad enough as an adult, but especially when you're a child. You know how vicious kids can be. They're nothing but half-tamed beasts."

"That's probably why he kept running away and going back to the old neighborhood. Lived on the streets, at least in the summertime. I don't know what he thought he'd find there, because there was no other family."

"You think he went back to avenge his mother?" Jake asked.

"Hadn't thought of that. Maybe. It might fit, 'cause he somehow got caught up in the rivalry between a couple of gangs. But she was no angel—that's for sure. Her sheet is a long one: possession, theft, prostitution. In and out of clinics, but I guess the methadone never worked for her. She always went back."

"What was her name?"

"Evelyn."

"Huh…" Jake couldn't suppress a crooked half-smile.

"What?"

"Excuse me, folks." Emma served their breakfast, then filled Jake's coffee cup. "Can I get you folks anything else?"

"Thanks, but no thanks." Jake smiled. "Not right now."

Samantha poked at her blintzes until Emma walked away. "I'm scared for those girls he's got. Really scared. Especially the young one. What is he going to do with them? To them?"

"You know more about Jamal than any of the rest of us. What are you afraid is going to happen? That's he's going to rape and sexually abuse them?"

"If you go by the F.B.I guidelines—and there is the whole thing with the…the mutilations."

"Forget the F.B.I. And the Baron doesn't own those mutilations. That's copycat, signature business."

"I don't know. Maybe not. I keep thinking about the little girl. Could he…"

"No. I don't think so."

"Why?"

"Don't get me wrong. They are very much in danger. He could kill them and may well do it…if he hasn't already. But this is not about—this is not a sexual thing."

"How do you know?" Samantha stared directly at him.

"I can't say—I mean I don't know how I know. I just know. Trust me." Jake held her gaze and whispered, "Trust me."

Samantha nodded and shrugged her shoulders. "What choice do I have?"

"Come on, let's eat. Try the blintzes."

They ate in silence.

"You were right," Samantha said. "These are good."

"E.J. Holmes, right? Did you find out what the 'E' stands for?"

"Yes. Enoch."

Jake froze in mid-bite. He dropped his fork to his plate.

"What? It was some prophet from the Old Testament."

Jake picked up his coffee and drank. He looked away, around the dining room.

"What?"

Jake looked back. He smiled and shook his head. *Son-of-a-bitch.*

"What is it?"

"This isn't about sex. Not at all. He's on a mission."

"Mission? What kind of mission?"

"Damn it, I don't know." Jake sighed. "Could you go back and double check whether Evelyn was really his mother or if she might have been his grandmother?"

"Why?"

"Please? Just humor me."

***~~~**

Amy

Jamal entered the room, dragging his bentwood chair noisily across the floor.

Not again, she thought from beneath the quilt. She heard him firmly plant the chair at the end of the bed. She felt his presence over her, then the chair creaked a bit as he sat. She lay still, pretending to be asleep, but knowing it would not work.

"I know you are not sleeping."

With a huff, waitress Amy rolled on her back and pulled the quilt off her face. She stared at the ceiling. The smell of coffee teased from the mug he had silently set on the nightstand.

"It is a beautiful morning," Jamal crooned in his low baritone.

"Yeah? How would I know?"

"I just told you."

"Yeah, well, thanks for that." Amy sat up and reached for her mug. The chain between the bed frame and the cuff on her ankle clinked. "You've made my day."

"You amuse me."

"Super."

"Was Jake so amused?"

Amy snorted and took a drink of coffee.

"I wonder…"

Amy waited. "What?"

"Do you think he has been faithful to you while…while you have been with me?"

She scowled.

"Hmmm…just a passing thought."

"What do you want?"

"What do any of us want? To be treated justly. Rewarded fairly for our sacrifices."

"Yeah. So you've said—*repeatedly.*"

"Yes, of course. Too bad in this world it is rarely so."

Amy's brow furrowed in thought.

Jamal smiled. He drank from his mug.

Amy put her coffee back on the nightstand. She threw back the quilt and swung her legs off the side of the bed.

Jamal watched closely.

Amy slowly unbuttoned the top of her pajamas. She slipped it off her shoulders, letting it fall free from her arms. She turned towards him, naked from the waist up.

The Baron's smile wilted. He was at once aroused and repulsed at the temptation before him.

"I could…" Amy listened to the deepening of his breaths. "…if I were fairly rewarded…"

Jamal sat back and smiled. "So…you would betray him."

She said nothing but met and held his stare.

In the next room, orphan Amy let Stephanie brush her hair. The first few times, she resisted, but once she gave in, came to crave the small act of kindness. She liked being cared for. She liked how Stephanie told her she was a pretty young child. Amy liked listening to her softly hum melodies as she tenderly pulled the brush through her hair. Today, though, the woman was silent.

"Miss Stephanie…what is it?"

"Nothing, child. Nothing."

"He isn't going to hurt me, is he? I don't want to die."

"We all pass, but not until our time."

"But I don't want to."

"Don't you fret, child. Don't you fret."

"But—"

"I have a nice, new dress for you. I'm sure you'll like it. You will look so very pretty."

Amy nodded but felt herself fill with dread.

"Don't you fret, child. Don't you fret."

~~~

The Invisible Mind

Q lay on his back on the cot he set up in the server room, staring at the ceiling. He waited for the bells to start clanging on the antique windup alarm clock he brought from home. Nine minutes or so later—the old mechanical clock was a little fuzzy in its timekeeping—the alarm on his phone would go off at precisely the time it was set for according to the U.S. Naval Observatory Master Clock. They were both unnecessary now, as Q's natural sleep cycles were finally in sync with the Black Tier.

He sat up and grabbed a hand full of Fruit Loops out of the cereal box by the cot. The sugar fix perked him up. He grabbed the box and went over to roust his laptop out of sleep mode.

"Oh…no…" Q said out loud, even though he was the only one in the building.

He sat down and watched in dread as the graphs on the server monitoring app updated, showing a massive tsunami of outbound network traffic, which redlined three hours prior—w*hile I was sleeping.*

Just as Q was about to start investigating, his phone dinged with a text message:

> My Dear Companion — Thank you so much for keeping me company, but the time has come for me to be on my way. Attached is the encryption key to what

you seek, but, alas, there is no longer much to find there. Not even breadcrumbs. Until we meet again, warmest regards, The Baron.

Q used the key to unlock the Black Tier and confirmed its data drives had been wiped clean. He shut down his monitoring app.

His phone dinged again. It was an alert from his sniffer algorithm. The Baron had sent the Munchausen instruction set for the next Ripper Gang killing in the clear.

Q called Lt. Sands to warn him, then forwarded the text to Samantha.

He shut down his laptop and waited ten minutes, then called Jake. "Did you talk to Sands?"

"Yeah, he just called," Jake answered. "We figure somewhere along the Nickle Plate Road. Maddie and Wally are taking the east side. Derek and I will cover the west tracks. Sands is calling Lakewood, Rocky River, Bay, and Westlake to have them step up patrols out their way. Do you have an A-VIN on the synthoid? Can you track it?"

"I sent the info to Samantha to work the trace and trap. But Jake…"

Jake stayed silent on the other end.

"I think it's a diversion."

"What do you mean?"

Q explained the data dump, the Baron's text, and the empty Black Tier.

"Did you tell Sands?" Jake asked.

"No."

Silence on the line. "Good. Call me if there's more."

Q replied with a nod of his head.

"Q? You there?"

"Yeah, Jake."

"Call me. You hear?"

"Of course."

Q tossed his phone on the table beside his laptop. He grabbed a folding lawn chair and went up to the roof. He looked north and saw where the "Crooked River" passed beneath the Detroit Superior and Main Avenue bridges on its way out to the lake.

Q opened the lawn chair and sat, trying to imagine the invisible fury which had been unleashed on the world while he slept.

~~~

The White City

Jamal and orphan Amy sat on a bench by the Fountain of Eternal Life in Veteran's Memorial Plaza downtown where caretaker Bill had dropped them off in the big black *Denali* SUV. She wore her new dress and a delicate layer of makeup Stephanie had applied which made her beauty glow. Amy's wrist was handcuffed to Jamal's.

Before they left, he warned her not to cry out for help and held a handgun up within an inch of her face to emphasize the point, an unnecessary gesture. He told her no one would care and no one would notice and most likely no one would help—at least not in time to save her—but she already knew that cold, hard reality well. When she lived on the streets, Amy always felt invisible. No eye contact or smiles, winks or nods. *Invisible.*

After being locked up indoors for so long, Amy savored the breeze on her face and the warmth of sun on the back of her neck. She was back in her natural element. Jamal held her hand in a warm, firm grip which, ironically, made her feel safe and relaxed. Surviving on her own meant always being on guard against human predators. She might be his captive, but the Baron would protect his possession.

At least I mean something to someone.

They sat in silence. Soon, the outflow of downtown workers from the buildings began, human rivulets joining into streams to puddle at bus stops and in parking lots for the evening commute home to the suburbs.

The Baron smiled. He looked all around and shook his head.

"What is it?" asked Amy.

"The ripple effect." He pointed at the fountain. "You would do well to consider how such small splashes can reach so far."

"What do you mean?"

"This place here where we sit, the Mall, reminds me of long ago. Of home."

"Where's that?"

"Chicago. It is a ripple from 1893. Look at them. Most people do not even have a clue."

"A clue about what?"

"Note these buildings." Jamal pointed to the library and the United States Courthouse to their right, then the old Board of Education Building and Public Hall on the other side of the Mall. "Classical architecture. Big white buildings lined up in neat rows. City Hall and the County Courthouse at the other end. The landscaping. Open space. Beautiful views, all the way to the lake. And a certain symmetry to it all. A ripple from long ago"

"Is this, like, history stuff?"

Jamal shook his head. "It reminds me of home. That's all. They copied the World's Fair to beautify their own cities. But we're all copycats. It's what human beings do." Jamal checked his watch. "Speaking of which…come, child."

He stood. He smiled down on Amy and gently pulled her up to her feet. They headed north hand-in-hand, crossing St. Clair Avenue and walking up the long grassy slope of Mall B above the underground Convention Center until they got to the end which overlooked Lakeside Avenue. Jamal leaned on the clear retaining wall and searched to the east.

"There." The Baron pointed at a woman coming down the steps of City Hall. She turned their way. "There she is."

Amy watched the woman walk towards them. "Who's she?"

"Oh…just a bit of entertainment I've arranged for our law enforcement friends." Jamal scanned the sidewalk back behind the woman. "She works in the City Planning Department. Now, that's ironic, given our conversation just a moment ago, no?"

"Are you going to—"

"And there. Yes, there is our helpful friend for the evening." He pointed to a man following behind the woman. "He comes to us from a biowaste disposal company which services local hospitals. Again, ironic."

"Please don't."

The Baron smiled at Amy, then tracked the woman as she passed by on the sidewalk below. A short time later, her pre-programmed synthoid predator passed by, closing the gap bit-by-bit."

"Shall we?" Jamal asked Amy.

"I don't want to see. *Please.*"

"Oh, no. Nothing like that."

"Then what are we going to do?"

Jamal thought for a moment. "We're going to make a little splash of our own."

They went back down Mall B to St. Clair, then walked west into the Warehouse District. They crossed West 6th Street and went to the corner at Lakeside to wait.

The rush of homeward bound workers had slowed back down to a trickle when caretaker Bill pulled up to the corner in the black SUV. Waitress Amy got out of the back, her wrist held tight in the hydraulic clutch of a synthoid.

"Let me go! Let me go! Let me—" she cried out before the Baron muffled her plea by grabbing her mouth hard with his hand.

Orphan Amy noticed a few pedestrians look their way. They all kept on walking.

Jamal shook his head in disgust at waitress Amy until she submitted. He released her and pointed up the West 6th Street exit ramp off the Shoreway.

The synthoid dragged waitress Amy out into the middle of the street and began walking up the ramp.

"Stay by me," Jamal said to orphan Amy as he followed close behind the synthoid, who calmly waved its free hand at the oncoming traffic.

Cars skidded and sideswiped one another as they careened to avoid hitting the four crazy-drunk pedestrians heading upstream.

Jamal smiled when he heard the cry of sirens rise up nearby. Soon after, one last car drifted past. The driver honked and shook a fist at them in anger.

The four walked to the center of the span of the now empty Main Avenue Bridge and waited.

~~~

The River Styx

By the time Maddie arrived with Wally and Jake arrived with Derek, the span of the Main Avenue Bridge had been cleared of wrecks with patrol cars blocking off each end. They met EC at the SWAT tactical van parked at the top of the Lakeside Avenue exit ramp off the Shoreway next to the Archer Apartment building.

"He's been asking for you two," Sergeant Kovacic said, pointing at Maddie and Jake when they got to the back of the van.

"Yeah. No surprise there," Jake said. "What's the situation?"

"We've got snipers up on the Ernst and Young Tower and up on the roof here. Not the best, but workable. There are two perps. One has a child with a gun to her head. The lunatic is sitting on the south wall a hundred feet up."

"Where's the girl," Maddie asked.

"Standing between his legs. We've got a clear shot, but it looks like they're cuffed together at the wrists—which kind of limits our options." Kovacic zoomed in the camera view from the sniper's nest on his *iSlate* to show them. "The other is holding a woman. From the thermals, it looks like that one is a droid. They're out a quarter-mile over the river."

Maddie drew her Glock. "Shall we?"

Jake unholstered his Smith and Wesson *eM&P* to take down the synthoid. It whined as he cycled the charging sequence. He looked at Wally and Derek. "You guys in?"

"Got your back," Wally said, pulling out his pistol.

Derek drew his weapon, too.

EC unshouldered his shotgun.

The five started walking west into the twilight, spreading out across the three traffic lanes as they went with Jake and Maddie out front slightly.

"Jamal!" Jake called out as they got near. He signaled for Wally and Derek to hang back. To EC on his right, he whispered, "Wait, and when we get up there, hop the median and get on the other side of them."

"Hello, Jake, my old friend," the Baron said loudly. "So glad you could make it."

"Can Maddie and I come up there?"

"Sure. *Come on down.*"

Maddie and Jake hugged the concrete median wall, keeping as much distance as possible between them and the Baron on the south side of the roadway. EC climbed over the wall and used it for cover to move to the west of the group. Wally and Derek inched a bit closer on the east flank, their weapons at the ready.

Orphan Amy felt the handcuff come off her wrist, but Jamal held her tight by the collar of her dress. She felt the press of his pistol on her shoulder again.

The synthoid held waitress Amy in front like a shield with a firm grip on each of her biceps.

"Jake, help me," waitress Amy screamed in panic. "Please, help me."

"Shut up!" Jamal yelled angrily at her.

The synthoid shook her into silence.

"It does appear we've got a, mmm, whaddaya call, a

situation, here," Jake said with a big smile, his *eM&P* discreetly aimed at the synthoid from the hip.

"Yeah. Look at us. One big happy family of man out here together," Jamal answered, his baritone voice calm and smooth again. "It is a beautiful evening. You missed a gorgeous sunset."

Maddie held Jamal in the sites of her Glock. She noticed orphan Amy's new dress and the makeup that gave her a more mature beauty.

"I have to admit, you've got a great view here," said Jake. "The lake. The city. You've got it all."

"So, what should we talk about?" asked Jamal. "The weather, perhaps."

"We don't need to talk," Jake said. "There's nothing to discuss, really. Is there?"

"You want to know why, though, right?"

"Nah. I know evil when I see it," Jake dismissed. "I don't need to read a manifesto or hear a speech. They're usually pretty boring anyway. And in the end…it's just evil."

"Quite the moralist, are we?"

"Maybe we could talk about how—like how you want this to end, but I think I know that, too. You're not really much of a man of mystery, Jamal. Or should I call you *Enoch?*"

"So, you know it all, do you?"

"No. I don't know where that crazy brain experiment you had down in the Flats went, but I'm sure it'll turn up again. Right?"

"It is block-chained everywhere. You'll never root it all out."

Jake laughed. "I guess that means job security for me and EC, no?"

"Do not mock me." There was a harsh growl in the Baron's voice.

Jake stared Jamal down.

"*Jake…*" Maddie whispered.

"This whole scene is a mockery," Jake said, waving his pistol. "Like a bad 'B' movie."

"I deserve respect."

Jake rubbed his chin with his left hand. "No…I don't think so."

"And I…will…have it." Jamal raised his voice and looked up to the stars as he cried out, *"Father!"*

Jake caught a slight movement in the triggered synthoid. He raised his *eM&P.*

"Jake, no," Maddie pleaded.

Jake fired, but the electro-magnetic pulse only weakened the synthoid. It still effortlessly tossed waitress Amy over its shoulder and off the bridge like a rag doll.

As the scream faded in the hundred-foot fall to the water, orphan Amy felt Jamal release his grip on her collar. She instinctively ran towards Maddie.

Maddie fired ten rounds from her Glock. The forty-caliber slugs slammed into Jamal's chest pushing him back and over the south wall. She grabbed Amy in a hug and turned, putting her body between the girl and the synthoid.

The Baron fell in silence.

Jake dropped the synthoid into a twitching spasm on the road bed with a second EMP round.

A faint splash was heard from below.

✳✳✳～～～✳✳✳

A Beautiful Friendship

Q sat in a chair on the visitor's side of his own desk next to Jake, watching Lt. Sands on the other side oversee the city IT technician scrubbing Q's desktop, laptop, and *iSlate,* deleting his log-in IDs and wiping his data files. Two uniformed officers stood outside his office on either side of the door.

"Are you sure you don't want your union rep here?" Lt. Sands asked. "I think I'd feel better about this if he was."

"Nah, I'm good with Jake," Q said. "I trust him."

"And why not?" Jake asked with a touch of bitterness. "I shot a Councilman's son dead and I've still got my badge."

"That is not funny, mister." Sands shot his finger across the desk at Jake.

"Yes, sir."

"And don't call me sir."

"Yes, sir."

"Damn it." Sands pointed at Q. "Such misplaced trust was probably your first mistake."

"Sadly, no. Just the latest in a long, long chain of errors and miscalculations," Q said. "And, it likely won't be my last."

Lt. Sands shook his head and turned back to observe the IT Tech.

"You know," Q said to Jake, "I was up on the roof at White Chapel that night."

"Oh, yeah?"

"Yeah. I saw the Baron fall."

"Really."

Lt. Sands crossed his arms against his chest and pinched his eyes shut, trying hard to ignore their banter.

"Man, he pancaked into the river good," Q said. "Real good."

"That Maddie…she's a hell of a shot."

"Couldn't have happened to a nicer guy."

"Yeah, it could have," Jake said. "But I'm glad it didn't"

"All done," said the IT tech. "I just need his phone and *iNode.*"

Q pointed to the credenza behind his desk, where a single cell phone was neatly placed next to his *iNode.*

"Just one?" Sands asked, then changed his mind. "No-no-no, I don't want to know."

The IT tech scooped them up. Sands, Jake, and Q watched him leave.

"Finally, I need your passkey, dongle and department ID." Sands held out his hand.

Q took off the lanyard with the requested items from around his neck and dropped it into the Lieutenant's hand.

Lt. Sands pulled a letter from his leather portfolio. "Here is your official notice of suspension—with pay, for now. You will get notification of the date and time of the administrative hearing by certified mail."

Q took the letter. The smile fell from his face.

"I'm sorry about all this, but…"

"It's okay. I'm the one who screwed the pooch," Q said.

Lt. Sands sighed. "Anyway, I need to get down to Public

Square for a meeting with the Director and you have to be escorted from the building."

"I want to collect my pictures and some personal items." Q pointed to the Mondrian and Warhol prints on the office wall. "Can Jake walk me out?"

"Yeah, I can take care of that, Lieu," Jake said.

Lt. Sands looked at Q, then Jake. "All right. But the uniforms stay."

Q and Jake nodded like scolded school boys.

The Lieutenant stepped out, spoke with the uniformed officers, then left the building. The patrolmen turned to watch Q and Jake through the glass front wall of the office.

"It's not his fault," Jake said to Q. "Sands is just an errand boy for the Captain, who's in overdrive CYA mode. You know management."

Q shrugged. "What is it you always say about the Captain?"

Jake chuckled. "I'm only six numbers away from telling that guy what I really think of him."

"Yeah, well, now we're only three…maybe even two." A smile slowly grew on Q's face.

Jake looked over and cocked his head.

Q exaggerated his lip movements as he silently formed the words, *Four…Hundred…Fifty…Million…Dollars…*

"Courtesy of esquires Howard, Fine and Howard?"

"Stooges by any other name are still stooges."

"You found it?"

"I'm close." Q gave Jake a conspiratorial wink. "I'm just surprised there wasn't a bigger uproar when it went missing."

"I'm not. Something about that whole deal always gave me pause." Jake frowned. "Wait a minute…*We?*"

"I'm selfish, but I'm not greedy," Q said. "Besides, I might need a helping hand along the way."

"Louie, I think this is the beginning of a beautiful friendship." Jake grabbed Q's shoulder and squeezed.

"Who's Louie?" Q asked.

"Who cares. Let's get your stuff and blow this pop stand."

~~~

Maddie and Jake

"I'm sorry, Jake." Maddie reached across the booth and took his hand. She squeezed.

"Yeah, I figured. Why didn't you say something?"

"Frankly, I knew you would talk me out of it." Maddie sighed. "So, I waited until I interviewed and made up my mind for sure."

"Can't talk you out of it?"

"Too late now."

"Why?"

"I need to break the cycle. With everything that's happened…" Maddie looked away. She scanned the deli dining room. "You'll be fine."

"I really don't think I will be fine." Jake smiled. "But I'm happy for you. Quantico. A fed, huh?"

Maddie nodded.

"And here I took you at your word, you'd be going back to Robbery/Homicide."

"When the Bureau came to town after, Sands and the Captain played me up, and…well, the suits bought it. They must be desperate to staff the new unit with experienced people."

Jake took a sip of coffee.

"It really should have been you, though."

"No. I get it. Too much baggage." He shook his head. "And I was never the Captain's favorite. You hungry?"

"No, really. I've got to get going. A million-and-one things to tend to before the move."

"What about Amy?"

"She's doing very well. She's with folks in Westlake—real close to me. I've seen her a few times. She seems happy."

"And when you leave?"

"She's a tough cookie."

"Like you?"

"Tougher, I think. She'll be fine." Maddie stood up. "We'll talk, okay?"

Jake nodded. He looked up from his mug. "I love you, Mads."

"Oh, Jake…I—I—" Maddie leaned over and kissed the top of Jake's head.

"Take good care. *Please.*"

Maddie smiled, turned and walked away. She stopped at the register and wiped a tear away. "Uncle Cutty…"

Cutty set down his butcher knife, took off his apron and came out from behind the meat counter. He gave her a big hug. "We'll all miss you, Missy *Mad-de-line.*"

Maddie sniffed. She looked back over Cutty's shoulder at Jake.

Jake waved.

I should have told him… Maddie buried her face in Cutty's shoulder. *But no…I'll wait a few months, when I'm starting to show.*

~~~

Home

Amy left her suburban foster home in Westlake at the regular time for school but went to Crocker Park instead. She boarded the RTA Cleveland State Line bus with the morning commuters headed downtown for work. She stared blankly out the window at the passing shops, restaurants, office buildings, and strip malls on Detroit Avenue, then at the big houses of rich people lining Clifton Boulevard.

Forty minutes later, she got off at the West 117th Street stop. It was a longer walk from there, but the bus would continue down the Shoreway and over the Main Avenue Bridge. Amy just could not bear returning to that place above the river again.

Amy walked south to the Rapid Transit station and took the next eastbound train to West 65th Street. She walked north to Franklin Avenue, then turned towards downtown until she got to West 44th Street.

"Welcome home, child," Stephanie said when she answered Amy's knock at the front door. "What took you so long?"

~~~

Thank you for reading my story.

About M.T. Bass

M.T. Bass lives, writes, flies, and plays music in Mudcat Falls, USA.

www.mtbass.net

Murder by Munchausen Sci-Fi Thriller Book #4
Available in Paperback, eBook & Audiobook

Just when you thought you could trust the robots again…

A senator's son is strangled by a synthoid in AsiaTown and, just like two other victims, tattooed with an indecipherable barcode.

Jake and Kim, his new partner, battle political corruption, the Chinese Triad, and Internal Affairs, discovering a disturbing Fourth Law of Robotics as they decode the tattoos to stop the deviant series of murders.

www.mtbass.net

White Hawk Aviation Adventure Stories #1
Available in Paperback & eBook

Hollywood, 1950 — Former P-51 fighter pilot A. Gavin Byrd is on location for a movie shoot, when he gets a call from the police that his older brother, a prominent Beverly Hills plastic surgeon, has been found dead on his boat. The Lieutenant in charge of the investigation is ready to close the case as a suicide from the start, but "Hawk" doesn't buy it and decides to find out what really happened for himself.

With help from a former starlet ex-girlfriend, a friendly police sergeant whose life was saved in the war by his brother and a nosy Los Angeles Times reporter, Hawk's search for the truth takes him through cross-fire, dog fights and mine fields in Hollywood, Beverly Hills, Burbank and Las Vegas, and leads him into some of the darker corners of his brother's patient files and private life that he never knew existed.

www.mtbass.net

White Hawk Aviation Adventure Stories #2
Available in Paperback & eBook

"There are only two types of aircraft: fighters and targets."
~Doyle 'Wahoo' Nicholson, USMC

Sweating it out in the former Belgian Congo as a civil war mercenary, with Sparks turning wrenches on his T-6 Texan, Hawk splits his time flying combat missions and, back on the ground, sparring with Ella, an attractive young missionary doctor, in the sequel to My Brother's Keeper.

www.mtbass.net

White Hawk Aviation Adventure Stories #3
Available in Hardback, Paperback & eBook

"If everything seems under control, you're not going fast enough."
~Mario Andretti

Strap down the 5-point harness in the cockpit of a Formula 1 air racing plane and join Hawk as he chases victory! First on their amateur make-shift course over Antelope Acres, then on the re-emerging pylon racing circuit in the early 1960s. And finally, as Hawk battles 7 other top-level pilots at the very first National Air Racing Championship event in Reno!

And then one day cruising home to Van Nuys airport, Hawk spies Allison, a beach-blonde surfer girl, insanely wing walking on the top of a Stearman PT-17 bi-plane. He quickly sets his sights on her.

Fly low…Fly fast…and Turn Left…

www.mtbass.net

Available in Paperback, eBook & Audiobook

She was one in a million…and the day I met her I should have bought a lottery ticket instead.

Griffith Crowe, the "fixer" for a Chicago law firm, falls for his current assignment, Helena Nicholson, the beautiful heir of a Tech Sector venture capitalist who perished in a helicopter crash leaving her half a billion dollars, a Learjet 31, and unsavory suspicions about her father's death. As he investigates, the ex-Navy SEAL crosses swords with Helena's step-brother, the Pentagon's Highlands Forum, and an All-Star bad guy somebody has hired to stop him. When Griff finds himself on the wrong side of an arrest warrant he wonders: Is he a player or being played?

Lawyers and Lovers and Guns…*Oh, my!*

www.mtbass.net

Available in Paperback & eBook

Anchorage, 1976 — Albert and Waxy flunk their Intro to Philosophy midterm and drunkenly decide to drop out of *The Ohio State University* and go to Alaska to "strike it rich" working on the Trans-Alaska Pipeline. After Albert's father cuts off his credit card, they get bartending & dishwashing jobs at an Anchorage bar, where Albert becomes involved with the bar owner's girlfriend, CiCi, who is also the lead singer in the house band. Albert "acquires" a union card to get a pipeline job for himself, but then learns that Waxy has become part of a crazy scheme with Jimmi the Pilot, Beantown Bob and Moe the Eskimo to find and recover a long lost government payroll from an Air Force cargo plane that crashed in the Alaska Mountain Range decades ago.

www.mtbass.net

Available in Paperback & eBook

Kansas City, 1965 — Y.T. Erp, Jr. can't wait to leave for college at the University of California, Berkeley to escape not only the work, but especially all the phlegm-brained idiots at his father's aerospace company. Leaving behind a pregnant auburn-haired cheerleader, a sensuous red-headed siren plotting to usurp his familial ties, and his two best friends—one who ends up in Vietnam and the other in the Weather Underground—his "trip" on the wild side of the Generation Gap takes him from the psychedelic scene of Haight-Ashbury to the F.B.I.'s Ten Most Wanted list. Meanwhile, his father is consumed by the task of managing his unmanageable corporate team in the quest to help fulfill a President's challenge to "land a man on the moon."

www.mtbass.net

Available in eBook

Cleveland, 1977 — Grappling with a foreign policy crisis, the U.S. Government targets a hapless rock-'n'-roller as a Russian spy in a classic case of mistaken identity for an innocent, 'Wrong Man' hero…or *is he?* Think of an unholy fictional union between the Rolling Stones and Alfred Hitchcock's *North by Northwest*. Unlike any novel you have ever read, this one has a soundtrack. After all, a story whose characters are musicians should have…well…*music*. Right?

www.mtbass.net

Available in eBook

*Lodging — bending of the stalk of a plant (stalk lodging)
or the entire plant (root lodging)*

While World War II engulfs every nation on the globe, Rebecca and her high school friend Sarah can only dream of escaping a dreary, wind-blown existence in western Kansas, until their boring, stodgy old hometown fills with handsome young men learning to fly Army Air Corps bombers known as *Liberators*, and their lives are suddenly filled with temptation and, perhaps, true love.

www.mtbass.net

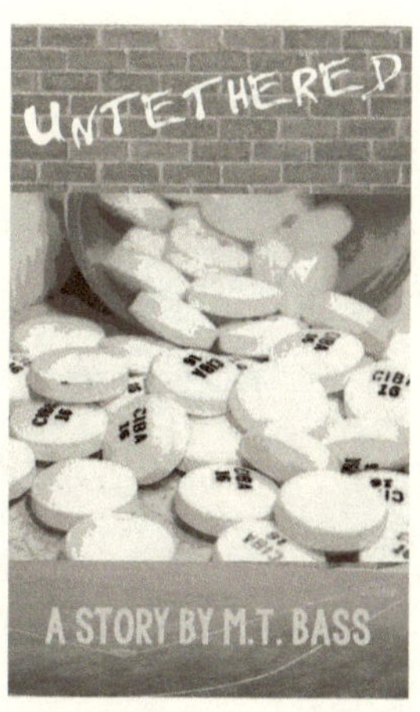

Available in eBook

At District High School #6241, Connor wants only to get close to Liz, the cheerleader whose locker is just across the hall, and forget the suicide of his father in jail, but his family's dark past and a rebellious nature force him to the fringes of student social circles and into an unlikely alliance to fight back against a tyranny of conformity.

www.mtbass.net

Available in eBook

The collected songs and verse of M.T. Bass

www.mtbass.net

www.ingramcontent.com/pod-product-compliance
Lightning Source LLC
Chambersburg PA
CBHW051424190726
48289CB00001B/37